BROTHERS

BROTHERS

A NOVEL BY

Michael Bar-Zohar

FAWCETT COLUMBINE • New York

A Fawcett Columbine Book
Published by Ballantine Books

Grateful acknowledgment is made to New Directions Publishing Corp.
for permission to reprint an excerpt from *Dylan Thomas: Poems of
Dylan Thomas.* Copyright 1943 by New Directions Publishing Corp.

Library of Congress Cataloging-in-Publication Data

Bar-Zohar, Michael,
      Brothers : a novel / by Michael Bar-Zohar. — 1st ed.
         p. cm.
      ISBN 0-449-90511-X
      I. Title.
      PR9510.9.B3B37   1992
      823—dc20   92-52666
                                        CIP

Text design by Debby Jay

Manufactured in the United States of America

First Edition: August 1993

10 9 8 7 6 5 4 3 2 1

BROTHERS

Preface*

IN THE WINTER of 1949 Stalin's secret police arrested the leaders of the Anti-Fascist Writers Committee. The committee was an association of Jewish writers that had been established during the Second World War in order to gather support for Stalin's war effort among Jews in Russia and abroad. The most prominent Jewish writers, poets, and philosophers of the Soviet Union had been among the founders of the committee. Their representatives had even visited the United States, where Albert Einstein and other personalities had pledged support for their initiative.

Now that the war was over, Stalin was worried by the budding Jewish nationalism in the committee. Chairman Solomon Mikhoels, the poets Fefer and Halkin, and Professor Lina Stern had presented him with a petition asking for the settling of Jewish survivors in Crimea; they also asked Stalin to condemn anti-Semitism in the USSR.

The Soviet dictator, furious, moved to crush the Jewish nationalists. Solomon Mikhoels was brutally murdered during a visit to Minsk. A few months later all the committee members were arrested, tortured, and condemned to death in a mock trial.

Some of them were shot immediately. The others were executed in

*The preface describes true historical events

3

January 1953, shortly after Stalin initiated one of the most hideous frame-ups in his bloody career: the Doctors' Conspiracy. The paranoid dictator accused the leading Jewish doctors in the Soviet Union of a plot to assassinate him and other communist leaders. He even claimed that the Jewish doctors, obeying orders from Washington, had already assassinated party chiefs Zhdanov and Shcherbakov. The late Mikhoels had allegedly been the intermediary between the evil doctors and some American Jewish organizations.

Before the Doctors' Conspiracy trial started, all the surviving members of the Anti-Fascist Writers Committee were shot in the inner courtyard of the Lubyanka Prison, in Moscow.

Stalin died on March 5, 1953, and the execution of the Jewish doctors was called off.

This story begins on January 23, 1953.

It ends today.

PART ONE
Youth
1953–1967

Chapter 1

A COLD, BITTER NIGHT had settled over Russia, and snow was falling on the sleeping city of Moscow.

Watching the lacy snowflakes dance outside the barred window of her cell, Tonya thought that tomorrow Moscow would look like an enchanted kingdom. Red Square would be covered with an immaculate carpet; the Spasskaya Tower would loom, tall and dazzling, like the Ice Castle in the fairy tale; white patches would gleam on the onion domes of St. Basil's and lay thick on the ramparts of the Novodevichny Monastery. In Gorky Park the small pine grove would turn into a forbidding forest, children anxiously trudging into its dark, cold shadows, looking for the Winter Queen; while by the frozen pond other children would play with snowballs and build white giants with carrot noses and eyes of black coal.

Tonya loved the white Russian winters; they always made her feel like a child again. One of her most famous poems, "My White Kingdom," described Moscow in the snow. She had once read it to the boys, but only Alex had seemed to understand; Dimitri was still too little. But she knew she would never write again, and never again see her enchanted kingdom. By the time the first child galloped into Gorky Park tomorrow, she would already be dead, shot in the base of her skull and buried in an unmarked grave, like all the others killed by the KGB in the inner court of the Lubyanka Prison.

She didn't want to look at the snow anymore, and turned the other way. The narrow cot smelled of urine, tobacco, and disinfectant. How many people had tossed restlessly here on their last night of life, she wondered, waiting for the firing squad? A single bulb illuminated the corridor, and faint yellow light crept into her cell underneath the iron door. The walls were covered with names, inscriptions, and dates, engraved in the mortar by the former inmates. "Revenge!" somebody had scratched on the far wall. "Stalin-murderer," another wall proclaimed. "The blood of a communist . . ." The author of that inscription had probably been dragged to his execution before completing his testament. The guards hadn't bothered to erase the graffiti, and for a good reason: all those who read them had carried their knowledge into the grave.

On the far wall somebody had scratched a Magen David, a Jewish star. Tonya raised her hand to her throat and touched the thick gold chain and her own star, which her sister Nina had given her before leaving Russia. Her forefinger followed the contour of the three Hebrew letters engraved upon the old symbol of her religion.

Tonya had almost no ties with the faith of her people. Her communist teachers in Kiev had taught her to despise religion; when she was a teenager she regarded her father's prayers and her mother's kosher cooking as backward customs of a dying world. Yet, when the KGB officers had stripped her of her possessions — watch, bracelet, earrings — she had asked to keep the chain. After she died, they could give the chain to Morozov; but as long as she was alive, she wanted to hold on to something tangible that would remind her of who she was and where she was going.

In a few hours it would be all over, she thought. Her blanket was thin and threadbare but she didn't feel the cold. She didn't feel anything, just a crushing emptiness, an immense lassitude. She had hoped until the last moment that something would happen and the execution orders would be revoked. Perhaps Morozov would get through to Stalin himself. After all, Stalin couldn't let innocent people die just because they were Jewish.

But yesterday evening, when they brought her the children for a last good-bye, she had realized that there was no hope. She had been taken to a bare office on the ground floor by a sour-faced KGB matron; the boys were already there, standing by the far wall under a faded picture of Lenin. It was a special favor to Colonel Morozov, the matron had said. Visits were never allowed in the Lubyanka. Yes, the colonel himself had brought the children; no, she wasn't allowed to see him. She'd better kiss the children now, the matron said, Colonel Morozov had to take them back.

Tonya had hugged the boys strongly, one then the other. Alex was wearing his new gray coat with the rabbit-fur collar, of which he was very proud; Dimitri was huddled in Alex's old sheepskin, which was still too large for him. Alex might have sensed something, with that amazing instinct children have, for he'd started to cry. "Are you coming home with us, Mommy?" he asked repeatedly, and she had mumbled, "Soon, Aliosha, very soon." Dimitri, who had barely started to speak five months before, hadn't said a word; he just clung to her, burying his face in her skirt and clutching her forefinger in his tiny hand. Even the matron seemed to be moved; when she herded the children out, she avoided Tonya's eyes.

And now Tonya lay here, alone with her memories, waiting for her executioner. Her comrades, the greatest Jewish writers and thinkers of the Soviet Union, waited in the nearby cells. They, too, would be shot at dawn. Why, God, what had any of them done? Tonya asked herself. Hadn't they faithfully served the Soviet Union? Why did she deserve such a fate? She so intensely wanted to live, she had so much to tell, there were so many unwritten poems in her heart!

She felt the tears welling in her eyes, and bit the coarse blanket to muffle her sob. Her guards shouldn't hear her crying; she wouldn't give them that pleasure. Perhaps it was only a nightmare, and she would wake up in her house, with her family. After all, only three years ago she had received the Mayakovsky Award, and her poems had been read in schools, factories, army camps; the *Literaturnaya Gazetta* had printed two of them together with an interview; she had even been mentioned as a candidate for the Lenin Medal. And here she was tonight, waiting to be shot for some nebulous crime she had never committed.

It had all happened because she and her first husband, Victor Wolf, had joined the Anti-Fascist Writers Committee during the war. That foolish step had sealed their fate. But in fact they weren't given any choice — the government had urged them to join. It was in 1941, exactly a year after she had run away from home and married Victor. They were so much in love, both young, both poets, totally involved in the socialist society, dreaming of a new world they would help build as soon as the war was over.

The committee had been created at the darkest hour of the war, when the Germans were already on the Volokolamsk road, barely fifteen miles from the Kremlin, preparing for their final onslaught on Moscow. Victor had come home very excited one night, and told her of the anti-fascist committee, which was to include the most prominent Jewish writers and philosophers of the Soviet Union. The committee's purpose was to gather support for the war effort in the Jewish communities abroad. They had asked Victor to be one of the founders. He was so flattered, he was only twenty-eight years old! He accepted, and they had both been elected members of the board.

Victor had also participated in the first delegation the committee had sent to the United States. On his return, he brought Tonya news from her older sister, Nina, who lived in New York. Nina had sent her a fluffy white blouse and three big bars of chocolate; she knew Tonya's weaknesses. Victor was thrilled to have met Albert Einstein in America, and the professor had pledged support for the committee's work.

The troubles had started after the war. Some of their friends had suggested that the committee should disband. "We are members of the Soviet Writers Union," she remembered Slavin saying, "we don't need a Jewish organization."

But Slavin was in the minority. Most members of the board thought that, on the contrary, they should even intensify their activities, and speak for the Jewish community. "The Soviet Jews need moral leadership!" their chairman, Solomon Mikhoels, had said at the plenary meeting, and everyone had cheered. Tonya remembered Victor's passionate speech in support of Mikhoels. Looking back now, it seemed they had become intoxicated with their success in Russia and abroad. They had forgotten that the Kremlin resented nationalism of any kind, especially Jewish.

In September 1948, on the day Victor had been appointed lecturer at Moscow University, the committee had taken another step down the road to their doom. Mikhoels and his deputy, Professor Sapojnikov, petitioned Stalin to settle Jewish survivors in Crimea. They also asked Stalin to condemn anti-Semitism in Russia.

They had gone too far. They should have realized this when the writer Ilya Ehrenburg, known for his close ties with the Kremlin, resigned from the committee. Another bad omen they disregarded was that Stalin didn't answer the petition. Tonya and Victor didn't worry; they were too busy furnishing the tiny apartment they'd gotten through Victor's connections at the Ministry of Culture. But in January 1949 they were shaken by news that Mikhoels had been brutally murdered during a visit to Minsk, apparently by young hoodlums. His wife could not find out exactly how he had died.

Odd, alarming rumors circulated among the committee members. It was said that Mikhoels's killers were not hooligans, but officers of the secret police; the murder had been ordered by the KGB. An obituary, scheduled to be published in *Pravda* was removed from the paper at the last moment. A committee meeting called to commemorate the chairman's death was canceled by orders of the *militzia*, the state police; no explanation was given.

Victor didn't believe the rumors; he told Tonya such things couldn't happen in Soviet Russia. Still, an uneasy tension pervaded the Anti-Fascist Writers Committee, and some voiced grim forebodings.

"I have the feeling that a noose is tightening around my neck," Yasha Slavin told them one night, after a meeting with French communist poets. Slavin, a gangly youth with a huge Adam's apple and brooding black eyes, was their best friend. He knew Politburo member Mikhail Pashko, a high party priest. "Pashko says Stalin was beside himself with fury when he received our petition." There was fear in Slavin's eyes.

Victor shrugged. "Come on, Yasha, these are not the dark ages," he said without conviction.

But Tonya knew better. In eastern Europe, show trials were being held, and democratic leaders were hanged for "conspiring against the state." In Russia, people disappeared without a trace. According to some, millions were imprisoned in labor camps beyond the Arctic Circle, and thousands of others were being executed. Tonya and Victor never spoke about them. Perhaps it was out of cowardice, or perhaps they didn't want to admit that their red flag could be marked by any stain.

Still, Tonya was deeply shocked when her downstairs neighbor, a stout Ukrainian woman always dressed in black, confided in her one rainy Sunday. She had just returned from church — the authorities didn't prevent old women from going to churches — and Tonya found her by the door, crying. Her big flat face was puffed, and her mouth quivered; she kept wiping her tears with her pudgy fists. Tonya made her some tea, and the Ukrainian told her about her son. He had been taken prisoner by the Germans and spent two and a half years in a POW camp. Two months after his release, at the end of the war, he had been shot by a Red Army firing squad.

"They said my Pavka was a traitor, Tonya Alexandrova. Would you believe that? My son — a traitor! His only fault was to be taken prisoner. Do you shoot somebody for that? And let me tell you . . ." The wretched woman bent toward Tonya, lowering her voice. There was fear in her furtive eyes, fear and secret knowledge. "He is not the only one. They say that our little father" — Tonya nodded at the allusion to Stalin — "gave orders to shoot thousands of former war prisoners. Our own sons! He called them traitors. I think that he himself — " She bit her lip, realizing she had said too much. Hastily, she crossed herself and disappeared into her small dark room beneath the staircase.

A FEW WEEKS after Mikhoels's death a man came to the Wolfs' apartment. They had not been expecting anybody that evening and when Tonya opened the door, the stranger had stood frozen on the doorstep, staring at her intently. He was a big man, with wavy brown hair and a broad face, and he was dressed in a government-issue civilian suit. He had a pugnacious chin, a full mouth, and straight eyebrows. Tonya was struck by his black eyes, which were sheltered in dark sockets. They were imbued with profound sadness and carried an oddly tormented look.

After a moment Victor came over, and the man introduced himself as Major Boris Morozov. He spoke at length with Victor in the living room, while Tonya sat in the kitchen, sorting the old baby clothes her sister-in-law had sent her; she was four months pregnant. She was deeply worried. What did a major want with her husband? Worse, a major in civilian clothes; that could only mean KGB. She had the feeling she had seen him before at the monthly committee meetings, which were open to the public. He might have been one of those who had asked for her autograph after she had read her poems.

Tonight she entered the living room twice, to bring the men tea and some biscuits; at both times Morozov stared at her so openly that she felt embarrassed. When he was about to leave, Victor called her and she came to the door. Morozov bid them good-bye, formally shaking their hands. He stared at Tonya a last time before vanishing down the dark staircase.

When they were alone, she turned to Victor. "Did you see how he looked at me?" she asked. But Victor didn't even hear her question. He was badly frightened. Morozov, he told her, was a KGB investigator. He wanted to know about the committee — did they have contacts with Jews in America and in England, did they meet Western diplomats, did they engage in activities against the regime?

She was astounded. "But that's . . . preposterous," she stammered. "We only had contacts with the Americans when the government asked us to. Didn't you tell him that?"

Victor was shaking his head. "I told him that the last time we met an American was during the war. He didn't seem to believe me."

"But he must, Victor, he must! Go to Fefer right away and tell him about this man!"

"Major Morozov said that several officers are talking tonight to the board members. The KGB suspects we are involved in an imperialist plot against the Soviet Union."

"My God!" she said. "If he thinks so, then . . ."

". . . then that's the end of us," Victor whispered.

VICTOR SPENT THE NIGHT huddled in the living room armchair, chain-smoking his Bielomorsk cigarettes. Early the next morning, without even bothering to shave or eat breakfast, he rushed to see the other members of the board. A violent storm was raging outside, and howling winds swept the frozen city. This wasn't a day to walk the streets, but Tonya had to see her doctor for her monthly checkup. When she stepped out of the house, a figure approached her out of the bleak, swirling curtain of snow. Only when the man was at arm's length did she recognize him. It was Major Morozov. White frost had formed on his eyebrows.

"Do you mind if I walk with you, Comrade Wolf?" he said. He was bent forward against the strong wind.

She shrugged, her feelings a mixture of fear and helplessness. "But I'm going to — "

"I'll accompany you to the doctor and back," he said, and she winced. He knew where she was going, of course, the KGB knew everything, and still he sounded awkward, ill at ease.

She expected him to question her, but he walked beside her in silence, staring at her with the same tormented expression she remembered from last night. He was a man of about forty, barely four or five years older than Victor, but his sturdy build and broad face made him look much older. When she entered the clinic, he vanished, but when she came out he was beside her again. At the doorstep of her house he took two parcels from the large pockets of his heavy sheepskin. "This is for you," he said. "Some smoked ham and a jar of honey. It will be good for your baby. And some chocolate, you'll like it."

She stared at him, astounded. "I cannot, I mean — "

"Take it, Tonya Alexandrova," he said softly. "One doesn't refuse food in Moscow these days."

He was right; she hadn't tasted smoked ham for months. But she was scared. How did Morozov know she was so fond of chocolate? Was this mentioned in her KGB file? He had addressed her as Tonya Alexandrova, which meant he knew that her father's name was Alexander. What else did he know about her? And why was he taking such an interest in her? Perhaps he was attracted to her. She knew she was beautiful, and she was accustomed to the hunger in men's eyes. But no man had ever stared at her with such pain and intensity.

She accepted the food only because it came from him, a KGB officer. It created a sort of complicity between them, made him her friend; perhaps he would also help her and Victor in the investigation. She wanted to ask him about it, but couldn't.

The next morning, when she went to the food store he was there again, in a Zil sedan at the corner. He must have been waiting for her to come out. At the store he flashed his special card, and she was given twice her regular ration without having to wait. The women lined up before the fish and meat counters shot venomous looks at her but didn't dare open their mouths; they knew a KGB officer when they saw one.

For the next couple of weeks Morozov miraculously appeared beside her almost every time she left her house. By the few words he exchanged with her, she realized he knew all about her work and had read some of her poems.

She finally found the courage to ask him about the investigation. Victor had spoken to all the committee members, who had also been questioned; but nothing had happened since, and her husband had somewhat calmed down. Morozov, though, would say nothing about it. He only shook his head and stared at her with his haunted eyes.

One morning, barely five minutes after Victor had left, there was a knock on the door. It was Morozov, with some parcels of food and a package that turned out to contain a piece of fine woolen fabric.

"I cannot accept that," she said. "I am very grateful, Major Morozov, but — "

He didn't listen. "Can we sit down?" he asked, and without waiting, he walked into the living room. She hastily removed a clothesline that had been stretched across the room. At that time of year it was impossible to hang anything outside.

"Would you like some tea?" she asked awkwardly, but he shook his head. He sat facing her, joining his hands on the table. She was already familiar with his tense silences, but today he seemed different, more preoccupied.

"This morning," he said slowly, "my colleagues arrested Fefer, Halkin, Slavin, and Gurevich. They didn't pick up Sapojnikov because he is on a lecture tour in Romania. The Securitate will take care of him. All the people we arrested are accused of being enemy agents. We have solid evidence about their contacts with the imperialist powers. They will be tried and probably executed."

She felt a sudden chill and her hand jumped to her throat. "But that's not true! I know them, they haven't done anything!"

"The orders came from above, Tonya Alexandrova," he said quietly. In slow, measured movements he lit a cigarette and inhaled deeply, holding the cigarette in his cupped hands, the soldiers' way. "But there is worse news. Your husband, yourself, and the other members of the board will be arrested during the night. You, too, are going on trial."

"But for what?" She was choking. "On what charges? We haven't done anything. I haven't, and I know that Victor hasn't."

"Your husband is dead meat already, Tonya Alexandrova," Morozov said. "They all are. When we get orders to arrest somebody, it means that the evidence is there. Nobody I've ever arrested has been found innocent. Ever."

She slumped in her chair. The room was spinning around her. Morozov went into the kitchen and came back with a glass of water. "Drink this," he said to her in a gentle but firm voice.

She gulped down the water. "Why are you telling me all this?" she stuttered.

He shrugged. "It is not a secret. What can your husband do? Or you? Run away? There's no escape. You're under surveillance twenty-four hours a day."

He suddenly seemed at a loss. He sat silent for a while, frowning. "I am telling you this" — his voice was different now, insecure — "because I think I can save your life."

"My life?"

He nodded, his eyes searching her face.

"How?" she uttered.

He shrugged and said nothing.

"I don't believe you."

He didn't speak, stubbornly staring at her, so she leaned over and grasped his arm.

"And Victor? What about Victor?"

"I told you, your husband is finished. There is nothing I can do for him. But I can save you. You came to very few meetings. You are a woman, and you're pregnant. I can protect you."

Her question burst out of her mouth before she even could think of it. "But there's a price, right?"

He held her eyes. "I want you to divorce your husband and marry me."

She looked at him, speechless, then buried her face in her hands. He was trying to buy her. It was unbearable. He would spare her life if she became his property, and if she left the man she loved. A wave of indignation surged inside her. She couldn't believe all this was happening.

"I know these are not the right circumstances for a declaration," Morozov said quietly, "but I am very fond of you."

"How can you — " she started, but he was already on his feet, reaching for his coat.

"Think about it," he said. "Talk it over with your husband. Whether you say yes or no, he will be tried and sentenced anyway. The only question is about you. And your baby. Do you want to have the child? Do you want to die or live? You've got to decide. I don't demand that you love me."

She slowly got up. Her knees were shaking.

Morozov stopped at the door, looking oddly vulnerable, his shoulders slightly hunched. "You don't know me, Tonya Alexandrova, but you must believe me. I know you love your husband. I never wanted to propose to you in such a way. This is a sad situation, and you don't deserve to be humiliated. You are a fine woman. I am embarrassed to talk to you like this. But I care about you, and you have no other way out."

* * *

SHE HAD COME to meet Victor at the Turgenevskaya underground station. Since Morozov's visit, she had felt she was losing her mind. What could she do, dear God, was there no hope for them? "Your husband is dead meat," Morozov had said. She was suffocating in the empty apartment, so she had run out of the house and wandered in the streets for hours, oblivious to the freezing cold, till exhaustion and the falling night had chased her back. Morozov's voice kept ringing in her ears. "Your husband is dead meat."

Victor came out of the station in a crowd of merry schoolgirls wearing ribbons in their braids and the red scarves of the Communist youth. The girls swept by them, eagerly chattering, and their happy, careless laughter left a silvery wake in the crisp evening air. She shuddered. Victor hugged her strongly and glanced nervously around. She realized that Morozov hadn't been lying. Victor apparently knew about the arrests. They didn't exchange a word till they were home. Then she told him about Morozov's offer. "It's disgusting," she said, "disgusting and degrading. Am I a slave to be bought and sold?"

"Disgusting or not, he's right," Victor said, his voice barely a murmur. She looked at him. His face was white as a sheet. They were standing in the kitchen, and through the paper-thin wall they could hear their drunken neighbor yell at his wife.

"What he told you about the arrests is true," Victor went on. "They picked up Halkin at the university. I saw them. One of my students said Fefer was arrested in front of his house."

She stared at him, stunned, refusing to believe he was saying this. "You want me to do as he says?"

He shrugged, and suddenly reached for her, pulling her close to him. "It's your life, Tonya, don't you understand? They'll kill you like a dog. They'll kill all of us."

"But I love you," she cried out, as tears flooded her eyes. "I love you, I don't want to live without you." She buried her head in his shoulder.

"I love you, too," he whispered. "You're my life. But there is no other choice, don't you see?" He was stroking her hair, his fingers trembling. "Do it for the child, my love," he said. "For our baby, Tonya."

"How can you say this? Can you bear the thought that I'll let Morozov kiss me, undress me, sleep with me?"

Victor cupped her face in his hands and stared at her. He was crying, too, the tears leaving glistening paths on his ashen skin. "Do it for our baby, Tonichka," he repeated.

THEY DIDN'T SLEEP all night, lying on the bed fully dressed, their unsolved dilemma rising like an invisible wall between them. She stared at the shadows crawling on the ceiling, and her memories carried her back to her youth in Kiev, to the day she had seen Victor for the first time, his smile bashful, disarming, as he addressed her class at the Kirov high school. "I am your new literature teacher." And the same shy, handsome youth, metamorphosing before her eyes into a charismatic poet, passionately reciting the verses of Pushkin, Mayakovsky, Lermontov, and his own. She was instantly infatuated with the young dreamer. On her way home she thought of nothing else but his black eyes, the proud bearing of his head, his delicate hands, moving gracefully as he spoke, accompanying his powerful performance.

She recalled the first time he had looked at her, the first time they were alone, the first time he had touched her. She thought of their secret meetings by the Bogdan Khmelnizki statue, his husky voice and trembling lips when he murmured, "I love you, Tonichka." Their decision to elope still seemed unreal, like a dream. She remembered her flight from home, their marriage, the exhausting train ride to Moscow. She loved him so deeply, so totally, and now he was asking her to leave him in order to save her life.

She got up and stepped to the window. It was a starry Moscow night, and their snowbound street stretched before her, serene and calm. Morozov was nothing but the fruit of her imagination, a character out of a bad dream; soon it would be morning and she would wake up. But she heard Victor move restlessly behind her. He wasn't sleeping; he was frightened, like her. At that moment she made up her mind. She would do anything, anything in the world, to save him. If he died, she would die, too. She returned to her bed, reached for Victor, clutched his feverish hand and pressed it to her cheek.

Shortly before dawn there was a knock on the door. Victor opened it. Morozov entered, escorted by two uniformed KGB lieutenants. "You're under arrest, Comrade Wolf," he said softly.

Victor grabbed his coat and stepped outside without turning back.

Morozov closed the door behind him, looking at Tonya. "I am sorry," he said. She clenched her teeth. After a short silence, he spoke again. "Have you thought about our conversation, Tonya Alexandrova?"

She got up from the bed and went to the window. A big black car was parked by the sidewalk, its exhaust pipe spewing thick white smoke. She had to make her decision, "I have one condition," she said without looking at him. Her throat was constricted. "I'll do what you say if you promise that Victor will not die."

"I cannot promise such a thing," Morozov said coldly. "There's going to be a trial."

"I know all about your trials." Down in the street she saw the KGB officers pushing Victor into the black car. A woman passing by quickened her pace, looking away. "You can have Victor sentenced to a prison term," she went on. "You have connections. If he is sentenced to death, I'd rather die with him."

She heard Morozov's steps, then he seized her by the shoulders and made her turn around. His eyes burned with anger and his mouth was a thin black line. She shivered.

"If he isn't executed, he'll be sent to a labor camp," he said. "Is that what you want? It's worse than death. He won't last more than a year, he's so frail."

"In a year, a lot can happen," she said stubbornly.

"Not to him," Morozov said knowingly. Then he added: "But I can't promise that. He is accused of treason."

"Then you'd better take me with you," she said.

"That's a foolish thing to say," he snapped, shaking his head.

"You are dealing with a foolish woman."

He stepped back and lit a cigarette, his eyes never leaving hers. "And if I manage to save his neck?"

She didn't answer.

"I'll see what I can do," he muttered, and walked out.

The trial started on July 1 and lasted three days. Except for KGB clerks and officers, nobody was allowed to attend. Tonya spent most of the time in the waiting hall of the Seventh District popular tribunal, together with the families of the other Jewish writers. They didn't speak; everyone was terribly scared, and Fefer's wife had warned her to keep quiet. "There are KGB agents among us," she whispered, wringing her hands.

At the end of the third day, eight of the ten members of the committee board were found guilty of treason and sentenced to death. They were executed after their appeal was rejected. The only survivors were Victor Wolf, who was condemned to life imprisonment in a labor camp, and Tonya Wolf, who wasn't brought to trial at all. The KGB report established that she had been unaware of the committee's illegal activities and therefore couldn't be accused of crimes against the state. The seventeen members of the committee council were severely reprimanded but not punished. The committee was disbanded and its archives were seized by the KGB.

Tonya had divorced her husband shortly after his arrest and resumed her maiden name, Tonya Gordon. A month after the trial she gave birth to Victor's child, a boy whom she named Alexander, after her father. In the early fall of 1949 she married Boris Morozov.

THE SOUND of heavy steps startled her, and she propped herself on her elbows. Cold sweat broke out on her forehead. Were they coming for her already? But the steps faded away and she closed her eyes, letting out a deep breath. The faces of the boys sailed out of her tormented memory, followed by Victor's gaunt profile, the way she had seen him last, three years ago. It was an evening in mid-July, and the humid breath of summer was smothering the city of Moscow. Tonya had waited for hours outside the Yaroslavski railway station where the political prisoners were herded aboard a Siberia-bound train. She had barely recognized Victor when he trudged, in chains, in the middle of a group of prisoners. He was bareheaded; his skull had been shaven. He'd looked old and withered without his shock of black hair. She called his name but he didn't hear, and she suddenly realized that she would never see him again.

She couldn't write to him. Morozov had warned her that if she maintained any contact with her ex-husband, the KGB prosecutors would come after her like bloodhounds; he wouldn't be able to protect her. She heard about Victor only once, from his old mother, who lived in Leningrad. He had contracted tuberculosis and was in critical condition at the camp's hospital. That was more than two years ago. She had mentioned it to Morozov, hoping he could help, but he only shook his head. "I told you," he said gently. "Vorkuta is the living Hell. They don't last long over there."

She wouldn't give up, and had secretly asked her brother, Valery to write Victor; friends and relatives could write to the prisoners once every three months. But Valery's letter had been returned with the word UNKNOWN stamped in purple over the address. The purple stamp meant that the prisoner was dead. Poor Victor, at least his suffering was over.

With Morozov she'd lived a few sheltered years. He had been good to her, and treated little Alex with tenderness. Ten months after their wedding, Tonya's second child was born: Morozov's son, Dimitri. Neither boy was circumcised, for their own safety.

Morozov was very much in love with her, and he refused her nothing. They lived in a modern apartment on the Kalinin Prospect, and the KGB car with the driver was at her disposal all day long. She shopped at the special stores for government and party officials; food was abundant in their home, and she could buy clothes she had never dreamed of. One summer they vacationed in a guest house for high-ranking officials in Sochi, on the Black Sea; she tasted caviar and champagne for the first time in her life.

After Morozov was promoted to full colonel, they received a six-room dacha — a country house — by Lake Biserovskoye, barely a two-hour drive from Moscow. They spent most of their weekends and vacations there, and the children couldn't have been happier. Occasionally she would even recover enough of her peace of mind to return to her writing for a few hours. But her poems were different now, bitter and cynical, full of anger.

She had a good life with Morozov, but she didn't love him. Victor had been her only love, and she remained faithful to him, at least in her thoughts and feelings. She did her best to conceal her pain from her family. The first time Morozov made love to her, she lay cold and inert as a corpse under his heavy bulk. As soon as she felt his climax inside her, she scurried to the bathroom and threw up, disgusted, feeling like a prostitute.

When she returned to bed, Morozov wasn't there; he spent the rest of the night in the other room. But the following night he made love to her again, very patiently, very tenderly. She clenched her fists, trying to restrain herself, but her body instinctively responded to her husband's lovemaking. She was swept by self-hatred for her weakness and for betraying Victor. But she was young, lonely, and desperately needed love and tenderness. Morozov was the only person who could release her from her agonizing solitude.

Still, Victor never left her thoughts. During the day she behaved more or less normally, but when she turned off her bedroom light and closed her eyes, she was assailed by terrible nightmares, the memory of Victor haunting her dreams. She was obsessed by feelings of guilt for being alive while Victor was already rotting in some mass grave in Siberia. When she became pregnant, she thought she was going mad. Inside her a child was growing; not Victor's, but the child of a stranger. This was her ultimate betrayal, she thought, as Morozov's seed grew in her body. Victor kept returning in her dreams night after night, his caressing voice haunting her, his dark eyes a silent accusation. Often she woke up screaming, and found herself in Morozov's arms. He watched her in silence, never asking why she'd screamed; he knew.

Still, his compassion couldn't dispel her loneliness. Victor had been not only her husband, but her closest friend; they'd had no secrets from each other. Morozov was different: a reserved man, he spoke little, and refrained from discussing his work. He told her very little about himself, and seemed unwilling to reveal even the most banal episodes of his life. When he would finally divulge a trivial detail from his distant past, he would behave as if parting with a fateful state secret. Perhaps it was because of his profession, she thought: Information is power, and you never disclose information unless it is absolutely necessary.

He reluctantly revealed that he was a worker's son, from the village of Shepetovka, in the Ukraine; he had enlisted in the Red Army before the war and gone to the Frunze Military Academy. Yes, he had fought in the war. Where? Oh, here and there, in Poland, in Russia, abroad . . . He had gotten married very young, but his wife Marina had been killed during the war. Yes, there were also children. Two little girls, Natasha and Vera. They had died, too. At that point he abruptly stopped, his eyes acquiring a distant look, and he withdrew into himself. At such moments, he would step heavily toward the old cupboard in the living room and take out the bottle of vodka, which he drank alone, his head bent low over the glass, a deep frown etched in his forehead.

Yet, on the few occasions when he had a reason to rejoice — like when she announced she was pregnant, or on Dimitri's first birthday — Morozov would discard the shield of self-control and an utterly different man would emerge, lively, spontaneous, totally uninhibited. He had a surprisingly warm voice, and when he sang, golden specks would dance in his eyes. A couple of times, when Ukrainian *kazatchok* had blasted from their old radio, he had danced for the children, shouting and whistling, bellowing with laughter, sticking his thumbs in his belt, slapping his boot heels with his open palms. His mass of undulating brown hair roguishly swaying over his forehead, an impish smile fluttering on his mouth, he suddenly appeared young and mischievous. Still, he never told her what had transformed the young Ukrainian with the melodious voice and the infectious laughter into the lonely, tormented man she had married.

LATELY Morozov had changed. He had never raised his voice to her or the children before; now he became tense, preoccupied. In the evenings he would sit for hours by the table, the bottle of vodka at his elbow. Often he would enter the boys' room and stand by their beds, watching them sleep. Tonya sensed his anguish and kept asking him what was wrong; he stubbornly refused to tell her.

. . . until that night, a couple of weeks ago, when he had awakened her. He looked distressed, and for the first time ever she discerned a note of despair in his voice.

"Something terrible is happening," he said, and she jumped out of bed, alarmed. She shivered in her thin nightgown. He lapsed into silence, apparently trying to collect his thoughts. "Lately the Kremlin is waging a war against the Jews. We have been secretly arresting Jewish leaders all over the country. The orders come directly from Stalin. He has become obsessed with the Jews."

She stepped toward him, awkwardly tying the belt of her robe. He had never spoken like this, not about Stalin, whom he worshiped.

Morozov's breath was shallow, and he fired his sentences in short, abrupt outbursts. "Stalin is not himself anymore," he went on. "He is convinced there is a Jewish plot against his life. An international plot. Concocted in Washington. Controlled by the American Jews."

She was stunned. "That's insane," she said.

"Last night we got direct orders from Stalin to arrest nine doctors. In Moscow and Leningrad. All but one of them are Jews. Stalin accused them of planning to assassinate him and some other communist leaders. Beria even has a witness."

"A witness? I don't believe it."

He nodded slowly. "Dr. Lidia Timashuk. She is a former KGB agent who used to work at the Kremlin hospital. She says she has proof of the conspiracy, that she heard the doctors planning the assassinations. She also went through the files of high-ranking patients, and can prove that the Jewish doctors gave them the wrong treatment in order to cause their deaths. She will testify against the Jews." He touched her shoulder. "Your brother is among them."

"Valery?" She shivered. Valery Gordon was one of Russia's leading hematologists. "Valery planning to assassinate Stalin?"

Morozov nodded. "Valery, yes, and Professor Kaplan, Professor Rodoy, Dr. Kozlovska . . ."

"That is insane," she repeated, her heart thumping wildly. "Nobody will believe this rubbish. Stalin believes that?"

"Stalin wants them shot," Morozov said bluntly. "He claims that they have already poisoned Zhdanov and Scherbakov."

She was overwhelmed by the enormity of the accusation. "But they . . . they're long dead," she stammered. Both party dignitaries had died of natural causes.

"Stalin says the Jewish doctors murdered them on orders from Washington. He also says" — Morozov hesitated a second — "that the intermediary between the Jewish doctors and their American manipulators was Solomon Mikhoels."

"My God," she murmured.

"The Jewish doctors will be tried and shot in the next few weeks," Morozov said, then averted his eyes. "But there is worse. Stalin ordered the arrest of all surviving members of the anti-fascist committee. All the former council members."

She suddenly understood and looked at him in horror.

He slowly nodded, his face livid. "You, too. They'll come for you tonight or tomorrow. I have no power in this affair. Beria has taken the matter out of my hands and given the entire operation to the First Directorate."

The First Directorate, Tonya knew, was in charge of operations abroad. Counterespionage inside Russia was under the control of the Second Directorate, of which Morozov was deputy director. "I tried to stop them," Morozov said, "but they wouldn't even talk to me. This time I am helpless."

"My God," she murmured again. "And the children? What about the children?"

Morozov looked at her, then shuddered, as if under the impact of a physical blow. A shrill, desperate wail burst from his chest, and his huge body was shaken by hoarse, spasmodic sobs. He turned his back to her and leaned against the wall, crying. Tonya was looking at a broken man.

THEY CAME FOR HER on Sunday, four KGB officers. Morozov stood in the living room, head sunk between his shoulders, and watched them take her away. She knew this meant Morozov's end, too, in a few weeks, perhaps a couple of months. First he would be kicked out of the KGB, then arrested and probably shot. In Russia they didn't do things halfway.

They brought her to the Lubyanka and threw her in this cell. She was supposed to be isolated from the other prisoners, but one of the guards told her that all the Jewish writers were in the same block. Her brother and the other doctors were in another prison.

She wasn't even brought to trial, and in a way, she was grateful to the KGB for that. She was relieved that she wouldn't have to go through the same charade as Victor had. She was ready to die. She had gotten used to the idea years ago, when they had taken Victor away. But the children, good God, who would take care of the children? They were so small! She loved them both, but feared most for little Alex. Boris would protect Dimitri; he was his child, perhaps he would send him to his mother; but Alex, a Jewish boy of three, would be thrown into the street! What could she do, how could she help?

She got up and approached the near wall. Boris had told her once about a heroine of the French resistance, Suzanne Spaak, who had covered the walls of her cell at Fresnes Prison with more than three hundred inscriptions, all intended for her husband. After her death, Claude Spaak had found her messages. Morozov must remember that story, she thought; he'll certainly ask to examine her cell. She removed the Star of David from its chain and, with its sharp point, etched in the mortar her last message for her family.

Boris, she scratched. *Save the children Nina can help with Alex love love to you all . . .*

But before she signed her name, the sound of marching boots filled the corridor, and the door of her cell squeaked on its hinges.

SHORTLY BEFORE DAWN the guards led them into the east court of the Lubyanka. The blizzard had finally died, the courtyard was covered with pure white snow. The guards herded them toward the far wall, where they stood in line, facing the rough, irregular stones. They were not allowed to look back. The stones were pockmarked with a multitude of black scars and grooves. Bullet marks, Tonya thought, bullets that had ricocheted from the stone wall after accomplishing their grisly task.

She shivered. On her right she heard low, muffled sobbing. She turned her head. Bodenkin was standing beside her, holding his baggy pants with his hands, his coat open; tears streamed down his unshaven face. He looked so helpless, Tonya thought, so vulnerable. She remembered his powerful verses, his moving "Ode to the Unknown Soldier." She recalled the fire burning in his eyes; and his ringing, defiant voice, echoing in Moscow's Taganka Hall as he read his electrifying poems.

Beside him she made out a humped shape. Laufer. And farther down, Segal, and Belkind, and Ribitzky. The gentle Bronstein, the gaunt, brooding Halperin, and of course Plotnikov, the cancer-ridden philosopher. They were all here, the greatest Jewish writers and poets of the Soviet Union, destined to die like traitors at the hands of a paranoid dictator.

Perhaps it was at this very place that KGB officers had also shot Fefer, Halkin, Slavin, and the other members of the committee board after their mock trial four years ago. Would the story of this infamy ever be told? Would they be remembered?

She stood ankle deep in the snow but didn't feel the cold. She tried not to think about what was going to happen. On her left, Horowitz had started to pray, swaying back and forth. *"Shema Yisroel,"* he chanted loudly, *"Adonai Eloheinu . . ."* Other voices joined him, hesitant at first, then confident and strong.

She didn't know how to pray, she had never been in a synagogue in her life; Lenin had said that religion is the opium of the masses. But now she joined the chorus, trying to repeat the unintelligible words after the men. *"Shema Yisroel,"* she murmured, turning for the first time in her life to the ancient god of her people. God, have mercy on the children, please help my children, they are so vulnerable, please protect them, they carry me in their blood, and Alex is Victor's son.

A shot echoed on her left and she heard the soft thud of a body in the snow. Her heart leapt wildly in her chest. The executions had begun.

Chapter 2

From a barred window on the third floor, Colonel Boris Morozov was watching the inner court of the Lubyanka. His eyes were riveted to the slender woman facing the execution wall, her long golden hair spilling over her shoulders. He had been waiting by that window since midnight; he had seen Tonya come out of the cellars, together with the other prisoners. In a few minutes she would be dead. He shuddered. God, how he loved her! She was the second woman he had ever loved, and the second one he was going to lose.

He had married Marina, his first wife, two and a half years before the war. He was then a young officer in the NKVD, the Soviet security service, with brilliant prospects for the future. He was a fervent Bolshevik, an admirer of Stalin, willing to devote his life to the defense of his country and the triumph of communism. He owed the party everything he had achieved: the house by the railroad depot, his education at the Shepetovka high school, and his training at the Frunze Officers Academy.

Actually he owed all this to his father, a burly railroad worker and a dyed-in-the-wool revolutionary, who had been killed in 1917 during the assault on Tzaritzin, the royal city. Tzaritzin was now Stalingrad, and his dead father a hero of the revolution. As the family of a fallen hero, Boris and his mother, Varvara, enjoyed special privileges: a pension for her, free tutoring for him, and a decrepit wooden house expropriated from a Polish merchant who had escaped across the Polish border, only twenty miles away. Shepetovka being a border town, it had a mixed Polish-Ukrainian population. During the civil war and the ensuing Polish-Soviet conflict, the region had passed back and forth several times, and many people had relatives on the other side of the border.

Boris had known Marina Arbatova since their childhood. She was a willowy, mischievous girl with irresistible dimples in her cheeks. Marina's mother was Polish; after the Polish-Soviet war of 1920, her brothers had escaped to Poland. One of them, Henrik Leshchinski, had joined the Polish army.

For Boris, Marina was the prettiest girl on earth. And he was the happiest man when she agreed to marry him, shortly after his posting at the local headquarters of NKVD border intelligence. Their marriage had been a three-day feast, with guests flocking from all over the Ukraine. Through his connections, Boris had even arranged a special visa for Marina's uncle Henrik, who was serving with a Polish border garrison. Henrik came in civilian clothes; none of the guests suspected he was a Polish officer.

After the wedding, Boris brought Marina home to his mother's house. The slender, blue-eyed girl with the silvery laugh and the heavy golden braids gave him two children, two little daughters. The day Boris's younger daughter, Vera, was born, Hitler attacked Poland and the Second World War began.

One night, two weeks later, Boris and Marina were awakened by the roar of engines; from their window they watched the clumsy T-35 tanks race through the unpaved streets of Shepetovka, heading for the border. The Red Army, too, was invading Poland. Only later was Boris to learn about the secret pact between the USSR and Nazi Germany, dividing Poland between them. Boris was thrilled. Radio Ukraine, broadcasting from Kiev, announced that Stalin was getting even with Poland, which had treacherously attacked the Soviet Union after the revolution.

The radio commentators kept warning the nation about the danger of a foreign aggression against the motherland. The day of the first winter storm, Boris reported to the NKVD headquarters at Gorodok and was dispatched to Moscow. There he was assigned to the seven hundred-man Battalion 121, made up entirely of NKVD officers. An old barracks of the czar's dragoons in Petrovskoye forest served as the battalion's headquarters; the camp was heavily guarded, and the battalion's very existence was shrouded in secrecy. Boris was elated; he was now a member of an elite unit.

Morozov was driven by a burning ambition to make his way to the top. The pay in the NKVD was much better than in the regular army; officers who won the trust of the Kremlin could be swiftly promoted, achieve important status in the party, and even reach the holy of holies of the Soviet regime, the Politburo. Besides, Morozov had always been thrilled by the secrecy of intelligence work. The NKVD's formal status was merely that of a government ministry, dealing with internal affairs. Actually, it was the most powerful organization in the country. It had swallowed the former secret services, the revolutionary Cheka and the bloody GPU. The NKVD tracked down enemies of the state and carried out secret operations abroad. The organization was headed by Stalin's trusted companion, Lavrenti Beria.

Beria was a dreaded man. His name was never pronounced aloud, but always whispered; he was feared even by the members of the Politburo. He controlled the secret police, the militia, parts of the army and the secret services; he ruled over the prisons and the labor camps. Beria was rumored to be a ruthless master spy who wouldn't hesitate to kill with his bare hands for Stalin. Boris had seen him when he came to inspect the battalion: a short, balding man in a general's uniform, with a sallow face, wire-rimmed spectacles, and thin, bloodless lips.

In August 1940, Battalion 121 was dispatched to White Russia. The officers were ordered to remove the epaulets, medals, and stars of rank from their uniforms. They were issued revolvers and submachine guns; heavy crates of ammunition were loaded on the trucks that were parked outside their barracks. Boris and his companions could hardly hide their excitement: they were on their way to a top-secret mission.

Their journey lasted more than four days. In the early morning of the fifth day, after passing through several roadblocks and turning onto a bumpy dirt road, they reached their destination. As the engine was turned off, Boris impatiently pulled aside the tarpaulin that covered their truck and looked around, stretching his arms. His whole body ached from the long journey. They had stopped in a large clearing, in the middle of a forest. Several tents stood in the shade, and a couple of soldiers were cooking thick yellow porridge in a field kitchen. He jumped down, enchanted by the beauty of a forest awakening in the summer dawn; in the luxurious foliage, morning birds were singing.

Boris lit a cigarette and inhaled the acrid smoke. "What's the name of this place?" he asked a soldier who was leaning on a tree.

"Katyn, comrade," the soldier said, "the forest of Katyn."

THEY SPENT THE MORNING setting up their tents. In the afternoon they were assembled in the middle of the clearing. All other personnel — soldiers, drivers, cooks — were ordered to leave the area. Colonel Gregoriev, the battalion commander, came to face his men. He was a wiry man with a hawkish, pockmarked face. He was accompanied by a cadaverous civilian in a leather jacket.

"We are here to accomplish a task for the motherland," he said curtly. "It is not a pleasant task, but it is a vital one. Very shortly, a number of Polish officers will be brought over. They were captured in Poland during our recent operations. Those officers have fought against our country and are dangerous enemies of the Soviet nation. Since 1920 the Poles, helped by an international capitalist conspiracy, have been trying to smother the socialist revolution. We are here to assure that they will never again lead their soldiers against the Soviet Union."

Boris and the officer standing beside him, a young Armenian, exchanged baffled looks. What did Gregoriev mean? But their commander went on, in the same dry, matter-of-fact voice: "Each platoon has been assigned its part of the operation. Your platoon commander will brief you on how to proceed. Dismissed!"

"What does he mean?" Boris asked the Armenian.

"Don't you understand?" a third officer said, grinning. "We're going to bump off the bloody bastards."

Good, Boris thought, excellent. It's time to get rid of the Polish sonsofbitches. As a Ukrainian, he knew how treacherous they were. He recalled the revolutionary years, when the bloody Poles had received with open arms any enemy of the Reds who crossed the border; they had let the Whites use Polish territory as a springboard for their assaults on the Ukraine. After the civil war, when Russia was on her knees, the Poles had stabbed her in the back, starting a war against her. It would be a privilege for him, a Ukrainian, to help settle his people's account with the Poles.

In the evening, the Polish officers started arriving in covered trucks, escorted by Soviet soldiers. They were dressed in the mud-stained uniforms in which they had been captured. The operation was carried out with utmost efficiency. The Katyn forest was divided into large lots, and each NKVD platoon was assigned several lots. As soon as a truck arrived at the clearing, a platoon would take charge of the Poles, tie their hands behind their backs and march them to one of the lots. Then the NKVD men would position themselves behind the prisoners, their weapons drawn, and wait.

At every hour, on the hour, they would shoot the prisoners in the back with automatic weapons and finish them with pistols. At those moments, bursts of gunfire would reverberate throughout the forest, as if a formidable battle were being fought. There was a strict order not to fire a weapon at other times, in order to prevent rioting among the prisoners, who didn't know what fate awaited them; they had been told they were being transferred to a new camp. The bodies were left where they fell, to be buried by other units. Then the platoon would return to the clearing, to receive the next shipment of prisoners.

The operation lasted three days and nights. Boris Morozov accomplished his task to the best of his ability. The first time, he had hesitated, just for a split second; he had never killed a man before. But he had quickly recovered and shot the Pole, a young boy with disheveled blond hair, whose shoulders were shivering; he had guessed he was going to die. Boris hoped nobody had noticed his hesitation. After the first one, the rest were easy.

For three days he behaved like a robot, herding the prisoners from the clearing, arming his weapon, killing, and killing again. He knew he was doing the right thing; at the NKVD school he had heard rumors about mass executions of enemies of the revolution, not only foreigners, but even Russians. It was a necessary evil; the Red Terror was the self-defense of the revolution. Lenin himself had said that class enemies should be mercilessly annihilated.

Still, Boris felt oddly confused: he hadn't expected there to be so many Polish officers; they were killing thousands. Most of them were young, almost kids; they didn't look like enemies of the revolution. But he kept his thoughts to himself. An NKVD officer from the Third Company who had questioned the orders had been court-martialed and shot by Colonel Gregoriev himself, in front of his comrades.

On the second day new orders were issued. The killings couldn't be concealed from the arriving prisoners anymore; bodies were strewn all over the forest. The Soviet officers were instructed to force the Poles, at gunpoint, to run to the closest lot, and shoot them without delay.

On the morning of the third day, while the forest was echoing with gunfire and desperate cries for help, a lean, swarthy officer appeared beside him. "Are you Morozov?" he asked.

Boris nodded.

"You'd better come with me, somebody wants you."

They ran across the forest, between the heaps of freshly killed bodies. Giant bulldozers were digging common graves and shoving the corpses in; soldiers from an auxiliary unit were pouring quicklime over the dead; it was summer, and the bodies had to be buried quickly to prevent an epidemic.

"Here we are," the officer said, short of breath. They were both sweating profusely.

In a small clearing, about twenty bodies were strewn in the grass, apparently shot only minutes ago. But another Pole, a major, was squatting under a tree, guarded by a couple of Russians.

"That's him," the swarthy officer said.

One of the Russians, a big fat man, turned toward Boris. A cigarette was dangling from his lower lip. "You're Morozov?" he said. "We've got a surprise for you. This guy here kept yelling your name, so we decided to save him for you."

Morozov stared back in astonishment. "My name? How did he know —"

"He didn't," the fat Russian said. "He kept yelling 'Morozov! Boris Morozov! Does anybody know Morozov?' Sacha, here" — he pointed at his friend — "said that there was a Morozov in the seventh platoon, so we sent for you. You know him?" He approached the Pole and kicked him, not too gently, to make him turn around. The prisoner raised his face. His cheeks were covered with bristle; a purple welt ran from his left eye to the line of his jaw. His lips were cracked and his eyes were filled with horror. They suddenly lit up as he saw Morozov. "Boris!" he groaned in Russian. "Borka, that's you! Thank God!"

Morozov froze, thunderstruck. The man was Henrik Leshchinski, Marina's uncle.

"Borka, dear, tell them who I am!" Henrik tried to get up, but the fat Russian hit him viciously and he fell back, blood trickling from the corner of his mouth.

"Yes, who is he?" the Russian asked, suddenly suspicious.

Morozov stared at Henrik, unable to utter a word. He recalled Henrik's warm hug at his wedding with Marina, the beautiful vase of fine Dresden china he had brought them. They had drunk for hours, then danced the gopak, arms on each other's shoulders. In a flash he saw Marina in her long white dress and colorful Ukrainian hat, clapping her hands and laughing.

"Borka, help me," Henrik implored, his voice breaking, "for Marina's sake. God will bless you, please!"

Feverish thoughts raced through Boris's mind. Henrik was Marina's uncle, he was family, he wasn't an enemy of the Soviet Union! But he was a Pole, he had seen the massacre at Katyn. He had to die. Nobody could save him now. And what about me, Morozov thought, what about Marina and the children? If it was reported that a relative of his was a Polish officer, he would be exiled to a prison camp, or even shot as a security risk. And Marina, too, would be taken away and never seen again; he knew how these things were done. He felt a sudden surge of hatred toward the bloody Pole who was threatening his career, his family, and his life by popping up right now. You motherfucker, he muttered inwardly, you shouldn't have joined the Polish army in the first place. You've asked for it. And he reached for his gun.

"Well, what is he to you?" the fat Russian repeated, his porcine eyes gazing at him suspiciously.

Henrik understood what was going to happen. "For the love of Christ, Boris, don't do it!" He joined his hands in prayer, tears streaming down his face. "God will never forgive you, Borka, I beg you . . ."

Morozov pointed his gun at Henrik's distorted face and squeezed the trigger.

THEY COMPLETED their grisly task late that night. A convoy of trucks was awaiting them at the campsite. Before boarding the vehicles, they had to line up by a long table and sign oaths of secrecy by the flickering light of petrol lamps. According to Boris's friends, they had shot between twelve and fifteen thousand Poles. When their trucks left the forest, the bulldozers were still at work, burying the bodies, layer after layer, in the black Byelorussian earth.

Inside the dark truck an ebullient atmosphere reigned. Boris's friends were joking and singing, releasing the heavy tension that had built inside them in the last few days. He didn't take part in the rejoicing. He was haunted by Henrik's desperate plea and his imploring eyes. Boris shuddered, recalling Henrik's last words. "God will never forgive you!" He wasn't a believer, of course, only his old mother believed in God; still, he couldn't overcome his torment. He had murdered Marina's uncle, a man who had done him no wrong. And all the others he had killed, were they all enemies? What had the young kids done? If there was a God, he thought, he would be punished for his crime.

These maddening thoughts continued to haunt him during the long, bitter years of the war. They left him no peace when he served in Latvia, where the NKVD was laying its security networks; when he was attached as a counterespionage specialist to Koniev's army after Hitler's invasion of Russia; when he became intelligence officer of the autonomous Smolensk partisans, following the Viazma debacle; and when he marched into the ruins of Shepetovka with Zhukov's victorious forces, in the spring of 1944.

The Ukraine had been under German occupation since the summer of 1941. Boris hadn't seen his family for almost five years; now he gunned his American-made jeep past the black, gutted houses of Shepetovka. He was tortured by dark forebodings. The railroad depot was a heap of rubble; most of the houses behind it had been razed. His own house, though, had remained miraculously intact. He ran toward it, but stopped at the threshold, alarmed by the silence. A house with children couldn't be so silent.

"Borka? Borka, is that you?"

At the top of the narrow staircase stood his mother, older, bent, dressed in rags, yet apparently healthy. She had survived! But he only had to look at Varvara Morozova's face to know that his darkest premonitions were true.

Marina had been hanged by the Nazis a few weeks after they had occupied Shepetovka, his mother told him that night. A traitor had informed them she was the wife of an NKVD officer; they had shot his little daughters, too. There was not even a grave to visit, Varvara Morozova whispered, wiping her tears; all the civilians murdered by the Nazis had been buried in mass graves outside the town.

Boris listened in horror. In a strange way, his mother's story only confirmed something he had known all along. He hadn't expected to find his family alive. He didn't tell his mother a word about Katyn; this was a secret. But deep in his heart he felt that the deaths of Marina and his children were his punishment for the murder of Henrik Leshchinski. In spite of his atheism, he couldn't escape this feeling. And he knew he was going to be haunted by his deed for the rest of his life.

It took him three weeks to track down the man who had betrayed Marina to the Nazis. He was Genadi Arkhipenko, one of the Ukrainian traitors who aspired to create an independent Ukraine with German help. Morozov found him hiding in a barn outside the village of Polyanka. He settled his score with Arkhipenko using a sturdy bayonet he had taken from a dead German soldier.

Soon afterward, he left Shepetovka, determined never to return; he wanted to wipe out that chapter of his life. He asked to be attached to Smersh, the top-secret unit created by General Abakumov. Smersh was an abbreviation of the words *"Smiert Shpionam"* — Death to the Spies. Smersh had been charged with tracking down spies, traitors, and collaborators with the enemy, and liquidating them without mercy.

Boris, now a captain, plunged into his new job with fanatical devotion. In Russia, then Poland and Germany, his unit advanced with the Red Army and combed the liberated lands for Russian traitors, Polish fascists, and SS officers on the run. Boris was particularly keen on hunting down Ukrainian traitors; he felt he had to avenge Marina's death on each and every Ukrainian collaborator. Marina's memory haunted him wherever he went; he never touched a woman.

After the war ended, he spent some time in Berlin, hounding families of Ukrainian traitors who had been sent over by the German authorities; he dispatched the women and the children to prison camps in Siberia. Back home, he was promoted to major and assigned to the hunt for Ukrainian counterrevolutionaries.

After a crash course in English, he was sent to Western Europe to track down Ukrainian emigrés who were planning to set up subversive cells back home. He personally chased two Ukrainians who were on their way to America to establish an organization financed by the CIA. He followed the two traitors onto the Paris–Le Havre train and shot them in their compartment.

His next task was to set up penetration routes and communication systems for Soviet agents tracking Ukrainian exiles in the West. In 1948 he operated in New York, posing as the driver of the Soviet consul. This chapter in his career came to an end when his cover was blown by Yuri

Sossnov, one of the first KGB defectors. Morozov barely escaped to Mexico.

Back in Moscow, he was summoned to the office of General Takachenko in the Lubyanka KGB headquarters. Takachenko, an old Chekist with a hollow chest and a drooping mustache, was in charge of the Second Chief Directorate. "We are creating a department of Jewish Affairs," Takachenko said, and went into a coughing spasm that seemed to rip his frail body. "Comrade Beria expects some trouble from that direction." He didn't specify what kind of trouble. "We want you to head the department."

Morozov accepted the appointment without enthusiasm. He wasn't interested in Jews and had had little to do with them in the past. As a child in Shepetovka he used to drift with the other kids through the streets where the Jews lived. They threw stones at their windows and taunted the bearded men in the funny hats. Or they pulled the sidelocks of the children, who ran away screaming in a strange language. But he had never gone beyond that.

One of the first assignments of his department was to investigate the charges of treason against the members of the Anti-Fascist Writers Committee. The instructions had come directly from Beria's desk, accompanied by a thick file. Actually, no investigation was needed; all the evidence had already been diligently gathered. Still, Morozov had put his men on the job, and being a field man himself, had directed the inquiry in person.

One night, at a public meeting of the committee, he thought he saw a ghost, Marina's ghost: a young woman with the same golden hair, the same smile, the same lithe body. For years he had thought a part of him had died and he would never look at a woman again. But that night he didn't sleep; as old wounds reopened and the old pain pierced him like a knife, he also felt, for the first time in years, a faint glimmer of hope. The woman he had seen was a Jewish poet, Tonya Gordon-Wolf.

The following morning he sent his secretary to buy Tonya Gordon's books, and he stayed in his office until late, bent over the small volumes. He liked Tonya Gordon's poems; but the reading turned into a torment, as Marina's face kept appearing in his mind. Her voice echoed in his ears, reciting the verses printed on the white pages. He could hear Marina's voice ringing with youthful enthusiasm when he reached the poem praising the heroes of the national war; it whispered huskily in his ear when he turned the page and plunged into a passionate love poem; it broke into a thousand chimes of crystalline laughter as he read the funny children's tales. Boris even imagined hearing the gleeful laughter of his little daughters, echoing their mother's delight.

In the following days he put his hand on every poem, tale, or essay Tonya Gordon had written. He sent a KGB photographer with a concealed camera to her address, and made him wait in the street for hours till he got some pictures. When the photographer brought him a batch of glossy portraits, he studied them for a long time, drinking in every detail of Tonya's face. He put most of the photographs in his right-hand drawer, but kept four of them on his desk. In one of the pictures, his favorite, she was smiling at somebody while the wind spread her long hair across her face; for him, it was Marina smiling at him again, Marina laughingly pulling aside the strands of her golden hair.

He requested Tonya's file from the department's archives, and found out all about her: her childhood in Kiev, the departure of her sister for Palestine and then America, her brother's medical studies and present employment at the Vassiliev Hospital in Leningrad; Tonya's elopement with Victor Wolf in 1940, their marriage and their move to Moscow, which had probably saved their lives. Two months after their departure, the Nazis had occupied Kiev and brutally slaughtered its Jewish population.

It dawned on him that he had become obsessed with Tonya Gordon. He caught himself inventing excuses to justify — to himself! — his passing by her house on Kirova Street almost every day. At the meetings of the anti-fascist committee, he listened to her reading her poems; he even dared asking for her autograph. She agreed with a smile. No, she didn't have the same dimples as Marina, nor the same silvery laughter. But she was poignantly beautiful; and in her eyes, her voice, her work, he discovered a romantic streak and a shrewd intelligence that Marina never had.

He realized that he would stop at nothing to conquer this woman.

STANDING NOW before the window, he passed an unsteady hand through his hair. He had won Tonya, using all the tricks of his trade. First, to earn the confidence of his superiors, he had volunteered to carry out the liquidation of Mikhoels in Minsk; he had driven the huge Gaz truck that had run Mikhoels over on Oktyabrskaya Street when the old man was on his way to his cousin's home. After delivering the writer's dead body to KGB headquarters, he was given free hand in the Anti-Fascist Writers Committee affair. He never told Tonya, of course, that he was Mikhoels's assassin.

But the most terrible secret he kept from her was his role in her husband's downfall.

The truth was that Victor Wolf was as pure as the driven snow. In the files Morozov had received from Beria, there was not one shred of evidence against Victor and Tonya Wolf. Their names weren't even on the list of suspected Jewish writers. That was bad. As long as Victor Wolf was free, Morozov knew he couldn't even dream of conquering Tonya Gordon. If he wanted to possess the woman, he had to remove the husband. He spent some sleepless nights planning his scheme and fabricating false evidence against Victor Wolf. He planted in the Jewish writers' file phony reports about Victor's contacts with foreign diplomats, phony letters presumably exchanged between Wolf and Jewish leaders in America. Morozov got the false documents from the forgers of Service A, First Chief Directorate. He only had to tell them what he needed, and they delivered the goods. Nobody questioned the orders of a high KGB official.

In less than two weeks he had built an ironclad case against Victor Wolf. The frame-up was perfect; when the file was transferred to the prosecutor general, Victor was accused of treason and arrested. Morozov was too excited with his success to dwell on the moral aspects of his deeds. What counted was that Victor Wolf had been removed from the scene. And Tonya, alone, pregnant and frightened, had dropped into his hands like a ripe fruit.

He wasn't so young anymore. The years, the war, the loss of his family, had made Morozov a bitter man. Even his promotion to deputy director of the directorate hadn't dispelled his melancholy. But Tonya's presence at his side made him happy again, although he knew she didn't love him. He treated little Alex like a son, perhaps because he had sent his father to Vorkuta. When he came home in the evening, he liked to play with the little fellow. When his own son, Dimitri, was born, his joy had no limits.

He had managed the impossible: to pick up the pieces of his shattered life. He had a family again, a beautiful wife, a little son. When Dimitri was two years old, they traveled to Shepetovka to visit his old mother;

he wanted her to meet her grandson. He looked forward to that trip with a mixture of exhilaration and secret apprehension; he feared the surge of painful remembrances from the past. How could he stand to see the places that were so closely connected with Marina's memory? But to his surprise, nothing happened. When he saw the old house at the end of Goats Lane — since renamed Red Cavalry Street — he felt a slight pang, no more. He realized with wonder that Tonya had gradually supplanted Marina in his heart.

But just when his suffering seemed to be over, the troubles had started. Like distant thunder heralding the storm, the first bad omen had appeared far away, in Czechoslovakia. The former foreign minister, Rudolf Slanski, and twenty other men, most of them Jews, were arrested, tried, and found guilty of spying for the British. Most of them were hanged. The communiqués stressed their Jewish origins. Zorin, the KGB liaison officer with the Czechs, told Morozov the trial had been remote-controlled by the Kremlin.

A few weeks later, the anti-Semitic wave reached Moscow. On arriving in his office one morning, Morozov found out that all high-ranking KGB officers of Jewish origin had been arrested. They included General Raikhman, head of counterintelligence, General Grauer, deputy director of the Fifth Chief Directorate, and Colonel Gorsky, who had handled the famous Kim Philby in London. The same day, Mikhail Borodin, Lenin's old companion and Chiang Kai-shek's Soviet adviser, was thrown in prison, where he was to die; his son was incarcerated in the Lubyanka cellars.

"It seems, Boris Artemovich," General Takachenko said to him between bouts of coughing, "that somebody" — he looked up, then lowered his eyes — "has declared war on the Jews."

Morozov nodded, acknowledging the allusion to Stalin. "I didn't know — " he started.

"No, you didn't." The skeletal general was staring oddly at him. "And that's rather disturbing, my boy."

"We should be the first to know," Morozov said. "After all, I'm in charge of Jewish Affairs."

"The matter is out of your hands." Again the odd, meaningful stare. "Perhaps somebody doesn't trust the department anymore."

The meaning of Takachenko's hints hit him only when he returned to his office. He had fallen from grace because he had married a Jewess, a former member of the anti-fascist committee.

Besides, like anyone else in the KGB, he had his enemies; officers who held a grudge against him for something he had done, others who coveted his position. They needed only a hint that he was vulnerable, and they would throw themselves upon him like a wolf pack. They had certainly noticed the signs: he wasn't trusted anymore. They could tear him to pieces.

His suspicions turned to certitude in the following weeks. A wave of anti-Semitic measures swept the country, but Morozov's department was the last to learn about it. The Jewish theater, the Jewish newspapers, and the Jewish restaurants in Moscow were closed, and many Jewish employees of various state bodies were fired. The Jewish wives of Soviet officials were arrested; among them was Zhemchuzina Molotova, the wife of Stalin's former foreign minister.

Morozov learned all that from bits and pieces reaching his office. He was kept out of the operation. All the arrests and the dismissals were carried out by the First Chief Directorate, although its function — foreign espionage — had nothing to do with Jewish Affairs. For the first time in his life Morozov felt real fear. In the KGB, being bypassed by one's superiors was equivalent to a first step toward the gallows.

What could he do, he kept asking himself, how could he save Tonya and the children? And his own neck? But there was nobody he could turn to. The only possible escape was defection to the West. But he knew that he would never turn traitor to his country.

While he was helplessly wondering what blow would come next, the affair of the Jewish doctors exploded. Then came Tonya's turn.

Desperate, he requested a meeting with Beria. But Beria flatly refused to see him. And Morozov understood what this refusal meant: soon after Tonya died, it would be his turn.

YESTERDAY, after the children had seen Tonya for the last time, he had taken them home, then returned to the Lubyanka. He had spent the night in his office, slumped behind his desk, swallowing glass after glass of fiery vodka. As a faint gray light crept into his room, he had woodenly stepped to the window. And now, at dawn, Tonya was going to die.

Morozov tried to look away. When they had given him this office, the administrative officer had joked about the "show" that he could watch once in a while from his window. No twisted mind could have ever imagined, though, that the "show" might turn into the most painful torture ever inflicted on a man — having to watch his beloved's death. He could turn his back to the window or go out, but he wouldn't. He was morbidly attracted to the sight down below, as the hare is mesmerized by the deadly stare of the snake.

He closed his eyes, then looked down again. The execution courtyard was small, sunk in deep shadow. Several officers were moving behind the prisoners lined against the wall, leaving deep tracks in the snow. A colonel came out of the building and stood in the middle of the courtyard. He must have said something, for the soldiers quickly retreated. A sturdy Georgian officer approached the prisoner on the extreme right and drew his pistol.

Boris leaned forward and felt the cold glass against his burning forehead. There she was, the woman he loved with such passion and despair. And he couldn't do anything to save her. God, he felt so terribly helpless, watching her as she stood facing the wall, waiting for the single shot in the base of her skull. They had taken her because they didn't yet dare touch him. But he was living on borrowed time. Soon they would come for him as well.

He looked down again. The execution was under way. Several bodies lay in the snow, their limbs twisted, red stains expanding around their heads. He swayed as the squat Georgian officer trudged through the snow and stood behind Tonya. She must have heard him, for she straightened up, defiantly throwing back her head. The Georgian raised his pistol. Morozov painfully swallowed. He was paralyzed, unable to move, unable to utter a sound. He didn't hear the shot; the double windows were too thick.

He saw Tonya shudder, then she slumped slowly, almost gracefully, the golden hair fanning around her head, her blood trickling on the pure white snow.

He reached for the table beside him for support. Tonya is dead, he said to himself. Tonya is no more. It is not a nightmare, it is for real. Tonya is gone. Soon he would be gone, too, perhaps the same way — a bleak dawn at the Lubyanka Prison.

HOURS LATER he was startled by a hesitant knock on the door. He had been sitting in his armchair, shoulders sagged, eyes unseeing, sunk in black torpor. He painfully got up; he felt as if every drop of energy had been drained from his body. "Come in," he muttered, and turned to the window.

The stone-paved courtyard was empty. The bodies had been taken away, the snow swept clean; nothing indicated a bloody execution had taken place down there a couple of hours ago. A wild thought flashed through his mind; perhaps it had all been a nightmare, perhaps Tonya was still alive. As the door behind him opened, the routine sounds of a day in the office invaded the room — phones ringing, steps in the staircase, the distant laugh of a young man. Perhaps it had all happened only in his sick imagination.

As he turned back, he saw his orderly, the cadaverous Arkadi Dookhin, standing awkwardly at the door, avoiding his eyes. "They said I should give you this, Comrade Colonel," Dookhin said. In his outstretched hand gold gleamed dully.

He took from Dookhin the heavy gold chain with the Star of David. Tonya's star. She had worn it until her last moment. He absently fingered it, suddenly noticing that one of its edges was slightly twisted and some grains of uneven gray dust had stuck to it. He stared at the piece of gold, crushing the tiny gray particles between his fingers. Then it all came back to him: his conversation with Tonya about Suzanne Spaak and the inscriptions she had etched on the walls of her cell. "I'll be back," he mumbled, shoved Dookhin aside and hurried to the elevator.

A few minutes later he was standing in Tonya's cell, reading her last message. *Boris save the children Nina can help with Alex love love to you all . . .*

He clenched his fists, a fierce determination taking shape in his mind. Now that Tonya was dead, he had a last duty toward her. To save her child.

And he knew how.

Chapter 3

CHASED BY the bitter February winds, Nina Kramer stopped in the cold lobby of her Brooklyn brownstone to catch her breath. As she wiped her spectacles, she noticed an envelope sticking out of her broken mailbox. She rubbed her frozen hands and picked up the envelope. It was stamped with the logo of the Jewish refugee relief agency. Inside there was a stenciled form, with the empty spaces filled in square block letters. Mrs. Kramer of 49 Elm Place in Brooklyn was asked to come to the agency headquarters in Manhattan on a matter concerning her nephew, "Alexander Gordon, age three, born in Moscow, Soviet Union, to Tonya and Victor Wolf."

Her heart pounding, she scurried to the subway station on Flatbush Avenue. She couldn't understand the letter. What did the refugee agency have to do with her sister's son? He was supposed to be in Moscow. Something must have happened to Tonya, something very bad, otherwise why would they want to talk to her about Alex? All during the ride she racked her brains for a possible explanation. When she reached the agency offices on Park Avenue South a few minutes before closing, she was haunted by grim premonitions.

She was received by Mr. Lipshutz, a small, bald man who obsequiously offered her a chair, sat down behind his decrepit desk, cleared his throat, suggested a cup of tea, and finally broke the horrible news. Her sister was dead, Mr. Lipshutz said. Then he lowered his voice, although they were alone. According to the agency's sources, Tonya had been shot for treason. Her husband, Morozov, had arranged for the child to be sent to America.

It took her a moment to digest the meaning of the man's words. "No," she cried out. Her mouth went dry. "You don't know my sister. Tonya isn't a traitor. This is all a lie."

Mr. Lipshutz was nodding compassionately. "I understand you," he said softly. "But we have good sources in Russia, you know. We check every visa application. Your sister's husband pulled quite a few strings to obtain an exit visa for the boy. I understand he is your sister's child from a former marriage. Is that correct?"

She didn't answer. She suspected Lipshutz's story was a lie, but why should he lie to her? Perhaps it was an FBI frame-up, but what purpose could it serve?

"Alexander is three years old," the elderly clerk was saying. "He is in Vienna now, and our people are taking care of him."

"When is the boy arriving?" she stammered, rising from her chair. Her knees were shaking.

"By the end of the week," Lipshutz said, offering her his small, cold hand. "We'll bring him to your apartment."

Three days later Mr. Lipshutz himself knocked on her door. He held a little boy by the hand and carried a small suitcase. Nina took the child into the living room, where he stood awkwardly, furtively peeking at her. He was pale but robust. Feeling her glance, he lowered his eyes, clenching his little fists. He seemed lost in his frayed coat, made of rough brown fabric. He wore high black shoes and a visor cap two sizes too large for him.

"Now, Alexander, tell me — what did they call you at home?" Nina asked in Russian with forced cheerfulness.

The boy didn't answer.

"They called you Aliosha, didn't they?" Nina went on. "Well, we'll call you Alex. Alex Gordon."

As she unbuttoned the child's collar, her fingers touched the gold chain. She clutched the Star of David, her heart thumping. She recognized the star; she had given it to Tonya on the eve of her departure from Russia. Looking the other way, she clumsily wiped a tear from her cheek.

*   *   *

LATER, as evening shadows sneaked into the cold, silent rooms, Nina sat in a chintz-covered armchair, watching the little boy sleep. She had no spare room — her husband Samuel slept in the far bedroom, and she used the tiny alcove by the kitchen — so she put little Alex to bed on the sofa in the living room. The exhausted boy was asleep before she even started to undress him. As she removed his clothes, she kept speaking softly, although the child didn't hear. Since Samuel's stroke, which had rendered him a deaf and dumb invalid, she had become accustomed to dispelling her loneliness by speaking to herself.

"Aliosha, *golubchek moi*, my little dove," she kept mumbling, recalling how she used to undress his mother, little Tonya, when she took care of her back in Kiev; her small sister, with her long blond hair and starry blue eyes, looked like a little angel. She was a blue-eyed angel, indeed, although Nina used to call her a naughty devil. Nina remembered the way Tonya used to hug her, clinging to her with her supple body; tears, so ruthlessly suppressed for years, gushed from Nina's eyes.

After taking Alex's clothes and shoes off, she gently laid him on the crisp linen sheets she had brought from the plywood cupboard, along with a large fluffy pillow. The sleeping child yawned and rubbed his eyes with his little fists, then curled up and buried his face in the pillow. He had his mother's long, silken eyelashes and her delicately arched eyebrows.

"You have your mother's face," Nina said, "you know that, Aliosha?" She covered Alex with her own eiderdown; she would get used to a rough woolen blanket from now on. Once the child was tucked between the sheets, she sat by him, studying every line of the little face, comparing it with Tonya's features, which surfaced in her memory. And with another child's face, inert and chalk-white, that she had all those years tried to erase from her mind.

She was so immersed in the contemplation of her nephew that she almost missed her regular ritual, which took place every nightfall, when the streetlights came on and the Brooklyn kids ended their street softball game and hurried home to dinner. She turned off the lights, stepped to the window, pulled the curtains aside and looked down at the street. The FBI automobile was there, as it had been every night for the past four months. It was a tan-colored car — the boys who lived downstairs said it was a Plymouth — with a dented fender and a patch of brown paint on the front left door. There were two men inside; she could tell by the two glowing cigarette tips. Did they know everything, she wondered, about Alex and Morozov and Tonya?

Tonya shot for treason, she thought. Tonya had betrayed the Soviet Union. It was a disgusting lie, of course. Tonya was a wonderful poet, a source of pride for the Soviet Union. Nina had always admired — and envied — her sister, for her beauty and her talent, but mostly for her participation in the building of Marxism. She hadn't seen her since she left Russia in 1928, but had met her first husband, Victor, back in 1943. Victor had visited the United States with the Soviet Anti-Fascist Writers Committee. He had brought her a book of Tonya's poems, with Tonya's affectionate dedication. "To my beloved Ninochka, from your little devil." Nina had barely contained her tears when she read the inscription.

After Victor left, she read the book often, until she knew all the poems by heart. She would visualize her sister in military uniform, her bright eyes sparkling, her long blond hair blown by the wind, reciting her inspiring verses to young Red Army soldiers on their way to the battlefield during the darkest days of the Great Patriotic War.

She envied her, Nina admitted to herself. She wanted to be there, too, with Tonya, at Russia's fateful hour, fighting the Nazis. But Tonya took part in the war effort, while Nina sat in an office in Brooklyn and scribbled in ledgers. She had made so many mistakes, Nina thought, while her sister had chosen the right path. Tonya had taken the road that she should have chosen. Tonya's life was the fulfillment of her own secret dreams.

About three years ago a letter from Tonya had brought astonishing news. Victor had been arrested and sentenced to a life term of hard labor for crimes against the Soviet Union. Tonya had divorced him and married Boris Morozov, a colonel. She was carrying his child. The letter had been cautiously worded, hinting at various events, not all of which Nina managed to figure out. One hint she had decoded, though. Tonya wrote: "Boris comes home every night, although he watches relentlessly over the security of our nation." Nina had understood: Morozov was with the KGB.

She had dispatched Tonya an anguished letter, full of questions, but it had remained unanswered. She couldn't believe that Victor had betrayed the Soviet Union. But some of communism's worst enemies came from the hard core of Bolsheviks. True, Nina couldn't imagine Victor committing any crime against his country. But who could have imagined that Trotsky, Zinoviev, and Kamenev would also turn into enemies of the revolution? Perhaps Victor, too, had slipped; perhaps his visit to America had turned his head.

Nina hadn't heard from her sister since. What had happened? What had Tonya done? Why had Alex been sent to America?

The news about Tonya all but made her world crumble. Nina was a communist, a staunch believer in the gospel of Marx, Engels, Lenin, and the fourth surviving giant, Yosif Vissarionovich Stalin. Never in her life had she doubted the just cause and the sublime ideals of her native country. She had fervently hoped to see communism triumph all over the world.

But today she was deeply confused. Even her total devotion to communism couldn't make her buy this nonsense that Tonya had betrayed her country. Nina's only explanation was that Soviet justice had committed a monstrous mistake and Tonya had died for nothing. Errors did happen, even in the Soviet Union. In the historic events that shook her country, individuals didn't count; they were nothing but oil on the revolution's wheels. Lenin himself had said: "When you chop wood — splinters fly."

Still, she couldn't digest the idea that her lovely sister had become such a splinter, an ugly mistake of the Soviet bureaucratic machine. And what about Victor? Had Victor's conviction also been a bureaucratic mistake? Could both Victor and Tonya be traitors? For the first time ever, she was at a loss; her faith in Russia was shaken. There must be an explanation, she said to herself, there must be a reason for this tragedy. She had written a letter to their brother Valery, in Leningrad, but Valery hadn't replied.

She stared down at the tan Plymouth. Alex had been officially admitted to the country, so the authorities must know about him, about Tonya and Morozov. One more reason for the FBI to stick close to her. Turning away from the window, she tiptoed to the kitchen to make herself some herb tea. While the kettle was softly purring on the gas ring, she sat erect by the kitchen table, her hands joined before her.

A few months ago, the New York *Daily News* had printed a picture of her in that posture, face drawn, forehead ploughed by a deep frown, eyes magnified by the wire-rimmed glasses. The headline above the picture said: SUSPECTED COMMUNIST NINA KRAMER TESTIFYING BEFORE HOUSE COMMITTEE ON UN-AMERICAN ACTIVITIES.

She had never done anything against her adopted country, of course, although McCarthy's gangsters had accused her of being a Soviet agent. They had finally let her go. Her lawyer told her she was small fry, she wasn't worth the effort. Nevertheless, she was forced to resign from her position as a bookkeeper with the Department of Health. Soon after, she found a job at Spiegel's Furs and things quieted down.

She was glad that her spell of notoriety was over. After her photograph had been printed in the paper, several people had yelled at her in the street, shaking their fists; a store owner had thrown her out, calling her "a bloody communist." It took a while until people forgot about her. But the FBI didn't forget. Since the proceedings, she was kept under surveillance. They followed her openly, and watched her house from their parked automobile. What did they expect, to catch her handing documents to Soviet spies?

Tonight, because of Alex's arrival, she had skipped a meeting of the Peace Movement. There was talk of a march on Washington, to demand that the President grant the Rosenbergs clemency. She was ready to go. The Rosenbergs were not spies. If they had delivered nuclear formulas to the Soviets, they had done it for peace. But American imperialism had decided to murder Julius and Ethel Rosenberg. Truman was determined to drag them to the electric chair.

She suppressed a sigh, and glanced at a picture of the couple that she had cut from a newspaper and fastened to the wall with thumbtacks. Ethel looked so gentle, almost pretty, in her buttoned-up coat with the fur collar; she wore a pointed, coquettish little hat. Julius was bent toward her, with a smile on his lean face. He was wearing glasses and had a small mustache. There was wire mesh between them; the picture was perhaps taken in court, or in the van that carried them back to prison. One could sense, even in this grainy picture, the deep bond between Julius and Ethel. Nina wished she could have met the Rosenbergs and told them how much she admired them. She couldn't suppress a pang of envy. They had not only believed in communism, but had taken action; not like her.

The water in the kettle was boiling. She poured the steaming brew into a glass, then sat down by the kitchen table and drank it slowly, sucking it through a cube of solid sugar she had placed between her front teeth, the Russian way.

Her Russian habits hadn't changed, although she had been an American citizen for more than twenty years. She still thought and counted in Russian, her English broken and inadequate, the book rack in her tiny bedroom laden with the works of Dostoyevski, Tolstoy, Lermontov, and Lenin. Every morning she bought *Russkoye Slovo,* the Russian daily, at Hershie's newsstand on Foster Avenue. She hated the reactionary ideas of the *Slovo,* but couldn't overcome her desire to read a Russian newspaper. She didn't read American newspapers and books, never went to the theater, rarely saw a movie. Once in a while she went to a concert, or to the ballet; she didn't need English for that. She plaited her hair in a tressed bun on top of her head, and wore dark, buttoned-up dresses and square-heeled shoes, those unmistakable trademarks of the middle-aged women in the country of her birth.

After twenty-four years in America, she had remained a stranger in this land. She disliked Brooklyn, with its incessant din and bustle. She had heard about the Dodgers but had no idea who they were; she had never ventured as far as Coney Island or Manhattan Beach. Jazz and popular music were alien to her ears. She disliked the taste of the American foods — hot dogs, hamburgers, and meat loaf. Once a week she walked all the way to the Russian grocer in Williamsburg to buy salted herrings, country sausage, and black bread. Her days were divided between her work at Spiegel's Furs and caring for her invalid husband. But her nights were hers, to dream of the life she could have had. If she had only dared.

Her whole life, she often reflected, was suspended between her reluctance to get involved in risky underground work and the burning desire to join the front line of communist activists. The result of those contradictory impulses was a maddening frustration, and she was constantly haunted by the feeling that she had deserted the battlefield and was wasting her life.

She sipped her tea, watching Alex. The child stirred, blinked a couple of times, then stretched his arms and sank back in sleep, his little face calm and serene. She bent over him and arranged his blanket. "What's the matter, my little one?" she murmured. "Sleep well."

He had the blond locks of his mother, but not her eyes. The child's eyes were gray with a greenish hue, strikingly luminous. Alex was thin and pale. He looked little for his age, but he seemed to be in good health and had good bone structure. She wondered if he was as fond of chocolate as Tonya. Nina used to stand on line for hours before the Narodnii foodstore on Leninskaya Street to buy Tonya a bar of chocolate, hard and dry, but chocolate all the same.

"Tomorrow," she whispered to the sleeping boy, "I'll give you a bath and scrub away all the filth you've collected during your trip. I'll make you look like new, *golubchek.*"

She would also do some laundry, and perhaps go to Polack's used garments store; Alex had no clothes but a heavy turtleneck pullover, worn-out pants, and a coat. The pants were made of the same rough fabric from which her mother used to cut the clothes of her younger brother, Valery, thirty years ago.

Nina's thoughts pulled her back in time, to the far provinces of her past. She belonged to the ill-fated Russian generation that was old enough to understand the October revolution but too young to take part in it. She was in her early teens when Czar Nikolai was shot and the Bolsheviks seized power in Russia. A student in the renowned Pobedo-noszev School for Girls in Kiev, she breathlessly followed the revolutionary events, the Brest-Litovsk peace negotiations, then the civil war. At school passionate debates broke out among the girls. She voiced her admiration for the Reds, who wanted to erect a new brotherly society on the ruins of backward, reactionary Russia. She and her friend, the dark, intense Katya Tiomkin, spun dreams of joining the legendary Red Guards, who included many women, even in command positions.

But when a Red cavalry battalion briefly stopped at Kiev, Katya was the only one to leave with the fiery horsemen. Nina remained behind to take care of a wounded soldier, Sasha Kolodny. This was the moment, Nina later realized, when she had made her crucial mistake. She should have followed her impulses, gone off with the Red Guards and taken part in the revolution. But she had stayed in Kiev, and her choice changed the course of her life.

And yet . . . she was only sixteen at the time, a small, chubby girl with a rather plain face, a strong chin, a large forehead, and long silky hair. She was proud of her hair, and secretly enjoyed admiring in her bedroom mirror the way it cascaded onto her shoulders. It gave her something of a dreamy look, like one of Chekhov's young heroines, she thought. But she never dared to wear her hair that way; when she went to school, she plaited it on the top of her head or drew it back in a tight bun.

No one had ever suspected that behind her homely features burned a fierce romantic fire, that her vivid imagination spun the dream of an adventurous life dedicated to a noble cause. Nor had anyone guessed that the quiet, plain girl longed for all-consuming, passionate love. But when she and Katya had gone to visit the wounded Red Guards at the military school's stables, and Sasha Kolodny had squeezed her hand and looked at her with his gentle gray eyes, she had cast aside all her revolutionary dreams and settled down on the edge of his bed.

And there she had stayed for the following three weeks, until Sasha recovered from the bullet wound in his thigh. By the time he limped out of the stables, leaning on her shoulder, the Red battalion had left town. She brought the young man home, something she wouldn't have dared to do before. But these were revolutionary times, the young made the rules and the old had no choice but to comply. Her parents meekly capitulated and agreed to give Sasha the maid's small room behind the kitchen. Their maid had returned to her village after the outbreak of the civil war.

Two weeks later Sasha and Nina moved to Zhitomir and settled in the expropriated house of a fur merchant who had been executed by a revolutionary squad. They shared the upper floor with four families of factory workers; Nina found work in a rope factory, and very rarely traveled to Kiev to visit her parents.

They had become lovers the first night they spent together; but Sasha didn't mention any plans for the future until three years later, and then in an odd, disturbing manner. Sasha was an odd young man indeed. Stocky, rather heavyset, with curly blond hair, a heavy jaw, and calm gray eyes, he was the most self-controlled boy she had ever met. He wasn't talkative, and he carefully weighed every word before pronouncing it. He had been very polite with her parents, and had told them he came from a Jewish family living in Omsk. He was kind and gentle with her; in bed, he was an eager, passionate lover. But even in those moments of closeness, Sasha wouldn't completely open up. He was a secretive youth, suspicious and ungiving. He reminded her of a character out of a novel; one of those shady, silent men who had turned *konspiratzia* — conspiracy — into a way of life.

When Sasha fully recovered from his wound, he didn't return to his former unit. Instead, he was assigned by the party to the Zhitomir

Narkom, the people's commissariat. Once Nina glimpsed a German Nagant handgun hidden behind a pile of his clothes. A friend of hers who was a secretary at the Narkom told her Sasha was with the Cheka, the new security and intelligence organization. But when she asked Sasha, he just smiled.

She soon realized that she would never get to know all about her lover. There was a part of Sasha's life that he wouldn't reveal to anybody. He would often go out at the oddest hours of the night, and afterward would meet her inquiries with a blank stare and a smile. When the civil war ended, he would often disappear for weeks, even months; a couple of times he brought her presents — a rabbit-fur hat, leather gloves, a pair of boots. She could tell by the names of the stores, stamped in purple on the cheap cotton lining, that he had bought them in Moscow. She asked him what he had been doing, but he only smiled in his gentle, disarming manner.

One winter night after he had been absent for six weeks, he came home late and woke her up. He was wearing his old military coat, and his shoulders were covered with snow. He looked excited. "Nina," he said urgently, "I am going to Palestine. Let's leave together."

She stared at him in dismay. "Palestine? What will we do there? Have you become a Zionist, Sasha?"

He shook his head. "It will be better for both of us."

"You're a communist," she murmured. "You have nothing to do in Palestine. Our future is here, in Russia."

He took a deep breath. "Trust me," he said.

But she persisted in her refusal. She couldn't tell him she was pregnant and his child was due by the following spring. He had told her many times that he didn't want children, they were nothing but a burden for a communist in these times. She feared he would be angry at her, or worse, he might regard her pregnancy as a cheap trick to force marriage upon him.

True, he kept repeating to her that they were as good as married, and they didn't need to go through the decadent ceremonies of a dead era; still, she nourished a secret dream of a white wedding. She would wear her mother's magnificent silk dress, and Sasha his long black jacket and tall, shiny boots. A couple of girls from the rope factory had been married in bridal dresses, and nobody had protested. Yet, she had never dared to share her dream with Sasha, lest he think her a bourgeois and a reactionary.

Finally he left for Palestine by himself. "If you change your mind," he said to her when they parted, "come, I'll be waiting."

His train had barely pulled out of the station before she started having second thoughts. Perhaps she should have gone with him. But how could she go, with the baby already kicking inside her? There was no other way, she had made the right decision. As soon as the child was born, she would write to him, and he would understand.

The baby, a boy she named Vladimir — there were many Vladimirs in those years, all of them named after Lenin — was born in March, in the first week of the thaw. A year later, the Great Famine swept through Russia, leaving millions of corpses in its wake. During the last days of his life, Vladimir didn't even have the strength to cry; he could only stare at her with his large, inflamed eyes, in which she read a terrible accusation. He died in her arms.

As she rocked the emaciated corpse of her little son, Nina felt she was going out of her mind. She had loved the child with all the fire burning inside her; but she hadn't been able to save his life. Other mothers had managed. She had failed her little Vladimir, and she had failed Sasha, too, by letting his son die. The terrible feeling of guilt never left her.

Tormented by grief and remorse, Nina returned to her parents' home and devoted herself to raising her brother Valery and her little sister Tonya. When her pain subsided and she was able to reason again, Nina decided to join Sasha in Palestine. By then, however, the Soviet Union had sealed its borders and was granting no exit visas. Three years passed before she finally sailed to Palestine on a rusty Italian steamer, to search for her lost lover.

Lost, for he hadn't written even once. Utterly lost, for when she arrived in the Promised Land, Sasha Kolodny had vanished. He had entered the country all right; she discovered the proof in the immigrants lists kept by the Jewish Agency. His name in a black ledger she perused in a dusty office in Jaffa. Sasha Kolodny, born in Omsk, 1898, arrived February 27, 1925. Those details had been entered by an expert foreign hand, but the signature was Sasha's — big, square letters, the K massive and wide, the y ending in a long upward stroke, the entire name underscored by a thick line, etched in the white paper.

But Sasha wasn't in Jaffa. Nor was he in Tel Aviv, nor in the famished settlements throughout Galilee, nor among the malaria-ridden kibbutzim of the Izreel valley. For months Nina traveled the country, living in utmost misery, subsisting on one meal a day, searching for Sasha.

As she wandered throughout the land, she met Russian immigrants who knew him, mostly young left-wing radicals. A couple of Moscovites had worked with Sasha in a Judean orchard; an old man had approved his application to the Palestinian communist fraction; a Haifa docker had been arrested with him by the British for subversive activity. The docker, though, gave her the most disturbing piece of news: Sasha Kolodny had been expelled from Palestine by order of the British High Commissioner. The British claimed that he was a Bolshevik agent, sent to Palestine by the Communist International to put in place a subversive organization.

"I saw Kolodny brought to Haifa under police escort," the docker said. "They put him aboard the first ship leaving the country. I think it was a French freighter."

The longshoreman's story explained quite a few things. Sasha had decided to go to Palestine not on a sudden whim, or because he had embraced Zionist ideas. He had been sent on a mission. He was one of the myriad young communists dispatched all over the capitalist countries to lay the groundwork for world revolution. Now that she knew the truth about him, Nina lost any hope of seeing him again. He was somewhere in Europe, or back in Russia, probably engaged in another dark scheme.

In a pioneers' camp in Galilee she met a gentle, frail youth named Samuel Kramer. His health was bad and his body weak; he had a rather awkward manner, and seemed unable to cope with the hard life in Palestine. Perhaps she was attracted to him because he was so helpless and stirred her motherly instincts, or because he was the opposite of Sasha, lacking confidence and self-control. One month after they met, she married Samuel and sailed with him to America. It was her declaration of defeat; failing to find Sasha Kolodny, she had given him up.

She couldn't pretend she was in love with Samuel; for her, it had been a marriage of convenience. She didn't want to stay in Palestine, she couldn't go back to Russia, and in Europe fascist regimes were taking over. Samuel was her ticket to America. He had American citizenship; his parents had emigrated to Buffalo in the 1880s. He had come to Palestine with the Jewish Legion that had fought alongside the British in the First World War.

But he was an only son, and rather spoiled; he had lost his Zionist faith after falling sick with malaria. He had drifted to the left, become a Marxist, and now wanted to go back to America and help organize the workers. As for Nina, she thought that after losing Sasha, she could patch together a new life with Samuel. They believed in the same ideals; love and affection would come later.

They sailed to America together, but soon after they moved to the small Brooklyn apartment, Samuel suffered a massive stroke and turned into a salivating, grinning idiot, unable to move. For years now he had been lying on the large bed in their former bedroom, soiling his sheets, panting, sighing, and moaning. He had lost all his hair and his teeth, was unable to speak, and could only utter squeaky, unintelligible sounds. She would have to wash, change, and feed him for the rest of his wretched life.

She assumed responsibility for their existence, and found a job as a bookkeeper. During the day, when she was at work, an old woman from across the street took care of Samuel; but Nina suspected she stole a part of his food, and never cleaned him as she should have. Very often, coming back from work, she found Samuel lying in his urine-soaked sheets, grinning foolishly. But sometimes he would grasp her wrist with his right hand — he had a remarkably strong right arm, the left was just a withered bough, hanging beside his flank — and stare at her with intelligent, wise eyes. It was the sanity and the despair she suddenly perceived in the pale blue eyes that almost drove her mad.

Had it not been for Samuel's malady, she often said to herself, she would have long ago joined the struggle for communism. But deep in her heart she knew this wasn't true. She knew her shortcomings; there wasn't enough steel in her backbone, enough dedication to the cause, for her to drop everything and go.

She was gnawed by the feeling that great historic events were passing her by while she didn't budge. When the Second World War broke out, she became restless. She could go back to Russia; she could enlist as a volunteer with the Women's Auxiliary forces of Great Britain or Canada. She knew people who did it, ordinary people like herself. She even found out the address of the British recruitment office, and once spent a couple of hours standing on the opposite sidewalk, watching young people enter through its massive wooden doors. But she was unable to cross the street, and after a while she went home.

Another option was to sail to Europe. Before Pearl Harbor, Americans could travel freely in France, help establish underground networks, smuggle refugees out of the country, carry documents. Besides, Nina had a secret reason to go to Paris. A letter she had received carried news that should have prompted her to catch the first boat to the continent. It had been dispatched by Emily Mayer, an American communist, who was in France helping the anti-fascist movement. Sasha was in Paris, the letter said.

"Come," Emily wrote to her, "I saw your Sasha, he is worth the trip, this man is a dream!"

But it was to remain a dream; she never set foot out of Brooklyn. Her frustration with herself knew no limits.

Samuel groaned in his bed. He wasn't asleep; the poor wretch rarely slept. Sooner or later she would have to take Alex in to meet his uncle. She hoped it wouldn't be too traumatic for the little boy.

As she watched Alex sleep, it occurred to Nina that he could change her existence. Alex could bring her sweet Tonya back to life. He could become the little son she had lost. She could raise him, inspire him with her ideals, mold him into the person she had so desperately wished to become. She could live again through him, a different and better life.

Yes, she thought with sudden determination, she would make Tonya's little boy a worthy son to his family, a Russian patriot, a communist in the pure tradition of Stalin.

MOROZOV heard of Stalin's sudden death from two KGB officers who pounded on his apartment door the night of March 5, 1953. He woke up immediately. He was all alone in the apartment now, and his light sleep was regularly assailed by the same grisly nightmare, in which he saw Tonya, her golden hair fanned on the bloodied snow. He couldn't get used to his loneliness. One of the children was already on his way to America. He had sent the other to the Panfilov Orphanage in Leningrad, an institution for the sons of fallen Soviet heroes. Little Dimitri, the principal reported to him over the phone, had quickly made friends with the other children in his class.

The officers kept hammering on his door till he opened, shivering in his old dressing gown. At first he thought they had come for him, as they once had come for Tonya. But the young captain at the door only said he was to report to KGB Center immediately. The car sent for him darted madly through the sleeping streets of Moscow. Morozov saw troops in combat gear jump out of trucks and take positions by major government buildings. Other units were setting roadblocks at several intersections. When he got out of the car, at Dzerzhinski Square, he heard the distant rumble of tanks.

KGB Center was ablaze with light. Phones rang incessantly, orders thundered from the loudspeaker system, messengers dashed through the corridors. Military automobiles discharged high-ranking personnel at the Lubyanka gates. The massive doors, whose brass coating was engraved with the hammer and sickle emblem, weren't locked as usual; for the first time in Morozov's experience, they were wide open. Every KGB officer from second lieutenant to lieutenant general seemed to have been summoned to headquarters.

At the armory, automatic rifles were issued to everybody present. Truckloads of junior officers were rushed to the Kuznetsky Most annex and to the Radio Moskva complex, while most superior officers were ordered to deploy around the Kremlin. Officially, the operation was meant to protect the vital government centers from a takeover by hostile forces, but Morozov suspected Beria of following a secret plan that would give him absolute control over the Soviet Union. Beria himself was now speaking at an extraordinary session of the Politburo, assembled in the Kremlin.

By sunrise, though, it became clear that Beria's action, although swift and brutal, hadn't been swift and brutal enough. The KGB officers were instructed to hand back their weapons and resume their regular duties. Morozov was shaving in his office when Takachenko came in with the news. The Politburo had elected Georgi Malenkov as the new Soviet leader. "Malenkov is a good man," Takachenko said cautiously. "A moderate. Do you know him?"

They looked at each other, communicating with their eyes what they couldn't say aloud, for fear that the office might be wired: Beria and the hard-liners had apparently suffered a defeat at the Politburo meeting.

One of Malenkov's first decisions was to put an end to the witch-hunt against the Jews. Barely a fortnight after Stalin's death the Jewish physicians who had allegedly participated in the Doctors' Conspiracy were released from prison. Among them was Valery Gordon. Dr. Lidia Timashuk, the chief witness against the doctors, admitted publicly she had fabricated the evidence in order to achieve promotion.

Morozov felt a surge of fury. The war against the Jews had ended, but eight weeks too late. If Tonya's execution had only been delayed, she would be safe now, probably released from prison. Only eight weeks, he thought, and his family would have been spared. But Tonya was dead, the children were gone, and their apartment was empty and silent as a tomb. Every night, on returning from the office, he would open a fresh vodka bottle and drink in silence, till he slumped unconscious over the kitchen table.

Still, for the first time since Tonya's death, Morozov had a flicker of hope, as far as his own fate was concerned. Things were changing in Russia. Jewish Affairs were back in his hands. Nobody spoke to him about Tonya, as if she had never existed. A couple of friends awkwardly asked after the children, and he vaguely answered that they were staying with relatives. This seemed to be an adequate response. Everybody knew that his mother lived in Shepetovka and Nina's brother was in Leningrad.

Morozov wasn't harassed, there was no surveillance of his apartment, and nobody interfered with his work; he began to feel secure again. Strange rumors wafted through the KGB Center corridors, that Beria was in disgrace, that his life hung by a thread. Perhaps a miracle would happen, Morozov thought, and he would survive.

But such an idea disregarded the irreversible motion of the KGB. Since Tonya's arrest, Morozov had been labeled an enemy; and an enemy had to be destroyed by the KGB machine no matter who was running it. Morozov was a doomed man. He had a last surge of hope in June, when Beria was arrested by his cronies and shot in the Lubyanka, like so many thousands of his victims. The operation had been meticulously prepared; Beria was dead before his closest aides even learned of his arrest.

But even after Beria's death, his former subordinates diligently continued to carry out his bloody decrees. A month after Beria's death, Colonel Boris Morozov was arrested. He had just visited little Dimitri in Leningrad and received news that the other child, after safely reaching Vienna, had been admitted to the United States. He now lived with Nina Kramer in Brooklyn.

A KGB inner board — not even a court — stripped Boris Morozov of his rank and sent him to the maximum security camp in Vorkuta. A year later his mother received official notice that her son was dead. No further details were given.

Varvara Morozova was a pious woman. Braving the communist law, she slipped into the deserted Pravoslav church and lit a candle for the soul of her dead son.

Chapter 4

ON HIS FIRST DAY at school, Alex realized he was different from the other children. As he stepped into the classroom, he was amazed; he had never been in the same room with so many kids his own age before. The first-grade teacher was a silver-haired lady named Miss Murphy. She was wearing a neat gray dress with a starched white collar and shiny black shoes. In a pleasant voice, she told the students to sit down, then asked them to tell the class their names and where they were born. When Alex's turn came, he said: "Alex Gordon, Moscow." Everybody looked at him strangely, even Miss Murphy.

After they introduced themselves, Miss Murphy asked the students various questions, to help them get to know one another. The most popular question was: "Name your favorite sports team." Most of the children announced: "The Dodgers!" to the sounds of loud hand-clapping and some catcalls. The Dodgers, at last, had won the World Series. Some kids said, "The New York Yankees," and only a few timidly applauded. When it was Alex's turn, he said: "Dinamo Moscow." He had read all about them in a Russian magazine.

Silence fell in the classroom. The children eyed him suspiciously. "What did he say?" a little girl with pigtails asked; the boy sitting behind her threw his arms up in the air in mock despair, triggering a ripple of laughter. "Who are those guys?" he quipped. "Never heard of them."

Miss Murphy appeared perplexed.

"Where is Moscow anyway?" wondered another girl.

"It's in New Jersey," a boy with slick hair and a fat ass said knowingly.

"What do they play?" Miss Murphy asked Alex encouragingly. "Baseball or football?"

"Soccer," Alex said, and sat down amidst stares of bewilderment.

That was all for that day, but the following morning, before class started, three boys barred Alex's way. One of them was big and strong, with a protruding chin and small black eyes; Alex remembered his name was Ralph. He had short-cropped reddish hair and a snub nose. The second boy's name was Stacy; he was small and wiry, with bleached hair and a large mole on his left cheek. The third kid, Burt, was thin and pale, with a narrow face and a small, colorless mouth. He was wearing a red baseball cap.

"My daddy said Moscow is in Russia," Ralph said, "and you are a connu . . . connu . . ."

"Connumist," Burt helped. Several children clustered around them, listening.

"And my daddy said," Ralph went on, "that you want to fight us and kill all Americans."

"Aren't you American?" Burt asked, peeping from behind Ralph; but before Alex could answer, Ralph hit him in the face. Stacy stepped forward, menacingly shook his fists, and tried to kick Alex in the shin. Blood gushed from Alex's nose, and his attackers ran away, Burt chanting: "Connu-mist! Connu-mist!"

Alex entered the classroom and went straight to his seat, followed by the hostile stares of his classmates. He was in pain, and he clenched his teeth to keep from crying. He tried to wipe the blood off his face with his sleeve, but the child sitting behind him, a neat little boy with a freckled nose and candid blue eyes, gave him his starched white handkerchief. "Here," he said kindly, "clean your face." As Miss Murphy entered the class, the little boy whispered: "My father is from England, and he says soccer is the best game in the world." Then he added, seeking reassurance: "You're not a connumist, are you?"

The boy's name was Joey. He was the only one who spoke to Alex that day. The other children looked at him awkwardly and kept their distance; Burt, Stacy, and Ralph had spread the word. When he went home, Alex knew he had made his first friend; still, he was utterly miserable. He had so much looked forward to the day when he would go to school with other children. He wanted to make many friends, and hoped to be liked by his fellow students. Now he felt he was going to be quite lonely in his class.

This was not new for him; he had always been a lonely boy. Aunt Nina didn't like him to play with other children; she said the kids in the neighborhood were stupid little brats and he shouldn't waste his time with them. She didn't let him play softball with the boys in the street, so he could only watch their games longingly from the living room window. He left the house with his aunt only when she went shopping, and twice a week she took him to the children's playground on Myrtle Avenue, where she sat upright on a bench, knitting, watching him play.

These were the only times when he could meet children; but Aunt Nina didn't like him talking to the other kids, so he didn't stay with them long. He loved his aunt more than anything in the world, and didn't want to displease her. When Aunt Nina was at work, he wasn't allowed to go down by himself. Old Mrs. Schneider would fix him his meals, and he would spend his days in the living room playing with the few toys his aunt had bought for him.

Aunt Nina was the kindest person in the world. She devoted most of her time to him, teaching him Russian, arithmetic, geography, and history; she told him marvelous stories about animals. She always had a severe look on her face, and very rarely smiled; but she spoke to him kindly and never spanked him. She sat with him throughout every evening, and took care of Uncle Samuel only after Alex went to sleep.

Alex was afraid of Uncle Samuel and hated the sight of his twisted body, the sounds of his mumbling and retching, and the bad smells that filled his room; he avoided going near it. Sometimes, in his nightmares, he would see his uncle get up and come toward him, his outstretched hands trembling and his mouth twitching. With his bald head, toothless mouth, and pinkish, hairless skin, he looked like a grotesque, old baby turned into a monster.

When Alex had those bad dreams, he would wake up screaming, and in seconds Aunt Nina would be beside him, hugging him, soothing him with words of affection spoken in soft, caressing Russian. At these moments her morose face would light up and her eyes would fill with warmth; sometimes there were even tears. He would hug her closely, breathe her fresh smell and cuddle in her embrace. He loved her so much, she was like a mother to him.

His real mother and father, his aunt had told him, were killed in an automobile accident in Russia. He was born in Russia, in Moscow, and had a brother Dimitri, who was a year younger. He and his brother had survived because they were not in the car the day of the accident. Dimitri had stayed in Russia, with some relatives.

Why hadn't Dimitri come to America like him? Alex asked. Well, his aunt said, Dimitri's relatives didn't want him to go abroad. How come, Alex kept asking, didn't they have the same relatives? They were brothers, weren't they, and brothers always have the same relatives. Actually, Dimitri was only his half brother, Nina explained, because they had the same mother but not the same father.

"Which of our two fathers was in the automobile the day of the accident?" Alex pressed on. "Mine or Dimitri's?" He was secretly hoping it was Dimitri's father who had died and that his father was still alive.

For a moment Aunt Nina seemed upset, but then she said curtly: "Both your fathers are dead, *golubchek.*"

Alex wanted to ask if both their fathers had died in the same accident — that seemed rather strange — but Aunt Nina looked very nervous, so he decided not to ask her. He thought he dimly remembered Dimitri, though. In his vague memories of their house, back in Moscow, he recalled another child playing with lead soldiers on the wooden floor — a quiet boy with a shy smile and almond-shaped black eyes.

He also remembered his beautiful mother, her smiling blue eyes and her long blond hair; but perhaps he was only imagining things from the photographs of his mother that Aunt Nina had shown him. His aunt had a few of his mother's photographs, and he had pasted one of them on cardboard and put it beside the sofa where he slept. She was so beautiful! It made him proud. He was sure that none of his classmates had a photograph like this one by their bedside. He also saw photographs of his grandparents, wearing dark clothes; and of his mother when she was still a baby, held in the arms of a giggling, plump girl who turned out to be his aunt. Those photographs, some of them yellowed by age, were arranged in an old album that Nina kept in her alcove.

Nina — she wanted him to call her "Nina," not "Aunt" or "Auntie" — was his mother's sister. She told him she had actually raised his mother, back in Kiev. She used to dress her, like a doll, then plait her golden hair into long braids; she bought her chocolate and sweets. His mother had craved candy just as he did.

His mother and father had both been poets, Nina said. His mother's name was Tonya, and his father's Victor; they were Jewish. His grandparents had died during the war, they had been murdered by the Nazis. Only Nina's brother Valery had survived. He was a doctor and lived in Leningrad. As he grew up, Alex repeatedly questioned Nina about his family, collecting every bit of information that she would disclose, although at times she seemed reluctant to answer his questions.

His most precious possession was an old book of his mother's poems, which his father had brought to Nina when he visited America many years ago. Almost every night before going to bed, Alex would read a couple of the poems. He knew several of them by heart. The one he liked most was "A Soldier's Letter." It was a ballad about a young soldier writing to his beloved before going to fight for Russia and die in battle. The soldier wrote to his sweetheart:

No bullet can destroy my heart, for you're in it, my only love —
and there's no weapon in this world that can vanquish love.

Alex didn't care very much about love between men and women; it was a subject that bored him. Yet, reading "A Soldier's Letter," he was moved by his mother's intense romantic feeling, which made her seem very young. Another poem he liked was "My White Kingdom," depicting the Moscow winter. It spoke of towering castles and palaces, of valiant princes and fair maidens, of the Winter Queen, the Kremlin fortress, and the evergreen firs in Moscow's parks, caressed by the north wind. He longed to be there, to see the beautiful ancient town, "a legend dressed in white, a city in a cloud, a dream for the pure at heart . . ."

Thanks to Nina's limitless patience, Alex knew how to read and write in Russian even before he learned to read English. Nina didn't know English, really, and they spoke in Russian; but he picked up his English from Mrs. Schneider, from the children at the playground, and from listening to the radio in its massive cabinet that stood in a corner of the living room. When Nina was out, he listened to sports broadcasts and talk shows. When she was home, she would tune the radio only to stations that broadcast music.

There was no book of his father's, only five poems that Nina had cut out of Russian literary magazines and glued to long sheets of white paper. His father's poems were different, more austere, more concerned with freedom, the fight against oppression, and social justice. He still didn't fully understand them — he was only a child, after all — but there was a verse that impressed him deeply.

> I'd gladly die a thousand deaths,
> and hang from a thousand trees,
> or burn in a thousand fires —
> if then my bones, my heart, my soul,
> into an iron fist would turn
> to crush the chains that man has put on man.

Victor Wolf, Alex thought, was a man of strong convictions, devoted to the truth, respectful of his fellow man. His poetry wasn't as moving as Tonya's, but his ideas were much more powerful. They expressed a passionate dream of changing the world. Sometimes Alex felt angry with his mother for having taken a second husband. She should have remained faithful to Victor Wolf.

Alex had no photograph of his father. He often tried to imagine how Victor Wolf looked, and nagged Nina with questions about his height, his clothes, his face, the color of his hair and eyes. Nina had met his father in New York during the war. She told him he was thin and pale, with a broad forehead, abundant black hair, and large dark eyes that expressed "an inner torment." Alex didn't understand what inner torment meant exactly, so Nina explained that there was sadness in his father's face. "He was very handsome," she summed up, "a dark and handsome man."

Alex looked at himself in the mirror and was disappointed. He saw a blond boy with bright gray eyes. He so much wanted to look like his father, but Nina said he had taken almost entirely after his mother, "except, perhaps, for the mouth." Alex often tried to visualize his father, over there in Russia, writing his poems in an obscure study at night, or teaching his students at Moscow University. Sometimes he imagined him reading his poems to a crowd of workers and peasants in Red Square, according to the Russian tradition.

He knew exactly how Red Square looked. He could describe, with his eyes closed, the Kremlin wall, its turrets and gates, St. Basil's church, the Lenin Mausoleum, the huge Gum department store across the square, the gently sloping avenue leading to the Moskva River. From reading magazines and books, Alex had become more familiar with the sights of Moscow than he was with Brooklyn. Nina said that he knew more about Russia than many Russian children.

He had learned to read at the age of five, and devoured scores of books, which Nina kept bringing from the Russian library in Gravesend. He knew many Russian songs by heart, especially those performed by the Red Army choir. Nina would play their music almost every evening on her hand-powered record player, which he was not allowed to touch. At the age of six Alex already knew how to sing the workers anthem, the "Internationale." He knew about the October revolution, the victorious struggle of the Russian people against its oppressors, the Great Patriotic War against the Nazis, and the heroic effort that had turned Russia into a paradise for the peasants and workers. And for the children, too. He longed to grow up like the children in Russia, wearing the red scarf of a pioneer, a member of the national youth movement.

Brooklyn was unimportant. Alex was a little Russian boy, speaking Russian and growing up in a Russian house that might have been transported to America by the touch of some magic wand, across lands and seas, soaring mountains and forbidding forests, as in one of Tonya Gordon's poems.

WHEN NINA CAME HOME from work, the day of Alex's fight with Ralph, Burt, and Stacy, her nephew was waiting for her in a belligerent mood. "I don't want to go to school anymore," he said sullenly. "I don't like it."

She took off her coat and hat, sat down on the sofa beside him and hugged him gently. "Now, *golubchek*, my little dove, your face is bruised. Tell me what happened."

Alex narrated the incident with Ralph. When he described the taunting and the chanting, his eyes welled with tears. "Afterward, when I got into the class, a boy called Joey — "

"What do you mean afterward?" she asked, feigning surprise. "You let Ralph get away with it?"

Alex looked up at her, puzzled. "What do you mean?"

"I mean that when somebody hits you, you should hit back," Nina said firmly. "You shouldn't let yourself be bullied by anybody. No matter who hits you — you should fight back. Instead, you run away and come home crying like a baby."

"But Nina, Ralph is much stronger than I am!"

She shrugged. "Nu? So what? In a couple of fistfights, he might win. But the next time you may win or hurt him enough that he won't want to fight you again. Then he'll let you be. All the children will leave you in peace, if they know you could be dangerous. Go now," she said, abruptly ending the conversation. "Go read something. And think about what I told you."

Alone in her tiny room, she wiped a tear from her cheek. Poor little Alex! This was the first time that her boy was being beaten for his opinions, but it wouldn't be the last. Today it had been Dinamo Moscow, tomorrow it might be the principles of communism. It was not easy for a child to be different; children tolerated nonconformity even less than adults. The boy must learn to fight and defend himself. Otherwise he might just give up, discard everything that she had taught him, and try to become like the others, one of the herd.

The next evening, she again found Alex with a bruised face. She pretended to ignore the scratches on his cheeks and the ugly welt above his upper lip, and the boy didn't say a word about it. He looked even worse the day after. But on the fourth day, although he had a black eye, he hurled himself upon her in triumph as she walked in. He hugged her and kept jumping around her in excitement. "Ralph hit me again today," he announced, "but I fought back. I kicked him right in the kneecap. You should've seen him crying in the dust, twisting like a worm."

"Good for him," Nina said. "Now he won't bother you anymore."

Indeed, Ralph didn't bother Alex again, nor did the other children, who grudgingly learned to tolerate their odd classmate. He didn't make any friends, though, except for Joey Simpson, a bright, curious child, the son of a teacher. Joey was fascinated by the strange boy who seemed to live in a world so different from his own, wearing those funny clothes, able to read Russian and tell amazing stories about Russia, and above all — a fan of Dinamo Moscow! The two boys became inseparable friends, and Alex didn't feel so lonely anymore. But Nina soon discovered that a danger far worse than loneliness was threatening her nephew.

Slowly, imperceptibly at first, school was changing Alex. Nina had been worried about his going to an American school. Now she realized she had been right. For the child had emerged from the protective cocoon she had woven around him, and was now exposed to all the temptations America could offer. He was spending his days with American children, speaking English, learning about America, its values, its people, its breathtaking beauty. He was fascinated by history — the Mayflower, the American Revolution, the Civil War. Listening to Alex as he enthusiastically described the highlights of American history, Nina felt a pang of anxiety. At these moments Russia wasn't present in his mind at all. The child could drift away, she feared, and then nothing would bring him back.

And after all, he was just a child, so easily tempted! He played softball with his schoolmates, read books in English, and was spellbound by the first movie he saw: *Robin Hood,* starring Errol Flynn. He saw Jewish boys with skullcaps and sidelocks, and for days on end pestered Nina with questions about his origins.

"What am I more?" he asked seriously, "more Russian or more Jewish? Can I be an American too?" He was still a fan of Dinamo Moscow, but now he also liked the Dodgers and the Yankees. When the Dodgers left Brooklyn and crossed the continent to settle at Chavez Ravine in Los Angeles, Alex was infuriated, like his American-born classmates. "They betrayed us," he said to Nina that night, his eyes burning with fury. "They betrayed Brooklyn!"

He started dressing like the other children and using the same language; he asked Nina for eggs and cornflakes, Hershey bars and chewing gum. He found hamburgers and hot dogs irresistible. He brought home children's magazines and comics, avidly followed Superman's adventures, enjoyed the cartoons of Mickey Mouse, Pluto, and Donald Duck. After school he often went with Joey to the Hollywood Soda Fountain, where they had a real television set.

But the event that alarmed Nina most happened the day Alex came home and told her he had learned the national anthem at school. He stood before her, an earnest, bright-eyed child of seven, placed his right hand over his heart and with a sweet, melodious voice solemnly sang "The Star-Spangled Banner." When he concluded, he stared at her, his face transformed with emotion.

She suddenly realized he was expecting her to say something.

"Wonderful, *golubchek,*" she managed. "Very good, *ochen khorosho.*"

* * *

THE TELEPHONE seldom rang in the Kramer apartment. It was mostly Mr. Spiegel, who called Nina on business. Sometimes it was one of her friends from the Peace Movement. But that autumn evening, Nina handed the receiver to Alex. "It's for you," she said.

He had spoken on the telephone only twice. He pressed the receiver tightly against his ear. "Hello," he said tensely.

It was Joey. "Did you hear the news?" He sounded jubilant.

"What news?" It had to be something quite extraordinary to make Joey so excited.

"Wait, I asked my father to write it down," Joey said, and quoted solemnly: " 'The Soviet news agency Tass announces that the Soviet Union has put a satellite into orbit around the earth.' "

"Wow!"

" 'The satellite,' " Joey went on, " 'is called Sputnik' . . . Hey, what does Sputnik mean?"

"Companion. Go on," Alex said urgently.

" '. . . and has been put into orbit by one of the Soviet Union's missiles, which are used for peaceful purposes. Sputnik continuously sends radio signals to earth, and they can be captured all around the globe. The Soviet Union,' " Joey triumphantly concluded, " 'has launched the first artificial satellite in the history of man, and begun the conquest of space.' "

Alex was so excited, he could hardly find words to express his feelings. "Wonderful, Joey, wonderful," he shouted into the mouthpiece. "We won!"

"Well, you did!" Joey conceded. "Congratulations."

Beside himself with joy, Alex grabbed Nina by the waist and led her in a wild dance around the room. "We won!" he shouted. "We won the space race!" Between shouts and leaps and bits of singing, he told her the great news. His enthusiasm was infectious. She finally burst out laughing, and obediently spun with him in the living room. He had never before seen her laugh like that. "Really, *golubchek*? Sputnik? What a beautiful name. Yes, my sweet, it's a great day indeed!"

"The Americans bragged they were about to launch a satellite, but they did nothing," he babbled excitedly, holding tight to her waist. His head was spinning and he almost slipped and fell. "While the Russians — they didn't say a word and — poof! We are in space!"

Nina nodded, smiling. He suddenly had an idea. He left his aunt in the middle of the dance and ran downstairs. At Louie's stall he bought an evening newspaper, which already heralded on its front page: RED SATELLITE IN SPACE. The photograph released by the Soviet news agency was printed under the banner headline: a shining round sphere, from which several thin antennae emerged.

Back home, under Nina's benign gaze, Alex cut out the front page of the newspaper, then pasted it on cardboard and thumbtacked it to the wall over his desk. Sputnik looked great on the wall, beside a color print of Red Square and a black and white photograph of Soviet soldiers hoisting the red flag over Berlin at the end of World War II. On the wall there were also pictures of Marx, Stalin, and the famous cruiser *Potemkin,* which had fired on the Winter Palace in Petrograd in 1917, starting the October revolution. Completing Alex's private collection, a tiny bronze bust of Lenin reigned over his desk.

In ensuing years other photographs, paintings, and press cuttings were to join Alex's picture gallery. A portrait of Yuri Gagarin, the first Russian "cosmonaut"; a bright-colored poster of the Bolshoi Ballet; the Dinamo soccer team, clad in red shirts, in their Moscow stadium. Every year, Alex would select his "picture of the year" and hang it on the wall, diligently inscribing the date in its right corner. In 1960 it was the wreck of Gary Powers's U-2 spy plane, downed over the Soviet Union by a SAM missile; in 1961 a smiling picture of bearded, cigar-smoking Fidel Castro inspecting the Bay of Pigs, where the CIA imperialist operation had ended in dismal failure.

Alex had also wanted to hang a couple of pennants on the wall, a poster of the Beatles in concert, a funny print of Bugs Bunny that Joey had given him, and a photograph of Johnny Weissmuller as Tarzan. But Nina had been furious. "I shall not allow such trash in my living room," she said.

She had also refused to let him display his favorite picture of John Kennedy. The young President was wearing a sport shirt and walking in a field, with ominous black clouds in the background. But Nina had said no again, even though it was before the Bay of Pigs invasion. Alex felt she was being unfair. Actually, Kennedy had boldly criticized President Eisenhower for lying to the Russians about the U-2 plane. Eisenhower had said to the Soviet leader Khrushchev that he had no knowledge of the U-2 missions over Russia. That had been a lie, and Kennedy had said so, although the American people could have turned against him for saying such unpleasant things about their beloved Ike.

But Nina didn't want to hear any of that. She angrily tore Kennedy's picture off Alex's wall. "No friends of mine will find an American President in my living room," she snapped, and he complied, although he failed to understand what could be so wrong with an American President.

Besides, friends of hers almost never came to see her, now that he was sleeping in the living room. He understood that before his arrival they had held some of their meetings there — the Brooklyn chapter of the Peace Movement, the League for the Rosenbergs, who had since been executed, and other organizations manned mostly by elderly people, shabbily dressed, with strong foreign accents. "That's why those men in the cars are watching me," Nina had told him. Alex didn't know who the men in the cars were, but he understood that Nina was being watched by American agents because she supported the Soviet Union.

Still, the men in the cars were very rarely around now, once every few months. They came mostly in the evenings, sat for a couple of hours watching the house, then drove away. Sometimes they came on foot and lingered on the sidewalk for hours, or followed Alex in the streets. They thought they were clever, but Alex had learned to spot them; they couldn't fool him.

He was quite observant, had sharp senses, and developed his own methods for finding out if he was being shadowed. As he grew up, it turned into a game he enjoyed playing: he would always look out for strangers on the street and check to be sure the mailman, the milkman, and the laundry and grocery delivery boys who passed by their house were people he knew. He would closely inspect the commercial automobiles in their neighborhood, and memorize the names of the companies that owned them, looking for cars that didn't belong in their part of the city.

On his way to school he would always vary his routes, cross and recross the street several times, use shop windows as mirrors to see if he was being followed, stop suddenly and go back, watching the other passersby for any unusual reaction; he would also memorize the faces of people he saw in the street. Alex's sharp memory was his best asset. A couple of times he noticed that two men, whom he had seen outside their house, followed him on his way back from school. Shaking them off was easy; he was amused by their clumsiness.

He was in seventh grade now, a student at Jefferson Junior High. His friend Joey was still in his class, but so were his enemies, Ralph and Stacy. He was doing quite well in school, except for mathematics, which was his weak spot. He was thirteen years old and growing up fast. He had started looking at girls, although he wasn't interested by anyone in particular. Joey was madly in love with a girl from their class who already had breasts, Laura Hendel, but Alex found her too fat for his taste.

He was becoming a tall, athletic boy. Since his fights with Ralph, he had become obsessed with improving his ability to defend himself. He ran around their block every morning, swam in the ocean during the summer, and doggedly exercised at home. In his free afternoons he went to Big Jack Macmillan's boxing school, where he would help clean the rings, collect the towels, and sort out the soiled garments of the trainees. He watched the training sessions and tried to memorize the fighters' moves. Every once in a while, Big Jack, a huge, florid-faced man with a fighter's broken nose, would give Alex a pair of gloves and let him punch the heavy bag, or even give him a couple of boxing tips.

"When you fight," Big Jack would say, munching his cigar, "remember rule number one: left foot forward, bent at the knee, right foot back; your weight is on the right foot, then throw all your body forward, shift your weight to the left foot, your power to your right arm, and — bang!" Alex did it time after time, but Big Jack would dejectedly shake his head. "No way, lad, you're never going to be a fighter. There's no fire in you, no killer instinct. That's the important part, see? The killer instinct."

Still, his workouts were bearing fruit; Alex's biceps became bigger, and he enjoyed the feel of his hardening muscles when he clenched his fists. His shirts became too tight at the shoulders. Nina was constantly repairing his clothes, or buying him longer trousers and larger shirts to keep up with his growth. This year, at Marshall's summer sale, she bought him a beautiful flier's jacket made of genuine leather. It had that wonderful leather smell, and when he pulled up the soft fur collar it felt so good against his skin. The jacket was brand-new too, not like most of his clothes, which Nina bought him at Polack's used garments store. Alex was very excited about the jacket, and couldn't wait for the cooler weather so he could wear it.

But on the first cold day of the fall, when he went to school proudly clad in his flier's jacket, he saw a small group of boys waiting for him outside the gate. Ralph was there, and Stacy, and two other boys named Brad and Tommy. Burt, who had called him names back in first grade, had left the neighborhood because his father had gotten rich and they'd moved to Manhattan. Alex looked at the four boys, noticed that they abruptly stopped talking when they saw him, and realized he was headed for trouble.

HE KNEW what the trouble was. The previous night, President Kennedy had dramatically announced that Russian missiles in Cuba were threatening the United States. American reconnaissance planes, overflying Cuba, had taken photographs of the missiles. Alex had watched the evening news on television with Joey, at the Hollywood Soda Fountain, and seen the photographs. Kennedy also stated that the missile bases were manned by Red Army crews. Joey had said America must invade Cuba and kill Castro.

The discovery of the missiles had shocked the world, and Alex had also been surprised. The Soviet Union was a peace-loving nation; why should she threaten America with missiles? But Nina explained to him that it was the other way around: America had missiles all over the globe pointed at the Soviet Union; American bombers were constantly in the skies, ready to drop atomic bombs on the Soviet Union if the President gave the order. America was the aggressor, plotting to destroy Russia. The Soviet prime minister, Nikita Khrushchev, had to defend his country!

Alex didn't like Khrushchev. At a meeting of the United Nations' General Assembly that Khrushchev had attended, he had been infuriated by an anti-Soviet speech, taken off his shoe and pounded it on his desk, shouting angrily. Alex thought that was childish, hardly what he expected of a proud leader of the Soviets; but Nina said there was nothing wrong with Khrushchev's behavior.

"The United Nations," she said, "has been turned by the Americans into a propaganda machine against the Soviet Union. Russia should show them she will not tolerate this anymore."

Alex didn't argue with Nina. But last night, during Kennedy's speech about Cuba, he recalled Khrushchev pounding his shoe on the desk, waving his fist and yelling.

As Alex approached the school gate now, Ralph barred his way. "We don't want you in our school," Ralph said spitefully. "This is an American school, we don't want Russian spies in it." Saying that, he caught Alex by the sleeve.

"Let me go," Alex muttered. "I don't want to fight." He hadn't fought with Ralph since first grade. They disliked each other and almost never spoke.

"Chicken," Ralph taunted him. "Yellow chicken."

Easy, Alex said to himself, it's one against four. You must be very careful.

"Are you going to shoot your missiles now?" Tommy asked mockingly. Tommy was a very handsome boy with bleached hair and clear blue eyes.

"You're a spy!" Stacy said, taking a step toward him.

"No, I'm not," Alex answered angrily. He shook off Ralph's hand.

"We saw on TV how you spied on our ambassador in Moscow. You're a sneak, you used our seal," Tommy said. "Aren't you ashamed?"

On the television news the night before, a silver-haired man named Henry Cabot Lodge had displayed the seal of the United States that had hung in the office of the American ambassador in Moscow. The seal was engraved on a round piece of wood. The Russians had sliced it open and planted a listening device in the hollowed interior, right in the beak of the American eagle carved on the seal. This enabled them to listen to all the ambassador's conversations.

Alex had asked Nina about it, and she'd said the Soviet Union had to protect itself, that everyone knew that the American embassy collected intelligence about the Soviet military forces.

"You're spies, all of you," Brad intervened. He was a squat boy with pockmarked cheeks. His black eyes were small and suspicious. "All your family are spies, we know."

"That's a lie!" Alex protested. Other children had gathered around them, their angry stares converging upon Alex. "Go back to Russia!" a thin voice called out from behind his back.

"Your parents are in jail for spying," Brad insisted.

"They're not," Alex flared. "They were killed in an accident."

"You're lying," Ralph said venomously. "Your sweet aunt is a spy, too! My father told me that her name is Nina Kramer, and she was tried for spying, he saw her picture in the paper."

"That's not true!"

"We saw your aunt Nina when she came to pick you up at school," Ralph went on. Nina had indeed come two or three times, and waited for him by the gate. "She came to spy on our school, so you could fire your missiles at us. She'll go to jail, too, like all the other spies." The crowd of children cheered him.

"Alex, Aliosha!" Stacy called, theatrically holding out his arms to him. Stacy started walking in circles around Alex, mimicking Nina's gait and her heavy accent. "Come, Aliosha." He had apparently overheard her talking to him. The children now bellowed with laughter.

"She'll hang," Ralph said, encouraged by the cheering audience, "or maybe we'll fry her in the electric chair."

"You jerk!" Alex exploded. He couldn't let the repulsive Ralph insult his aunt. He lunged forward and hit Ralph in the face; but Ralph saw the blow coming and stepped back. Alex's fist barely touched his cheek. Ralph kicked Alex in the groin. The pain was excruciating; Alex moaned and doubled up. He heard some of the students clapping their hands and cheering for Ralph. Ralph's three friends hesitated for a moment, then joined the melee.

The boys stepped in each other's way as they attacked, and most of their blows were ineffective. This allowed Alex to catch his breath, though he was still dizzy and in pain. Brad tried to seize him by the waist, and Alex kicked his ankle, making him lose his balance. As Brad fell, he grabbed Alex's arm and pulled him down. Alex heard a ripping noise; Brad had torn the sleeve of his leather jacket. Enraged, he shook Brad off and drove his right elbow into Stacy's belly. Stacy recoiled, gasping for air. Tommy bent to help Brad get on his feet.

Suddenly Ralph was standing before Alex, looking confident, his face unprotected. Now! With crystal-clear precision, Big Jack's instructions surfaced in Alex's memory. Weight on the right foot, left foot forward, slightly bent, then a shift of the weight to the left foot, all your force in the fist, go! He hit Ralph's exposed chin with all his concentrated power; the angry blow came from beneath in an upward arc. Ralph was flung backward, then he collapsed on the sidewalk, his eyes glassy.

But Alex's triumph was brief. Brad and Stacy, back on their feet, grabbed his arms from both sides. Then Tommy, his face set in ugly determination, drove his fists into Alex's belly four or five times; when Alex jackknifed in agony, Tommy struck him in the face. Alex squirmed, trying to kick, but they held him tight as Tommy punched him again.

"You damn spy!" Tommy kept repeating. A blow landed on Alex's eyebrow, and blood trickled into his left eye, blurring his vision. A burning sensation spread on his cheek where Tommy had scratched it.

"Stop that, at once! What are you doing?" It was an adult voice, and the boys let go of Alex and fled. "I saw you!" the man shouted. Alex recognized the voice of Mr. Lieblich, the math teacher.

The teacher, in the blue suit and wide-brimmed black hat he always wore, chased the boys into the schoolyard. Alex swayed, then squatted on the dirty sidewalk, holding his stomach. He was going to be sick. His new jacket was a mess; aside from the torn sleeve, there were ugly scratches on the brown leather. What would Nina say? he wondered. But he forgot his troubles when he saw Ralph still spread out on the sidewalk, groaning, then dazedly trying to get up, shaking his head like a dog coming out of the water. Big Jack should have seen me, Alex thought proudly. It was the perfect knockout punch, worthy of a killer.

THE NEXT MORNING, Nina and Alex were summoned to the principal's office. Mister Holloway stood behind his desk, nervously tapping his pen on an open file. A large portrait of Thomas Jefferson hung on the wall behind him, beside the American flag. On his right, in a cupboard with glass doors, stood scores of gleaming sports trophies won by the school teams. A stale odor of sharp tobacco hung inside the small office.

The principal was a thin, middle-aged man with sparse, graying hair, tired eyes, and salient cheekbones. His worn-out suit hung loose from his skeletal frame, and the collar of his gray shirt seemed a couple of sizes too large for his scrawny neck. He had bony hands with long, gnarled fingers. Alex knew him as a soft-spoken man who never raised his voice. But today his eyes had a cold, mean look, and angry spots flourished in his cheeks.

He didn't ask Nina to sit down. "I'll be brief," he said. His voice was sharp with anger. "Yesterday's events were a shame to Jefferson Junior High. Your conduct, Alex Gordon, has no excuse. I shall not tolerate any violence among my students."

"There were four of them against me," Alex protested.

"The school will not easily overcome yesterday's scandal," the principal said. He reached for his pipe, which lay in a round ashtray, then changed his mind. "Many students saw the fight. Some were scared, a few were hurt." He glanced at Alex's bruised face. "Ralph Barr has two broken teeth and is receiving medical attention."

Good for him, Alex rejoiced, but kept his thoughts to himself. "My new jacket was torn," he said, averting his eyes from Nina.

Mr. Holloway raised his hand. "I shall not tolerate my school being turned into an anti-American institution."

"What did he say?" Nina asked Alex, but he motioned her to wait. It was clear that Mr. Holloway regarded him as totally responsible for yesterday's fight.

"You, young man," Mr. Holloway went on, "can hardly be suspected of giving your fellow students an example of American patriotism."

"But I didn't — "

The principal did not pause to let Alex speak. "Since you've become a student in this school, you have not ceased expressing opinions hostile to this country and favorable to our greatest enemy, Soviet Russia. I am well aware of your behavior in class. You act as if you don't belong in this country. Perhaps it's not your fault, but that of your . . ." Holloway looked at Nina. ". . . of your family, which has raised you in such a way."

"What you say about boy's family?" Nina managed in her limping English.

"Since yesterday morning the telephone hasn't stopped ringing," Mr. Holloway said, turning to Nina. "I have had complaints from many parents, who demand that your nephew be expelled from school."

"Who are this parents?" Nina asked belligerently. Last night, when he had narrated the incident to her, she had kissed him warmly. "You did right, *golubchek*," she'd said.

"There's Mr. Barr, for one, and Mr. Warzsawski, Stacy's father. And also Mr. John Simpson, who is a teacher."

"Mr. Simpson?" Alex was stunned. It couldn't be. Mr. Simpson was Joey's father.

"Yes," the principal said. "He claims that you have a very bad influence on his son."

Alex felt afraid for the first time. If even Joey's father didn't want them to be friends anymore . . . In spite of everything, Alex liked the school, some of the teachers, and quite a few of the children. If he was thrown out, he certainly wouldn't be able to see Joey anymore.

"No, please, Mister — " Nina began, recognizing Mr. Holloway's threat.

"I have decided, however, not to expel you," the principal said, looking sternly at Alex. "You're a good student, and this time you'll get away with a warning. You should be grateful that your adoptive country is a democracy in which you are free to express the most revolting opinions. That is not the case in the Soviet Union." He wiped his brow with a gray handkerchief. "You will be transfered to another class. You'll be separated from Ralph Barr and his friends."

And from Joey, Alex thought.

"And I am also officially advising you that the next time I hear any complaint about you, I'll expel you from our school without any further warning. Is that clear?"

"Yes," Alex whispered. His throat was constricted. This is unfair, he wanted to protest, it was not my fault! But he was afraid he would be thrown out of school, and so remained silent. He had never felt so humiliated.

BUT IT WASN'T Mr. Holloway's warning, nor the prospect of another fight, nor even the fear of losing Joey's friendship that made Alex stop voicing his opinions.

One afternoon, a few days after the Cuban crisis began, he was again at the soda fountain with Joey. Joey's father had forbidden him to see Alex again, but Joey didn't care. He was now happily blabbering about Laura answering a note he had sent to her, but Alex wasn't listening. He expected a war to break out at any moment between the United States and the Soviet Union, especially now that Kennedy had imposed a naval blockade on Cuba. On the television screen harried speakers kept announcing that a special news bulletin was due any minute.

"So she came up to me," Joey narrated rapturously, "and said: 'Was it you who wrote that sweet note to me, Joey?' And I said — "

"Not now, Joey," Alex said, and Joey clammed up, visibly hurt. The words Special Report had flashed on the screen, and a newscaster's face appeared. "Soviet Premier Nikita Khrushchev," he solemnly intoned "announced today that Russia will withdraw all its missiles from Cuba. This action, Khrushchev said, is being taken in the interests of peace."

"What?" Alex gasped.

Joey was shaking his head. "I don't believe it."

"The Soviet Union will provide to the international community all necessary proofs and guarantees that her intentions are serious," the newscaster went on. On the screen, his face was replaced by film sequences, taken from low-flying aircraft, in which Soviet ships could be seen sailing away from Cuba. Long cylindrical forms covered with tarpaulin were stacked on the ships' decks. At the sight of the approaching American craft, the Russian crews removed the tarpaulin, uncovering the missiles. They waved to the Americans; one of the shots had been taken from a very short distance, and the Russians could be clearly seen grinning and cheering.

"I must be dreaming," Joey murmured. Alex was too dismayed to speak. He felt as if someone had punched him flush on the temple. Why did they do it? What was going on?

He slowly came to his senses. The Russians had capitulated before the Americans, they were unconditionally retreating. They were pulling out of Cuba "in the interests of peace," which meant that by bringing the missiles to Cuba in the first place, they had acted against peace. Had Russia made a mistake? Was Kennedy right when he called the Russians aggressors?

Alex jumped from his seat and darted toward the door. "Where are you going?" Joey called after him, but he didn't answer. He ran all the way home and burst like a hurricane into the apartment. Nina was standing in the kitchen, cooking. "Khrushchev is pulling the missiles out of Cuba," he announced breathlessly. "He gave in." He watched Nina intensely as he spoke.

For a moment she was at a loss. She blinked several times, frowned, then said halfheartedly, "What is this, Alex, a joke?"

"No, not a joke, I saw the Russian ships carrying the missiles back. They showed them on TV!"

She stared at him for a while, then slowly settled into a chair, pursing her lips as she always did when she was thinking. "Nu," she said, "that proves, once again, that the Soviet Union is ready to do anything for peace, even — "

He couldn't take it. "How can you say that!" he exploded. "How can you still defend them? They almost caused a world war."

"Now, Alex — "

"But you always defend them, don't you? You always find an excuse for what they're doing. You'll never admit they could be wrong, even once!" He ran to the living room and tore Castro's smiling picture off his wall. "He has nothing to smile about," he muttered furiously.

* * *

BUT THE HARDEST BLOW came right after the festival of Shavuot.

Lately Alex was becoming more interested in his religion. Last year he had turned thirteen, but Nina had refused to celebrate his bar mitzvah, which she regarded as a barbaric custom. Alex was unhappy with her decision. He was intrigued by Jewish survival throughout the ages, and he wanted to learn more about his origins. There must be something in our religion, he thought, that helped overcome all the disasters, persecutions, and massacres. He had hoped that the religious training in preparation for a bar mitzvah would unlock the mysteries of Judaism, but he didn't want to confront Nina. One day, he thought, when I grow older, I'll look into this myself.

On the day of Shavuot, the Jewish Pentecost, he visited their neighborhood synagogue. He hadn't told Nina he was going. But he left the service disappointed. People in skullcaps and prayer shawls were reciting and chanting in Hebrew. He understood nothing, he didn't know the meaning of the prayers, he didn't know when to get up and when to sit down; he was a stranger among his own people.

The following morning, he saw Ralph Barr coming out of his classroom. They had bumped into each other in the past, but they didn't talk. They were afraid to get into another fight that could cause their expulsion from school. But this morning Alex noticed a malicious grin on Ralph's face. Alex was startled, and walked to his desk, wondering about the reason for Ralph's attitude.

On his desk was a plain white envelope.

He opened it. A newspaper clipping fell out. It was an article from the *Daily News,* dated the previous Thursday. The headline said: SOVIETS SECRETLY MASSACRED EMINENT JEWISH WRITERS. The article was illustrated with several portraits: a bespectacled man named Mikhoels, a man with a gaunt face and large forehead named Fefer. But his attention was drawn to two names, circled in vivid red.

Victor Wolf and Tonya Gordon-Wolf.

His knees buckled and he slumped into his chair. His heart was suddenly pounding in his chest. Somebody called his name and said something, but he couldn't hear. He swallowed hard and tried to continue reading. The words were dancing before his eyes. He had to read each sentence three or four times to understand it.

In the years 1949 and 1953, the article said, the KGB had secretly executed some of the greatest Jewish writers and philosophers in Russia. In mock trials, they had been accused of spying for the United States and Great Britain. Most of the writers had been shot, the rest had perished in concentration camps. They were all victims of Stalin's persecution mania.

The massacres had been kept secret, the article continued, until the defection of a Soviet diplomat last month. His revelations explained, at last, the disappearance of so many famous writers from the Soviet literary scene in the early fifties.

The list of the writers murdered by Stalin followed. It included the names of his mother and father.

He got up from his seat and walked out of the class. The math teacher was saying something, looking at him strangely, but Alex didn't hear. It was raining outside, a warm, early summer rain. Heavy drops splashed on his face as he crossed the schoolyard. Ralph was behind all this, he knew, but he didn't care about Ralph. The jerk had only cut out the article and put it on his desk.

Alex walked down the street, the rain soaking his hair and clothes and streaming down his face. As he crossed Flatbush Avenue, he was almost run over by a car. The driver, a round-faced man with a huge cigar, angrily waved his fist and yelled at him.

Alex entered Spiegel's Furs and went straight to the back of the store. Two salesgirls came toward him, and one said: "It's Nina's nephew, he looks a mess." His water-soaked shoes left muddy prints on the carpet. Mr. Spiegel, a fat, bald man with gold-rimmed spectacles and a blue suit, got up from his seat glaring at him.

Finally Alex saw Nina. She hurried toward him, her face a mixture of puzzlement and concern. She had told him never to come to the store, Mr. Spiegel might get upset.

Nina asked something, but he didn't hear. He reached into his shirt pocket and his hand came out clutching the newspaper clipping, now wet and dripping.

"Did you — " he began, but his voice was oddly thin, almost inaudible. "Did you know about this? Did you know that Stalin murdered my parents? Did you?"

Nina stared at him. Her trembling hand rose to her mouth, and her eyes filled with anguish.

*   *   *

IN RUSSIAN, Alex wrote to his brother.

Dimitri, my beloved brother,

For many years I tried to write to you, but I didn't find you. I sent you greetings for the New Year and your birthday (Aunt Nina, mother's sister, said you were born on July 6, 1950), but the letters were returned by the Moscow post office. Perhaps I have the wrong address. I am therefore writing on the envelope that they should forward the letter to your new address. This time I hope it will reach you. This is important because I've got terrible news.

An American newspaper published an article saying that our mother and my father were executed for treason by the Soviet security services. Did you know that? I don't believe my parents were traitors. You know that our mother wasn't a traitor, she was a great Soviet poet. Your father wouldn't have married her if she, or my father, had done anything wrong. This must have been a terrible mistake. Perhaps your father can help us find the truth? I know he is an officer in your security services, can you ask him? I often read Mother's poems, and I can't believe that she has been shot for treason, she was so devoted to the Soviet Union. I often dream at night about her death, and I wake up crying.

Please write to me when you receive this letter. I so much want to meet you. I think I remember you. Do you have brown hair and black eyes? That's how I remember you. And how are you doing at school? I am doing fine, except for math, which I hate; perhaps it is because we have a bad teacher. I love reading books, I like movies, rock music, mostly the Beatles, and color television. How is the television in Moscow? Aunt Nina says it's the best in the world. Do you like the Beatles? I am also boxing a little and playing softball. We have no soccer in America.

Please write to me. Your loving older brother,

Alex

Three months later the letter was returned to Alex's home. The envelope was stamped with a large purple inscription in Russian: UN-KNOWN AT THIS ADDRESS.

Chapter 5

AT FIVE MINUTES TO EIGHT Nikita stuck his egglike head in the door and beckoned to Dimitri. "Get ready," he rasped, revealing his tobacco-stained teeth, "they're here. Good luck."

"Thank you, Nikita," he said affectionately. Nikita was one of the few adults in the institution who had ever been kind to him. The old janitor waved a gnarled hand and was gone.

He stood up, pulled his uniform jacket tight, buckled up his heavy belt, and rubbed the tips of his shoes against his ankles, to polish the leather with the backs of his trousers. From the dented mirror by the door, a slim youth angrily stared back at him. He critically examined his reflection, the cropped brown hair, the pale forehead, the gaunt, saturnine face. There was smoldering hostility in the black almond-shaped eyes, sheltered under thick eyebrows. His stubborn mouth, clamped with bitterness, was a thin line under the straight nose; a brown mole was placed like a stranded punctuation mark over his upper lip. The jawline was sharp and the square chin defiantly jutted forward. It would have been a handsome, passionate face, had it not been so fierce and accusing; his black stare made people ill at ease.

Relax, he thought, calm down, don't look so aggressive. They want you tame and subdued. That's the secret of climbing the ladder in Mother Russia: only the tame and subdued are allowed to become fierce and brutal. And you, Dimka, you already bare your fangs like a wolf, when you're still expected to bleat like a baby lamb.

The far door of the deserted dormitory opened, and Vanya burst in. He was short of breath; he must have been running. Vanya waved at him with both hands. "I wanted to catch you before you left," he called. "Good luck, Dimka!"

He waved back at Vanya and went out. The corridor was cold, but his forehead and palms were sweating profusely. His knees were shaky and a sensation of emptiness lingered in the pit of his stomach. His footsteps echoed loudly in the long passage, where the portraits of legendary Russian generals stared at him from their frames on the peeling, light green walls: Suvorov, the eighteenth-century master; Kutuzov, who drove Napoleon out of Moscow; Budienny, the revolutionary commander of the Red cavalry; Zhukov, the conqueror of Berlin in the Second World War. From the spaces between the portraits, slogans painted on thick cardboard praised the glorious Red Army and its heroes. The largest slogan, fixed above the refectory door, proclaimed: "The Panfilov Institution for Orphans of Soviet Heroes salutes the Motherland on the Anniversary of the October Revolution." Some joker had erased the H from Heroes and painted a Z instead.

He entered the office of Lev Brudny, the new administrator. He could see the vegetable garden by the window, still buried in deep snow. "You can go right in," Brudny said to him, half rising from his chair, a greasy smile on his stupid face. He knocked on the heavy door, made of thick oak plates. THE PANFILOV INSTITUTION, the chipped enamel sign read, COLONEL PAVEL BORODIN, PRINCIPAL.

He stepped into the principal's office. Colonel Borodin wasn't there. Three chairs had been placed behind his large desk. Two men and a woman were seated close together, smoking and quietly talking. On the desk were steaming glasses of tea and a bowl of sugar cubes. When they saw him enter, they fell silent. From the far wall a portrait of Lenin observed them with a benign smile. When Dimitri had first entered this room, as a little child, it had been Stalin who scornfully surveyed him from the same spot.

"Good morning, comrades," he said, and stood at attention.

"Good morning," answered the man in the middle, apparently the commission chairman. Before him lay Dimitri's application forms. The chairman was a corpulent man of about fifty, dressed in a gray suit. He had graying blond hair, watery eyes, and his mouth was large and rubbery. He was wearing a crimson tie. A small pin, representing a red flag crossed with a bayoneted rifle, was stuck in the lapel of his suit jacket. The pin indicated he was a Red Army veteran.

"I am Genadi Bodrov," he said, "from the Committee of State Security." The committee was better known by its initials, the KGB. "This is Comrade Helena Kraiova, deputy director of the Higher School of State Security." The woman, dressed in a conservative blue suit and a white blouse, had a stout torso; her forehead was mottled with tiny spots, sprayed over sharp, alert eyes. She held her cigarette like a pencil, between her thumb and forefinger. "And Colonel Oleg Kalinin, from the GRU." The GRU was military intelligence. The handsome colonel was wearing an elegant, dark blue suit and a dazzling white shirt. As he nodded at Dimitri, a quick smile flashed on his face. A friend, perhaps, Dimitri thought. A groove of white scar tissue ran across Kalinin's left cheek, below the salient cheekbone.

"You may stand at ease," Bodrov said briskly, pretending to study Dimitri's application forms. He suddenly raised his head. "I see that your mother and father have been shot for treason. And that your half brother lives in America."

A chill ran up his spine and he nodded woodenly.

"That makes you a security risk, don't you think?" the woman said coldly, exhaling a puff of smoke.

"If you were in our place," Bodrov followed, "would you admit somebody with such a record into the KGB?"

"Now, now, comrades," Colonel Kalinin said pleasantly. "We know that both Tonya Gordon and Boris Morozov have been fully rehabilitated." He picked up Dimitri's application forms and glanced at them for a moment, then put them back on the desk. "Dimitri Morozov is a fine young man, and his record is commendable. We don't want him to pay for what Stalin did — wrongly — to his parents."

Dimitri felt a surge of relief. Thank God for Colonel Kalinin, he thought. The colonel was openly siding with him.

Bodrov, forehead thoughtfully puckered, slowly nodded, then looked at Dimitri. "Tell the commission, why do you wish to study at the Higher School of State Security?"

Dimitri cleared his throat. Kalinin smiled at him encouragingly. He was much more confident now. "If they intend to reject you," General Takachenko had told him the day before, "the interview will be over in thirty seconds. That's the ritual."

So let's proceed according to the ritual, he thought. "My name is Dimitri Morozov," he started. He had learned the trite formulas by heart. "I want to participate in the building of socialism. I am a member of the soviet communist youth, the Komsomol. I want to serve the Soviet Union and protect our just society against its enemies from within and from without. I want to join the KGB and follow in the footsteps of my father, Colonel Boris Morozov."

Do you really want to know why I am joining you? he bitterly reflected while declaiming the banal answers they expected. Do you want me to describe the life of a helpless child, abandoned in this accursed orphanage? Do you want to hear about a childhood of privation and abuse? Do you want to know how I learned to cheat, and lie, and steal, in order to survive? And how in despair I swore I would escape from this place?

He didn't remember the day he had arrived at the Panfilov orphanage; he was barely two and a half years old then. At times, a succession of blurred images would surface in his mind, like an enigmatic message from a former existence: fragmentary glimpses of a stocky, dark-haired man with severe features, a faceless woman with long golden hair and a sweet smell, and another child, a merry blond boy. He recalled riding in an automobile with a driver through large, snow-covered avenues, the blond child jumping and giggling beside him.

He never mentioned these memories to his classmates at Panfilov; he was a quiet, lonely child, and kept mostly to himself. He often painfully longed for a mother, for a hug, a loving touch; sometimes he would dream about the woman with the golden hair. But he didn't know if she was his mother. She was probably dead. She couldn't have knowingly abandoned him to his fate. And the blond child, was he his brother? What had happened to him?

Dimitri felt that there was something unclear about his origins. He had asked his teachers about his father, but his questions had been met with cold, silent stares. To his friends' questions he answered that his father had been a colonel and had perished fighting for the motherland. "How was he killed fighting?" his classmates would ask. "There was no war when you were born."

"And what about you?" he countered. "We are the same age."

Their own fathers, they replied, had been heroes of the Soviet Union, but had died years after the war. He bowed his head, confused; he didn't know what to say.

Not until the age of thirteen had he heard about his parents' executions. Panic-stricken, he had retreated even further into himself, raising his ramparts and pulling in his bridges, determined to preserve his shameful secret. Nobody at Panfilov, he decided, should ever find out what fate befell Boris and Tonya Morozov.

The Panfilov orphanage was located in an old barracks of the czar's Seventeenth Cavalry Regiment, outside the Leningrad suburb of Pushkin. The barracks was a compound of drab, dun-colored structures, stuck in the middle of an exercise area that froze solid in the winter and turned into a muddy mire in the spring and fall. The soldiers' dormitories and most of the stables had been hastily rebuilt to lodge three hundred boys, aged from two to eighteen. The orphanage was named after a general who had been killed defending Moscow. It was run by a retired colonel, and organized as a regular military unit.

Dimitri and the other children were issued uniforms — a dark woolen set for winter, and two light khaki outfits for summertime. Each boy was also given a cap and an overcoat, a pair of high shoes and a pair of felt boots. Their hair was cropped short; their beds and lockers were subject to constant inspections. The dorms were often fumigated, but the lice and ticks of Panfilov didn't seem to mind, and kept sucking the children's blood.

Each dormitory corresponded to an age group and a school class. Older boys, attached to the dormitories, served as "duty sergeants" and ran the classes as military platoons. There were roll calls, drills on the parade grounds, physical exercises, paramilitary training sessions. The teachers and instructors, most of them former officers, lived in the compound with their families.

No student was allowed to leave the orphanage without special permission, which was almost never given; the only way Dimitri and his friends could catch a glimpse of Leningrad was during the class trips to various museums and stadiums in the city. Girls were not allowed in the

Panfilov compound, except for the families of the staff. The staff quarters were several tidy cottages, separated from the orphanage by the parade grounds. A shady chestnut grove stretched behind the cottages.

At Panfilov, Dimitri learned to live in constant, degrading poverty. He never received a new garment, or a new pair of shoes. The uniforms issued to him were threadbare hand-me-downs, repaired and patched countless times; so were the shoes. Private property wasn't allowed. Any clothing, underwear, money, pocketknives, or food discovered in the students' lockers were immediately confiscated. The school was in a constant state of disrepair. In the winter, icy gusts of wind invaded the decrepit buildings. The children almost froze to death in their poorly heated dorms, shivering under their thin blankets.

Dimitri was constantly hungry. Black bread and gluey porridge for breakfast, black bread and potatoes for lunch, black bread and watery soup for dinner: this was the invariable menu in the refectory. On national holidays the students also received meat, fish, or sausage. The vegetables they grew in the backyard never reached their plates. "Rotten," the chief cook always said in response to their timid inquiries. "Everything was rotten this year." He was a burly man with huge arms and a malevolent face. Nobody dared to contradict him — that was considered insubordination. The punishment for insubordination could be expulsion from the school; and they had nowhere to go.

But there was a priceless subject that Dimitri mastered at Panfilov: the art of survival.

AS LONG AS HE LIVED in the small children's wing, home to the kindergarten, first, and second grade kids, Dimitri had been protected. But on the first night he spent in the third-grade dorm, somebody stole his shoes. In the morning he trudged, barefoot, to the "duty sergeant" and reported the theft. The older boy, a sturdy youth with tallow hair, a round face, and small porcine eyes, shrugged. "That's your problem," he drawled. His front teeth were rotten. "You must be more careful next time."

Dimitri didn't know what to do. He was only nine, and classes were about to start. He ran to the administrator's office to complain, but on the way there bumped into the janitor, Nikita. "Lost your shoes, little one?" Nikita asked kindly. He was bald and frail; he always wore a worn-out *rubashka* and walked with a funny, gooselike gait. But he had a warm voice and good, soft eyes.

"Yes, and I'm going to report it to the administrator."

Nikita sadly shook his head. "Don't," he said, gently touching his cheek. "You'll be punished; they won't help you. Do you have any money?"

"No," Dimitri said, surprised. "Why?"

"That's what I thought," Nikita said. "If you had money, or anything of value, you could have asked your duty sergeant to help. He would have found your shoes."

"I have some books," Dimitri said hopefully. He was devouring travel and adventure books, and had won *Gulliver's Travels, Treasure Island,* and *Oliver Twist* at school contests.

Nikita shook his head. "Books are no good. Money, that's what you need. If not . . ." He stared fixedly at Dimitri. "You can wear your boots to class today, nobody will mind. But if your shoes are missing at the inspection on Saturday, you'll be in big trouble. You'll be punished, and they'll enter a warning in your file."

"But why would anybody steal my shoes?" Dimitri asked, his eyes welling with tears.

The janitor took a tin box full of black tobacco out of his pocket and rolled a cigarette in a piece of gray paper. "To sell them, of course," he said. Noticing Dimitri's puzzlement, Nikita added: "Back to you, or at the market in Pushkin. People would pay a good price for a pair of shoes, even secondhand."

"But," Dimitri stammered, "we aren't allowed out of school."

Nikita lit his cigarette and let out a murky puff of smoke. "There are ways, little one, there are always ways."

Only when Nikita had gone, did Dimitri understand. He was expected to buy back his shoes, and if he didn't have money or valuables, to steal a pair of shoes from another child.

He went to class in his felt boots. During the day, he kept thinking about Oliver Twist, the hero of Dickens's novel, how helpless he had been, all alone in the orphanage! At nightfall Dimitri lay awake on his cot, listening to the regular snoring of his roommates. Long after everybody had fallen asleep, he slipped down from his bed and crawled to the far end of the dorm. His arms and legs were trembling with fear. Stealing was wrong, he knew; he had never stolen before. If he was caught, he would be thrown out of the orphanage. But if he didn't get another pair of shoes, he would be punished. He had to succeed.

One of the children stirred in his sleep, and he froze, holding his breath. But the boy turned the other way and Dimitri continued to crawl. Shoes were nowhere to be seen; apparently the other boys, smarter than he, had safely hidden them in their lockers or under their pillows before going to bed. He was too naive, that's why his shoes had been stolen.

By the last bed he saw a pair of shoes. He approached and crouched in the dark. Nobody moved. His heart was thumping wildly. Twice he reached for the shoes, but withdrew his hand. He couldn't do it; he didn't want to become a thief. But he didn't want to be punished on Saturday either. He didn't want a warning in his file. He hadn't done anything wrong, why should he suffer? Oliver Twist had also been forced to steal when he escaped to London, he'd had no choice.

Finally he grabbed the shoes and lunged back. But the shoes jumped out of his hand! They clanged against the iron bedpost, and the sharp noise made his heart leap with dread. The shoes had been tied to the bed! He darted in panic toward his bed. On both sides of the passage heads were rising from pillows.

"Catch him," somebody yelled. "He tried to steal my shoes!"

"Catch the thief!" others shouted.

He kept running, but one of the boys stretched his leg across the passage between the beds. Dimitri stumbled and fell on his face. Several pairs of hands grasped his arms and feet and pinned him to the ground. He fought wildly, kicking and striving to yank his arms free. "Let me go!" he groaned, tears choking his throat. "Let me go!"

"A blanket," somebody called urgently, in a low voice. The duty sergeant! "A blanket, and keep quiet!"

Somebody threw a blanket on him, and a strong hand clamped over his mouth. Then they fell on him, perhaps five or six boys, hitting and kicking him with all their might. The pain was terrible; he was suffocating, gasping for air, and tears were streaming down his face. The boys beat him up silently, viciously, and he could hear their rasping breath as they threw punches at him. He couldn't protect his face, since his arms were held behind his back. A blow smashed his nose, another landed on the side of his mouth, and he felt the salty taste of blood. Somebody kicked him in the spine, and he jerked in pain. But he didn't moan, and he bit his lips rather than shout.

The blows stopped suddenly and someone removed the blanket. At first he didn't open his eyes, he felt so humiliated. Finally he looked up. In the darkness, he made out the group of boys surrounding him, staring down at him. "Dirty thief!" one of them said, and spat at him. A child standing behind the others tried to kick him. A dazzling beam of light shone in his face; somebody had turned a flashlight on him. He blinked in the light and looked away.

"Look at him," the duty sergeant said. He was the one with the flashlight. "That's the thief, one of your own. Remember him, and don't let him come near your belongings. And not a word to the teachers. We settle these matters among ourselves."

He lay on his bed, aching and humiliated, and cried silently. Once or twice he sank into fitful sleep that lasted only a few minutes. When he woke up, he couldn't believe that he'd been caught stealing and that the children had beaten him up. It hadn't happened, he thought, he'd only had a nightmare. But as he turned on his bed, he felt the raw pain from the beating. It hadn't been a dream after all; his nightmare had just begun.

As morning came, he experienced the ignominy of being an outcast. Nobody spoke to him. The boys grimaced at him, spat on the floor, or called him names. At breakfast, when he sat down, his classmates moved to another table. In class he heard those around him whispering, "Thief." When he came back to the classroom after the lunch break, he found that somebody had chalked a skull and crossbones on his desk.

"What happened to your face?" the arithmetic teacher asked him. In the mirror today, his face glowed with all the colors of the rainbow. His upper lip was swollen, and a crust of coagulated blood had formed under his nose. Two long scratches ran across his left cheek. "I fell," he said. His classmates giggled.

The teacher, an old man with wise eyes, peered at him closely. "Be more careful," he suggested. He probably understood what had happened, but obeying the orphanage code, he didn't investigate further.

Dimitri knew that the following days were going to be terrible; he had been branded forever by his class. Still, his problem remained unsolved. He needed new shoes before the Saturday inspection. Tonight, or tomorrow at the latest, he had to try again. He had no choice, he had to do it.

This time, though, he prepared his operation carefully. He wouldn't steal the shoes of one of his roommates, but try another class. He would also have to choose the right time to do it. After spending another sleepless night, he devised a plan. In the morning, he studied the school schedule posted on a board beside the administrator's door. During lunch he stole a knife at the refectory and concealed it in his shirt. In the middle of geography class, at two-thirty, he suddenly doubled up in his seat, feigning a stomach ache, and raised his hand. "I must have eaten something bad," he moaned. "May I go to the toilet?"

The teacher, Comrade Lydia Raznukhina, stared at him severely, then reluctantly nodded consent. As soon as he was out of her sight, he dashed to the calisthenics hall, where the fifth grade was exercising in dark blue shorts and undershirts. Their clothes hung in the adjacent locker room; their shoes were neatly lined up on the floor, each pair tied together by the shoestrings.

Dimitri selected two pairs of shoes that looked roughly his size, then took the knife out of his shirt and cut the shoestrings. He took the right shoe from one pair and the left from the other, and stuck them beneath his shirt. Then he collected all the other shoes, cut the strings that tied the pairs together, and piled them in one corner. When the students came back, they would think somebody had played a practical joke on them. Everybody would try to retrieve his own shoes; by the time two of the students realized they were left with one shoe each, he would be safe.

Five minutes later he walked back into his class. His face was flushed and his breath shallow, but he was elated. The knife was securely hidden in his mattress, and the felt boots were back in his locker. He was wearing the stolen shoes. He returned to his desk and sat down. Nobody had seen the change in his footwear. Nobody but a Georgian boy named Vanya, who sat across the aisle. Vanya looked down at Dimitri's shoes, then slowly raised his head and smiled the cunning, knowing smile of an accomplice. Two nights ago, Dimitri recalled, Vanya had participated in the beating. But today he wanted to make up.

Dimitri wanly smiled back.

The inspection on Saturday went smoothly. A half hour later, in a ceremony on the parade grounds, Dimitri and his classmates received their red scarves, symbols of membership in the Lenin Pioneer Organization. Soviet tradition required that at the age of nine, every child join the pioneers, the communist children's movement. As they were awarded the neckerchiefs and their badges, the boys solemnly chanted the Laws of the Soviet pioneers:

"The pioneer adheres to the motherland, the party, and communism.

"The pioneer emulates the heroes of struggle and labor.

"The pioneer is persistent in studies, work, and sports.

"The pioneer is an honest and true comrade and always stands for the truth."

Vanya turned and winked at him.

A RUTHLESS DETERMINATION was born in Dimitri the night of his beating. The memory of his humiliation by the entire class never left him; he carried the pain and the shame of that night in his flesh. And he swore that never again would he let himself be hurt without hurting back, without making his enemy pay tenfold. Never again would he lie under a stinking blanket, his arms and legs pinned down, and let a horde of damned cowards beat him up.

He threw himself into physical training as if possessed. He got up in the morning earlier than the other boys and ran for an hour along the fence surrounding the institution, then did push-ups, chin-ups and sit-ups. He took classes in boxing and karate, which were held in the students' free evenings. He would spend hours at the gymnasium, venting his hatred and frustration on the punching bag, or splitting wooden boards with the hardened edges of his hands till the skin broke and started bleeding.

"*Molodetz*, Dimka, great fellow," his sports teacher would say, smiling, as he squeezed the boy's bulging muscles. The teacher was a bow-legged Don cossack with a balding head, a half-crescent mustache, and huge shoulders. "I wouldn't like to be on the receiving end of that fist."

He'd show them one day, Dimitri thought, he'd pay them back. He often dreamed of his revenge, although he didn't know against whom.

He expected the theft of the shoes to be his first and his last. He had stolen because he had been forced to. He wasn't a thief, he was a student and he wanted to become an important man. He did well in his studies. He excelled in geography and in the history of the Soviet Union. He devoured more books by Dickens, the works of Jules Verne, Alexander Beck's trilogy on the world war, and the *Young Guard* by Ostrovski. Some of the boys in his dorm started speaking to him, and he answered curtly, smothering his hatred. The shameful episode of the theft was slowly fading away.

The next winter was the harshest since 1937. As the terrible Leningrad cold settled in, the Gulf of Finland and the river Neva froze solid, and the orphanage and its grounds disappeared under a deep layer of snow. The water pipes inside the orphanage building froze as well, and the washroom faucets grew sparkling beards of icicles. Each morning the staff had to work for hours to get the pipes to yield a trickle of ice-cold water. Frost glazed the windows, crept into the poorly heated dorms and settled in the corners, like some living, alien presence, blowing its icy breath on the children.

The weaker boys couldn't fight the cold; six Panfilov students, two of them from Dimitri's dorm, were rushed to the Chapayev Hospital with acute pneumonia; two of them died. At the funeral of the second boy, Vanya approached Dimitri. "We might be next, you know," he said. He cocked his head toward the group of teachers. "They wouldn't care if something happened to us."

Dimitri nodded. "What should we do?"

"We'll need warmer clothes, and more blankets," Vanya whispered.

"And better food, too," Dimitri added.

That night, Dimitri and Vanya broke into the workshop and stole several saws, hammers, and screwdrivers, which they concealed in the coal cellar. Soon they were stealing whatever they could — money and personal objects from the boys' lockers, bags of potatoes and flour from the kitchen, jars of alcohol from the biology lab. One of the cook's helpers, an Uzbek named Kolya, sold the stolen goods at the free market outside the church. In return he brought them woolen sweaters that they wore under their uniforms, extra blankets, canned meat and vegetables which they would heat late at night in the deserted kitchen. Some nights they smoked Prima cigarettes in the backyard. Their duty sergeant, Kuzma Bunin, cooperated in exchange for a cut of the profits. He told them that a network of students from the higher grades was smuggling stolen goods over the school fence. They had never been caught.

When he lay on his cot at night, Dimitri was assailed with guilt feelings. What had happened to him? He, the son of a colonel in the Red Army, had become a thief, robbing his friends and his school. He despised himself for what he was doing. But he didn't want to die! Besides, he didn't owe them anything. During the remaining months of that terrible winter, three more boys were taken to the hospital. One of them died, and one was too sick to return to the orphanage; they never saw him again.

Dimitri and Vanya, on the other hand, started the eleventh year of their lives in excellent physical shape. Dimitri emerged as a brilliant student. In a paper he read in class, he explained why life in the Soviet Union was so much better than life in America. "The decay of American society," his paper began, "can be seen in the high rate of crime and narcotics addiction, encouraged by the capitalist regime. People in America become swindlers, robbers, and thieves because their families are hungry."

"Excellent," exclaimed the teacher, Karmiya Tolbukhina. She came from an old communist family, and even her unusual name had a patriotic meaning. It had been composed of the words Krasnaya Armiya — Red Army. "Proceed, Dimitri," Karmiya said warmly.

Dimitri went on to describe the suffering of the American workers, exploited by the capitalists; how armaments manufacturers fomented wars in South America and in Asia; the social injustice; the persecution of intellectuals. "America is an imperialist country that sucks the blood of smaller states, robbing them of their wheat, their steel, and their oil." The Soviet Union, by contrast, helped small countries, protected its workers, and struggled for world peace and fraternity.

"I am lucky I was born in the Soviet Union," Dimitri's paper concluded, "because in America children are starving."

Karmiya Tolbukhina, deeply moved, stepped toward him and kissed him on the forehead. At the end of the term, Dimitri was awarded a prize: a small bust of Lenin.

"DIMITRI! Dimitri, wake up!"

He tried to push away the hand that was shaking him. He was immersed in a dream about a beautiful tropical island. A girl was holding his arm and looking into his eyes. She loved him. All his dreams lately were about girls, and all had the same wet ending. But not this one. "Dimka, wake up!" the voice in his ear kept whispering urgently, and the hand continued shaking his shoulder.

He opened his eyes. "What — "

The hand swiftly covered his mouth. "Keep quiet." He recognized Vanya's voice. "Come with me. Something is going on."

He grabbed his clothes — it was late spring and the weather was warming up — and tiptoed after Vanya. Kuzma Bunin, the duty sergeant, snored loudly in his bed by the door. They sneaked into the dimly lit corridor. "What happened?" Dimitri asked while dressing. His mouth had a foul, bitter taste. "What time is it?"

"Two-thirty. Don't put your shoes on, they'll hear us."

"Who?"

But Vanya was already dashing ahead. "Come, I want you to see something."

Vanya led him to the kitchen, then through the dark backyard to the kitchen storage building. They crouched behind the backyard fence. A truck was parked beside the storage building. Two men were loading heavy bags on the truck.

"That's the cook," Vanya said, "and the driver."

"What's in the bags?"

"Flour," Vanya said, "and potatoes. They already loaded several crates of vegetables, all that we grew this year. And blankets from the other storage building."

A third man came out of the small building and joined the two others. "That's the administrator," Vanya said.

Dimitri gasped. "The administrator? I don't believe it." He thought of the friendly, elderly clerk who used to lecture them about the hard times and the shortages of food and fuel in the Soviet Union. "We all have to make sacrifices for the sake of our country," the administrator would say. Now he was stealing from the school, together with the cook.

"How did you find out?" he whispered.

"I was hungry. I went to heat a can of vegetables in the kitchen. I heard a noise."

Dimitri thought of his own guilt feelings. His thefts were nothing compared to what the cook and the administrator did. They robbed the school by truckloads!

"Did you take down the truck number?" he whispered.

"Yes," Vanya said. "I also heard them talking to the driver. His name is Rodion."

"Let's go," Dimitri said.

The following morning they asked to see the principal. They were wearing their red pioneer scarves. Dimitri was the one who spoke. "We believe, Comrade Colonel, in the glorious tradition begun by Pavlik Morozov."

"What's that?" The colonel smiled. "Dimitri Morozov follows Pavlik Morozov?"

Dimitri smiled back nervously. "It's only a coincidence that we have the same last name, Comrade Colonel."

"Of course." Colonel Borodin nodded. "I was only joking."

Only a week before, Dimitri and Vanya had learned about Pavlik Morozov at class. Pavlik was a hero of the Soviet children. He was a twelve-year-old pioneer who lived in the Urals. During the famine of 1932 he overheard his father and his uncle plotting to conceal a part of their grain and not deliver it to the government as required. As a good pioneer, Pavlik reported his parents' crime to the authorities. His father went to trial, and Pavlik testified against him. Pavlik's uncle mercilessly murdered the boy. The police arrested Pavlik's uncle, and he was hanged.

Pavlik emerged as a martyr of the revolution and became the subject of countless stories and poems. The Soviet pioneers sang songs and put on plays dealing with Pavlik's heroism. His deed was taught in schools as an example of the Soviet citizen's duty toward the state. A good pioneer had to report even his parents to the KGB, if they caused harm to Soviet Russia.

"We asked to see you, because we want to follow Pavlik Morozov's example," Dimitri said. "Last night, Vanya felt dizzy. He thought he was going to be sick. He woke me up, and I helped him get outside, for some fresh air. We didn't want to wake up the duty sergeant. And then, by the kitchen storage, we saw . . ."

Half an hour later a militia automobile arrived at Panfilov. The chief cook and the administrator were arrested; the truck with the stolen goods was found the same afternoon. Dimitri and Vanya were honored at the weekly pioneer meeting, and a reporter and photographer for *Red Pioneer* magazine came to interview them about their noble feat. Colonel Borodin himself pinned the pioneer medal of honor on their chests.

In a special ceremony on the parade grounds, the two little heroes raised the red flag, while all the students and teachers stood at attention, the officers saluting. The pioneer choir sang the "Youth Anthem." Dimitri watched the faces of his roommates who had beaten him four years ago. They're singing in my honor, he thought. I am the pride of the school. Let them dare call me a thief again.

* * *

SHORTLY AFTER Dimitri's thirteenth birthday, the principal entered his class. "Excuse me, Yakim Efremovich," he said to the geometry teacher. "Dimitri Morozov, step outside, please."

Dimitri exchanged alarmed looks with Vanya, then got up and left the class. "Did anything happen, Comrade Colonel?" he inquired, trying to keep his voice casual.

"You have a visitor," Colonel Borodin replied, and led Dimitri to his office. He opened the door and let the boy in. "I'll leave you now, Comrade General," he said in a respectful tone. "You can use my office for as long as you need."

A general? Dimitri stared in apprehension at the old man who stood behind the principal's desk. "Thank you, Comrade Colonel," the man said. Suddenly he was seized by a spasm of dry coughs that seemed to tear his lungs apart. His face grew ashen and he grabbed the edge of the desk for support. "Sorry," he muttered as his cough subsided, wiping his mouth with a crumpled handkerchief.

"My office — " Borodin repeated.

"No, no, Comrade Colonel, I won't bother you anymore." The general kindly patted Dimitri's back. "I'll talk to Dimitri in his dormitory. I'd like to see how he lives."

Puzzled, Dimitri led the man to his dormitory. The large room was deserted, except for the duty sergeant, who was asleep on his cot after night duty at the infirmary. The bleak October sun cast a fuzzy light inside the dorm, and dust particles, caught in its beams, briefly turned into specks of gold.

"My name is Takachenko," the general said. "I am a KGB officer, and I was a Chekist. I was your father's friend."

Dimitri felt tremendous relief. When Borodin had called his name, he had feared that his thefts had been discovered. Thank God it was a false alarm. He examined the general. He was tall and thin, with a caved-in chest and a scrawny neck. His hair and eyebrows were snow-white, but the edges of his drooping mustache had turned yellow, apparently from too much smoking. He had several gold teeth in his mouth. He was dressed in a plain brown suit, and his red tie was carelessly knotted.

But his look was alert, and he expressed his thoughts in concise phrases. "Your father asked me to look after you. I couldn't do it until now, for reasons that I shall explain later. Your father was my deputy at the Second Chief Directorate of the KGB. He was an excellent man, a patriot, and a good communist. You have to remember that, Dimitri, always."

He took a cigarette out of a blue package of foreign manufacture, apparently French. Then he plunged into another bout of coughing. The cigarette had a pungent smell. "Do you kids smoke over here?" Takachenko asked.

"We aren't allowed, Tovarich General," Dimitri said.

"I didn't ask if you were allowed, I asked if you smoked," Takachenko said sternly, then threw him the package. "If you don't smoke, trade it for something else, I know how things are in these places. Don't worry about me, I've got another pack, I never go out without my poison." He patted his other pocket. "And don't call me General. My name is Anatoly Sergeyevich. Understood?"

"Understood," Dimitri said, grinning.

"Are they treating you all right here?" the general asked in a cloud of smoke. "Is the food adequate?"

Dimitri frowned. Was the general trying to deviate from the subject they were talking about, his father? "You said my father had asked you to look after me."

Takachenko nodded gravely.

"How did my father die?"

Takachenko stared at him closely. "Nobody told you," he said softly. It was a statement, not a question.

"How did he die?" Dimitri repeated. He felt suddenly anxious.

Takachenko bowed his head for a moment, then looked straight into the boy's eyes. "Your father was shot by an execution squad at the prison camp of Vorkuta, in April of 1954."

An execution squad. He stared speechless at the old general, unable to digest the shattering news.

"He was condemned to death because of his wife — your mother — a Jewish writer named Tonya Gordon. Your mother and her former husband, Victor Wolf, had been found guilty of anti-Soviet activities. Your father married Tonya Gordon after her divorce from her first husband. Your mother was later executed. You have a half brother, Alexander, living in America. He's your mother's son from her previous marriage."

He had a brother! "Is he blond?" he asked. He thought he noticed the duty sergeant stirring on his bed.

"What?" Takachenko looked at him oddly. "Oh, your brother. Perhaps he is. But if I were you, I wouldn't mention his existence. People who have relatives abroad are not trusted, you know."

"And you say both my parents were shot," Dimitri said slowly, as if awakening from a dream.

"Your mother was shot first, and your father a year later."

"But why? What did he do?"

"Your father will be posthumously rehabilitated," Takachenko said forcefully. "Two months ago, a special court was appointed by Chairman Khrushchev to review the verdicts issued before his time. I have no doubt that your father's verdict will be annulled and his rank will be restored. He did nothing wrong, and he died only because he had married this woman. Morozov is a hero of the Soviet Union. They will rehabilitate him, mark my words."

"And who will rehabilitate me?" Dimitri shouted angrily. All the shock and the pain caused by the general's revelations, all the frustration and suffering accumulated in eleven years at Panfilov, exploded in his furious outburst. "Me! Who will rehabilitate me? Who'll get me out of here?" He stared at Takachenko. "You?"

Takachenko didn't flinch. "No," he said. "I won't rehabilitate you, and I won't get you out of here. I wanted you to know the truth about your father."

"That he was shot as a traitor?" Dimitri threw back at him.

"That he was a good man, and an excellent officer. I wanted to come and tell you the truth years ago, but . . ." Takachenko smiled sadly. ". . . I wasn't in a very good position myself. I was forced to retire soon after the arrest of your father. They brought me back last year."

"Why?"

Takachenko shrugged. "I guess I can tell you, it's not a secret anymore. Have you heard of Colonel Oleg Penkovski?"

Dimitri shook his head.

"Penkovski was a colonel in military intelligence who committed treason and disclosed military secrets to American espionage agents. He caused terrible damage to the GRU and the KGB."

"What's the GRU?" Dimitri asked.

"Military intelligence." Takachenko cleared his throat, then wiped his mouth with his handkerchief. "We must now rebuild the service. The Politburo decided to recall some of the old Chekists who hadn't been involved with Penkovski in any way, like myself, to clean up the services. And here I am. I had to visit one of our facilities in Leningrad this week, so I dropped in to see you." He doubled up under another spasm of shrill coughing.

Dimitri waited quietly until it subsided. "General Takachenko," he finally said, looking up.

"Anatoly Sergeyevich."

"Anatoly Sergeyevich . . ." His voice was different now, dropping almost to a murmur. "Could you please tell me about my father?"

And for more than an hour, periodically interrupted by bouts of coughing, enveloped in the smoke of his pestilent cigarettes, sitting in the dorm or walking back and forth on the deserted parade grounds, his bony hand on the youth's shoulder, Takachenko described the life and times of Boris Morozov.

"Why did he marry Tonya?" Dimitri asked at the gate, before Takachenko got into his chauffeur-driven Chaika. This car could have been my father's today, he thought morosely.

The general spread his arms. "We all warned him, Dimitri. This woman was not for him. A Jewess, and besides, involved in that organization . . . But he was obsessed with her. He married her, although she was already marked for death. When she sank, she pulled him down with her."

Alone at the gate, shivering in the afternoon breeze, Dimitri watched the departing car. He felt, rising from the depths of his miserable life, a wave of hatred for Tonya Gordon.

JEWS, he thought on his way back, damned, hateful, disgusting Jews. They were everywhere, ministers, officers, party apparatchiks, professors, speculators, profiteers. Like the Jew Fagin from *Oliver Twist,* all of them a curse to society. His father had been a fine officer, he might have become a general by now, perhaps even the KGB director! Why did he marry that Jewess? Why did he let himself be bewitched by her cheap tricks? It was clear why she had lured him into marriage. She had lost her husband, she had a baby, she needed protection; so she cunningly spread her net at the feet of an unsuspecting Soviet officer. And he had fallen into her trap.

His mother was responsible for all the disasters that had befallen him. If his father had married a Russian woman, Dimitri would be living in a spacious apartment in Moscow, studying at the best schools, eating the best food, vacationing on the Black Sea or abroad, in East Germany or Czechoslovakia. It was all the fault of the Jews. One day, when he rose in the Soviet hierarchy, he would purge the government of Jews. Let them go to Palestine, where they belonged, or to Birobidjan, their autonomous territory in Armenia. Let them stew in their own juices, let them cheat and swindle and betray each other.

Vanya had told him that several students in the higher grades had formed a nationalist cell. They wanted Russia to be Russian again, Vanya had said, free of the foreign parasites that lived off the people's labor. They were inspired by the memory of old Russia, which for centuries had been kept pure of alien scum. "Pamyat" — Memory, the cell was called. Perhaps he'd ask Vanya to take him to one of their meetings.

Still, one of those Jews was his half brother. It didn't make him better than the others, of course, but he was his only living relative. It could be nice to meet somebody who was family. They might even like each other. But this could never happen. Alexander must have grown up like the other Jewish children in America. An American and a Jew, that was the worst combination. Yet, what if one day he just met him at a place where nobody knew them, and his blond brother would be standing in the middle of the street, and Dimitri would suddenly appear before him and say: "Alexander, I'm your brother!"

These thoughts were interrupted by the sight of his duty sergeant, Kuzma Bunin, who stood by the side entrance of the school, arms folded on his chest, lazily leaning against the wall. Dimitri hated him wholeheartedly, although Kuzma worked with him and Vanya in smuggling stolen goods. He could never forget that Kuzma had ordered him beaten under the blanket that night.

"You're in a hurry, I see," Kuzma said in a mellifluous voice.

Dimitri nodded, and quickened his pace.

Kuzma barred his way. "Why such a big hurry?" he said, his lazy smile revealing his bad teeth. "You have news for your class?"

Dimitri pushed him aside. "Kuzma, let me go, I'm late."

"You'll tell them about Tonya Gordon?" Kuzma called after him.

Dimitri stopped dead in his tracks. A sudden chill made him shudder. "What do you know about Tonya Gordon?"

"I know all about your mother," Kuzma scoffed. "I heard everything the old goat told you, back in the dorm."

Dimitri recalled him moving on his bed when Takachenko was speaking to him about his family. The swine, he thought, he must have been pretending to sleep while he listened to everything we said.

"I heard the touching story about your father, too," Kuzma said mockingly. "The great hero, shot at Vorkuta for treason. Your friends will be delighted to hear about that. Our Dimitri is not only a thief and a black marketeer, but also a traitor's son. I don't want to detain you. Go, go and tell them."

"Wait," Dimitri said, pulling Kuzma into a nearby doorway. Frantic thoughts rushed through his mind. If the truth about his father was exposed, it would be his funeral. He would become the laughingstock of Panfilov; the Pamyat association wouldn't accept a half-Jewish boy. But much worse, he would certainly be thrown out of school and branded an "enemy of the people." This label was even applied to relatives of those only suspected of anti-Soviet activities. An enemy of the people could never become a member of the Communist party, or reach an important position. He was condemned to the most miserable existence; he was banned from the upper circles of Soviet society. And for Dimitri, that meant the end to all his dreams, forever.

"Wait," he said, clutching Kuzma's sleeve. "Tell me, what do you want?"

"What do you offer?" Kuzma asked, studying him through half-closed eyelids.

"I'll give you five bottles of vodka," Dimitri said quickly.

Kuzma burst laughing. "You must do better, brother."

"I'll give you a uniform, brand-new," Dimitri said. "I have one, honest, it's yours."

Kuzma shook his head. "No. You've got much more than that."

"What do you want?" he asked in desperation.

"I want everything you have," Kuzma said softly, a sly, cunning flame lighting up in his pale eyes. "And I want a double cut in the operation you're running with Vanya."

Dimitri could have strangled the pig, right there. Kuzma left him no way out. How could he convince Vanya to double Kuzma's cut? And even if he managed to buy Kuzma's silence, the dirty bastard would keep blackmailing him forever. His secret would never be safe, not as long as he lived.

"I agree," Dimitri mumbled. His throat was dry. "I'll give you all I have." Think, he said to himself, think quickly, you must find a solution.

"I'll take you to my cache, all right? You can take whatever you want." He grabbed Kuzma's shoulder.

Then he realized, in a surge of boundless horror, that there was a way out, after all. The only way. He shivered. No, he couldn't do it. But Kuzma was looking at him with a confident smile, his eyes gleaming with malice. This stinking carcass held him in the palm of his hand. What shall I do, Dimitri thought in despair, all this can't be real, it's a nightmare. And yet, a plan was already starting to take shape in his mind. He looked around. There was no one else to be seen.

"What do you have in your cache?" Kuzma asked suspiciously, disengaging from his grip.

"Everything. I have all you could dream of." That was true. In the last year Vanya and Dimitri, instead of stealing, had become middlemen in the black market that flourished in the school. With Kuzma's complicity, they had continued to buy and sell stolen goods, skimming a fat profit.

"I have canned food, beef, chicken, fish. I have a uniform, brand-new. I have six bottles of vodka. I have cigarettes, and money, even a watch. German. I'll give you everything." I must make him come tonight, he thought, before he starts blabbing.

"Where is all that treasure?" Kuzma asked with forced indifference. "I don't believe you."

Oh yes you do, Dimitri thought, you know I'm telling the truth, you were part of all our deals. "I have a hiding place in the old quarry. I dug it myself, at the very bottom. Nobody ever looked there." The abandoned quarry was cut in the flank of a hill, about two hundred yards east of the orphanage fence.

Kuzma cocked his head. "So that's where you keep your goods. No wonder your locker was always clean. But I thought there was no access to the bottom of the quarry."

"There's no access for those who don't know the place," Dimitri said. "I know my way around." The old quarry was sixty feet deep, a rectangular pit dug in the limestone. In the nineteenth century it had been used as a cistern for the fields that stretched southeast of St. Petersburg. There were still black watermarks on the white stone walls.

Kuzma gave him a long look. Finally he shrugged. "Let's go and see what you've got," he said noncommittally.

"Not now. Tonight, after curfew. I'll go first, and you'll come five minutes after me. Be careful that nobody sees you." He paused. "And bring your flashlight with you, it's dark down there."

Kuzma nodded. "Go now," he said, again cocking his head and squinting warily at him. "And no tricks, Dimka. Remember."

HE CROUCHED behind a boulder, waiting. A crescent moon lay low over the land, but the quarry was plunged in shadow, illuminated only by the eerie incandescence of the naked limestone. Perhaps he won't come, he secretly prayed, perhaps he'll have second thoughts, and we'll find a solution tomorrow. The very idea of what he intended to do was maddening. There were about ten yards between the place where he hid and the edge of the pit; even if he pushed Kuzma hard, he couldn't shove him over the edge. He had to stun him first. He had no weapon, he would have to rely on his hands.

He saw Kuzma's furtive shadow and heard his cautious steps, then the old door in the quarry fence creaked on its hinges. "Dimka, are you there?" Kuzma called softly.

He didn't move. Don't come in, he thought, go away.

"Dimka?" The beam of Kuzma's flashlight pierced the darkness, and the duty sergeant stepped into the quarry. "Fuck your mother, Dimka, I know you're there, you little piece of shit!"

Dimitri hesitated another moment, then clenched his fists and lunged sidewise toward the hand holding the flashlight. But he had underestimated his enemy. As his clothes rustled, Kuzma swiftly turned the flashlight toward him, and Dimitri was briefly dazzled. At that moment something moved swiftly and a tremendous blow landed on his right forearm. Dimitri cried out in agony. The bloody bastard, he had brought a weapon. Kuzma hadn't trusted him.

Kuzma hit him again, and sharp pain exploded in Dimitri's thigh. He slipped and fell. And that probably saved his life, because for a split second he must have disappeared from Kuzma's field of vision. He felt the long, heavy club swishing over his head. He threw himself at Kuzma's feet and pulled him down. Kuzma lost his balance and collapsed, his flashlight clanging on the ground and rolling toward the edge of the pit. The duty sergeant held on to his club, but now he was crawling on the ground, striving to get up, and Dimitri didn't fear him anymore. He tried to get hold of Kuzma's neck, groping in the dark with outstretched hands. He caught him by the waist, and the club struck his exposed back, but with little force. Kuzma succeeded in shaking him off, and scrambled to his feet.

"Help!" the duty sergeant screamed shrilly.

You can yell until tomorrow, Dimitri thought, nobody will hear you. He grabbed Kuzma's waist again, from the back, spun him around, and brought his clasped hands down on the duty sergeant's right wrist. Kuzma cried out in pain, and his club — a length of lead pipe — clattered on the ground.

Dimitri encircled Kuzma's neck with his left arm and locked it tight with his right. He was smaller but more vigorous than his opponent. He could have strangled him now, but something made him stop. No marks, he thought, it must look like an accident. Kuzma was grunting and groaning, trying to tear himself from Dimitri's hold. Dimitri wrestled him to his knees; then, his hatred doubling his strength, he raised both arms and hit Kuzma's exposed neck with the edges of his hands. The duty sergeant slumped down like a bag of rags.

Dimitri didn't waste time finding out if Kuzma was dead or only dazed. He dragged him on the ground to within a couple of feet of the edge of the pit and swept the stone floor with his hand. His fingers felt the jagged rim. Kuzma's flashlight, which had rolled toward the pit, spread fuzzy light over its opposite wall. Dimitri stared down into the abyss and shivered.

Beside him, Kuzma stirred.

Dimitri swerved back in terror, his hands raised to strike. But the duty sergeant was shuddering and shifting. A gurgling sound came from his chest.

"Die!" Dimitri whispered. "Die, then!" He grabbed the boy and rolled him over the edge. He heard the echo of the body hitting the vertical wall of the quarry, then the sickening thud as it crashed on the bottom.

He got up, swaying. The flashlight lay to the right, its light weakening. He kicked it into the pit, then did the same with the piece of pipe. He could leave now. There was no danger of his cache being exposed; it had never been near the quarry, of course, he had said that just to lure Kuzma there. He stepped outside, leaving the door in the fence open. He wanted somebody to find Kuzma.

They found him the next afternoon, after his absence had been reported at roll call. Several teachers searched the school first, then the orphanage grounds, and finally the surrounding fields. The history teacher, Karmiya Tolbukhina, discovered the body and staggered back to the school in a state of shock. The news of Kuzma's death spread throughout the school, which buzzed with excitement, like a bee swarm. Colonel Borodin called the militia, and four investigators interrogated the boys. When his turn came, Dimitri calmly reported that he had seen Kuzma asleep on his cot while he spoke with General Takachenko; then he had strolled with the general on the parade grounds and escorted him to his car. In the evening he hadn't spoken with Kuzma Bunin. No, he hadn't seen him leaving the dorm after curfew.

The general's name produced the desired effect, and nobody asked Dimitri to testify again. The investigators reached the inevitable conclusion: Kuzma had wandered for some reason to the old quarry, stumbled, and fallen to his death. The only puzzling discovery was the length of pipe that lay on the bottom of the quarry, close to the body. But it could have been lying there for quite a while, without any connection to Bunin's death.

The next morning, Dimitri and Vanya were getting ready for Kuzma's funeral. Kuzma had no known relatives, so there was no use delaying the interment. Dimitri, wearing only an undershirt, was fumbling with the buttons of his trousers.

"Hey, what's that?" Vanya asked, pointing at Dimitri's forearm. It was swollen, and the skin above the elbow had a sickening purple color.

Dimitri shrugged. "I fell," he said.

For a moment Vanya stared at him, frowning. Then he nodded. "I see," he said. After a moment he asked casually, "You didn't get up the night before last, did you?"

"Me?" Dimitri said. "I slept like an angel."

Dimitri put on his shirt. There was something new in Vanya's eyes, he realized. Something he had never seen before. Fear. Vanya was afraid of him.

And he decided that he rather liked that.

ON CHRISTMAS EVE he was working out when Vanya popped up in front of him, a conspiratorial look on his face. Since Kuzma's death, Dimitri had spent every evening in the gymnasium, ferociously hitting the punching bag, groaning under the weights, torturing his body into complete exhaustion. He hoped that his physical fatigue would induce him to sleep.

Still, night after night, as he closed his eyes, the memories of that day in October tormented him. There was Takachenko again, describing his father's infamous death and his mother's revolting game; there was Kuzma again, threatening to expose him, then gurgling and kicking before he died. Dimitri knew that Bunin was a swine, a poisonous snake who deserved to be crushed. Besides, the duty sergeant had left him no other choice. But this didn't make him feel better. The infernal experience at the quarry haunted his sleep and instilled horror into his dreams, and he would wake up with a start, shivering, gasping for air.

But another feeling had been born in him the night of Kuzma's murder. Sometimes he enjoyed it; at times he feared it. It was a strange sensation of power; an awareness that he was able to have his own way by breaking the rules that ordinary people lived by. He knew that he could kill, without flinching, if necessary. He also knew that he was going to make it in life, and that anyone who dared to stand in his way might well end up like Kuzma Bunin.

Vanya never again spoke to him about that night. But Dimitri felt that the shrewd Georgian had guessed much more than he cared to admit. Since Kuzma's death, their relationship had changed. Vanya submitted totally now to Dimitri's authority and did his best to please him. Dimitri couldn't tell if Vanya acted out of friendship or fear. Vanya brought him presents — good food, vodka, two American cigarettes he had found somewhere — and he even agreed to accept Dimitri's old German watch in exchange for his own, a heavy steel beauty with a black dial and green phosphorescent digits.

Vanya also introduced him to the Pamyat circle, but Dimitri was disappointed. They met in the grove behind the staff cottages and performed an oath ceremony at candlelight, over a rusty revolver. This was ridiculous. There was a lot of bombastic talk about Mother Russia, and empty slogans against the Jews, but no apparent will to act. He didn't care about slogans, he wanted to do something, clean the Jews and liberals out of Russia. One day, he thought, when I get out of here.

Tonight Vanya looked different. His face was flushed and his eyes burned with a mischievous flame. He stood in front of Dimitri and pulled the punching bag aside, then asked loudly: "Don't you think it's time for you to fuck a girl?"

"What?" Dimitri stared at him, baffled.

"Come," Vanya said, "let's go, I've got it all set."

He was confused. "But the curfew . . ."

"It's arranged," Vanya said over his shoulder as he led the way across the parade grounds. "I gave a can of chicken to Aram." Aram was their new duty sergeant, a timid Armenian boy of seventeen who quickly understood that Dimitri and Vanya were calling the shots in their dorm.

"Where are we going?" Dimitri asked.

Vanya pointed at the staff cottages, visible against the shadow of the chestnut grove, where lights were on. "Remember Zoya?"

Did he remember Zoya! The voluptuous daughter of the biology teacher was the embodiment of all his fantasies. He saw her every morning at the gate, when she took the bus to her school in Leningrad. She was stunning. Her short hair was light brown, her eyes, too; her skin was milky, and her large, swelling lips bestowed upon her face a hungry sexuality. So many nights he had lain on his bed craving her full breasts, her firm buttocks, and her lovely hips. So many times he had masturbated wildly under his blanket, dreaming of the wet, warm depths between her thighs, imagining the moment she would part her legs for him and he would stick his penis deep into her till she screamed. As the semen burst out of his body, he would see her convulsions, her legs holding him, her juices mixing with his. Zoya was the symbol of all the women he wanted to conquer, of the wildest sex experiences he could imagine.

He swallowed hard. "Zoya will let me screw her? I don't believe you."

Vanya chuckled softly. "She'll let both of us screw her tonight." He pointed to the right. "We'll go around to the back of the cottage."

"Vanya, wait, what are you talking about? She's only fifteen, her parents would kill her."

"Exactly," Vanya said. He caught Dimitri by the arm and they stopped. "You don't know, but she's been fucking a guy from the eleventh grade, Misha Pugachev. Know him?"

He nodded. Misha was a gentle boy with a fragile body and a beautiful face, illuminated by two innocent blue eyes.

"I saw them, in the grove," Vanya whispered, "fucking like mad. So I went to see Zoya, yesterday. Her parents have gone to visit relatives in Odessa for Christmas. She didn't want to go. I guess she wanted to spend her holiday fucking Misha."

"What did you say to her?" Dimitri asked.

"I said that if she let us fuck her, we wouldn't tell anyone what she did with Misha. If she refused, all Panfilov would know. Her father would be fired, and she would never fuck her Misha again." He paused. "Yesterday she refused, but I saw her again this afternoon, and she said yes. She's waiting for us now."

"She spoke to Misha?"

Vanya shrugged. "I don't think so."

Dimitri followed him, feeling strangely light-headed. God, it couldn't be, he must be dreaming. He was going to fuck a girl at last. And not just any girl, the best, the sexiest, the most exciting. Zoya, he was about to fuck Zoya!

She opened the door of the cottage. She was wearing a long skirt and a sweater that was stretched tight over her heavenly breasts. Her face was puffed; she had probably been crying. Her lips were trembling. She led them across the kitchen and a living room, furnished with rustic chairs and tables. There was an old radio by the wall. A standing lamp, covered with a shade of oil paper, was surrounded by a circle of light. A pearl-gray Persian cat perched on a settee, staring at them suspiciously. Zoya opened a door. "Here," she said.

"You go first," Dimitri said, turning his back to Vanya. "I'll wait here."

"Don't you want to watch?" Vanya asked with a lascivious smile.

"No," he said. I don't want to watch you, he thought, and I don't want you to watch me.

On entering Zoya's room, Vanya flipped the light switch, and Dimitri heard the girl's muted protest. Dimitri stepped toward the door and closed it. He sat on a chair, then got up. The cat's eyes followed each of his moves. He picked up the *Ogonyok* weekly that lay on the table, flipped through it and threw it back. He idly turned the radio buttons, then moved away. His palms were sweating and he wiped them on his trousers.

He heard Vanya's rising moans and a final groan of ecstasy. Then there was silence. A moment later Vanya came out. His hair was disheveled and his eyes sparkled. He looked ecstatic. He was fumbling with his trousers. "Brother," he grunted, "that was something. Go, go, you'll see what paradise is all about."

Dimitri entered the room, closing the door behind him. Zoya's bedroom was lit by a lamp hanging from the ceiling. There were some stuffed toys in one corner and three racks of books by the window. An old cupboard, a desk, and a chair, were lined up along the near wall. A print of a ballerina graciously bowing, on a blue-gray background, was pinned to the wall, above the desk.

He looked at the bed and held his breath. Zoya was lying on the crumpled sheet, completely naked. Her arms lay limp at her sides; she didn't even try to cover her nudity. He felt his penis harden — he had never seen a naked woman before. His head swayed as he stared at her round breasts and pink nipples. Her crotch was covered with a thick mass of pubic hair, and that excited him even more. He approached the bed, unbuttoning his trousers. Her eyes were closed and she was silently weeping, the tears trickling through her eyelashes. He wanted to kiss her; he had so often dreamed of her full lips parting under his. He bent over her, but when she felt his breath, she jerked her head away. Then she burst out crying. Desperate spasms shook her body, and she covered her face with her hands.

He stared at her, bewildered. He hadn't imagined it this way. He wanted Zoya's abandon, her fire. He wanted her wildly making love to him. But before him lay a wretched girl, crying in shame and humiliation. She didn't want him to touch her. For a second anger surged in his chest, the same black anger he had felt before killing Kuzma. His blood was pounding wildly in his temples. Instinctively, he clenched his fists and his body tensed. But Zoya looked so defenseless, so desperate. His fury faded away. He felt disgusted and didn't know what to do.

He turned away and stared at the sylphlike ballerina on Zoya's poster, nimbly spreading her long white arms. His hardness dissolved and he shivered. He timidly reached for Zoya and touched her hair with his fingertips. Then he fled from the room.

"What happened?" Vanya was staring at him, puzzled, his stupid smile slowly fading away.

"Let's go!" Dimitri said fiercely, and rushed toward the back door. On his way, he stumbled against a chair, which fell to the floor with a crash. "Fuck your mother!" he muttered. The cat arched its back and hissed angrily at him.

HE LOST HIS VIRGINITY a year later, to Valya, the younger daughter of the new chief cook. Valya was a big-breasted, round-hipped girl of seventeen, with long bleached hair, a broad face, merry brown eyes, and rolling laughter. It took her barely a couple of months in Panfilov to gain a reputation as an easy lay. "Give her something, anything," Aram told him knowingly, "and she'll show you a great time."

Dimitri sent Vanya to her and they struck a deal immediately. Valya was ready to service Dimitri for two one-liter bottles of vodka "with the original seal, not a drop of water inside." She met him behind the kitchen and seriously inspected the bottles. "Let's go inside," she said, taking his hand. Her skin was soft and dry.

She led him to the kitchen storage room, where she had improvised a bed with a heap of bags. When Dimitri told her that he had never slept with a woman, her enthusiasm soared. The sullen girl turned into a hot-blooded woman with an insatiable appetite. She pulled him to her, apparently inspired by his lack of experience. "Come, my little one," she murmured, her tongue darting in and out of his mouth, probing his ear, then licking down his throat. "Let me take care of you, let Valya show you why we don't need storks and cabbage patches anymore."

On the soft flour bags, in the dark store room, she hugged and kissed him, undressed him, made him fondle her breasts and rub her swelling nipples, enveloped him in her long, strong arms and legs, rode him astride, caressed him with her expert hands, excited him with her plump breasts, her wet, pulsating vagina, and her gentle mouth.

She lay on him, kissed him, bit him, sucked him, drank him, ecstatically moaning, whining, and groaning over and over again. She feasted on him with such abandon and such uninhibited pleasure, interspersed by delighted screams and explosions of laughter, that Dimitri decided she was getting the better part of the deal. She was the one who should have paid him two bottles of vodka for her pleasure. Still, he had never imagined sex could be such fun. The hours he spent with that simple peasant's daughter, smelling of ripe wheat, fresh soap, and woman's musk, were to remain among the few sweet memories of his tormented youth.

GENERAL TAKACHENKO came to see him again a few months before his seventeenth birthday. Dimitri had just traded his pioneer scarf for full membership in the Komsomol, the organization of Soviet Communist party youth. Takachenko had barely changed since Dimitri had met him three years before. His clothes were as sloppy and his voice as alert as before; but the skin pouches under his eyes had grown more flaccid, and his cough had acquired a grating edge.

Khrushchev's demise two years ago, Takachenko said, and his replacement by Leonid Brezhnev, had somewhat delayed the work of the special tribunal that was to review his father's case. But the tribunal had finally ruled last month, and Boris Morozov had been completely rehabilitated. His military rank and medals had been posthumously restored.

Dimitri listened quietly. He had grown so used to misfortune that he didn't know how to receive good news.

"It's time for you to get out of here, my boy," Takachenko said, taking a sheaf of papers from his pocket. "I want you to fill out those forms. They are application papers for the KGB academy, the Higher School of State Security. In a couple of months a commission will come to interview you. I want you beside me, like your father. I think you have a great future."

Three months after the commission interviewed him, Borodin handed Dimitri an official government envelope. The commission chairman, Bodrov, informed Dimitri Morozov that he had been admitted to the KGB academy.

On October 1 he was to report to the academy compound in Moscow.

Chapter 6

ALEX GORDON came out of the subway station on Flatbush Avenue and trudged dejectedly toward home. Damn the consul's assistant, he thought, clenching his teeth, damn the sonofabitch. He recalled the stupid stare of the Russian he had just met. Had all his efforts of the last four years been worthless? All those letters and phone calls and months of waiting — for what? To almost get slapped in the face by a stupid Russian clerk?

Four years ago he had been devastated by the newspaper item describing his parents' deaths. His first reaction had been to find his brother and share the shattering news with him. Perhaps Dimitri knew something more about their parents. He had written Dimitri a long letter then, and sent it to their former Moscow address, but the letter had been returned with a stamp saying there was no such person at that address. That setback hadn't stopped Alex. On the contrary, finding his brother became an obsession with him. He wrote to Dimitri again, with the same result. He wrote to his uncle Valery, in Leningrad. There was no reply. He wrote to the American embassy in Moscow, to the Soviet embassy in Washington, to their U.N. mission. He besieged the Soviet consulate in New York with phone calls, asking for an appointment with the consul. They always told him to call next week, or next month, the consul wasn't there, he was in a meeting, on a lecture tour, on home leave.

Finally, last week, they had told him that his request had been granted. Today he had rung at the consulate door at four P.M. exactly, dressed in his Sunday best. He had been screened, searched, and inspected by two big, silent men in the consulate lobby. Then an aging woman, her square shoulders draped in a black woolen shawl despite the early summer heat, had appeared from nowhere and grudgingly led him to a small cubicle on the ground floor.

"This is the consul's office?" he asked.

"The consul is busy," she said. "You'll be received by one of his assistants."

The assistant was a portly middle-aged man with cropped brown hair and a moon-shaped face. He wore an ill-fitting gray suit. After he had formally shaken Alex's hand, he squeezed behind the cheap desk. The room was bare, except for a faded poster of Red Square hanging behind the assistant. There were no filing cabinets along the walls, and no files on the desk; the office was apparently used for interviews only. Alex spoke for ten minutes, in Russian. He had diligently rehearsed his discourse at home until he knew it by heart. He described his efforts to get in touch with his brother, the inscriptions on the letters that had been returned to him, his appeals to the Soviet foreign ministry, the ambassador, and the consul general.

The Russian listened, his face expressionless, his pudgy hand tapping on the desk with a ballpoint pen. He didn't flinch throughout Alex's speech, even when Alex stressed that Dimitri's father was a high-ranking KGB officer. When Alex finished, the assistant asked for his brother's name and address, and wrote them down in a small notebook. "Very well," he said, and got up. "We'll check on this and let you know."

"I can give you some more details about the family," Alex said. "Dimitri's grandmother lives in the Ukraine, near — "

The man in gray raised his hand. "No need for that," he said, and repeated his magic formula: "We'll check and let you know."

The sour-faced woman suddenly materialized by the door, and escorted Alex out of the building. He found himself on the sidewalk, boiling with anger and frustration. In spite of their promises, they hadn't let him see the consul. The man in the gray suit apparently was just a low-level employee. He didn't care about the request, hadn't even bothered asking him any questions that might help them to locate his brother. He didn't care, that was all.

All his efforts during the last four years had been flushed down the drain. How could people like this "assistant" be employed by the Soviet foreign service? Soviet diplomats, entrusted with representing the USSR abroad, were supposed to be the very best people; but here he had found himself facing a fat, dyspeptic bureaucrat who only wanted to get rid of him. The bastard, he thought, he could have at least pretended that he wanted to help me.

Alex glanced at the kids playing softball across the street. Two of them were shirtless, their naked backs glistening with sweat. It was only the beginning of June, but the heat was oppressive. He took off his jacket, which Nina had washed and pressed for his interview with the consul. What shall I do now? he wondered. Today's visit to the consulate might have been his last chance. He recalled the bovine stare of the assistant and the scowl on the woman's face. Furiously he kicked an empty garbage can and sent it rolling along the sidewalk. Then he turned the corner into his street.

The street was blocked by a huge movers' van, parked in front of his building. The van belonged to the World-famous Tramontana Movers, according to the huge flaming red letters stenciled on its side. People were unloading pieces of furniture and crates of housewares from the van and carrying them into the old two-story house that stood across the street from his own. As he approached the van, he saw that in addition to the employees of the moving company, dressed in blue coveralls, the group of unloaders included older men, women, and some younger boys and girls. They argued, shouted, laughed, conversed, mostly in English but also in melodious Italian. "Adriano!" an old man was calling, "Adriano!" And every time he shouted, a woman's head popped up in the open window of the Italians' new house and she shouted back: "Adriano has gone home, you fool!"

The Italians yelled at each other, joked with each other, warmly patted each other's shoulders, panted, cursed, and stopped once in a while to circulate a bottle of dark red wine or a tray of overstuffed sandwiches. The entire street echoed with their laughter, shouts, and quarrels. One of the movers, a black-haired man with a pink double chin, sang a melodramatic Italian song at the top of his lungs. Some of his friends joined him for the refrain, others, including an old woman with a mobile face, mimicked his theatrical gestures and erupted in laughter every time he embarked upon a new stanza.

Alex stopped by the van, staring in wonder at the cheerful crowd. An

Italian family was moving into the two-story house, and their relatives —
apparently the whole tribe — had come to help. He wanted to go home,
but the bubbling exuberance of the merry Italians fascinated him, and
he stayed there, planted in the middle of the sidewalk, grinning foolishly.
His bad mood had faded away.

Somebody bent under a huge bale of clothes blindly advanced toward
him, and he stepped aside to let the person pass. It was a girl. She slowly
lowered her load on the sidewalk, then straightened up and turned
toward him. He also turned, and stood still.

"Hi, I'm Claudia," she said. "What's your name?"

RESTLESSLY TURNING on his narrow bed that night, his face on fire and
a new, sharp pain throbbing deep in his chest, he remembered Claudia.
She haunted his sleepless solitude, as enticing as when he first saw her
yesterday: beautiful black eyes, full dark lips, satiny skin, and sensuous
figure. He wanted to kiss her, to bury his face in the silken mass of hair
that fell over her left shoulder in a dark cascade; to touch the gracious
line of her neck, the delicate contour of her chin. The thought of her
nude body drove him mad. A strange fever had awakened inside him,
and his imagination, suddenly unleashed, galloped drunkenly toward
unknown horizons.

First love is a love of torment. Joey had quoted this to him from a book
he was reading a few years ago, when Joey had fallen head over heels for
his fat, pimpled Laura. (Laura was gone now, replaced by fat, pimpled
Frida.) But only today did Alex realize how right the book was, how
painful and agonizing love could be. He had never been in love before.
He hadn't suspected that such emotions existed, that a casual meeting
in the street could turn into an obsession. As the morning light seeped
into his room, and the first rays of sunshine caressed his body, he
solemnly decided he could never love anyone the way he loved Claudia
Benevento.

Yesterday evening he had helped her carry her load into the old house,
where heavy, big-breasted women in dark dresses had already taken
control and were unceremoniously ordering the men around. The
younger men had welcomed Claudia's entrance with whistles and catcalls, which she accepted with unmitigated delight. As Alex stepped in
behind her, carrying her bale of colorful blouses and dresses, a wave of

good-natured laughter swept the living room. "Caught one already, Claudia?" a skinny youth called from the top of a ladder. His athletic partner, who was handing him a heavy chandelier, ominously added: "Wait till I tell Stevie!"

"My brothers again," Claudia groaned, then burst out laughing. She moved about like the princess of the household, obviously enjoying her role. "This is my friend Alex!" she solemnly proclaimed. To the old white-haired woman who trudged in, leaning on her walking stick and gazing at him in puzzlement, she repeated in a louder voice: "Alex, Grandmother."

"Who?" the old lady squeaked.

"Alex, Alexander, Alessandro."

After dumping his bale in the middle of the living room, Alessandro asked her to the Hollywood Soda Fountain.

"What?" she said, belligerently planting her fists on her hips. "You mean I should let my poor family sweat and slave while I lick ice cream with you at a soda fountain?"

"Well . . . yes," he stammered.

"Great," she exclaimed, mischievous sparks lighting her eyes. "Wonderful! Let's go." She merrily linked her arm in his, her firm breast brushing against his elbow. He was panic-stricken. No girl had touched him like that before. "I'm going away with Alex," Claudia shouted, and regally departed, dragging him behind her.

In their booth in the Hollywood, she gobbled down two orders of Our Special Double Banana Sundae; her delighted squeaks and carefree laughter infected everyone present. The soda jerk, fat Louie, who had a wooden leg and sparse silver hair plastered over his skull, whispered in Alex's ear: "This girl of yours, she's something!"

His girl. Gathering all his courage, he turned to her and blurted: "Who is Stevie?"

"Oh, you heard." She laughed, then shrugged. "My boyfriend," she said, and his heart sank. Claudia regarded him for a moment without laughing, and he had the impression that there was a message for him in those dark, ardent eyes.

Then her serious look dissolved and Claudia was her bubbly self again, animatedly telling him the story of her life. She was a natural storyteller, and had the gift of making every detail, even the most trivial, sound exciting. Her family had moved from New Jersey, where her father, after fighting corrupt politicians, local muscle, and organized crime, had become a respected businessman. They were second-generation Americans; her grandparents had been born in Calabria, "the tip of the Italian boot, if you know geography." She had inherited the blood of notorious Calabrese bandits, she darkly revealed, lowering her voice.

She had one sister, who was nurturing a secret, desperate love, and three brothers, one of them married and the father of twins. She was sixteen years and two months old, the youngest of the five children, "and the most spoiled, of course." She liked to sketch and paint, had won a couple of awards at school, and for a long time had wanted to study art. A famous artist had asked her to become his student; but if she told her brothers what he wanted in return, it would start the bloodiest vendetta on this side of the Atlantic.

Fortunately, she also loved clothes, she said, stressing the word "loved" and closing her eyes in rapture. "Do you like my blouse?" she asked coquettishly, turning around to enable him to better admire her bottle-green sweater. Her family, she added, unanimously agreed that she had very original taste in clothes, and they all believed she was going to become a great fashion designer. Wasn't that wonderful? Clothes and art together? And he said oh yes, great, absolutely.

Then she assailed him with questions about himself, and he readily responded, describing feelings, thoughts, hopes, and frustrations he hadn't revealed even to Joey. He told her about his parents' death, his lost brother, his efforts to discover the truth concerning his family. She seemed captivated by his story. When he described his mother's execution, he saw, to his surprise, tears streaming down her cheeks. "I'm sorry," she said, embarrassed, and looked away. It occurred to him that she was the first stranger he had seen shed a tear for his dead mother.

To change the subject, he told her of his ill-fated visit to the Soviet consulate that afternoon. Claudia laughed as he humorously described the assistant consul and his black-shawled dragon; later, she put a friendly hand on his arm and let it rest there for a while. He suddenly realized that he had never been as happy as he was right now, with this lovely girl, at the Hollywood Soda Fountain.

When he finally delivered her to the Italian tribe across the street, it occurred to him that the incident at the Soviet consulate had lost its importance. His disappointment with the assistant consul seemed to belong to the distant past. All he wanted now was to see Claudia again.

The following afternoon, he rushed home from school and immediately took a position by the living room window, facing Claudia's house. He had to speak to her again. He wouldn't budge from his observation post, he decided, until he saw her. Then it would be a matter of seconds, out of the apartment, down the steps, into the street. He would run to the corner, cross the street, come back and bump into her, so that their meeting would look accidental. "You shouldn't let a girl know you're interested," little Joey had sternly lectured him today, when he told him about his great love. "A woman is never attracted to a guy who's too available. And remember, if she asks you, say that you've had lots of girls before. If she knows you're a virgin, she'll leave you right away." The little Casanova looked at him severely and explained: "At this age, they're only attracted to guys with experience, see?"

And so he lurked in ambush by the window, watching the Italians' house. To avoid an interrogation by Nina, whose sharp eyes missed nothing, he pretended to be reading Alexander Beck's book on the Battle of Moscow in 1941. He answered Nina's occasional questions with monosyllables, unwilling to begin a discussion that might divert him from his task.

His relationship with Nina was back to normal after their painful dispute of four years ago. On that rainy day, when he had found out she'd lied to him about his parents' fate, his first impulse had been to run away from home. Seething with bitterness and frustration, he never wanted to see his aunt again. But after he confronted her at Spiegel's, she had followed him to the apartment. And they'd had a long, agonizing discussion, during which he had cried his heart out. Nina, too, had shed a few tears. She had tried, she said, to spare him the terrible shock of learning how his parents had died. That was why she'd invented the story about the car accident.

"I knew you would finally get to know the truth, Aliosha," she admitted sadly. "I wanted to tell you myself, but not yet. I knew it would be a terrible shock to you, and I didn't want you to go through hell while you were still a child." How could she ever imagine that the story would be published in the newspaper, and some evil little boy would put the clipping on Alex's desk, just to hurt him? Watching her distraught face, with the tears streaming down her cheeks, Alex finally embraced her. She was right, he admitted, she had lied to him for his own good.

They knew that the accusations against Tonya and Victor Wolf were phony, of course, a fiendish intrigue fabricated by deranged minds, and the Soviet government had made a terrible mistake. Nina hesitated for a while, then showed him a copy of a secret speech Khrushchev had made in 1956, before the twentieth congress of the Communist party. The speech, smuggled to the West, had been published a few months later. Khrushchev had denounced Stalin as a murderer and a criminal who had been responsible for show trials, torture, and terrible massacres.

"It is hard to believe, *golubchek*," Nina sighed. "Our little father Stalin, the man we used to call the sun of the nations, the prophet of communism — a murderer!"

"I read that Lenin, before his death, warned the party against him," Alex said.

"Lenin must have turned over in his grave at what Stalin did," Nina stated firmly. "This explains all that happened to Tonya and Victor. It's not the fault of communism. It was Stalin who ordered his henchmen to commit those terrible crimes, and for that your parents paid with their lives." Their deaths were a warning that the march toward communism might be diverted by enemies of the working class or by megalomaniac dictators. Therefore his mother and father hadn't died in vain.

Besides, she added, perhaps his father was still alive; nobody had seen him die in the camps. But Alex just looked at her and she fell silent. They both knew his father was dead; no prisoner could have survived more than a year or two beyond the Arctic Circle.

He was torn from his memories when he suddenly saw the door of the Benevento house open and Claudia come out, munching an apple. A couple of window cleaners working at the neighboring house stuck their fingers in their mouths and whistled shrilly. She didn't look up. She was dressed in jeans, flat ballerina shoes, and a white shirt embroidered with large green flowers. Green was apparently her favorite color. He was already on his feet, about to dart for the door, when, to his immense surprise, Claudia casually crossed the street and walked straight to his building, then disappeared in the entrance. She was coming here!

He panicked. He rushed to the door, then scurried back to his desk, frantically tidying books and writing pads, scooping up pens and pencils. He didn't know what to do, he had never received a girl in his apartment. But the doorbell was already ringing, and Nina's brisk steps coldly echoed in the vestibule. He heard the door open, and in floated Claudia's sunny, warm voice. "Hi, you must be Nina. I'm Claudia Benevento, a friend of Alex. Is he home?"

"Yes, he is home." There was surprise and reserve in Nina's voice. She could have been more friendly, dammit. He stepped toward the door, but Claudia was in the room already, grinning at him. "Hi, Alex," she called. God, how pretty she was! In the dusk reigning in the vestibule, he could make out the stern expression on Nina's face, looking at him over Claudia's shoulder.

"I came to see your picture gallery," Claudia went on. "May I?" He had told her last night about the photographs and posters he had hung over his desk.

"On one condition," he said.

"What?" She was already by his desk, staring at the wall. "This must be the Sputnik. And who is this? Lenin?" she asked. When he didn't answer, she turned back to him, the mischievous sparks dancing in her eyes again. "What condition?"

"That you give me one of your paintings, for my collection."

"Done!" she readily announced. "But on one condition."

He crossed his arms, amused, and bowed his head in solemn obedience.

"Will you have dinner with us tonight? We're celebrating our move to Brooklyn. My mother's been cooking all day, and my grandmother thinks you're very cute. 'Bring Alessandro,' she said, 'bring the blond *ragazzo*.' Will you come?"

He smiled. "I'm in love with your grandmother. For her, and for her only, I'd love to come." Then he realized that it meant leaving Nina alone. "Nina," he turned back, "my friend, Claudia — "

But Nina had vanished from the vestibule, and her quick steps, retreating toward her small room, carried a ring of loneliness and reproach.

NINA FADED out of his mind the moment he entered Claudia's home. Crossing the threshold of the Benevento house was like discovering another world, eons away from his own. He was used to the sepulchral silence of his aunt's apartment, interrupted only rarely by the ringing of the telephone, or by the playing of a Russian record. Claudia's house echoed with a fascinating mélange of sounds. Everybody was calling everybody at the top of their lungs, someone was always singing, and someone always quarreling with someone else. The radio was blasting in the living room; Mother Benevento was shouting orders to the tribe from her kitchen; and the telephone was always in use, transmitting business discussions, young girls' chatter, boys' bragging, cooking recipes exchanged by the women of the house, young voices speaking English with the pungent accent of New Jersey, older voices flowing in rich, musical Italian.

Tantalizing smells of cooking, garlic and spices, grilled fish and meats, frying butter and pungent sauces, wafted from the large kitchen at the back of the house. There was continuous movement; a distant cousin coming or going; Claudia's brother's twins crying or laughing or embarking on a wild spree through the house; her mother carrying bags bursting with food; the grandmother diligently tap-tapping with her walking stick; associates of Mr. Benevento arriving to discuss business.

Even the decor was alive. In sharp contrast to the austere furnishings in Nina's apartment, the Benevento house was densely populated with colorful rugs, heavy Italian sofas dressed in faded velvet and laden with fluffy pillows, carved wooden cupboards ornamented with lace doilies, big lamps with shades made of tasseled fabric or colored glass, china statuettes, massive tables, ramshackle armchairs, and bright paintings of Italian landscapes and scenes of rural life beside pictures of saints, angels, apostles, madonnas, and the Lord Almighty Himself in various costumes.

The Beneventos obviously thrived in delightful disorder. Claudia's father was a stout man with a big belly, who bustled about the house in collarless striped shirts. Her mother, whose cameo face still carried traces of beauty, controlled the household with an iron hand, scolding her flock from her kitchen, loudly complaining of her misery, sharing her troubles with the Almighty in loud, poignant monologues. Claudia, her brothers, and her sister all treated their parents with amused irreverence. Alex was soon to discover that the shouting and fighting were not even half as serious as they seemed, that beneath the thunderous vocal exchanges the family ties were close and warm.

But the most disturbing truth Alex discovered at the Benevento house was that life could be exciting even if it was not devoted to the fanatical pursuit of an idea. Fiercely individualistic, these people didn't want to blend in faceless masses, marching toward glorious achievements; they were happy with their lot, living for the present, not for future generations. They wanted to make the best of life, today. If Karl Marx had known the Beneventos, Alex suspected, he might have written a different book.

These heretical thoughts invaded his mind that evening as he ceremoniously shook everyone's hand and was then led to the living room, where the huge dining table — covered with a checkered cloth and napkins, an array of glasses, trays, bowls, and old, massive silver, seemed ready for an extraordinary feast.

And a feast it was. Slices of red carpaccio in piquant sauce were followed by prosciutto and melon, delicious lasagna, fresh tomatoes swimming in olive oil, grilled jumbo shrimp, breaded veal, hot Italian sausages, and sharp cheeses, all served in gargantuan quantities. Chianti and Soave flowed into their wineglasses. The meals at Nina's apartment were consumed quickly, mostly in silence. Here there was not a moment of quiet. Everyone cheered and clapped at the appearance of every new dish; talked, laughed, and shouted their compliments at the lady of the house, who shouted back, her face flushed with contentment, enjoining her guests to clean their plates.

Dinner was almost over when a newcomer walked in and was greeted by a merry chorus. "Hi, Stevie," Claudia's brother Ricky called. "How was the game?"

"Okay," he answered. His voice was tired. "We won."

Claudia's sister Maria ran to him and hugged him warmly. She was wearing a tight wine-red blouse. "Claudia, come over!" her middle brother, Michael, yelled, and threw an odd look at Alex. Her second brother, the wiry, agile Ricky, bent across the table, his Adam's apple pulsating in his open collar, and explained to Alex: "Stevie is a basketball player. Great athlete." Claudia's boyfriend seemed to be the hero of the Benevento household.

Claudia, who sat beside Alex during the meal, had just gone to the kitchen to help her mother. Now she came out and briefly hugged Stevie, who kissed her on the cheek. She turned to Alex, looking ill at ease. "This is Stevie, my boyfriend," she said. "Stevie — Alex." Alex looked up at Stevie, whom he already considered his rival. Stevie was his own age, very tall, with dark hair and eyes, a straight nose, and an angular jaw. He was dressed in tan chinos and a blue oxford cloth shirt, and he had a white athletic bag hanging on his shoulder; he looked very handsome. "Hi, Alex," he said, and smiled.

Alex smiled back. "Hi," he said. He hated the guy.

He felt utterly humiliated. He didn't belong here. Why had Claudia asked him over? To meet her boyfriend? Evading Stevie's stare, he looked up at a painting of Saint Sebastian that hung over a Livorno chest. The saint, painted in gloomy dark colors, was tied to a pole, his body pierced by arrows. Alex got up. His face was burning. Maria was looking at him sideways, her plump hand smoothing her red blouse. Don't blush, he said to himself. His palms were sticky. Don't blush. "I've got to go," he said. "I left my aunt alone at home. Thank you very much. Thank you, Mrs. Benevento, it was the greatest meal of my life."

"Wait, Alex!" Claudia's mother called, wiping her hands on a dish towel. "The dessert is coming, wait!"

"Alessandro," Grandmother Benevento rasped.

"I'm sorry," he said. "Excuse me, I've got to go." He made a vague gesture with his hand. "'Bye everybody, thanks." Claudia was staring at him, her face distressed.

" 'Bye, Claudia," he said. "Thank you."

He all but ran out of the house. The street was dark and the night air cool against his flushed face. He began to cross the street, then changed his mind. He couldn't go home yet, Nina would still be awake, and he couldn't face her critical stare. He decided to walk a little, to do some thinking. But Claudia's face filled his mind, her voice whispered in his ears. Why the hell had she invited him? he asked himself. Did she want to tease him, or to make her boyfriend jealous when he found him at her table, eating her mother's lasagna? Women were like that, Joey had told him, they loved using men for their sneaky little games.

He saw the neon sign of the Hollywood Soda Fountain and turned the other way. Damn Claudia, he thought. And yet, she didn't seem that sort of girl. Yesterday she had cried when he'd told her about his mother. And today, in his apartment, he had shown her Tonya Gordon's book of poems and recited his own translations of "My Magic Kingdom" and "A Soldier's Letter." Claudia had reached over and squeezed his hand. He could swear she'd been deeply moved. She said that "A Soldier's Letter" was one of the most beautiful poems she'd ever heard. She also said that she'd never met anyone as nice as Alex. She had looked at him with something more than friendship in her eyes.

That's nonsense, an inner voice immediately countered, a girl wouldn't fall for you the first time she met you. You only thought so, stupid, because of that romantic streak you inherited from your parents. What did you think, that she had been waiting all her life just for you? Of course she has a boyfriend, she even told you that yesterday. Why didn't you ask her if she loved him? If he didn't mind her seeing other guys? Perhaps they're even sleeping together, it happens a lot nowadays. He clenched his fists. The very thought of somebody touching Claudia's naked body drove him crazy. And he had only met her yesterday!

Could she really be sleeping with Stevie? She was young, but a lot of girls started young. Joey had told him he and Frida were very close to doing it already; Joey thought they would do it in a couple of weeks. Girls want it as much as we do, Joey had said knowingly, but we have to play it cool and detached, don't show them you care, and then, at the right moment, just help them come across. Alex wondered where Joey had got all this wisdom; after all, they were the same age, and he'd only had a couple of ugly girlfriends, Laura and Frida.

He had to find something to keep himself busy, Alex decided. Lately, he had neglected his swimming, and he hadn't been to Jack Macmillan's boxing school for years. Tomorrow he'd start again. In a year, at most, he could become a great athlete, much better than Stevie. He would also devote more time to his studies. He was not just muscle, like Stevie, he had brains too. He visualized himself graduating from high school at the top of his class, and Claudia hearing about it from the neighbors. Just you wait and see, Claudia, he thought, one day you'll be sorry for letting me go.

It was almost midnight when he returned home. As he stepped into the entrance of his building, a shadow detached itself from the darkness and moved toward him.

"Claudia," he gasped. "What are you doing here?"

"You weren't home," she said. "I called your house. Your aunt said you hadn't come back."

"I went for a walk," he said uneasily. "Where's Stevie?"

"Why did you go away?" she asked. "I wanted you to stay, you were my guest. Why did you leave?" The entrance hall was dark, but he could see her face was pale and troubled.

"You know why," he said.

"No, I don't."

"You have a boyfriend," he said. "Why did you ask me over for dinner?"

"Because we had lots of fun yesterday evening," she said, "so I wanted you to come to my house. We're friends, aren't we?"

"And Stevie doesn't mind?"

"I didn't know Stevie was coming," she said defensively. "But why should he mind? We didn't do anything bad, did we?"

"We might." He recalled Joey's advice: play it cool and detached. Well, the hell with Joey. "Let me tell you something, Claudia. I don't know you, I don't own you . . ."

"Of course not," she said.

". . . and I have no claim on you. But I don't want to be just the kid next door, okay? I met you last night, and I liked you very much. I don't have a girlfriend and I've never had one. I thought of you all night, and I thought of you all day. I don't want us to be 'good friends.' And I don't want to be a replacement for Stevie when he isn't there."

"Things between me and Stevie are not what you think," she said.

"Oh? I've heard that one before, believe me, it's a great line from the movies. My husband doesn't understand me, things between us are not what you think."

"Don't make fun of me," she said. "He's not my husband."

"I don't know how things are between you and Stevie, but . . ." He hesitated, and finally blurted out: "It so happens that I want you all to myself. No Stevie, no good friends, just you and me. Now I said it. Do you understand? Do you?"

She stared at him for a long moment. "You're really something, you know?" she said in wonderment. "I've never met a boy like you before. You talk like you come from another planet. You say what you feel and you don't play games. You make me think of something your mother wrote: 'A dream for the pure at heart.' You know what? I think you're pure at heart, Alex Gordon."

She ran away before he could answer.

He slowly climbed the stairs, puzzled by her words. Did she really like him? Would he see her again?

The door to their apartment wasn't locked. All the lights were on. Nina was sitting in the living room, her hands in her lap. She looked up at him, but there was no rebuke in her eyes, just tired resignation. "Alex . . ." She took a deep breath. "It's your uncle Samuel. He died tonight."

THERE WERE VERY FEW people at Samuel Kramer's funeral: Alex and Nina, two distant cousins of Samuel's who came all the way from Buffalo, a couple of salesgirls from Spiegel's Furs — Mr. Spiegel himself couldn't come to the cemetery, he sent a wreath and a telegram — and three elderly women with unhappy faces and burning eyes, Nina's friends from the Peace Movement. An old man who lived in their building had arrived first; he could hardly walk, and had to lean on a tree to catch his breath. He said to Nina that perhaps it was for the better that dear Mr. Kramer was released from his suffering at last. The poor man, Alex thought, he was talking about Samuel Kramer but thinking of himself.

There was also a strange car, a Chevrolet, parked at a distance, with two men in the front seat. Alex briefly saw the glint of a camera lens. He recalled the men who used to watch their apartment and follow him once in a while in the streets of Brooklyn.

Joey was the last to arrive, short of breath, and he warmly hugged Alex, beckoning with his eyes to the left. "Is that her?" he whispered. There, to Alex's great surprise, stood Claudia in a severe dark blue dress, and two of her brothers, Michael and Ricky. They were both wearing skull-caps and looked very solemn.

"Thank you," Alex said, walking over and shaking Ricky's hand. "Thank you very much for coming. You didn't even know him."

"But we know you," Ricky said. "You are our best friend in the neighborhood. You helped us move, you came to our celebration. If you need anything, just open your window and yell. Okay?"

Claudia didn't say anything, she only held his hand and looked at him searchingly, as if expecting an answer to some unspoken question. Yes, he wanted to say, I love you. As she moved to shake Nina's hand, he saw his aunt's back stiffen. Nina regarded Claudia as a rival, he thought, as somebody who might steal his love. Well, perhaps Nina's instincts were right. Claudia's appearance on their street had completely confused his feelings. For him, nothing would be the same anymore. He had assumed that his love for Nina and his infatuation with Claudia were two different things, but perhaps Nina knew better.

Back at home, they prepared the living room for the traditional seven days of mourning, which Nina, after a long hesitation, had agreed to observe. They covered the mirrors with pieces of cloth and arranged the sofa and the chairs in a half circle, for their guests. Nina made him sit on the sofa. She sat upright in one of her straight-backed chairs, facing him.

"There are some things we should discuss, Alex," she said. "First, the apartment. Tomorrow some workers will come, and a cleaning woman.

We'll take your uncle's things out of the apartment. His room is going to be yours now, it's time for you to have your own room."

"But Nina, you need a room, too," he protested. Yet, deep in his heart he felt a surge of exultation. He was going to have his own room at last! He wasn't going to sleep and work in a corner of the living room anymore. And his uncle's room was the largest room in the apartment. He only prayed that his uncle's sour, repulsive smell would vanish together with his old furniture.

"I'm fine where I am now," Nina was saying. "I've already ordered a new bed for you, a nightstand, and a couple of chairs. We'll transfer your desk to your room, and of course" — she smiled faintly — "your picture gallery."

He was about to thank her, but she raised her hand. "There's something else, Alex. Your uncle had life insurance. I've been taking care of the payments for years. I don't need the money. We'll use it to pay for your studies. You can pick the college you like. Have you thought about it?"

It couldn't be true, he must be dreaming. He had never dared to hope that he could pursue his studies. "Brown University, in Providence, Rhode Island," he blurted. "Sovietology."

Nina nodded contentedly. "I hoped you'd choose Soviet studies," she said. "Why Brown?"

"They have a student exchange program with the Soviet Union and East Germany," he said.

"And you want to find Dimitri," she said, completing his thought.

"I must find him," Alex said forcefully. He leaned toward Nina. "What about you? Don't you want to find him?"

"Of course," she said. "He's my nephew, exactly like you." But after a moment she laid her hand on his arm. "No," she said, "not exactly. I raised you, Alex, you're like a son to me. I could never care about anybody else as much as I care for you, even if I wanted to."

He called Brown that same day, long distance, and asked them to send the application forms and curriculum brochures. He still had ample time to apply, but he was burning with impatience to know where he was heading.

Even in these moments of exhilaration, Claudia was in the forefront of his mind. Going to Brown meant he wouldn't be able to see her, he would be away for most of the time. Perhaps it would be for the best, though; he couldn't bear the thought of living close to her, seeing her daily from his window, yet unable to be with her. If he stayed in Brooklyn, his obsession with Claudia wouldn't leave him for a single moment; he would go mad, imagining her in the arms of that vain, dandyish boyfriend of hers.

Nina was watching him closely with her sharp, clever eyes. It occurred to him that she had probably guessed what he was thinking, and wasn't displeased to see him go away, for the same reason.

The brochures arrived on a balmy afternoon a week later. As the day drifted to its end, he sat in his new room, cleaned, sprayed and newly furnished, reading the application forms for the umpteenth time. The windows were wide open, letting in the dusty smell of early summer; darkness was already settling in. There was a knock on his door. Nina appeared on the threshold, her face dour. "You have a visitor," she said.

She moved aside, and before him stood Claudia. She was very pale, and looked thinner. She was wearing a tight, sleeveless blouse made of thin blue fabric, and a knee-length zippered skirt. Her face was drawn, and her breath was shallow, as if she had run up the steps.

"Claudia, come in," he said. "What's wrong?"

She stepped inside and closed the door behind her, leaning back, her hand clutching the handle. "I came to tell you — " she began, then paused and took a deep breath. Her eyes carried an uncertain look. "I came to tell you that Stevie and I broke up."

He stood and faced her, unable to speak. His heart was thumping and a strange tremor rose inside him. He didn't know what to say. "What happened?" he finally managed. She didn't answer. Her mouth was trembling.

Suddenly nothing else mattered but Claudia's trembling lips, which now she offered to him. As in a dream, he moved toward her and awkwardly bent toward her, staring into her eyes. He could feel her breath on his face. Her lips were hot and dry, and as they parted under his, he forgot everything else, sinking into an abyss of sensations — triumph and elation, passion and boundless love. And a slight twinge of fear.

LATER IN THAT WEEK, while Nina was at work, the only sound in Alex's room was the soft rustling of their clothes. With fevered hands he pulled off her skirt and blouse, then he was cupping her breasts and caressing her silken thighs. His impatient mouth closed on her nipples, and his heart, a wild sledgehammer, pounded madly inside his chest. He carried her to the bed, overwhelmed by the beauty of her naked body, which was the color of ivory. He had never undressed a woman before, had never felt such an explosion of passion in his heart. She gasped as she opened herself to him, and suddenly he was inside her, his mouth drinking hers.

"I love you, Claudia," he murmured, "I love you," pressing her against him, feeling her breasts against his chest. "Tell me you love me, tell me you feel me inside you, tell me you want only me."

And her hoarse murmur slowly rose in his ear, her uneven breath turning into moaning, her nails digging into his flanks, her breasts suddenly taut and her body arching toward him, her fiery embrace telling him she was his now, his only, until he exploded inside her and collapsed in her throbbing depths.

Only later, when he propped on his elbow and leaned over her in a surge of tenderness, did he notice the stain of blood spreading on the white bed sheets.

"I thought . . . I didn't know you were a virgin," he whispered.

She didn't answer, holding him tight, softly kissing him, softly crying.

PART TWO

Love

1967–1977

Chapter 7

IT WAS RAINING hard, gray, slanting sheets of rain, as the Lear jet landed shakily on the deserted runway. Grimaldi gazed wistfully out the plane window at the dark mass of trees that bent low, beaten by the wind. He didn't recognize the airfield. His guess was that they had landed in Virginia, possibly at the Farm, the CIA training facility; or perhaps somewhere along the East Coast, between New York and Washington. Judging by the heavy air traffic they had encountered before landing, they were probably near a major airport, possibly JFK or Dulles.

The aircraft was private, unmarked, and Grimaldi was the only passenger on board. The steward handed him his overcoat and bulging handbag, flashing him a quick smile. He was a slim, graceful boy, with matte skin and slightly slanted eyes, and Grimaldi felt a sharp pang as a bittersweet memory surfaced in his mind, then slowly dissolved. He placed the neatly folded coat beside him, checked the knot of his vivid blue silk tie and smoothed the contour of his mustache. The plane slowly taxied on the runway, and Grimaldi sank back in thought. For the last two days, and during the long journey from London, he had tried to figure out the purpose of his sudden recall, and the reasons for the cloak-and-dagger procedures that had surrounded his precipitate flight.

For some nebulous reason CIA headquarters had organized his return as an emergency rescue operation, as if he were in mortal danger. First there was the cable to his London apartment: Top Secret — Immediate — Eyes only — Decode by own hand. Then, the explicit instructions not to reveal anything to his colleagues at the CIA liaison office. The convoluted scheme of establishing contact, the phone calls from public booths, the meeting at crowded Charing Cross Station. And finally the night trip in the black Rover, with a driver he had never met. Taking a tortuous route, designed to avoid surveillance, they had made it to Basingstoke Air Force Base, where his plane was waiting on the runway, engines droning. He hadn't played these games since Berlin, and that was more than fifteen years ago.

Not that he didn't like games. On the contrary, since he had shed the naiveté of his younger years, Grimaldi regarded life as a never-ending, fascinating game. It was a charade, he believed, a perpetual contest of wits. He had boldly stepped into the charade at the age of eighteen, when he had adopted his Corsican stepfather's name and country of origin and metamorphosed from Frankie Flanagan into Franco Grimaldi.

This mutation had crowned a strange and painful process young Frankie had gone through in his teens. He had always been different from the other boys. Effeminate, artistic, attracted by flashy colors and flamboyant clothes, he was a smart but weak youth. The neighborhood boys hounded him, calling him a sissy; he often returned home beaten and bruised. He was seventeen when he met a soft-spoken saxophone player at a jazz concert. He returned home in the morning, horrified yet thrilled by the discovery of his homosexuality. Now he understood why he was not attracted to women. But he also realized he had to conceal his sexual urges if he wanted to succeed in life. New Orleans, in 1937, didn't tolerate homosexuals; neither did any other city, as far as he knew.

Frankie was driven by a burning ambition to make it in life. But how could he? He was weak, ridiculed and disliked by his classmates. There was nothing special about him. He was half Italian, half Irish. His mother had been born in a small village near Ancona, on Italy's Adriatic coast. She had met Colin Flanagan in Louisiana, where she had immigrated with her family. His father had died when Frankie was a baby. He had seen him only in some old photographs: a slight, ferret-faced Irishman. Frankie had been raised and taught French by his mother's second husband, a warm-hearted man with a booming laugh.

The birthplace of Napoleon, Corsica was famous for its fierce brigands. Frankie, thrilled by their romantic aura, desperately searching for something that would make him intriguing, took his stepfather's name and appropriated his roots. He also changed his Christian name to Franco. Since the age of eighteen, when he left school and moved to the East Coast, Franco Grimaldi claimed to be descended from Corsican bandits. The truth was that his family operated two restaurants in New Orleans, where the only acts of banditry were valiantly performed at the cash registers.

The deception had been successful for years. Grimaldi was known to all his friends as a Corsican. His colleagues at the CIA had nicknamed him "Napoleone." They also made fun of his flowery vests, colorful bow ties, silk scarves, and heavy gold jewelry, but that was sheer envy and their jabs left him indifferent.

He had been drawn to espionage because he liked adventure and was ready to take risks — as long as he could fight with his mind or tongue, and not with his fists. It had not been the Corsican legend he had spun around himself, but his Italian-sounding name and his knowledge of the language that had gotten him his first assignment. It was 1943; the war was at its peak, and he had landed in Sicily with a group of Italian-born agents. Their mission was to reach the Mafia strongholds, on General Patton's behalf, and negotiate an agreement with the local dons against Mussolini.

He was just a kid then, barely twenty-three, the youngest man on the team. He would never forget the smoke-filled huts in the Palermo hills, when he faced the tough Mafia dons and stared down the long barrels of their Luparas. He knew that each of those men could be a fascist in disguise or a German-paid assassin. But he had survived and the agreement had been concluded; the mafiosi had launched a rebellion against Mussolini and the Germans. Since Sicily, Grimaldi had started believing in his lucky star.

He had continued teasing danger in Berlin, after V-day, when Russian and American agents were already dying, the first casualties of the cold war. He had struck a unique relationship with a Russian officer and embarked with him on many an adventure. But their last joint operation had ended sourly. Alone again, he became involved in his most ambitious initiative: the Gehlen gambit.

These were the days when the American wartime intelligence organization, the Office of Strategic Services, was breathing its last, and the OSS founding fathers — a team of endearingly clumsy blue-eyed and blue-blooded Americans — were striving to build an organization capable of confronting the Soviet spy machine. To Grimaldi they looked like Boy Scouts declaring war on the Chicago mob, gullible crusaders waving the cross in front of Saladin's ruthless hordes. The KGB had infiltrated the vital centers of the West with thousands of agents. The newborn Central Intelligence Agency had nothing similar in Russia: no resident agents, no networks, no highly placed moles. Here Grimaldi, still a young man, but already a cold-blooded cynic, had stepped on the stage and produced a solution called Gehlen.

Strangely enough, he had learned about Gehlen from the Russians, in one of the rare instances when he had joined forces with them, hunting escaped Nazi criminals. General Reinhard Gehlen was the Russians' nightmare, he learned, a man they had sworn to annihilate. Gehlen, the wartime chief of espionage against the Soviet Union, had spun an excellent web all over Russia. At the end of the war most of Gehlen's networks were still intact, his spies unidentified. That drove the Russians mad with frustration. Among them, in their army headquarters and their government offices, thrived treacherous Nazi spies. The KGB officers wanted Gehlen's files, the lists of the traitors who worked for him; most of all, they wanted his head.

Grimaldi used every trick he knew. He bought information from former German officers for food, liquor, and cigarettes scavenged in the U.S. Army stores. He sweet-talked the secretaries who typed reports for his bosses; but mostly he shamelessly traded secrets with two British intelligence experts, baiting them with the minutes of the Russian-American negotiations about the future of the dismembered German empire.

After months of groundwork, he succeeded in locating Gehlen's hideout in the Taubenstein Mountains. He secretly traveled to Lake Schliersee, where he got hold of the gaunt spymaster and whisked him to safety. Gehlen could be the jewel in Grimaldi's crown. If he succeeded, it meant rapid promotion, high position, a substantial salary. And a lot of power to play his games. They hadn't nicknamed him Napoleone for nothing.

In his talks with Gehlen, Grimaldi displayed cold logic and a cynical attitude. He offered Gehlen a deal: his personal safety in exchange for the German networks in Russia. He pointed out that Gehlen's networks were not worth much to the general if his own life was not protected. Besides, since Gehlen couldn't turn to the Russians for help, he didn't have a choice. Thus, General Reinhard Gehlen, once Hitler's master spy, became America's best asset in the secret war against Russia.

In the ensuing years, Gehlen put Hitler's former spies at the service of his new masters. And Grimaldi took residence at the dreary compound in Pullach where Gehlen had established his headquarters. He was the CIA watchdog, peering over Gehlen's shoulder, supervising his operations, perusing his lists.

He knew that he now was a target for the KGB, which would have paid dearly for the secrets passing through his hands. But it was not the KGB that led to Grimaldi's downfall. It was Willie Schiller, a beautiful Pullach youngster he had met in January 1952, a lithe boy with graceful limbs, a soft mouth, and dark eyelashes.

Grimaldi had been very careful since joining the CIA. Except for one secret adventure in Berlin, he had suppressed his sexual urges. If his superiors found out he was a homosexual, he could be thrown out of the Company. Homosexuals were regarded as high security risks who could become blackmail targets for the enemy.

He didn't know what made him lose his head. Perhaps his excessive confidence, perhaps Willy's enticing sensuality. Grimaldi fell desperately in love with him, and spent a few unforgettable nights feasting on his soft, docile body. When the boy finally broke up with him, Grimaldi lost his self-control. He began following Willie in Pullach's streets, phoned him at all hours, and pounded on his house door, begging him to return. Finally Willie's parents — the boy was only seventeen — complained to the local police.

The following morning, Grimaldi was summoned to a suite at the Vier Jahreszeiten Hotel in Munich, where his superior officer, Colonel James Macpherson, Jr., confronted him. Macpherson was seething with rage.

"You're a piece of shit, Grimaldi," he hissed at him. "You got the top slot in Europe, with the best promotion chances, and you blew it. You fucked this kid and you fucked up your future. I want you on the next flight home. You'll probably be kicked out of the service as soon as you get to Langley."

Grimaldi was listening dejectedly, his head bowed. He didn't know what to say. "Can't you help me, Jim?" he finally managed. "The Company is my whole life, you know."

Macpherson shook his head. "I tried my best to save you, but nobody would listen." He looked away, shaking his head. "You fool," he rasped, "you bloody fool."

Macpherson interceded on Grimaldi's behalf, though, and finally saved his hide. They didn't kick him out — he was one of the Company's best Soviet experts. But his operational career was over and he was exiled to a desk job in Washington. In 1957 they sent him to France, five years later to England. Everywhere, he held positions of high responsibility; but the closest he came to field operations was in his dreams. The Pullach scandal barred him from the job he coveted: control of the Russian networks.

Now, in the fall of 1967, fifteen years after the German scandal, there was no longer any chance he would ever take part in field operations again. Time had blunted his lust for action, and his frustration had simmered down. He had gotten used to the comfort of a less tumultuous existence. He enjoyed grooming his Clark Gable mustache, and he had let his wavy brown hair grow longer. His catlike green eyes were in startling contast to his swarthy Gypsy's face. The only vestige of his swashbuckling years was his flamboyant taste in clothes, jewelry, gourmet foods, and fine wines. It suited the role he had chosen, that of the daredevil, pleasure-loving adventurer.

Tonight, during the long transatlantic flight, he had slept fitfully, alone in the cabin. A tiny blue light shone at the far end of the aisle, where the flight attendant dozed in his seat. Even in his sleep Grimaldi was haunted by the secrecy that cloaked this journey. Why had they summoned him? Why all the precautions? An important assignment probably waited for him at the end of this voyage. But what assignment? He had gone through some turns in his career; they had not always been for the better.

The airplane slowed and came to a stop. The steward unlocked the cabin door and beckoned to Grimaldi. He threw his coat on his shoulders like a cape and stepped outside. It was a nasty morning, with a low, dark sky, and a cold, gusty wind. The folding stairs were slippery from the rain, and the wind slapped his exposed face. The heavy raindrops were cold against his skin.

A black Chevrolet waited on the tarmac, close to the aircraft. Grimaldi opened the rear door. A gush of warm air enveloped him, and he smelled the aroma of sandalwood-scented tobacco.

"Come in, Napoleone," said a husky voice with a New England accent, and Grimaldi looked up, startled.

"Good morning, Jim," he managed. "Well, this is a surprise."

JIM MACPHERSON, his former boss in Germany, had made it to the top, and was now deputy director for Plans. Macpherson held the number-three position in the Company hierarchy, after the director and his deputy for Operations. Grimaldi hadn't expected the DDP to come in person to meet him. He stepped into the car and settled uneasily beside Macpherson on the back seat.

"How was your flight?" the DDP casually inquired, apparently without expecting an answer. "And how's London these days?" His rebel shock of hair had grown white, but still bestowed a boyish air on his handsome features.

The second man in the car, the driver, turned around, his skull-like face cracking in a lopsided grin. His pallid eyes had the cold, calculating look that Grimaldi recalled only too well. *"Bonjour, cher ami,"* he drawled in heavily accented French.

"Hello, Walt," Grimaldi said, hardly disguising his displeasure. "Driving the boss now, I see. I always believed you'd climb the ladder one day." Walt Reiner's smile vanished. Grimaldi couldn't stand the DDP's assistant, who was nothing but a pompous ass. Years ago Walt had acquired the habit of spicing his conversations with Grimaldi with high school French, and he believed this to be very funny.

"We didn't want to bring a driver along," Macpherson explained. "We want to keep our meetings with you as discreet as possible."

"Why?" Grimaldi asked. If they had come in a car, the landing strip must be close to Langley Woods. "Why all this secrecy?"

Macpherson took his pipe from his mouth and glanced out the car window. "I'd rather talk about this over breakfast somewhere."

"I'd rather talk about this now," Grimaldi said, his voice quiet but firm. "I'm fed up with being ordered around, Jim. I'm a big boy now. I don't like being instructed to leave my job in the middle of the night, then fly five thousand miles without knowing what it's all about. So let's skip the breakfast and talk now."

Macpherson didn't answer right away. He morosely studied the moist stem of his pipe, then threw a look at Walt Reiner, who shrugged. In the silence that ensued, the drumming of the raindrops on the car roof rose to an angry staccato. Finally the DDP turned to face Grimaldi. "All right," he agreed. His finely lined face was suddenly very earnest. "We want you to go to Moscow," he said.

For a second Grimaldi was speechless. He felt a surge of disbelief mixed with nascent joy. "Moscow? What for?"

"We want you to run an agent," Macpherson said, his brown eyes studying him closely.

Grimaldi returned his stare. The entire situation didn't make sense. "I've been in mothballs for fifteen years, Jim. I thought you had better qualified men in Moscow."

"I certainly do," the DDP agreed. "But this one needs special attention. He's an extraordinary man."

"Now, wait . . . wait . . ." Grimaldi stammered, then blurted out the question that burned on the tip of his tongue. "Why me?"

Macpherson and Reiner exchanged sour smiles. "We wouldn't have ever done this of our own free will, *bien sûr,*" Reiner said breezily, enjoying his wit. "We had quite a few other candidates. But the man asked for you. *Comprenez-vous?*"

MACPHERSON'S NARRATIVE started in the car, then continued in the vinyl-padded booth of a Denny's roadside restaurant where Grimaldi, softened by the good news, had finally agreed to have breakfast. The talk ended in a small apartment in downtown Washington, which had been prepared for him by the Company.

"We'll call our Russian comrade Top Hat for the time being," Macpherson suggested, and Grimaldi nodded agreement.

The Russian had been recruited in Vienna three weeks before, Macpherson's story went. He had established contact with Bob Collier, the CIA man at the embassy, which proved he was well-informed. He sent Collier's wife a dozen roses. Stapled to the bunch was the florist's envelope, but inside it the Russian had slipped a note to Bob with instructions for a meeting. When he met Collier, in a car parked outside the Museum of Fine Arts, he identified himself as a colonel in Soviet military intelligence. His office was in the Kremlin complex, and he had access to highly classified documents. He was in Vienna for the debriefing of an agent who worked in the entourage of a European leader.

"We think it's either Herr Erhard or *mon cher* General de Gaulle," Reiner interjected, then shrunk in disappointment as his revelation failed to provoke any response.

The Russian told Collier that he wanted to defect, Macpherson continued; he had been a communist all his life, but his dream had crumbled.

And how did that happen? Collier had asked. After some hesitation, Top Hat revealed his motive. His sister, a scientist at the Michurin Institute in Volgograd, had discovered that the famous heredity theory of Soviet geneticist Lysenko was nothing but a fraud. She reported her findings to the Institute director. As a result, she was arrested and taken to a mental hospital, where she was still imprisoned. "My sister is not mad," the Russian said to Collier, "and a regime that throws scientists into nuthouses doesn't deserve to exist."

Collier, Macpherson went on, immediately perceived the tremendous potential of the Russian. The man was a treasure; he moved in the highest circles of Soviet intelligence. Collier didn't want him to defect; he wanted him back in the Kremlin, working for the CIA. The Russian's lust for revenge could make him the greatest spy the CIA had ever had in Moscow.

At a second meeting, Top Hat was more relaxed, and revealed his name to Collier. The CIA carried out some discreet inquiries, and found that the man was speaking the truth. Collier then suggested that he return to Moscow as a CIA agent. He offered him a tempting salary and the rank of colonel in the U.S. Army. In ten years' time, maybe less, he would be brought over to the United States, be given a new identity, and would live happily ever after. The Russian had agreed, under certain conditions. Now he was back in his Kremlin lair, waiting to be contacted.

"I met Top Hat," the DDP said. "Jim Nolan — you know, the chief of the Soviet division — suggested I look into the matter myself. So I flew to Vienna. There wasn't even a breech of security involved." He smiled wanly. "The Russian knew all about me. He even showed my picture to Collier."

"Didn't it occur to you it might be a setup?" Grimaldi suggested. "Double agents are the KGB house specialty. They've been planting double agents in the West since 1945, and we've been swallowing all their bait. If we buy this guy now, he might feed us red herrings for the next ten years."

"It's a possibility," Macpherson admitted, "but my feeling is the man is honest." He sunk into a long silence. "Anyway," he finally said, "that's why we want you to go over there and hold his hand. You've got enough experience to spot a double, if he is one."

"Did he bring any samples?" Grimaldi asked.

Macpherson nodded again. "A couple of reports. One was a memo to the Politburo, signed by Major General Pugachev."

"The deputy defense minister?"

"Yes. It deals with the missile program. It says that testing has been stopped since an SS-20 exploded on the launching pad at Baikonur last May. More than a hundred people were killed."

Grimaldi took a sleek gold-plated cigarette case out of his pocket and chose a thin black cigarillo. "Is it true?"

"We sent an SR-71 to verify," Reiner said. "They almost shot it down, but the pilot made it, with half a dozen photos. The ground is scorched in a radius of two hundred yards around the launching pad. Lots of debris all over the place. *Voilà.*"

The telephone beside Reiner buzzed and he picked it up.

"We had two long meetings, and I liked him," Macpherson frankly confessed, then suddenly smiled. "You wouldn't guess the first thing he asked for."

Grimaldi looked at him sideways. "I give up. You tell me." Reiner was whispering into the telephone, glaring at Grimaldi.

"He asked to see his colonel's uniform," Macpherson said. " 'If you make me American colonel' " — he mimicked the Russian's accent — " 'I want to see my uniform.' " Macpherson resumed in his normal voice: "I had to send Collier to the Ramstein air base to find a colonel's uniform. You should have seen our Russian trying it on in front of the mirror. He was the happiest man on earth."

Macpherson had asked the Russian how he would pass the information he collected, and he had been amazed by the answer. "He asked for you," the DDP said. "He met you in Berlin, after the war. He said he knew you were in the intelligence business, and he would work with nobody but you. His name is Kalinin."

Grimaldi stared at him, stunned. "I'll be damned," he finally mumbled. "Oleg Kalinin. I'll be damned." He frowned, staring at Macpherson suspiciously. "You're not kidding, are you?"

Macpherson shook his head.

"I don't believe it." Grimaldi's memory took him back to the black ruins of postwar Berlin. "He made it," he murmured, shaking his head in wonder. "He made it, he's alive!"

Perturbed by a surge of recollections, he didn't immediately realize that Macpherson was speaking to him. "What I want to know," Macpherson was saying, "is why he wants you, of all people, after all these years."

"We were involved in several operations together," Grimaldi said cautiously. "They had to do with Nazi criminals."

Oleg's face sailed from the dark niches of his memory as he had seen him first, that evening at the Berlin *kommandatura* bureau. Those were the days of the Nuremberg trials, when Russians and Americans had briefly joined forces in the hunt for Nazi criminals. Many wanted Nazis had assumed false identities and gone to ground. Some had escaped to villages and forest hideouts. Most had blended into the hordes of famished Wehrmacht soldiers roaming the ruins of the defunct Reich, looking for homes and families that no longer existed. Grimaldi had been instructed to report at the *kommandatura* to meet with a Russian officer, Captain Kalinin.

Tall and handsome, broad-faced and sandy-haired, with a child's curiosity, a dimpled chin, and eyes sparkling with life, Oleg Kalinin had shattered his image of a Russian officer. Grimaldi had expected the run-of-the-mill Russian: stiff, stolid, suspicious and hostile. The young officer with the infectious laughter stunned him. Kalinin was outspoken, irreverent, and quick-tempered; they ended their evening in a glorious brawl with British military police at the notorious Fett Madchen bar. Grimaldi couldn't help succumbing to his new friend's charm. In many ways the Russian was a mirror of his own self: he was a gambler, he was ambitious, and he nurtured a sublime disregard for military hierarchy. And there was something in his look, his smile, the furtive touch of his hand, that conveyed to Grimaldi a message only he could understand.

Two nights later they became lovers. Never since then had Grimaldi felt such profound love for another human being, such a blend of physical satisfaction, intellectual challenge, and emotional harmony. His affair with Oleg lasted only a few months. But it was the love of his life. He still dreamed about him at night, still woke up longing for the touch of his skin, the warmth of his body.

"He was an adventurer," Grimaldi said loudly, looking searchingly at

Macpherson. Did he know, he anxiously asked himself, did he suspect? "A Russian," he went on, "a communist, a KGB officer, but a bandit all the same." On the sofa in front of him, Macpherson was sipping his black coffee, watching him over the rim of his cup.

Grimaldi accepted another coffee, just for the pleasure of having Reiner serve it to him. Kalinin was the man who had stirred his interest in Russia, that enigmatic empire, sworn to destroy his own world, still desperately trying to imitate it; a nation of men who could be warm, sentimental people, devoted friends — and yet ruthless, scheming enemies.

"We were very excited about the Nazi project," he said. "Kalinin spoke good English and understood a few words of German. We also had with us a British expert named Tony Whitcombe. He had been born in Berlin and spoke German fluently. We managed to unravel some of the escape routes the Nazis were using to get out of Germany." He smiled despite himself. "You should have seen us, excited as schoolboys, when we found out about the Spider."

Macpherson raised his eyebrows.

"*Die Spinne,* in German," Grimaldi explained. The organization was indeed a spider, spinning its web over several countries, smuggling criminals from southern Germany and Austria to Spain or the ports of Italy. "There was another network, *Die Schleuse* — the Lock Gate — that had established a route through Germany and Austria into Italy, ending at Genoa or Naples." From the Italian ports, the Nazis embarked for Peron's Argentina.

"The most dangerous criminals, however, escaped with the help of Odessa." He quickly explained: "*Organisation der Ehemaligen SS Angehorigen* — Association of ex-SS members."

The three of them, Grimaldi went on, were enthusiastic, willing to take risks. Dressed in civilian clothes, Whitcombe posing as a Bavarian sergeant, Grimaldi claiming he was a former French collaborator, they were able to sneak into SS circles. Kalinin was less fortunate. He carried the papers of a Russian officer in General Vlassov's pro-Nazi army, but they were of little use. Nobody wanted to mess with the Russians.

Whitcombe and Grimaldi participated in several Odessa meetings in Berlin. "Twice we succeeded in locating Odessa headquarters; the first time in the wing of a hospital where they treated contagious diseases, then in a farm off the road to Dresden." His frustration surfaced, as if it had happened yesterday. "We were so proud when we submitted our reports. But they were drowned in red tape. The liaison office was leaking like a sieve. Finally, when our special units arrived at the Odessa head-quarters, they found that everybody had flown the coop.

"That was too much for Kalinin and me," he went on. "We couldn't bear such mediocrity. Our superiors were unable to carry out an opera-tion — so we decided to do it on our own."

"Same old Grimaldi," Reiner quipped. Macpherson didn't say a word, his eyes watching him intensely.

"I had a plan," Grimaldi said.

He suggested to his friends that they "roll up" the Odessa network from the inside. The three of them, posing as fugitives, would ask for Odessa's assistance in their escape. They would follow the Odessa trail, memorizing names and places; after reaching one of the ports of Italy — the final destination of their journey — they would report to Berlin and lead the raid on Odessa's network.

At the beginning the plan had worked fine. The Odessa escape com-mittee in Berlin had subjected them to an intense grilling. But they had passed the test with flying colors. "At least we thought so at the time."

"Same cover stories?"

"Yes," Grimaldi said. "They sounded genuine. This time, we had no problem with Kalinin. The Odessa people had objected to a Russian participating in their meetings; but they didn't object to him joining us in our escape. The Vlassov officers had been even more cruel than the Nazis, during the Russian campaign." He paused to light another ciga-rillo. "So we were on our way."

It took them twelve days to travel across Germany and Austria, sleep-ing in mountain lodges, farms, a monastery, and once even in a police-man's house. They now embarked on the last stage of their trip — the crossing into Italy. They spent the night in a gamekeeper's home outside Ober Gurgl, and in the early morning sneaked to the Italian border, where the guide from Merano would pick them up.

Grimaldi remembered well the last time he had seen Oleg, that early dawn by the Brenner pass: tense yet thrilled, the dark eyes burning with anticipation under the visor of his cap, the hands stuck deep in the pockets of a thick brown jacket. Tony Whitcombe crouched beside him behind a low stone wall, shabbily dressed in a cracked leather coat, baggy breeches, and scuffed shoes. They were two tiny figures, barely noticeable against the backdrop of the Tyrolean Alps, peaks hidden in the clouds, slopes plunging into the narrow valleys, buried in the morning mist.

"I had stayed behind, to pack some food in my rucksack. I hurried to catch up with them, before the guide from Merano came from the forest."

All of a sudden he saw Tony grotesquely throw up his arms, then he heard the shots and realized that his friend's funny movements were the convulsions of a dying man. Oleg also rolled on the ground, kicked, then disappeared behind the stone wall. The shots echoed throughout the gorge, reverberating against the cliffs. There was no man from Merano waiting for them, Grimaldi realized, just a murderous ambush.

He darted toward a jagged outcropping that stretched from a hill on his right. Bullets cracked in his ears, one of them ricocheting between the boulders. In the shelter of the stone rampart, he stopped to catch his breath. His face was on fire and his shirt was soaked with sweat. He should go back, he thought, he must save Oleg! But he was unarmed, he couldn't fight the gunmen, and he was trembling with fear. He ran all the way to the village and alerted the burgomeister, who telephoned Allied army headquarters.

"We found Tony's body by the stone wall. He had been hit in the back by several bullets; he had died instantly. Kalinin had disappeared. We found traces of blood and followed them for about three hundred yards." The traces led into a ravine flanked by muddy slopes. One of the mountaineers, whose dog panted at the end of a short leash, found the footprints of three other men; they had either followed the wounded man or carried him away. All the footprints, though, disappeared at the stream that gushed through the gully. "I never saw Oleg Kalinin again," Grimaldi concluded. And I longed for him all those years, he thought.

"So you blew it," Reiner concluded. A police car's siren wailed in the street.

"I did," Grimaldi admitted. That had been the bloody ending of his scheme to defeat Odessa. Months of planning, intelligence gathering, and personal risks had produced the Brenner pass massacre; and the taste of panic, his running away in terror, his trembling hands, the cold sweat breaking on his forehead, had haunted him for years.

"And nobody blamed you when you came back?" Macpherson asked. "I would have court-martialed you on the spot."

Grimaldi crushed his cigar in a chipped ashtray shaped like a maple leaf. "A month later I brought them Reinhard Gehlen. So they chose to ignore the Brenner pass incident."

"What about the killers? They were never found?"

"No," Grimaldi said. "Our men raided the relays where we had stopped on our way; I gave them a detailed list." He took a deep breath. "They found nothing, all the Odessa agents had vanished. Odessa set up new routes and stayed in business for a few more years." He walked to the window and looked down. Two Hispanics in brightly colored windbreakers were loading suitcases into an old blue Chevrolet. He turned back. "Perhaps Kalinin will tell us how he managed to escape."

"He was your friend, wasn't he?" Macpherson asked coldly. "Didn't you try to find out what had happened to him?"

Grimaldi's throat was dry. The phantoms were rising from his past. "How could I? I thought he was dead. Either murdered by the Nazis, or, in the unlikely case that he had escaped, shot by the Russians for insubordination. The Soviet commissars shot people for much less than that. If by any chance he had survived, I would have only complicated matters for him by asking questions."

"You still think of him as your friend?" Macpherson pressed, while poking into his pipe with an ugly silver instrument. "You didn't act very gallantly by abandoning him there, wounded. Perhaps he hates your guts for that."

Grimaldi didn't answer, his eyes focused on an Andy Warhol print hanging on the wall.

"But you'll take the job, won't you? You'll go to Moscow."

"I don't know," he said. "Let me think about it."

Macpherson slowly shook his head. "Walt, would you leave us alone for a moment?" he said softly.

Reiner shrugged and left the room. Macpherson turned to Grimaldi. His face was distorted with anger. "You stupid old queen," he muttered. "I saved your ass, back in Pullach, remember? I protected you all these years, and turned a blind eye to all your sordid adventures with the scum you've been picking up in New York and London. You want me to make you a list of all the queers who've passed through your bed?"

"My private life — " Grimaldi started.

"I don't give a damn about your private life. One phone call from me will be more than enough to have you kicked out, and this time for good." He paused. "Do you want me to make that call? Or would you rather take the Moscow job and say thank you, sir?"

Grimaldi swallowed but kept quiet, staring blankly at Macpherson.

"That's better. Someone will drive you to the office later." Macpherson's voice had changed. It was brisk now, matter-of-fact, with a commanding ring. "You'll spend a few weeks with us, for briefing, procedures, and so on. Then a short stay at the Farm, and you'll be on your way. I want you there before Christmas."

The door opened and Reiner walked in, his sly eyes darting from Macpherson to Grimaldi.

"Cover?" Grimaldi asked, ignoring Reiner.

Macpherson examined his pipe and put it in the pocket of his corduroy jacket. "French Canadian," he said. "Representative of the Delices du Nord Company, of Montreal. They import caviar and fish from Russia. Their man in Moscow is going back home in six weeks."

"Canadian immigration is all screwed up," Reiner pointed out. "Lousy filing system, no records of passport numbers. You'll be absolutely safe."

Grimaldi leaned back against the window, feeling its chill like a cold breath down his neck. "You had it all sewn up, didn't you, Jim? You knew I was going to accept."

Macpherson shrugged. "You bet," he said bluntly. "Very few people get a second chance, Napoleone."

He was on his feet, preceded by Reiner, who had opened the door.

"I asked you before, but you didn't answer me, Jim," Grimaldi said. "Why all the secrecy? What was the rush?"

Macpherson turned back toward him, looking annoyed. "We wanted you out of England at once. We feared a leak."

"What kind of leak?"

Faced with Grimaldi's righteous puzzlement, the DDP reluctantly explained. "I told you Kalinin had brought us two documents. The first was the memo about the missile mishap. The second was a GRU analysis of Soviet espionage in England. It seems British intelligence is still riddled with Russian agents." He paused. "I didn't want the British, or our liaison office, to hear the news about your going undercover. That would have been reported to Moscow Center in twenty-four hours."

"But — "

"Any regular transfer would have raised questions, and people would have asked where you're going next," Macpherson went on. "This morning" — he consulted his watch — "London was informed by cable that you had to urgently fly home because your father was terminally ill. In a couple of weeks we'll inform them that you're resigning from the service to take care of the family business. It's a restaurant chain, isn't it?"

He turned toward the doorway and, without waiting for an answer, walked out. Reiner hurried after him.

Grimaldi didn't ask if they had told his stepfather about his ghastly malady.

GRIMALDI stepped out of the elevator on the fourth floor of the main Langley building, amiably nodding at the employees he saw on his way. He popped a mint in his mouth; a faint touch of garlic still lingered on his breath. It had been an excellent lunch, Fernand was as good as ever. He had recognized him immediately. "Monsieur Grimaldi, I can't believe it." The stout Parisian chef was exaggerating his French accent, as usual. It worked wonders with his Washington clientele. "How long since you were here last?"

"I've been away for years," Grimaldi had said. "In Europe, mostly in Paris. You're still the best, *mon ami.*" Fernand retreated, beaming, and sent Grimaldi's party a *mirabelle* on the house. It was a great ending to an excellent meal, Grimaldi decided. And productive, too. He had been extensively briefed by Jim Nolan, the director of the Clandestine Services, Soviet Division (S/D), and Steve Pershing of the GRU desk. They had chosen to meet at a Washington restaurant rather than the executive dining room at headquarters. That way their lunch looked like another of the many farewell meals offered to Grimaldi by his colleagues; the same meeting, held at Langley Woods, might have raised quite a few eyebrows. His superiors were religiously clinging to the cover story concocted by Macpherson: broken with grief, Grimaldi was resigning from the Agency and going back to Louisiana. As far as his colleagues were concerned, his future, from now on, lay in Cajun chicken wings and Bahamanian conch chowder. Only Macpherson's staff and six people at Clandestine Services knew that he was bound for a more sinister destination.

It was his last visit to Langley before starting his journey to Moscow.

On Monday he had returned from a refresher course at the Farm, which included, according to the local dialect, Mass, Wheel of Torture, and Gunsmoke — respectively, low-level briefings, physical training, shooting practice. And Sunday school, of course, an utterly irrelevant initiation to invisible inks, microdots, and James Bond gadgets, which Grimaldi knew, and S/D knew, he was never going to use.

The following morning he flew to Buffalo. In a small motel by Niagara Falls he handed his American papers to a man he had never met before. The stranger gave him the keys to a car with Quebec plates, and a Canadian passport. The same night Mr. Charles Saint-Clair, from Montreal, crossed the Canadian border on his way home.

SIX WEEKS LATER, an hour after sunset, Grimaldi got out of a Moscow taxi on Chkalova Street and entered the dreary low building that housed the Kursk railway station, the gateway to the southern USSR. The place was bustling with people: peasants from the Ukraine, swarthy cossacks from the Don, squat Georgians, their dark eyes bleary after the long train journey.

First he had to make sure that he would reach his destination without a KGB goon on his tail. Mixing with a group of Volgograd engineers, Grimaldi donned a cheap rabbit-fur hat and removed his coat, then plunged into a delegation of Tula teachers carrying red banners and signs proclaiming their support for the teachers of revolutionary Cuba.

He walked into the crowded cafeteria, cautiously navigating between families, children, old people, dogs, and heaps of packages and cracked suitcases. He had memorized his instructions. He entered the corridor leading to the rest rooms, but instead of going to the back, he pushed a door on his left, crossed a dark room full of cases of bottled water and jars of pickles, almost tripped on a couple of brooms, and went out by another door.

He emerged on the gloomy Kostomarovsky Prospect, crossed the street and casually sauntered into the parking lot facing the station. A bitter wind was blowing from the east, and he draped his coat over his shoulders. The instructions had been very clear: second row from the left, then to the left again. A black Moskvich with a broken radio antenna and a toy teddy bear on the dashboard. He tried the handle, and it gave smoothly. He bent down.

"Come in, Franco." He'd have recognized the deep voice with the clipped accent anywhere. "Long time no see."

He slipped inside the car and sat upright in the front seat, beside Oleg. He took off his hat. His mouth was sticky and his heart was pounding. His mission here, perhaps even his life, depended on the next few minutes. Twenty years ago Oleg Kalinin had been his lover. Today he could be his enemy. Perhaps he had walked straight into a KGB ambush. He imagined Kalinin raising his hand, or lighting a cigarette, and a swarm of KGB goons emerging from the darkness and dragging him to the Lubyanka cellars.

Grimaldi had dreaded this meeting since the moment he had accepted Macpherson's offer. Time after time he had relived those terrible moments from long ago, the nightmare in the Austrian ravine, when Tony Whitcombe had died and Oleg had disappeared. He had tried desperately to find an excuse for his behavior that day. He wondered what Oleg felt about him after he had abandoned him under fire. Was Oleg still his friend? Or did he hate him for running away? Perhaps Oleg had concocted some devious plan to make him pay for his betrayal, and he wanted him here, in his power. The idea seemed farfetched, but Grimaldi was a skeptical, suspicious man.

But as soon as he closed the car door, Kalinin leaned over and hugged him. "So good to see you, Franco, I am so happy we meet again." He warmly patted Grimaldi's arm. "When did you arrive?"

"Yesterday." He tried to sound natural. "I'm staying at the Ukraina Hotel until I find an apartment. My cover name is Charles Saint-Clair, from Montreal."

"Monsieur Saint-Clair." Kalinin chuckled. "Welcome to Moscow."

In the faint light emanating from the Kursk station's windows, Grimaldi glanced at his friend. Kalinin was still handsome, although he was losing his hair, and deep wrinkles surrounded his eyes. A pale scar ran below his left eye but didn't disfigure his face; on the contrary, it bestowed upon it a kind of roguish charm.

"Your scar . . ." Grimaldi began. He felt awkward.

"Yes." The Russian nodded. "From that day in the Alps."

"I never found out what happened to you," Grimaldi mumbled. "I tried, but you had vanished."

"I got hit in the face and in the ass." Kalinin grinned boyishly. "Remember the ambush? You were behind, I was beside Tony. He got hit first. They were firing at us from behind, so I had no choice but to run forward. I was bleeding, and my wounds hurt like hell. I limped down to the creek. I heard them running after me. Thank God for that stream — they lost me there. I spent the night up a tree. I heard people, and dogs — "

"That was us," Grimaldi said. "We were searching for you."

A man and a woman passed in front of the car, leaning forward against the wind, and Grimaldi slid down in his seat, then straightened up again. Kalinin's voice dropped to a murmur.

"I was too exhausted to call for help; besides, I wasn't sure you weren't the motherfuckers coming back for me." He turned toward Grimaldi. "You know, the funniest thing is that they never penetrated our cover. It wasn't Odessa that ordered us killed."

"What are you talking about?"

"I checked this out. It was a local initiative."

"I don't understand. The killers were not Odessa?"

"They were, but they acted on their own. They belonged to the local Odessa network. They had no idea who we really were — they thought we were genuine Nazi fugitives. We were not their first victims. Their game was knocking off fugitives they presumed to be rich. They killed for the money and valuables, and hid the bodies. Nobody ever lived to complain, and even if somebody survived, he couldn't report them to the authorities."

"But after the attack on us, the Odessa network vanished."

Kalinin shrugged. "Of course. The Odessa bosses heard of the incident, and ordered everybody into hiding until an alternative route was established. By the way" — he lightly touched his scar — "the Odessa people themselves bumped off the guys who attacked us. That was bad publicity for Odessa Travel.

"And your superiors didn't blame you for disobeying orders?"

Another man passed by. "It's crowded here," Grimaldi muttered. "I had a few unpleasant moments. There was a colonel who wanted me court-martialed for insubordination. But I had barely survived, I had been wounded by the Nazis, and my colonel realized he would have trouble explaining why he was court-martialing me. He finally agreed that I had been punished enough." He laughed softly. "And that's enough of that. We haven't seen each other for twenty years, we're starting the riskiest adventure of our lives, and all we care to talk about is that day at the Brenner pass.

"What happened since?" Grimaldi said. "You got married?"

"Married to the GRU and to a fine woman. And father of three beautiful daughters," Kalinin proudly added, then cast a sideways look at Grimaldi. "You haven't, I know."

Grimaldi nodded. They would never be lovers again, he realized. Oleg was married, he liked it, and he wanted him to know it.

A shadow passed over Oleg's face and he slapped his hands on the dashboard. "That's enough small talk for today. We have a lot of ground to cover." He paused. "We must be very careful, Franco, this is a deadly business. Two weeks ago they shot somebody in the Lubyanka, for treason. We don't know yet who he was."

Grimaldi kept silent, and Kalinin glanced at his watch. "Let's start with drops and crash meeting procedures."

"Good," Grimaldi said. He had barely heard Kalinin's warning. He was still thinking about their conversation. They were not lovers anymore, but they were friends, close friends. Everything was going to be all right, he could count on Oleg. He was pervaded by a blissful sensation of relief. It had started snowing, and large flakes fluttered gracefully down, melting on the warm windshield.

"Good," Grimaldi repeated.

Chapter 8

"COMRADES!" the short general pompously declared. "I welcome you to the Higher School of State Security."

The general was sitting behind a table, on a raised podium that overlooked the austere conference room. His thick eyebrows fused into a straight gray line over black beady eyes; a sharp nose hovered over a Cupid's-bow mouth. The general's uniform was neatly pressed, and his chest was covered with four rows of glinting medals hanging from multicolored ribbons. The narrow windows on his right, facing an inner court, cast a morose gray light upon the assembly. On the wall behind the general a color poster of Lenin, haranguing the working masses in a three-piece suit, was paired with a charcoal sketch of Marx and Engels, who stared grimly at the artist.

"You are being entrusted with a great responsibility," the general continued, "to defend the achievements of the October revolution. After you graduate, you will be dispatched to the front, where a bitter battle is being fought against a crafty enemy. The Western intelligence services intend to undermine the foundations of socialism, using the most despicable means. International capitalism is the enemy. In order to overcome this enemy you must know all about him."

"What's his name?" Dimitri whispered to his neighbor, a bulky young

154

man with curly blond hair and hard brown eyes.

"General Lubelski, the school commander." The blond boy chuckled. "They say he never stands up in public — he doesn't want people to see how short he is. That's why they call him the dwarf. He always delivers his lectures sitting on his fat ass."

"Your success," the general was saying, "will depend on how well you master the methods used by an intelligence agent, how well you study the fundamentals of Marxism-Leninism and the mentality of Western nations, and how well you can use your weapons and your hands, which might save your life in a desperate situation."

The small general surveyed his sixty-two students. "Remember," he said, his chin jutting forward, "an officer in State Security is more than a mere party member or a government official. He is a Chekist, meaning that he is a communist first, last, and always. Every act of his daily life must be bound to this premise: he eats, reads, loves, thinks, acts, and sleeps as a Chekist. He must remember, always, that the world is divided into two classes of people: communists and the others."

Dimitri couldn't concentrate, he was still overwhelmed by the new world unfolding before him. He had arrived in Moscow yesterday afternoon, after a twelve-hour journey in a crowded train. He had taken the metro, then walked to the four-story house at 19 Stanislavskaya Street. He had never traveled on an underground train before, never seen such large crowds and such bustling streets. Huge edifices from the Stalin era towered over the city; they were massive conglomerates of concrete from which pointed spires emerged, crowned with red stars.

Shortly after sunset Dimitri reached his destination — a red-brick building facing the drab East German embassy. This was the Visshaya Shkola, the Higher School of State Security, where he was going to live for the next four years.

On presenting his papers to the armed guards at the gate, Dimitri was sent to the school secretariat. A sour-faced officer took him to a medical inspection, then to the quartermaster, who issued him three new uniforms, a new overcoat, new shoes, new shirts, a leather belt, two khaki-colored ties, sneakers, and new underwear. Dimitri couldn't believe they were giving him all this. God, he thought, at Panfilov I could trade these goodies for a year's supply of food, vodka, and cigarettes! The quartermaster also gave him a smart military cap, adorned with a shiny emblem: a red star embossed with the Soviet hammer and sickle on the background of a sword and a shield. Dimitri had never been so excited in his life. He felt a surge of gratitude to General Takachenko, who had helped him get out of Panfilov, and to that handsome colonel, Kalinin, the member of the State Security commission who had stood by him when his loyalty had been questioned. Now here he was, a KGB cadet on his way to the top.

The school administrator, a bald major named Nekrasov, escorted him to his dormitory, where sixteen beds awaited the new students. Beside each bed there was a nightstand, a lamp, and a big locker. "You'll be sixty-two students," the major droned, "divided into four dormitories and two classes. Classes start at nine A.M. and end at ten P.M. The period from five to seven P.M. is set aside for individual studies. Sundays are free for rest and amusement, and only then are you allowed to leave the building. Your salary, during your studies, will be two hundred rubles a month."

Two hundred rubles! Dimitri gaped at him, amazed. He had never seen so much money. Two hundred rubles was a judge's salary. As a mere KGB trainee he was going to earn the same salary as a judge, and make more money than a teacher. At Panfilov the teachers made barely 120 rubles! "Reveille at six-thirty A.M.," the major was declaiming, "at seven, physical exercise in the courtyard, shorts, undershirt, sneakers. Breakfast at eight." He consulted his watch. "You can have dinner now, the mess is still open. That's all."

The major stopped at the door. "By the way, you are our youngest student. All the others are twenty-two or older, and most of them are army officers or university graduates. You're either very bright or you know somebody very high up." His face briefly contorted into a lopsided grin.

"Comrade Major!" He jumped to attention. "I request permission to go out tonight. It's my first night in Moscow. I know this is highly unusual, but I was born here and have been away for more than fifteen years."

To his surprise, the administrator smiled. "No, it's not unusual. Every new student has the same request on his first night in Moscow." He shrugged and nodded. "All right, you can go. Stop at the secretariat on your way out for a written authorization. By the way, you can dress in civilian clothes, that's one of our privileges here." He nodded again and was gone.

Civilian clothes! Nothing in the world could have prevented him from putting on his dashing new uniform. He would have paid dearly to have his schoolmates from Panfilov see him now, a smart young trainee walking the streets of Moscow, the KGB insignia shining on his cap. But what he really wanted — he felt a pang in his chest as the thought struck him — was for his father to see him, for Boris Morozov to know he was alive, that he had overcome all the obstacles and was going to be a KGB officer, like him.

His father's memory haunted him throughout this chilly October evening as he explored Moscow. He thought of his father when he stood in Red Square, staring at the government buildings that rose behind the sturdy Kremlin wall. He could imagine KGB Colonel Boris Morozov arriving on a night like this, entering the supreme center of Soviet power to brief Beria, Kaganovich, perhaps even Stalin! His shiny Zil limousine probably passed through the Spasskaya Gate, alongside the colorful onion domes of St. Basil's, and he'd wearily lift his fingers to his cap as the KGB guards of the compound recognized him and jumped to attention. Then, hours later, Morozov's car would dart out, like the luxurious automobiles Dimitri now saw speeding out of the Kremlin into the Moscow streets, respectfully saluted by KGB guards and militiamen. One day I'll also enter the Kremlin in my black limousine, Dimitri thought.

But the place he had most wanted to visit tonight, even more than Red Square, even more than the Kremlin, was Dzerzhinski Square. The famous Moscow square, named after the ascetic Polish aristocrat who had founded the Cheka, the precursor of the KGB, was where the KGB had established its formidable stronghold and its most notorious prison.

The square was deserted. A timid rain was falling from a cottony sky, and a sharp autumn wind swept the desolate sidewalks. Dimitri stood under the sinister statue of Felix Dzerzhinski — bearded and hollow-eyed, dressed in his black executioner's robes — and eyed the massive bulk of the Lubyanka, which loomed over the north side of the square, exuding an air of brutal menace, like the awesome, evil-looking fortresses of the Dark Ages.

His mother had died there, in one of the execution cellars, but he didn't really care about her. It was his father he thought of, visualizing that terrible moment when several officers — perhaps young like him, perhaps wearing the same uniforms and insignia — had walked into

Boris Morozov's office and ordered him to surrender his revolver and come with them. A humiliating scene would have followed, as his epaulets and medals were stripped from him; the insults, the dark cell, being branded a traitor. And finally the camps, the freezing cold, the hunger, the beatings, and the firing squad.

You who have taken part in killing my father, Dimitri vowed in a surge of black hatred, whoever you are, I'll find you one day and I'll crush you. But I will not act like a fool, I will not go for you in a suicidal outburst that will cost me my head. Revenge is a dish I intend to eat cold. First I'll climb to the top floor of the Lubyanka, I'll become a KGB general, your chief. And as your chief I'll use my power to get your hides.

The merry laughter of children jolted him out of his revery. He looked across the square, where a group of little boys and girls, accompanied by their parents, was screaming in delight, watching the illuminated windows of Detsky Mir — Children's World — the largest toy store in the Soviet Union. What an absurdity, he thought, to erect that toy palace, the symbol of innocence and children's joy, across the street from the torture cellars and execution chambers of the Lubyanka.

He stared for a long time at Dzerzhinski's black statue. Even Khrushchev, who had denounced Stalin's and Beria's crimes, accusing them of murdering scores of thousands of people, couldn't remove Dzerzhinski's statue from this place, and so it remained in the heart of Moscow.

What a strange nation we Russians are, he thought, in our present and our distant past. Hating power and yet admiring it; praising democracy, yet yearning for a strong hand; loathing the secret police but crawling on our bellies before it; speaking out against torture and violation of human rights, and still making torturers and executioners the princes of our society. What other nation would have raised a statue to the man who founded the bloodiest secret service in the world? What other people would have given that man's name to one of their capital's main squares, then turned one of their capital's main buildings into a prison and an execution site?

I will be a Chekist, he ruefully thought on his way back, and certainly one of the most reliable, the most dedicated. But I'll never be a believer. For whatever faith I had, whatever innocence I was born with, I lost it at Panfilov long ago, long before I lost my virginity to Valya, the cook's daughter.

*　*　*

"The sluggards in the artillery!" the burly drill sergeant roared, and sixty-two voices yelled back, their running steps marking the measure:

"Braggards in the cavalry . . .

"Drunkards in the fleet . . .

"Idiots in the infantry!"

The sergeant bellowed again: "And who are we?"

They yelled in unison: "All the smart ones — KGB! KGB! KGB!"

They had already been running for fifteen minutes in the inner court of the school, their weary feet pounding on the uneven flagstones. It was a freezing morning in February, but Dimitri felt good; he enjoyed the early morning exercises. His training at Panfilov was bearing fruit; he was in excellent shape, not like some of his classmates, who were panting, flushed and bleary-eyed, on either side.

The drill sergeant, a huge, bald Latvian, raised his voice again. He is more interested in having us yell his stupid slogans, Dimitri thought, than in having us do our exercises. This time the sergeant chose a joke on the initials of the OGPU, one of the secret services that had preceded the KGB.

"O Gospodi pomogi ubezhat!" the Latvian shouted, quoting the popular interpretation of the OGPU initials: O God, help me escape!

Dimitri and the other students shouted the answer, which was based on the reversal of the initials: "Ubezhish, poymayem, golovu otorvem!" If you escape, we'll catch you and cut off your head.

The drill sergeant brayed in laughter. Very funny indeed, Dimitri thought.

Still, he enjoyed the physical training as much as the intensive studies. Early this morning, after a sleepless night in the library, he had completed an essay on the history of the Soviet secret services. It was a fascinating story, which reminded him of a medieval succession war between fierce warlords, each coveting the throne, every new chief murdering his predecessor. The cycle started with Felix Dzerzhinski founding the Cheka — the All-Russian Extraordinary Commission for Combatting Counterrevolution and Sabotage — in December 1917. It continued with the Red Terror, the necessary liquidation of thousands of dissidents, ordered by Lenin in September 1918.

Dimitri liked the romantic aura of the Cheka. It soon metamorphosed into the OGPU, which pursued Lenin's war by unmasking and annihilating the surviving enemies of the revolution: the Whites, the aristocrats, the rich kulaks, the treacherous foreign agents. The OGPU was replaced by the NKVD, an excellent organization that unfortunately became Stalin's instrument for the purges of the thirties, in which countless innocent communists perished. In 1936 NKVD chief Heinrich Yagoda was shot on Stalin's orders, to be replaced by Stalin's bloodthirsty hangman, Nikolai Yezhov, whose murderous streak earned him the nickname "the bloody dwarf." Soon, Dimitri noted, Yezhov met the same fate as Yagoda: he was shot in the same Lubyanka cellar where he had executed his predecessor.

These were the dark years, Dimitri wrote, when Stalin used the Soviet security services for his criminal enterprises. In 1938 Stalin's henchman Beria arrived on the scene, taking over the organization, already known as the NKGB. Beria incorporated it into the Ministry of Internal Affairs, the MVD. Beria was the man who had ordered Boris Morozov's arrest, but he didn't live to see him killed. In 1953, soon after Stalin's death, it was Beria's turn to follow Yagoda and Yezhov into the execution chamber. At the end of Beria's rule, the new KGB was born. It was detached from the MVD and became its sworn enemy.

"With the creation of the KGB, a circle was closed," Dimitri wrote in conclusion, "the KGB acquiring the same political status and powers as the revolutionary Cheka. That was how the Cheka rose from its ashes." This year, shortly before Dimitri arrived in Moscow, a new chairman had taken over the KGB command: a scholarly looking man with sallow skin, graying blond hair, and pale eyes magnified by steel-rimmed glasses: Yuri Andropov.

Besides mastering KGB history, Dimitri penetrated into the organization's convoluted internal structure. The KGB chairman, he learned, was under the direct orders of the Politburo. The KGB headquarters, entrenched in the Dzerzhinski Square compound, were a cluster of separate branches: four chief directorates, seven independent directorates, and six departments. Those, in turn, were subdivided into an intricate web of directorates, departments, directions, and services.

Most of the KGB power was concentrated in three chief directorates and one directorate. These were the First (KGB operations abroad), the Second (counterintelligence and surveillance of Soviet citizens), the Fifth (struggle against dissidence), and the Armed Forces Directorate, which was responsible for the loyalty of all Soviet officers, from Red Army headquarters down to the company level.

Dimitri was amazed at the incredible scope of the KGB's powers. Its branches, he discovered, dealt with numerous activities, from espionage, subversion, and assassination abroad, to surveillance of foreign tourists, students, and businessmen; from planting spies in the West, and sexually blackmailing foreign dignitaries, to controlling the East European satellites, operating against China, watching Soviet leaders, and sending KGB special troops to fight border wars. KGB guards managed labor camps beyond the Arctic Circle and protected the Kremlin. KGB operatives granted travel visas, manned the telephone and radio systems, and carried out necessary disinformation campaigns. KGB sleuths shadowed potential enemies: dissidents, priests, Jews, ethnic minorities, emigré organizations, foreign right-wing movements. KGB officers investigated economic crimes and protected industrial secrets; KGB scientists manufactured deadly, untraceable poisons.

Dimitri was amazed by the incredible number of people employed in the gigantic machine of the KGB: 90,000 staff officers in the Soviet Union and around the world; another 400,000 special troops, border guards, clerks, and employees; and hundreds of thousands of informants and agents, most of them on the government payroll.

The KGB, Dimitri realized, had grown into a secret world, an invisible web that covered the entire Soviet Union and reached to the most remote corners of the globe. From the Lubyanka headquarters, known as Moscow Center, the KGB could reach to every village in the Soviet Union, to foreign capitals, army headquarters, and scientific installations. For their own security, Soviet citizens were watched, surveyed, vetted, and appraised; other nations couldn't imagine the range of the secret army that was protecting the Soviet Union while striving to penetrate its enemies' secrets.

Inside the Soviet Union the KGB had become a parallel nation, a closed caste that lived off the fat of the land. "Take Moscow, for example," Misha Ponomarev said to Dimitri one evening when they were alone in the library. "You think you know Moscow?"

Ponomarev, tall and clumsy, narrow-faced and round-eyed, was a twenty-seven-year-old White Russian whose parents had been hanged by the Germans in Borisov. He had been raised in orphanages and youth institutions, and had grown fond of Dimitri, perhaps because of their similar backgrounds. A fourth-year student, he expected to graduate in May. In his last year at the Visshaya Shkola, he was assistant lecturer on the structure and organization of the KGB.

"There are two cities in Moscow," he said eagerly; Misha was the happiest KGB student Dimitri had ever met. "One is the city that every tourist discovers: Red Square, St. Basil's, Novodevichny Monastery, Gorky Park, the Bolshoi, the Economic Achievements Exhibition.

"And there is the second city, our city."

Dimitri raised his eyebrows.

"The secret city of government and KGB," Misha triumphantly announced. He paused, apparently waiting for his words to sink in. "Imagine a street map of Moscow," he said, his long hands floating in the air, drawing an imaginary circle. "No, wait."

He disappeared between the book racks and was back a moment later, eagerly unfolding a large map before Dimitri. "Let's take the portion delimited by the Garden ring, and start with the Kremlin." His bony finger landed at Red Square. "A few hundred meters from the Kremlin you have the KGB official and secret compounds: Moscow Center at Dzerzhinsky Square, our offices at Dzerzhinsky Street, Malaya Lubyanka Street, Kuznetsky Most, see? Take Gorky Street and go by the special KGB living quarters at Mozhayskoye Road, First Meshchanskaya Street, the Arbat." Ponomarev's hands were dancing, shaping concentric circles on the map. "All this is within the Garden ring, see? Oh yes, and behind the Bolshoi conservatory we have the MVD headquarters."

Dimitri nodded. The MVD was in charge of the militia and the Special Interior troops.

"Farther down," — Ponomarev's enthusiasm soared to new heights — "at Kaluzhskoye Chaussee, we have a special unit of the KGB guard protecting the Academy of Sciences; and at Pokrovsky Boulevard, the compounds of two MVD and KGB divisions, kept in constant readiness."

Ponomarev shot a contented look at Dimitri, like a magician who had just pulled a string of colorful kerchiefs out of his wand. "We control the city, see? And I didn't mention the KGB club, nor the clusters of buildings — like Kutuzovsky Prospect — where the Politburo members, the Kremlin top brass, and our own chiefs live."

"Where does Andropov live?" Dimitri asked.

"Kutuzovsky Prospect, the same building where Brezhnev has his apartment." Misha briefly paused. "I didn't mention our secret safehouses, like . . . here, on 62 Novokuznetzkaya Street, 32 Bolotnaya, 11 Sirotzky, 17 Taganskaya, and the villa on Zubovskaya Square. . . ." His finger punched the map at different points. "Now, beside all this, we have scores of operational flats in town; we have our own farms outside the city, where we grow our food; our own slaughterhouses, for our meat; our own doctors, cooks, electricians, and handymen."

"Our own, you say?"

"Let me show you something." Misha chuckled. "Take your coat and let's go."

"Where?" Dimitri asked.

"You'll see."

Half an hour later they were seated at the elegant KGB restaurant, on the eighth floor of the Lubyanka, where Misha, because of his position, had the right to entertain visitors. It was the first time Dimitri had visited Moscow Center, and he was so awed, he barely dared to breathe. His heart thumped wildly when he showed his credentials to the KGB guards at the entrance and cast a quick look at the hammer and sickle emblems engraved upon the massive gates. In the elevator he stood silent, imagining the coups being concocted at this very moment in locked rooms, barely a few yards away.

At the restaurant he stared, wide-eyed, at the officers and civilians who moved about. He was sure some of them were daredevil secret agents, back from dangerous assignments abroad.

"Aren't you eating?" Misha said.

He ordered salted salmon, real sour cream, and the delicacy he craved most — chocolate. The waitress brought him a bar of real Swiss chocolate, not one of the cheap substitutes sold in Moscow's stores.

"As you can see," Misha was blabbering, "we have our own restaurants, our own stores, and our own schools."

"The ordinary citizens don't know about this?" Dimitri asked.

"Most of them know, but they wouldn't dare talk about it," Ponomarev chortled. He was marked with the cynicism and the obsession for food of the orphan child. He made a sweeping gesture around him, as if he owned the place. "Here you can get a royal breakfast for almost nothing. They serve you milk, eggs, bacon, sausages, and fresh fruit. At the KGB club across the square, we've got a gym, a sauna, a swimming pool, a restaurant, and a delicatessen. You can buy everything there — caviar, sturgeon, smoked salmon, apples and oranges. A bottle of scotch whiskey costs you less than in America — the equivalent of one dollar! That, brother, is what I call living!"

Misha loaded two thick slices of pink salmon on his buttered toast and bent forward. "But there is something much more exciting than food or drink in the KGB. Have you ever heard of Department Thirteen?" He cast a wary glance about him and lowered his voice. "Let me tell you about it."

COLONEL IGOR GUZENKO, tall, cool, looking very English with his trim reddish mustache and steely blue eyes, cleared his throat and surveyed the class. "Today we'll deal with the First Chief Directorate," he said, and pointed with his stick at a chart he had pinned on the blackboard. A storm was raging outside, and gusts of wind moaned through the cracked window frames, billowing Guzenko's chart like a ship's sail.

"The First," Guzenko announced, "is the KGB branch charged with clandestine activities abroad. As you can see" — his stick pointed at the middle of the chart — "it is subdivided into three subdirectorates, three services, and twelve departments."

Dimitri frowned. There was another department he knew about, but it didn't figure on the diagram.

"We'll start," Guzenko was saying, "with the Illegals Directorate. It infiltrates KGB agents into foreign countries, where they operate under false identities. Each agent is trained individually, for security reasons."

Dimitri listened as Guzenko proceeded to describe concisely the information and counterintelligence services, the ten geographic departments, the disinformation department, and, finally, the cover organs department.

"Cover Organs," the colonel pointed out, "places KGB personnel in cover jobs abroad with other government agencies, like Tass, Aeroflot, Sovtorg, Intourist, Sovfilm, and various newspapers. We also use foreign organizations, like the World Bank, the United Nations, the Red Cross, and international sports associations."

Guzenko surveyed his audience and laid down his stick. "And that, comrades, wraps up the First Chief Directorate," he contentedly said, puffing on his pipe. "Any questions?"

Dimitri stood up. "What about Department Thirteen?"

Guzenko stiffened. "What? What was your question?"

"Department Thirteen," Dimitri repeated, "Executive Action."

Guzenko stared at him sharply. "What is your name, student?"

"Dimitri Morozov, Comrade Colonel."

"Dimitri Morozov," Guzenko repeated. "There is no Department Thirteen in the First Chief Directorate. You may sit down."

"It is also known as Department V, Comrade Colonel," Dimitri insisted, then reluctantly released the last item of information he possessed: "It's nicknamed Mokrie Dela." Wet Affairs.

"I told you," Guzenko said tersely, anger exploding in his eyes, "there is no such department. Now sit down!"

Dimitri complied, feeling the stares of his classmates converging upon him. His cheeks were flushed. Fuck your mother, Guzenko, he thought, you lying carcass. There is no such department, hell! The Thirteenth is the most important department in the entire KGB!

He was morosely torturing his steak at dinner, his mind still on the afternoon's incident, when Major Nekrasov, the school administrator, appeared beside him. "General Lubelski wants to see you," he said, "right away."

The dwarfish school commander was sitting behind his desk in his austere office. He was going through a file, pursing his lips; he raised his eyes with a frown when Dimitri entered and saluted. "Student Morozov reporting, Comrade General."

Lubelski seemed angry, very angry. The deep frown made the straight line of his eyebrows plunge downward, bestowing a malevolent expression upon his broad face. He didn't waste time with niceties. "Who told you about Department Thirteen?"

Dimitri swallowed. "I heard about it from friends."

"Who? What are their names?"

Dimitri didn't answer.

"I want to know," Lubelski repeated. "How did you hear about Department Thirteen?"

I can't tell him it was Ponomarev, Dimitri thought. They'll kick him out, a few weeks before his graduation. "You know the school grapevine, Comrade General. We hear all kinds of rumors."

Lubelski picked up a sheet of paper covered with handwriting. "And all you said today — Mokrie Dela, Department V, Thirteen — was rumor? What other rumors did you hear, student Morozov?"

He didn't reply. The damned dwarf is going to kick me out, he thought in panic.

Lubelski was seething with barely contained anger. "I want you to know, Morozov, that behaving as you did today is an adequate reason for expulsion from our school." He scowled at Dimitri, his jaws clamped, until Dimitri lowered his eyes. "However, I found in your file that you were recommended by General Takachenko."

A sensation of relief slowly descended upon Dimitri. He tried not to show it, penitently holding his head down. "I spoke to General Takachenko, who assured me that I shall have no more reason to complain until the completion of your studies. Understood?"

"Yes, Comrade General."

"Good." The general angrily closed the file, and it dawned upon Dimitri that Lubelski wasn't as angry at him as he was frustrated for having to bend to Takachenko.

"Morozov!" Lubelski's voice caught him at the door, still irritated, but now tinted with a shade of curiosity. "Why this interest in Department Thirteen?"

"That's where I would like to serve, Comrade General." Dimitri saluted and left the office.

He wasn't interested in internal surveillance, in persecuting terrified Soviet citizens or harassing long-haired intellectuals and big-mouthed dissidents. He wanted to take part in dangerous operations in foreign capitals, cross swords with the aces of the British MI-5 and the American CIA, travel to exotic countries, conquer mysterious women.

Still, Dimitri didn't dream of becoming a Soviet spy abroad, nor even a *rezident* — commander of a KGB station in a foreign capital. He wanted something more challenging, something he could do by himself. He was a loner, and his childhood had taught him not to trust anybody. He remembered the sensation of power that had swept through him the night he'd killed Kuzma Bunin. He recalled Vanya's fear and respect. He felt he could kill again, but this time he wanted to win a medal for it. He had set his sights on the ultrasecret Thirteen — nicknamed "Wet Affairs" for the bloody trail its agents left behind them — because of the meteoric rise of its officers in the KGB hierarchy once they came back from field duty.

Thirteen, whose very existence was so vigorously denied, was in charge of violent operations abroad — kidnappings, sabotage, assaults on enemy safehouses. And murder.

Student Morozov wanted to become a killer.

*   *   *

BUT BEFORE THAT, he had to learn how to be a secret agent.

Two slant-eyed Tartars, officers of the Soviet commandos, instructed the students in hand-to-hand combat and in the use of small firearms. Sergei Grozny, an elderly civilian with a disfigured face and a glass eye, taught Dimitri and his classmates to use plastic and conventional explosives, build a bomb, and concoct incendiary devices from components they could buy at any pharmacy. The students joked that one of Grozny's homemade bombs had apparently blown his eye away. But Misha Ponomarev told Dimitri another story about Grozny.

"He was teaching a class in this very building," Misha said, "when news came that Stalin was dead. Grozny started crying; but his tears streamed only from one eye, as the other one was made of glass. Two students in the first row burst out laughing. Their timing was bad. They were never seen again."

The legendary colonel Rudolf Abel, who had spent many years as an illegal in New York and had been exchanged for the U-2 pilot Gary Powers, taught the trainees the basic rules of operating in an American city. Abel looked like a broken man. After his lecture, Dimitri saw the gaunt colonel sitting all alone at the officers' mess; but nobody approached him. "Since his return from America," Misha revealed, "Abel is not fully trusted anymore."

A comely employee of Communications, Vera Shevchenko, trained them to code, cypher, and transmit with miniaturized devices. "Many messages to our agents abroad," she disclosed, "are conveyed by means of Radio Moscow musical programs."

"You mean that you tell Radio Moscow what music to broadcast?" Dimitri asked.

She nodded. A British agent who had, unfortunately, been captured — she gravely explained — used to receive his orders by a code based on four popular tunes: "Kalinka," "The Nutcracker," "The Saber Dance," and "Swan Lake." Shevchenko also instructed the students to manufacture invisible inks and reduce photographed documents to the size of microdots.

Other retired KGB officers taught the rules of running field agents, servicing dead-letter drops, street shadowing, and dodging surveillance. The students practiced the acquired techniques in full-day exercises in the streets of Moscow.

The most sensational lecture was delivered by Kim Philby, the KGB spy who almost became chief of British intelligence before escaping to

Moscow. Dimitri drank Philby in with his eyes. He saw an aging, handsome man, with graying blond hair and a mischievous twinkle in his eyes. In spite of his swollen beer gut and his baggy suit, he still looked distinguished. Or perhaps Dimitri felt so because of Philby's irreverent style, which survived even the translation from English into Russian, performed by a fat civilian with a stony face.

Strangely enough, Philby used his lecture to launch a violent diatribe against the clumsiness and shortcomings of KGB foreign operations. He accused the KGB agents abroad of always repeating the same outmoded procedures. He criticized the political interference in analysis and evaluation. "Many brilliant researchers," he said, "write the wrong assessments of a situation not because they believe it, but to please their superiors."

Moscow Center, Philby said, was being defeated by Soviet bureaucracy. Instead of an aggressive, sophisticated organization, the KGB had become "a huge dinosaur" whose efficiency was in decline. "Soviet agents," Philby warned, "are easily recognized by their ill-fitting suits, their heavy accents, their archaic methods, their lack of imagination. If the KGB doesn't change soon, it will be routed by the Western services."

Philby's words were received with uneasy laughter and confused stares. Dimitri was surprised that Philby had been allowed to deliver such a lecture. He was impressed by the courage of the Englishman, who had dared to revolt against the KGB routine; Dimitri believed every word he said. One day, he thought, I'll remodel the First the way Philby suggests.

"A SOVIET INTELLIGENCE OFFICER must be *kulturny*," Colonel Helena Kraiova announced as she started her first lecture. Dimitri remembered her from Panfilov, where she had come to interview him with the KGB commission. She was deputy director of the school, and theoretical studies were her domain. She made the students devote two hours daily to the study of English or French. She invited to the school former *rezidents* in Western capitals, and they described the structure and modus operandi of foreign services, like the SIS, the CIA, the Mossad, and the French SDECE.

But that was not what Kraiova meant by the word "*kulturny.*" Her ambition was to instill in her pupils fine Western manners, for the good of the cause, of course. She taught the students etiquette, table manners, proper social behavior. Once a week she brought in a busload of young ballet dancers from the Bolshoi to teach the students dancing. Only years later was Dimitri to realize that while he had perhaps become *kulturny,* he hadn't really learned to dance. In the *kultura* lessons, he learned mostly mazurkas, Viennese waltzes, boleros, and schottisches, which were not exactly the hottest items in the discos of the swinging West.

One evening in May he cornered his dancing partner, an elfin girl with flaxen hair and very white skin. Her name was Ludmila and she reminded him of the dancer on Zoya's poster, back in Panfilov. "Can I see you on Sunday?" he asked.

"Why?" She stared at him with her enormous blue eyes.

"I think you're very cute," he said. She didn't respond, so he added: "I can bring some good food if you like — Hungarian salami, and caviar, some salmon. We can have a picnic at Sokolniki."

"Could you also get us a jar of French marmalade?" she asked in a little girl's voice.

"Sure." He wondered if she was a virgin, she looked so young.

On Sunday they had their picnic in Sokolniki Park. Ludmila was very sassy, gaily chattering about the Bolshoi, her girlfriends, the two sisters that she had left behind in Smolensk. They ate the food and drank a bottle of sparkling Georgian wine. He kissed her rosy mouth, and she returned his kiss with unexpected fire. Then she deftly packed the leftovers, gravely inspecting the volume of French marmalade left in the jar. She got up, brushing the crumbs from her skirt. "Let's go," her eyes said.

Ludmila behaved as if everything had been agreed between them beforehand. She led him to her room in the apartment she shared with three other girls. The moment she closed the door behind her, he kissed her again, and she responded at once, rubbing herself against his hardness, offering her breasts to his kisses. He didn't wonder about her virginity anymore.

Ludmila undressed quickly and lay naked on her bed, waiting for him. She had small breasts with bulging pink nipples, and a flat stomach culminating in a mound of thick, dark blond hair. That excited him. As he crawled into bed, she pulled him inside her, letting out short, contented screams. She made love eagerly, yet Dimitri felt there was something mechanical in her behavior, as if sex was the obvious dessert after their picnic lunch.

He returned to Stanislavskaya Street strangely dissatisfied. He knew he wasn't bad-looking, and there were women who found him attractive; he had seen some inviting looks in the streets of Moscow. Still, he had the feeling that he had bought an afternoon of sex for a jar of French marmalade.

The same sensation kept returning, time after time, during the following months. After Ludmila, there were other ballet dancers, or girls from the foreign language classes who took the English course with the students. They lit up at the prospect of a good meal, fancy foreign food, a tin of coffee, even a bottle of expensive vodka they could exchange for a bar of soap. "When you graduate, it will become much easier, brother," Misha knowingly whispered. He had graduated three days before. "Very few girls refuse to date a KGB officer. We get the choicest pieces, see?"

How could he tell him, Dimitri wondered, that it was not only sex he was after? That sometimes he felt a sea of love boil and churn inside him, but he had nobody to share it with? His loneliness was suffocating him. He had never experienced motherly love, and the dreams he'd had about his mother as a child had been shattered by Takachenko's revelations. He hadn't experienced brotherly love, either; his half brother had vanished, somewhere in America. He would have paid dearly to meet him, but he didn't even know how to get in touch with him. Anyway, Dimitri doubted if they had anything in common. How could love still exist between them?

He had never been loved by a woman. The women who had slept with him had done so out of routine or for a present; it was sheer whoring, even if disguised. He had never experienced true love.

He longed for a woman who would love him, make him feel the burning passion and total devotion he had read about in books. Sometimes he couldn't sleep, imagining how wonderful life could be if he had just one person, his girl, beside him, to share with him everything he achieved. But he always reached the same black conclusion, dictated by his morbid streak: he was condemned to live and die alone, and never experience real love.

He knew he could discuss his painful yearning with nobody, not even Misha. His friend would merely wink and announce: "I know the medicine for your trouble, brother. I'll get you a pair of silk stockings, and for that price you can screw Miss Komsomol herself, see?"

AT THE BEGINNING of his second winter in Moscow, four days before the Revolution Day parade, he was summoned to Lubelski's office. Only a week before, Dimitri had become a member of the Communist party, and Lubelski had firmly shaken his hand at the end of the short ceremony. This morning the dwarf was seated behind his desk, buried in his files. He was smoking a fat Cuban cigar. "Morozov," he said. He didn't look angry. "You have an hour to pack your belongings. You're leaving us."

Dimitri missed a heartbeat. What had happened? He hadn't done anything wrong. His marks were good, he was one of the best students in his class, and an excellent shot as well. "May I ask where I'm going, Comrade General?"

"You may," Lubelski said. "Remember our conversation, a few months ago?"

"Yes, Comrade General." He recalled the general's fury after he had mentioned Department Thirteen in class.

"You are transferred to the Foreign Intelligence School," the dwarf said, spewing gray smoke, "the private school of the First Chief Directorate. That's where we train our officers for operational assignments abroad."

It took Dimitri a moment to digest the general's words. An operational assignment abroad. God, this could be a first step toward Department Thirteen! He was transported, but didn't let it show. "Yes, Comrade General."

Lubelski spoke out of a cloud of smoke. "I think you'll like the place. It's three years of hard work, but it's worthwhile. Not everybody makes it, Morozov, remember this."

He saluted. "Thank you, Comrade General."

He packed hastily and ran down the stairs; he even didn't have time to break the news to Misha. A car was waiting for him outside, a battered Zhiguli, but a car all the same. The driver was a Red Army soldier. He didn't speak to Dimitri. It was already snowing, the first snow of the year. The tiny snowflakes melted as they landed on the sidewalks. The car drove past Red Square, and Dimitri glimpsed the grandstands rising along the Kremlin wall. Hundreds of people had worked around the clock for the last three weeks to have the stands ready for the Revolution Day parade. The streets adjoining Red Square had been freshly tarred, with yellow lines and arrows indicating the parade itinerary.

The car left Moscow by the Volokolamskoye Highway. About a kilometer after passing by the monument to the Defense of Moscow, it took a narrow road that plunged into the forest. The snow had turned into rain, and the drops tapped on the car's roof. They entered a village.

"What is this place?" Dimitri asked.

"Yurlovo," the driver said, revealing two steel front teeth. His breath carried an odor of onions. The Zhiguli passed through the village, scaring a flock of meager chickens. A turkey ballooned in anger and ran after the car, clucking menacingly. They drove through an open field, then entered the forest again. On the left side of the road, they came to a yellow masonry wall, about eight feet high, topped with broken glass and barbed wire. The car stopped at a gate in the wall, where two soldiers stood guard, armed with rifles.

"This is the place," the driver said, and Dimitri got out, dragging his knapsack. Two civilians huddled in windbreakers emerged from a booth whose windows were thick with condensation. Over their coats they wore leather belts with Makarov automatics in holsters.

"Papers," the smaller one said. Dimitri gave him his documents. The other civilian went to the booth, apparently to use the telephone. He was back in a minute. "You can go in," he said. "Across the parade ground, second door to your right — there's a sign saying 'Secretariat.' Welcome to Yurlovo." He stood by the gate, glowering suspiciously at Dimitri, his breath escaping from his mouth in short white puffs.

COLONEL YAKOVLEV was a heavy man in his late forties with a red beefy neck, wrestler's arms and feet, and a bulging belly. But the oblong eyes peering through layers of fat were keen and alert. The small mouth beneath the meaty nose smiled often.

"I'll be your personal tutor, Morozov. Your father, your confessor, and your most ferocious critic." They were walking around the compound, so that Yakovlev could show Dimitri the main facilities. "You may make friends in your class, but no serious friendships. No disclosure of personal information. You may visit the village in pairs, but no partying or dinners together. There will be a bus leaving for Moscow every Saturday night and Sunday morning, back from Sverdlov Square every Sunday night."

"How should I dress in Moscow?"

"No uniforms outside the school buildings. You'll be issued civilian clothes. For all practical purposes, you're a student of international relations, Moscow University, class of Professor Rudin. I'll give you a telephone number in case of emergency. You'll have to memorize it."

Dimitri nodded. A flock of geese flew low over their heads.

"In the school, we have 122 students, divided into five sections. In yours there are only fifteen students. You're not supposed to tell anybody what you're doing or what subjects you're studying."

Dimitri raised his head. It had started snowing again, large, soft snowflakes falling from a bleak sky.

Two civilians armed with Makarovs crossed their path. They held German shepherds on long leashes. Yakovlev followed them with his eyes. "They patrol the grounds twenty-four hours a day. In addition, the place is riddled with infrared sensors, triggered by body heat."

They came in view of the main cluster of buildings. "On the right," Yakovlev pointed at a three-story concrete house, "we have the class-rooms, two separate libraries — for classified and unclassified material — laboratories, mess, and offices."

"The dorms?" Dimitri asked.

"No dorms. Our students live in rooms, three men in a room." A room. For the first time in my life, Dimitri thought, I'll live in a real room, not in a human stable.

Yakovlev pointed at a new building across the yard. "Gymnasium and heated swimming pool. Firing range in the basement." He stopped by the door, tidying up his uniform with an air of finality. "Your status as of today is junior lieutenant. There is going to be a small raise in your salary. That's all, I believe." He paused. "I think you'll enjoy tomorrow's lecture, Morozov."

Dimitri looked at him searchingly. "Why, Comrade Colonel?"

"I read your file," Yakovlev said.

"IF HITLER had been assassinated in 1939, there would have been no world war," said the gaunt civilian, who had introduced himself by the pseudonym Oktober. "Remember that. Execution of criminal elements can be, at times, not only forgivable, but vital for the protection of society and the survival of democracy."

Dimitri sensed that the man believed every word he said. He had an ascetic, tormented face; sad, intense eyes; hollow cheeks; an aquiline nose; and two grim furrows plowing the skin all the way down to the sharp jawline, framing a large, bitter mouth. His white hair was long, drawn back and spilling over the black collar of his turtleneck shirt. A strange fire illuminated his face from within, bestowing upon it a sort of sinister magnetism. It made Dimitri think of a religious martyr about to be burned at the stake; or perhaps the very opposite, a Spanish inquisitor, his face exuding pain and compassion, but also the willingness to inflict horrible suffering in the name of Christ. Torturers during the great purges must have been people like this, he thought.

"You know him?" Dimitri whispered to his neighbor, a lanky Byelorussian named Tabenkin.

"I was told he is General Sudoplatov, who was deputy chief of Department V until 'fifty-three," Tabenkin whispered back.

Dimitri had heard the name. "It can't be. Sudoplatov was shot, shortly after Beria."

Oktober was looking at him. "As students training for executive action, you'll discuss and analyze operations performed by Chekists in the line of duty. But these discussions shouldn't turn into an academic seminar." Oktober wanly smiled. "Therefore, I'll start by telling you how I killed the Ukrainian reactionary Konovalenko in Rotterdam, in 1938."

So, with the concise description of a rigged box of Swiss chocolates that had blown Konovalenko to bits, Oktober began his lectures on the bloody story of Department Thirteen.

Dimitri followed these chronicles of violence with bated breath: the liquidation of scores of White emigrés in Paris, Hamburg, New York, and Macao in the thirties; the establishment, in 1936, of the Wet Affairs department, whose men murdered Leon Trotsky in Mexico; the transformation of Wet Affairs into the Spetzburo, which assassinated notorious emigrés in Germany and Austria.

After Beria's death the Spetzburo changed names again, becoming Department Thirteen. Its most efficient killer was a twenty-five-year-old Ukrainian, Bogdan Stashinsky. He had been recruited at the age of nineteen, Oktober said. Dimitri had the impression that Oktober was looking insistently at him as he spoke of Stashinsky's age.

In the late fifties, Oktober continued, Stashinsky killed two Ukrainian emigrés in Munich, Lev Rebet and Stefan Bandera. In both cases the assassin used a hellish device: an electric pistol loaded with poison bullets — ampules of prussic acid that blew up on contact with the victim's face.

At his next lecture, Oktober displayed the electric pistols. For a couple of hours they practiced loading and unloading the weapons. Oktober then led them to a clearing in the forest where fifteen dogs had been leashed to trees. Two KGB guards stood beside the dogs, but Oktober dismissed them with a nod. He opened a combination-locked attaché case and handed each student a gun, an ampule of prussic acid, and an ampule containing antidotes. No explanation was needed.

"Who is going to be first?" Oktober asked, his dark eyes surveying the young men.

Dimitri stepped forward and approached one of the dogs. The animal, a friendly Great Dane, playfully waggled his tail. Dimitri bent toward it and fired. There was no discharge, just a soft click. The big dog staggered, kicking awkwardly, then fell and died in frenzied convulsions. Dimitri inhaled the antidote from a second ampule, lit a Prima and sat on a log to wait for the others.

The other students followed, killing their dogs in silence. Oktober wants us to get the feel, Dimitri thought, to see how efficient this is, and how easy. When Tabenkin's turn came, he stood still, as if nailed to his place. His face was deathly pale and his eyes acquired a dull glint. He suddenly swayed and threw up. Dimitri yanked the gun from his hand and shot his dog, a German shepherd with a mangy hide. When he turned back, he caught Oktober watching him thoughtfully.

Tabenkin was expelled from school that day. Only fourteen remained in the class.

A week later Oktober took the untouchables — the name they adopted after watching the American series on the school television — to an isolated villa in Vnukovo known as the Kamara, the KGB institute for developing untraceable poisons. Oktober led them through a succession of laboratories where silent researchers in white smocks subjected guinea pigs to various experiments. "Their substances must satisfy two requirements," Oktober said. "First, they must kill, quickly and efficiently. Second, the target's death must appear the result of natural causes." One of the students stumbled and leaned on a table laden with vials. Oktober sharply turned back. "Don't touch anything!" he snapped. "You may die in a matter of hours." The students exchanged stares, wondering if they were supposed to laugh.

The visit to the poison chamber concluded the training of the untouchables in the use of exotic devices. The next lesson in Oktober's course was purely physical: the use of one's bare hands as a weapon. Sanakoyev, an old, heavily built Chekist with huge arms, described to the class the assassination of the defector Agabekov in Bucharest. When he narrated in detail the killing of Agabekov, Dimitri raised his hand.

"How do you know all these details?" he asked. "Agabekov and his killer were alone that day."

"I was the killer," Sanakoyev said.

WINTER was drawing to its close when Dimitri was summoned to Colonel Yakovlev. "Have you had any practice in surveillance?" Yakovlev asked pleasantly.

Dimitri shrugged. "The routine Visshaya Shkola exercises."

"Tomorrow we'll have a full-day exercise in Moscow. All the students will participate. Each will be given the name of a foreign resident in Moscow, picked at random. You'll have to follow him all day and report every detail of his movements. We start at six, so you'd better get to bed early."

It was a bleak dawn, with smoky fog rising from the frozen Moskva River and stealthily invading the neighboring streets. The streetlamps were smoldering globes of yellow light. The first cars out drove cautiously along the snow-lined streets, sometimes skidding on the ice that had formed during the night.

An old Zis sedan slid on the slippery road and nearly missed Dimitri as he crossed the Leningradski Prospect; he tripped and almost fell, then regained his balance and unsteadily covered the last few meters before the entrance to number 74. He had chosen that dark porch of a nineteenth-century town house as an observation post. His target was number 78, an apartment building mostly occupied by foreigners. The man he was supposed to follow was a Canadian businessman, Charles Saint-Clair. He had been assigned to somebody else, actually — an Italian visiting professor of Renaissance art — but one of the untouchables, Youri Savonov, fell sick toward midnight, developing a high fever. In the ensuing reshuffle, his assignment was transferred to Dimitri.

Dimitri was disappointed. He was fascinated by Italians, and it would have been a pleasure shadowing an art professor on a cosy promenade through Moscow's museums. But he found himself stuck with the Canadian, an importer of fish and caviar. He represented a Montreal company called the Delices du Nord, whose offices were on Gorky Street. The photographs in the file showed a dapper man in his fifties, with wavy brown hair which Dimitri suspected was dyed. His face was well-groomed, with a dandyish mustache and bright eyes. The photostat of his Canadian passport said the eyes of Monsieur Saint-Clair were green.

Saint-Clair's file had been established by the seventh department of the Second Chief Directorate. The seventh watched foreign residents. Its report also said that Charles Saint-Clair was a bachelor with expensive tastes. He liked stylish clothes, jewelry, and wore heavy gold rings. Saint-Clair spent a fortune at the Moscow foreign currency restaurants. He was also a ballet lover who went to the Bolshoi at least every other week.

Dimitri raised the collar of the heavy brown coat he had been issued. The sky over the Lenin Hills glowed with a faint orange hue, and the street was awakening. He could make out the huge sign fixed on top of the building across the street: LENIN LIVED, LIVES, AND WILL LIVE FOR-EVER. The spire of Moscow University emerged from the fog, the glint of its red star dulled by the frost. More cars passed, and people began emerging from the buildings. A couple of babushkas huddled in thick clothes were sweeping the sidewalks, calling at each other across the street.

A militiaman suddenly emerged beside him. He was young, with fair skin and red cheeks. "Waiting for somebody, comrade?"

Dimitri proudly flashed the red KGB card he had gotten last night. The young officer sullenly glanced at it and was gone. The militia didn't like the KGB. KGB officers were better paid, better dressed, better lodged and fed, and had much more clout.

At 7:45 Saint-Clair came out of the house and walked to a chauffeur-driven Mercedes with foreign plates. He was dressed in a tan camel's-hair coat with a fur collar, and an expensive mink hat. Dimitri crossed the street and entered the battered Zhaporozhetz he had been given for today's assignment. Saint-Clair was on his way to work; Dimitri didn't have to hurry. Fifteen minutes later he parked on Gorky Street, just in time to see Saint-Clair enter his office building. He noted the departure and arrival times, then slumped in his seat. What a bore, he thought. He had nothing to do but wait until lunchtime, when Saint-Clair would take his break.

The Canadian came out at twelve-thirty, on foot, and turned south. He behaved as if he had read the seventh department report, Dimitri thought: exactly the same routine as described. Dimitri followed Saint-Clair into the revolving doors of the National Hotel, and was admitted by the armed guards on presentation of his KGB card. In the Russalka Restaurant, Dimitri ordered a salami sandwich, watching Saint-Clair, who was devouring a steaming chunk of meat at the opposite side of the dining room. When Saint-Clair was through, Dimitri followed him back to the street.

It was after crossing the bustling Stanislavski Street that Dimitri realized Saint-Clair had spotted him.

It was nothing tangible at first, just a change in Saint-Clair's pace, then two unnecessary street crossings, and afterward a stop, then another, before some shop windows. Dimitri knew the routine of crossing streets and using shop windows as mirrors to see if one was being followed. But that was KGB routine, it certainly wasn't an art the Delices du Nord company taught its employees! Vaguely alarmed, he continued following Saint-Clair, who continued to expertly employ the tricks of Dimitri's trade. He walked into a large government store selling meat, fish, and fowl, on Gorky Street, and came out by the second exit on Ogarev; he repeated the trick again in the Krimskaya Cafeteria. Soon after, he abruptly turned back, retracing his steps, and Dimitri had to dive into the entrance to a bookstore. Saint-Clair wasn't trying to shake him off; he was on his way back to the office. Now it seemed he wanted to make sure that he was followed.

Saint-Clair entered a phone booth and picked up the receiver. That was odd. Why should he call from a phone booth when his office was barely two hundred meters away? Unless he wanted to use a line that wasn't tapped by the KGB . . .

Dimitri watched Saint-Clair hang up and walk straight back to his office. There were no more street crossings or stops before shop windows. Dimitri thought of calling Yakovlev with an interim report; Saint-Clair's behavior was certainly very unusual. But on second thought, he decided to wait. Saint-Clair might have felt that he was being followed, and simply tried to make sure of it, using techniques he had learned from espionage novels.

Shortly before sunset, Dimitri called the phone-tapping service of the Second Directorate. After identifying himself, he asked if Saint-Clair had made any unusual calls from his office in the afternoon.

No, answered the officer on duty, a woman with a low, grating voice. He had made no unusual calls . . . except for booking a seat for tonight's performance of *Giselle* at the Bolshoi.

And what was unusual about that? Dimitri asked.

"Well, he always books tickets a week in advance," the weary voice answered. "Besides, the telephone log shows that Charles Saint-Clair already saw *Giselle* last week."

WHEN THE CURTAIN ROSE on the first act of *Giselle*, Dimitri stood in the shadows of an unoccupied box, watching Saint-Clair. The Canadian had a seat in the sixth row, beside a group of noisy Americans in raincoats and sneakers. Getting here had been child's play. Dimitri had come to the Bolshoi a half hour before the performance, shown the assistant manager his card, and got what he wanted. Power made things so easy; Dimitri saw how it could be intoxicating.

At the intermission, Saint-Clair casually stepped into the aisle and walked out. Dimitri rushed after him, elbowing his way through the crowd, but when he finally reached the brightly lit lobby, Saint-Clair had vanished. Dimitri scrambled to the men's rest room, but Saint-Clair wasn't there. He was neither at the lobby bar nor at the mezzanine light buffet.

Dimitri felt a surge of panic. Could Saint-Clair have used the crowd to leave the theater? Dimitri knew he would become the laughingstock of Yurlovo tomorrow if he had to explain how an amateur had so easily given him the slip.

But the bell for the second act was ringing, and from a side passage Saint-Clair emerged, calm and relaxed, and strutted back to his seat, smothering his cigar in a standing ashtray. Dimitri continued to stare at the passage, watching people, mostly couples, file back toward their seats. Then, when the flow of people had almost ceased and the last bell rang, a solitary man appeared at the passage entrance.

Dimitri stood still. He knew the man; he'd met him before. He remembered the handsome face, the dimpled chin, the scar below the cheekbone. *Then it dawned on him.* It was Colonel Kalinin, the GRU colonel, the friendly member of the State Security commission who had interviewed him back at Panfilov! After Kalinin's remarks, the two other commission members had agreed that Dimitri's loyalty was beyond reproach.

He now stared insistently at the GRU colonel. Kalinin apparently recognized Dimitri, too, because he smiled at him as he passed, nodded amiably, and entered the theater.

Dimitri remained alone in the deserted lobby. What was Kalinin doing here? Had he met Saint-Clair in the passage? But he had seen at least another twenty people come out of that area. He entered the passage. It led to a flight of stairs that descended to a lower gallery, where an exhibition of Bolshoi posters was on display. At the far end of the gallery there were two doors. Dimitri tried them, and both were locked. Perhaps Kalinin had a key? Perhaps he had met Saint-Clair in one of those rooms? But that notion was farfetched. He hadn't witnessed any contact between the two men. Saint-Clair could have met any of the twenty-odd men and women who had visited the gallery.

When the ballet was over and Giselle had departed for a better world, Dimitri followed Saint-Clair to his apartment building and then drove back toward Yurlovo. He couldn't make up his mind about Kalinin. Should he mention him in his report? Casting unjustified suspicion on a military intelligence colonel could be risky; it could cost him his career. He decided to reconsider the matter the next morning, when he was supposed to prepare his report.

But his report was never to be written.

"Morozov! Wake up!"

The sharp, sinister face of Oktober sailed out of the dark, framed by wispy white hair. A nightmare, Dimitri thought, turning away, seeking refuge from the smoldering eyes; but the rasping voice invaded him, insisting, commanding, and a bony hand kept shaking his shoulder. "Get up. Get dressed. Parade uniform. Down at the gate in ten minutes. Repeat."

He sat upright, staring in the blackness. "Yes, Oktober." He repeated the orders, but Oktober was already bent over his roommate, Victor

Seletzin. In his loose black coat, with the rippling white halo of hair floating around his skull-like face, Oktober looked like a harbinger of death. Dimitri's third roommate, a Finn named Arno Tuuomi, was already dressing with quick, spare movements.

Dimitri threw off the covers. The room was freezing. His watch showed four-fifteen. Oktober had disappeared and Victor was waking up in a crescendo of curses. Fuck your mother, it's four in the morning, fuck this bloody school, fuck the KGB; and a final fuck you, addressed at Arno and Dimitri, who stared at him with forgiveness.

Dimitri's first thought was that the world war had started; but when he reached the gate and found only the untouchables, he discarded the idea. Perhaps a government crisis had broken out, or somebody had died. At Stalin's death, KGB troops had been deployed all over Moscow. But why only the untouchables, where were the other Yurlovo inmates? It didn't make sense.

An army Zil truck was parked outside, its engine hoarsely coughing, the exhaust spewing pale smoke. He climbed in the back, huddled in a corner and lit a cigarette. "I bet it's another exercise," grunted Victor Seletzin, slumping heavily beside him. "Fuck the day I met Oktober."

Once everybody was on board, the truck rumbled, squeaked, and was on its way. They were too tired to talk, and only a few cigarette tips glowed in the dark. As they crossed Yurlovo, a dog barked, joined immediately by others. Dimitri killed his cigarette on the floor, wrapped himself in his topcoat and dozed the rest of the way.

He awoke with a start as the truck abruptly braked. A high-powered flashlight beam swept the interior of the truck, dazzling him momentarily, and he recalled Kuzma Bunin, that night at the quarry. They were being checked at some kind of roadblock. He could hear voices, truck engines, running steps. The truck moved, then stopped again. Strong light seeped in from every crack in the tarpaulin cover. A voice rasped: "Everybody out." It was Oktober.

He jumped out of the truck. The place was brightly lit with floodlights and batteries of white, green, and blue lights along two straight lines on the ground. They were standing at the edge of a runway. Behind them hovered a huge building, all glass and steel; most of its windows were brightly lit. Across the runway, in a long, open garage, he could make out the contours of fire engines, tow trucks, and pale-colored ambulances. On the right loomed the enormous rectangular hangars. In a parking area on the left stood several passenger aircraft. One of them, a Pan Am plane, was being serviced by men in white coveralls. "Fuck your mother," Victor muttered behind him, "this is Vnukovo."

The international airport was in turmoil. Military trucks kept arriving and discharging KGB border troops who took positions around and inside the terminal. Harried civilians and militia officers scurried about, barking orders. Airport tractors started towing aircraft away from the VIP lounge, whose elegant interior they could see through the bay windows.

"Look at these flags," Arno murmured. Huge banners — orange, white, and green — were floating in the wind beside the Soviet flags. "What are those?" Dimitri asked.

"Indian," somebody said. "Indira Gandhi is arriving on a state visit." Dimitri and Arno turned to Victor, and he didn't disappoint them.

"Fuck Indira," he groaned.

"This way," Oktober ordered sharply. The man had a spooky ability to emerge from the dark without anybody noticing his approach. He led them, long coat floating behind his back, into a dark room, apparently a departure lounge. They gathered around him.

"Moscow Center has been struck by a disaster," he said. "A Department Thirteen officer, Colonel Lyalin, has turned traitor." His eyes glowed strangely in the dark. "He gave to the British intelligence service the names of one hundred five of our agents. They've all been expelled."

He paused. "There's worse. Lyalin revealed to the British the existence of Department Thirteen. We've been denying for years that we have a unit specializing in violent activities. Lyalin disclosed the names of our men serving abroad, and now they're running for their lives. Since early evening they have been fleeing from the major cities of Europe and America. I hope they all arrive home safely."

"What will happen to the department?" Arno asked.

Somebody struck a match, and in a flash Dimitri glimpsed the tense, perplexed faces.

"The department," Oktober said, "is dead."

"It can be rebuilt, though," Dimitri suggested.

"You're right, Morozov." Oktober cackled oddly. "But to rebuild it we need new men, totally unknown, who don't figure on any list Lyalin could have furnished. An entirely new team."

"You want us to form the new department," Dimitri said. The darkness and the atmosphere of crisis seemed to permit a certain familiarity between them.

"I have to convince the political level it's feasible."

"And the political level — " Dimitri began.

"Comrade Brezhnev has cut short a visit to Czechoslovakia. He will be landing in a few minutes. The KGB chairman and most Politburo members are already here. I hope we'll convince them."

Why is the meeting being held here, Dimitri wondered, and not in Moscow? He could guess the answer. Oktober wanted a decision from Brezhnev before he met the other KGB chiefs, who might advise him otherwise. With sudden clarity, Dimitri grasped Oktober's ploy. The man was using Lyalin's betrayal as a lever to carry out his own coup and take over Department Thirteen.

He had probably suggested to Andropov that the KGB chairman present to the Politburo a new operational unit that could replace Department Thirteen. Andropov had good reasons to accept Oktober's offer. It could take the heat off him, sparing him some embarrassing questions about Lyalin. Oktober had brought the untouchables to Vnukovo to prove to the Politburo that he had good men, ready for action. If he succeeded, their training would be over and the untouchables would become the new "Wet Affairs" team; Oktober's exile would be over as well.

"What about Indira Gandhi's visit?" Bosjanov asked. He was a Kazakh, from Alma Ata.

"She's arriving today," Oktober said. "The control tower will order her plane to keep circling the airport, till the Politburo meeting is over." He surveyed his small army. "I have to go. Stay here and keep quiet."

At the break of dawn, Brezhnev's Tupolev landed and taxied to the VIP lounge. Dimitri and his friends watched the bulky General Secretary descend from the aircraft, hug and kiss his Politburo colleagues. Large snowflakes were swirling and dancing over the Soviet leaders, then softly landing on their shoulders. Andropov himself was at the end of the receiving line; Brezhnev only stared at him and coldly shook his hand. The small crowd entered the VIP lounge. Oktober was nowhere to be seen.

They settled in the standard plastic chairs and waited. Arno and the resourceful Bosjanov started a card game, and several others joined. A moon-faced matron in a white apron brought them tasteless coffee and cookies. Dimitri didn't eat, nor did he play cards with his friends. He stood by the window, watching the snow-covered fields, the gray runway, and the line of graceful aircraft. This was the gateway to another world, to another life.

"On your feet, comrades!"

Oktober stood at the door. His face was blank. "Leave your overcoats here. I want you lined up outside in one minute." Dimitri threw a look over his shoulder. A convoy of Chaikas was slowly moving toward the VIP lounge to pick up the Politburo members.

"Chairman Andropov would like to shake your hands," Oktober was saying, a note of triumph finally sneaking into his voice. He paused, a cunning smile slowly cracking his face.

"Welcome," he rasped. "Welcome to Department Thirteen."

Chapter 9

NINA WAS RUSHED to Mount Sinai Hospital with a bleeding ulcer on the very day Alex left for Brown. It was a beautiful, crisp day in September. That morning, she had stood by the window, watching him load his bags into his first car, a bright red Mustang convertible. Alex had bought it, secondhand, after working the whole summer at a car wash in Brooklyn. Nina felt the first burning pains in her stomach when she saw him exchange a long good-bye kiss with Claudia. She was revolted. This girl was clinging to him with her whole body, holding him as if he were her property. She had no shame, behaving like that in the middle of the street, in front of everybody, like a slut.

Nina was happy that Alex was leaving town. At Brown, she was sure, her boy would meet other girls and forget the little Italian. She watched them from the window, her lips tightly clamped, until they finally parted and Alex drove away. Then she went to the kitchen to make herself a cup of tea, and collapsed on the checkered floor tiles.

She woke up at the hospital three hours later. She had been found by Myra, the cleaning woman. Thank God, Myra hadn't called an ambulance, but instead had asked their neighbor to help carry her to a taxi. Nina would rather have died than let herself be carted into an ambu-

185

lance, sirens screaming, red lights flashing, the entire neighborhood watching. She made Myra swear not to breathe a word to anybody, but Myra, of course, was unable to keep her big mouth shut and the news spread like wildfire through the neighborhood.

Alex arrived during the night. Nina later learned that he had just arrived at the campus and hadn't even started unpacking when the message from Claudia reached him. He drove to the airport and caught a plane back to New York. When Nina woke up, he was sitting beside her bed, his face unshaven. *"Ninochka, lyubimaya,"* he said in his soft, caressing Russian, "how could you do this to me, *dushenka maya,* my little soul?"

Despite Nina's protests, Alex stayed with her the entire six days until Dr. Sapirstein decided not to operate. He took her home and made her swear to take her medication regularly, watch her diet, and not get upset. He left on the seventh day. As the door closed behind him, a heavy silence settled upon the apartment. And a feeling of desperate loneliness sneaked into her heart.

Thus began Nina's bleak years of solitude. Samuel's death had put an end to an existence she hated, but to which she had grown accustomed. Then Alex had spread his wings and left her alone. Because of her illness, she had to stop working. Her friends from the Peace Movement were either dead or disillusioned; the only light left in her grim existence was Alex.

Throughout the next four years, she lived for Alex's letters, his telephone calls, his short visits home; she read his books, his university papers, questioned him about his professors. She knew all about Brown without being there. In the summers, when he returned for his vacation, she was the happiest person in the world. He was growing into a handsome, confident young man, and she had no doubt he was going to be a famous scholar.

But often, when she sat by the window letting her mind wander, she was pervaded by a sense of failure. Alex was slipping inexorably away from her. Alex, the boy she had shaped and educated, the man she had wanted to be worthy of his parents, had taken a different road. The gap between them was growing wider every day.

She recalled noticing the first signs when he was still a child and had been swept away by the temptations only America could offer — games, movies, sports . . . He had grown to love America more than Russia. Alex had admired John Kennedy, in spite of his reactionary policy in Cuba and Vietnam; Kennedy's assassination had devastated the boy. His next shock was when he learned the truth about his parents' deaths. He wasn't ready to cope with such appalling facts. His admiration for the Soviet Union was shattered; on top of that, he was deeply offended by the way the Russian bureaucrats had treated his letters.

Then this girl came, and turned his head. Nina was convinced that Claudia was the worst disaster that had ever befallen Alex. She didn't object, of course, to Alex having a girlfriend. But this one tore Alex away from her. At his age, sexual attraction was everything. She remembered her infatuation with Sasha Kolodny, back in Kiev, when she was only sixteen. Once, at the very beginning of Alex's romance, she had hinted that he should spend more time studying. "Don't worry about Claudia," she had observed. "Claudia won't run away."

"What's this, Nina, are you jealous?" Alex retorted jokingly.

"Stop that nonsense!" she snapped.

Perhaps she was jealous; she had a right to be. After all, Alex was her life, she had dedicated her existence to him. She so loved their evenings together, when they would listen to classical music or discuss Russian literature and history. Now all of a sudden he had no more time for her; his evenings were monopolized by a girl with a pretty face and big, young breasts.

Claudia was very nice to her, and Nina tried her best to reciprocate. But she couldn't help feeling a surge of anger whenever she saw the girl. Bitterness would grip her throat, the blood would drain from her face, and her voice would become cold and remote — the voice of an insecure woman confronting her rival.

Besides, Alex had fallen in love not only with the girl, but with her entire clan. He spent more time in the Benevento house than he did in his own home. The Beneventos simply swallowed him, treating him as one of their own. They had given him something he'd never had: a family.

Shortly before Alex left for Brown, there had been an ugly fight between him and Nina. She'd seen it coming for a long time, but she wasn't ready for it when it erupted, in the hectic summer of 1967. War broke out between Israel and her neighbors, and Alex came home from school cursing the Russians, ready to strangle Brezhnev with his bare hands. He admired Moshe Dayan, the handsome Israeli general who looked like a pirate with his black eyepatch. She tried to explain the Soviet point of view to the boy, but he yelled at her and left the house.

A year later Russian tanks invaded Czechoslovakia, and Alex organized a student rally on the Brown campus. It was even reported on television. They showed Alex speaking, condemning "Red imperialism" and haranguing the crowd against "Soviet brutality." She was so ashamed, she had terrible pains that night, but she didn't alert the doctor and didn't answer the telephone for several days, fearing it might be someone calling about Alex's speech.

After calming down, she decided to adopt a new strategy. She would avoid a confrontation, and instead employ logic and common sense. When Alex returned for a weekend, she made him a cup of coffee and served it on the kitchen table. Israel was an imperialist state, she said, everybody knew that; Moshe Dayan had fought with the British army. The Czech revolt was a Western ploy, and the Red Army had entered Prague at the people's request.

Alex was beside himself with frustration. "How can you say that, Nina? The Russians just whistle, and you click your heels. Can't you ever make up your own mind?"

She felt the familiar pain in her stomach, and put down her coffee cup. Her fingers were trembling and some coffee spilled on the tablecloth. "Is this what Claudia says about me?"

She had spoken without thinking, and she regretted her words immediately. She saw the fury exploding in his eyes.

"Leave her out of this, Nina. This is between you and me."

She didn't know what to say, so she got up and left the table. He ran after her and hugged her. "I love you very much, Nina," he said. "I shall always love you. But I can't stand your fanatical devotion to your Kremlin idols."

Since that conversation, he had come home very rarely. But Nina refused to humiliate herself; not even once, during Alex's studies, did she call Claudia Benevento to inquire about her nephew.

In January 1971 there was a soft knocking on the door. Nina was having her afternoon tea by the living room window, watching the dance of snowflakes over the street. The snowfalls of January always made her think of Tonya's last hours, and she sank into a morose, brooding mood.

When she heard the knocking, she got up and briskly walked to the door. Even when she was alone at home, she was properly attired. Today she was wearing her polka dot dress with the starched white collar and her black patent leather shoes.

A young man, no more than thirty years of age, stood on the landing. He was rather sloppily dressed in a beige woolen coat, frayed at the cuffs, a thick woolen scarf, brown corduroy trousers, and thick-soled yellow shoes. His big nose stuck out of a pale face, he wore thick glasses, and his untidy hair was covered with melting snowflakes. "Mrs. Kramer?"

"Yes?"

"I hope I'm not disturbing you," the man said, and before she even realized it, he was inside her vestibule, dripping water all over her carpet. "My name is David Hughes. I'm a writer."

He had a distinct English accent, which could also account for the old-fashioned clothes. "May I have a word with you?"

"About what?" she said. Can this be about Alex? she thought.

"About Sasha Kolodny."

It took her a moment to digest the name. Sasha Kolodny. Her Sasha. She hadn't heard his name in thirty years. She swayed and leaned on a chair for support. "Sasha? You know Sasha?"

"He was your husband, wasn't he?" Hughes's eyes were darting incessantly, searching the apartment.

"No, not my husband." When she was disturbed, her English became even worse. "Sasha, he dead?" she managed, her heart pounding.

"No, I don't think so," the Englishman said, and entered the living room. "May I sit down?"

"Where is Sasha?"

He settled in one of her armchairs. "As a matter of fact, I hoped you could tell me that." He glanced around and grimaced in disappointment. He probably had expected to see Sasha's picture on the wall. "I was told he was your first husband."

She shook her head. "No, no husband, just my friend."

"Of course," Hughes said, unbuttoning his coat. "I am writing a book about him, you see, and I hope you can help me."

She sat up, very tense, then stood up again. "A book? On Sasha? Why you write a book?" That was very suspicious, and so was the Englishman. She hadn't heard of Sasha since the beginning of the war, when Emily Mayer had seen him in Paris.

He smiled, revealing huge buckteeth. "Come on, you know why. Your Sasha is a big hero. Do you have any pictures of him? Or of you two together?"

"A hero?" Her hand darted to her chest, her knees buckled, and she sat down again, very stiff, facing him. "What hero?"

The Englishman shook his head. "You really don't know, do you? Well, you haven't been reading the European papers, I guess." He fumbled inside his pocket and produced a photograph.

She hastily adjusted her glasses. It was a man's portrait, taken from a low, unusual angle. The man was staring at the camera over his shoulder. His face was totally expressionless, his eyes sharp and cold, with a hint of contempt. He looked very elegant, wearing a jacket over a white shirt and a tie. His fair hair was cropped very short; gone was the unruly shock of honey-blond hair. The jowls and neck had thickened with the years. The mouth was powerful, almost brutal. But this was, unmistakably, her Sasha.

"This picture," the Englishman said, "was taken by the Gestapo, in Paris, when Sasha Kolodny was under arrest. He was known as Theodor Shroeder, but his friends in the Resistance called him the Chief." He handed her the picture. "Take it, this is a copy, I have another one at home."

She took the photograph, and her fingers, as if acting on their own, gently caressed the beloved face. "The Chief," she repeated. Her Sasha was the Chief. She leaned toward the Englishman. "Please, tell me what happened with Sasha." She was forgetting her manners. "Please excuse me. You want coffee? Tea?"

Sasha had reached Paris in 1929, the Englishman's story went, and had worked for a few years as a bricklayer, dishwasher, and carpenter. In 1936 he had crossed the border into Spain, where he had fought with the Republicans against Franco; he had been wounded at the Battle of the Ebro. Back in France, he had been appointed chief of Soviet espionage in Western Europe. Actually, that was why he had left Russia in the first place; he was sent to Palestine, then to France, to create his networks and recruit agents.

Nina recalled the night when Sasha had woken her up, saying: "Let's go to Palestine," and she had refused. They were not Zionist, she didn't know then that he had been assigned a special mission, and of course couldn't tell her. She had been afraid to tell him she was pregnant. It was such a stupid misunderstanding, yet it had shattered her life. God, how different things could have been!

"Kolodny," the Englishman was saying, "now changed his name to Shroeder." He emerged in the posh Sixteenth Arrondissement of Paris, posing as a wealthy businessman. He had lots of money, a large office on Avenue Victor Hugo, and influential connections. "And women," Hughes added, briefly avoiding her eyes, "young and attractive women."

She shook her head. Sasha was such a handsome man, of course he had many women.

After the German army conquered France, Shroeder had been among the first Parisian businessmen to deal with the Germans. But in secret, his network was transmitting vital information to Moscow about the German military machine. His greatest achievement was a message to Stalin announcing Hitler's imminent attack on the Soviet Union. The Chief reported the code name of the assault: Operation Barbarossa. And the date: June 22, 1941.

"But . . . this is impossible," Nina stammered. "The Red Army didn't expect an attack."

Hughes was nodding his head. "Exactly," he said. "Stalin didn't believe the Chief."

Shortly afterward, the Gestapo had captured the Chief, but he managed to escape. He gained the Gestapo's trust by promising to cooperate and feeding them some second-rate information about his networks. Then, one day, while crossing Paris, he had asked permission to buy some aspirin. The Gestapo car had stopped by the Lyons railroad station. Sasha had entered the large corner pharmacy, then calmly walked out by the back exit and vanished into thin air.

Nina was listening, enthralled.

"And at the end of the war," the Englishman said, "the most painful chapter in Sasha's life began."

Outside, night was falling and the wind whined in the kitchen window.

"A special Red Army plane came to Paris to take the Chief back to Moscow. Stalin wanted to see him, the Russians told him. He wanted to thank him and decorate him."

"Decorate?" she asked, puzzled. "What is decorate?"

"A medal, they said Stalin would give him a medal."

"And what did Stalin say to Sasha?" Nina bent forward, sensing a forthcoming blow.

"Sasha never saw Stalin. From the airport he was taken directly to the Lubyanka. He spent eleven years in jail, and was released only in 'fifty-six."

Nina was on her feet. "I don't believe you. Why . . . why does Stalin do this?"

The Englishman looked at her over the rim of his teacup. "Actually, Stalin should have given your Sasha a medal. But by doing so he would have been admitting that Sasha had been right, and he, the generalis-simo, had been wrong. He hadn't listened to his warnings, he'd preferred to trust Hitler. This blindness had cost millions of Russian dead . . ."

"I don't believe . . ." Nina said stubbornly. "I don't believe."

". . . so rather than admit his own failure, Stalin threw Sasha Kolodny in the Lubyanka Prison."

It suddenly occurred to Nina that Tonya and Sasha had been impris-oned in the Lubyanka at the same time; perhaps their cells had been in the same block. They might even have met, without knowing each other. The two people she had loved most had both been Stalin's victims.

"Where is Sasha now?" she asked.

The Englishman shrugged. "I hoped you would know. There were rumors that he was reincorporated in the KGB; then he disappeared from view. Now, let's go back, to the time when you met him. Can you tell me about him?"

"No," Nina said, panicking. "Is nothing to tell."

"Why? Because of the other women he had?"

"No, no, I not care about other women." She took off her glasses, then put them on again. She didn't know how to cope with such emotions.

"Don't you want to see Sasha again?"

"Why you ask this?"

"Because my book will be published all over the world. I believe it will also reach the Soviet Union. And if Sasha Kolodny is still alive, he'll know where his Nina is and how to find her."

"No," she said. "He will not want to find his Nina. Is nothing to tell."

But he argued, explained, insisted, and she finally gave in. Not to the ugly Englishman, of course, but to her own, long-suppressed desire to tell aloud the story of her love for Sasha Kolodny. She let herself go, and told the Englishman about Sasha and their life together as a married couple, "as man and wife, but no rabbi." She even brought from her room some yellow-edged letters and photographs, which she showed him, but refused to let him touch. As Nina spoke, she felt a wonderful sensation of deliverance, as if another woman, who had been jailed inside her for many years, had suddenly blazed her way to freedom and recognition.

It was late at night when Hughes left. Nina washed the teacups and the glass in which she had served him sherry, then turned off the lights and went to her room. Angry winds howled outside as she lay awake in her bed. She cried a lot about her lost youth, about the tremendous mistake she had made when she had refused to follow Sasha. But she also felt happy to think that the timid teenager she had been in those far-off days in Kiev had made the right choice after all. Sasha was a great man; she had known it the first time she saw him.

Her life wasn't over; not yet. She now had a new hope to light up her old age. Perhaps one day they'll find Sasha, she thought, perhaps the Englishman's book will help. And she might live long enough to see him again. A pang of delightful anticipation shot through her body. She had so much to tell him, they could speak for days.

What a pity that their child had died. Sasha would have been thrilled to find out he had a son. But the boy was gone, and this was the only part of her story she didn't tell the Englishman. Nor would she tell Sasha, if she ever saw him again.

DIMITRI DIDN'T KNOW the real identity of the old man who trained him in "modus operandi/deep cover in a Western city." The man was impressive: broad-shouldered, with a leonine head, a white mane that had been blond once, a big, straight nose, and a willful mouth. He wore a tired tweed jacket over a black woolen shirt, buttoned up to his chin; his gait was clumsy, deceptively slow. Oktober spoke of him with unusual respect, calling him "the Chief." Rumor had it that the Chief was a Lubyanka graduate. He had spent a long prison term there after a nebulous wartime mission. A morose, sardonic man, he didn't belong to the department's inner circle and had no access to operational files. He had spent many years in the West, and now trained the Wet Affairs' agents for their missions abroad.

"Your base and your headquarters will be a café, always a café," the

Chief told Dimitri. He had met the man at the gate of the black mansion on Balaklavskaya Street where Oktober had established Wet Affairs' new headquarters. Dimitri was about to leave on his first assignment abroad, and the Chief had been charged with his personal training.

"In Paris," he went on, "there's a café on every street corner, in Rome and Brussels as well." He had a grating, cavernous voice. "In England, Germany, and the United States not so frequent, but you'll find bars and cafés in every big hotel. You can carry out all your meetings in cafés.

"Remember, the best protection is a crowd. Wherever there are lots of people, you're safe."

He drove Dimitri to a KGB operational model at Gavrikovo, outside of Moscow. The complex was spread over a vast area, surrounded by a pine forest, protected by fences and guard towers. The Chief led him to the eastern wing of the sprawling structure and past the guards to the lower level. The room they entered was built like a Parisian café, with mirrors on the walls, Formica-topped tables, electric pinball machines, and a brass-topped counter. The place was empty, but Dimitri could easily imagine it full of men and women sitting at the tables, and waiters with long white aprons mincing between the patrons.

"Always sit with your back against the wall, close to the service exit," the Chief said, and nodded as Dimitri chose a convenient table. "Never raise your voice to call a waiter, never pull him by the sleeve, never order something that isn't on the menu. Never draw attention to yourself."

He spoke in a monotonous voice, and Dimitri realized he didn't care about his job. The old man's blank eyes indicated to Dimitri that the Chief was long dead, his body and mind functioning only by habit. He probably continued to carry on his routine duties because espionage was the only trade he knew.

"For all practical purposes, you're a Canadian," the Chief was saying. "We use their passports because they don't have computerized records of their citizens. We use their identities because there's no such thing as a Canadian."

"How's that?" Dimitri asked.

The Chief lit a Sobranie cigarette. It was black and gold-tipped. The fingers holding the cigarette were yellow around the joints; the Chief's teeth were also stained by nicotine. He saw Dimitri watching him and smiled wryly, offering him a cigarette. "Never do that when on a mission. Never smoke an unusual brand of cigarettes, it will cause you trouble. People and ashtrays remember such things."

He slowly exhaled. "Where were we? Oh, yes, the Canadians. Canada is a mosaic of immigrants, from all corners of the earth. The country is full of Italians, East Europeans, Portuguese, French, Greeks. Nobody is surprised if a Canadian doesn't speak English or speaks it with a heavy accent. Get it?"

Dimitri nodded. The Sobranie had a rich, sharp flavor.

"Now," the Chief said, "let me take you to the lavatory."

Dimitri followed him, puzzled. The Chief went through a door on which an enamel sign said: TOILETTES, TELEPHONES. The old man stepped into one of the cubicles and pointed at the water tank. It was a European model, fixed to the wall above their heads and connected to the seat with a long pipe; the water flow was activated by a chain, hanging from the tank.

"This is your dead-letter drop," the Chief said. "If you want to survive, stay away from the standard KGB nonsense. Don't ever establish your drops in woods or fields, beneath shrubs or in holes in trees. Our people in America do it, and regularly get caught with their pants down by the FBI. Good for them; the poor slobs don't deserve anything better."

Dimitri chuckled. The old boy didn't mince words.

The Chief's rasping voice was charged with utter contempt. "A man who sneaks into the woods alone is always suspect. A man who drives his car from his office to the woods, or to a deserted field, is always suspect. The same for a man who parks his car by the road, in the middle of nowhere. But a man who goes to pee in a café lavatory is not, see? So here's what you do."

He fished a small box out of his pocket, took a condom out of it and unrolled it. "You place your message or microfilm or whatever inside the rubber, tie it up, twice for security, and drown it." He climbed on the lavatory stool and deftly plunged the condom into the water cistern. "Nobody will look there, and if they do, they can never trace it to you or your contact."

He led the way back to the café. "The first thing you need whenever you get into a big city is a map of all the stores, underground malls, train stations, and hotels with multiple exits. Your case officer should have one ready for you before you set out on your mission. You memorize it and destroy it. We call these places sanctuaries. If you're shadowed, you head for the closest sanctuary, move in by one entrance, out by the other. It may save your life." He paused, looking at Dimitri. "I could tell you of a pharmacy in Paris . . ." He smiled, his eyes suddenly lighting up, and let his voice fade away.

As they left the place, he turned back to Dimitri and his cavernous voice boomed again. "Remember: you enter a café, a restaurant, a hotel as if they belong to you. Don't linger by the door, don't look uncertain. In the West there is no police guard on hotels. Everyone can walk in and out, and the more confident you look, the less likely they are to suspect you."

DIMITRI RECALLED the Chief's advice three weeks later as he walked confidently into the brass-and-leather lobby of the Hotel Universal in Frankfurt. The soft shirt and slacks of his custom-tailored Western suit caressed his skin. He smiled absently at the concierge, paused by the souvenir shop, where he lit a cigarette with deliberately slow gestures, then casually walked toward the elevators, swinging his leather briefcase.

He had arrived the night before on a direct Lufthansa flight, carrying a Finnish passport in the name of Timo Kuusinen. At the airport's lower level he boarded the direct train to the Hauptbahnhof, the main railroad station. The station restaurant was a poorly lit place with solid wooden furniture and hefty waitresses in white aprons. Dimitri ordered a couple of grilled sausages and two strong, cold beers — his first meal in the West, which he found excellent, especially when he plunged his spoon into the dessert, a cup of creamy chocolate mousse. He gulped down his coffee, then stepped into the men's lavatory.

Locking the door of the third cubicle behind him, he climbed on the seat, rolled up his sleeve, and plunged his hand inside the water tank. The condom he took out of the water contained an unmarked key, which he used to open the third upper locker from the left in the station's waiting room. Inside he found a handbag containing an entire new set of clothes, purchased in Hamilton, Ontario, and a Canadian passport in the name of Stefan Nagi. There was no photograph on the passport. This was done as a security measure, in case someone managed to open the locker and find the handbag. Under the clothes, packed in a leather pouch, were an electric-powered gun, three ampules of prussic acid, and three ampules of antidotes.

A sign in German at the other side of the hall offered showers to travelers for 4.5 Deutsche Marks. He changed in the dressing room; five minutes later he stashed his Finnish clothes and passport in the same locker that he had opened before. That way, no one could establish a connection between the Finn who flew in from Moscow and the Canadian who now left the train station and walked into the city of Frankfurt. If anything went wrong, and Stefan Nagi's role in the forthcoming operation was exposed, his trail would grow cold at the entrance to the Hauptbahnhof.

It was early evening when Stefan Nagi checked into the Globe, a tacky fleabag hotel in the red-light district, walking distance from the station. On his way he saw huge signs announcing the Buchmesse — the annual Frankfurt Book Fair. Enormous posters praised the latest bestsellers and their authors. Once inside his room, he ordered a couple of ham and salami sandwiches and two more beers. From a plain envelope he had brought with him, he removed his own photograph, which he carefully glued to his Canadian passport. He spent the evening and most of the next day in his room, valiantly struggling with a decrepit black-and-white television set. He kept turning the chipped button, since he didn't understand the German programs. Finally, he tuned in the U.S. Armed Forces network and watched some old American sitcoms which he found boring and utterly stupid.

He had lunch at a crowded bar down the street, where he was apparently the only patron who wasn't either pimping or whoring. Back in his room, he reluctantly turned the TV on again and wolfed down two huge bars of milk chocolate with hazelnuts while he watched. Once in a while he would hear steps in the corridor outside, men's hoarse voices and women's forced giggles. The Globe was apparently doing good business.

As the afternoon neared its end, he put on his Canadian clothes, picked up the elegant leather briefcase, then hailed a taxi outside the hotel. He stared out of the cab window at the opulent shops, the luxurious cars, the well-dressed people. The food stores were crammed with a variety of products; anyone could just walk in and buy whatever he wanted, without having to stand in line. It was an overcast afternoon, and the colorful neon signs were blazing merrily all along the Kaiserstrasse. A cascade of lights shaped like women's bodies invited him to a sex show. So that's the West, he thought — fat, rich, and decadent. And that's Germany. We won the war, we raised our flag in Berlin, and the bastards are living off the fat of the land.

As he walked into the Universal, he passed a blond woman in an expensive fur coat who flashed him an inviting smile. It jolted him. For a second he fantasized that he was alone in a hotel bed with such a ravishing woman, away from everything.

But as he entered the lobby, he cleared all other thoughts from his mind and concentrated on the mission ahead. His target was a man staying in room 1218, Lawrence Tierney. He was American by name and passport only; he was in fact Genadi Lyubimov, a former deputy head of the Soviet mission to the United Nations. Lyubimov had defected to the West six months before, and delivered a devastatingly accurate report to the CIA about Soviet infiltration in American government agencies.

Lyubimov was a greedy man, Oktober had said. Braving danger, he had emerged from hiding and come to the Frankfurt Book Fair. He had flown all the way to Germany to meet a Berlin publisher and convince him of the authenticity of his memoirs. And collect a fat check, of course.

But Dimitri knew enough about Oktober's methods to surmise that there was no German publisher interested in Lyubimov's memoirs — just Oktober. Dimitri's wily chief must have been the one who had smoked Lyubimov out into the open by dangling wealth before his eyes.

"I want him dead," Oktober had said to Dimitri at Sheremetyevo Airport before he boarded his flight. It was shortly before dawn, and they stood on the tarmac in the freezing cold. The wind billowed Oktober's black vestments and blew his long hair into a white halo around his skull-like face. That's the way Death probably looks, Dimitri mused, gazing at the emaciated features, the cruel mouth, the implacable resolve burning in the dark eyes.

"I want him dead," Oktober repeated. "For what he did, and for what others might do if they believe they can get away with it."

"You're trying to resuscitate Smersh," Dimitri observed.

Oktober's bony hands grabbed him by the shoulders. "Your father was a Smersh officer, never forget this."

I'll never forget, Dimitri thought now as he stepped into the elevator of the Universal Hotel. A bearded Jew with sidelocks and a large black hat got in after him. Dimitri had seen orthodox Jews only once before. Bloody bastards, he thought, they're everywhere. They also won the war, along with the Germans and the Japanese.

He got out on the tenth floor and climbed two more flights on the service stairs. Before stepping into the corridor, he stuffed his raincoat and jacket into his case and put on a white tunic embossed with the Universal logo. He had found it in the bag he'd collected at the station. He left his briefcase in the closet where the fire equipment was stored.

He entered the corridor. Its walls, decorated in beige and brown, were discreetly lit, and the thick carpet muffled his footsteps. Two men, laughing softly at something one of them had said, passed by him, and he politely bowed. On his right was room 1216, on his left 1215. His heart was beating faster, and he felt the familiar hollow sensation in the pit of his stomach.

He rapped on the door to 1218.

"Yes?" The voice was reserved, suspicious.

"Minibar check."

"No need, I didn't use it."

"Sorry sir," he said in German-accented English. "I must check, these are hotel regulations."

There was a long silence. "Okay, wait," the voice finally sighed. Dimitri stood facing the brown door, his right hand gripping the electric gun inside his pocket. The ampule containing the antidote was in his left hand. Lyubimov will now open the door, he thought, I'll step in, fire the poison ampule in his face, and it will all be over. He remembered the sharp odor of the antidote gas and the convulsions of the dogs he had shot in the Yurlovo forest.

The door opened. A middle-aged man wearing a silk robe stared sullenly at Dimitri. He was heavily built, with a broad face, a shock of dyed brown hair over white sideburns, and plump cheeks. A cigarette was dangling from his fingers.

"Mr. Tierney?" Dimitri managed.

The man nodded, glancing suspiciously at Dimitri's right hand, which was stuck in his pocket.

"Sorry to disturb you," Dimitri began, and the target moved aside, letting him pass.

"Get it over with," he said impatiently. "I'm busy."

Dimitri bowed subserviently and closed the door behind him. On the right wall, over the minibar, he glimpsed a print of two men wrestling, their muscles bulging with the strain.

All of a sudden he remembered that black night at the quarry outside the Panfilov orphanage, the crushing grip of Kuzma Bunin, the stunning blows of his iron bat. And the brief surge of ecstasy that had swept through him when he'd squeezed the life from his enemy's body with his hands.

He let go of the gun and dropped the antidote ampule. He turned back and hurled himself on Lyubimov, his clawed hands reaching for the defector's throat. For an instant Lyubimov was stunned, but he swiftly recovered and dove to one side. Dimitri crashed into one of the sleek Danish chairs and landed on the floor amidst broken pieces of wood.

Lyubimov grabbed the telephone. Dimitri rolled on the carpet and yanked the phone cord from its socket, then sprang again. This time he managed to seize his victim by the waist. Lyubimov screamed in terror, wildly kicking and punching Dimitri in the face. He tasted the metallic flavor of blood trickling in his mouth. His jaw ached, and his enemy's screams rang in his ears. But none of this mattered. While the defector squealed like a slaughtered pig, Dimitri's hands tightened on his beefy throat. And in one quick move, which transported him with rapture, he snapped the traitor's neck. He heard the crack of Lyubimov's upper vertebrae, and felt the heavy body go limp in his arms.

The following morning, after another night spent in the Globe, this time with a teenage prostitute — blond, slight, and freckled — the man named Timo Kuusinen boarded a flight to Berlin, and connected with Finnair Flight 118 to Helsinki, with stops in Prague and Moscow.

The electric gun and Nagi's clothes had been returned to a Frankfurt locker, whose key, tied in a condom of reinforced latex, now lay in a water tank in the Hauptbahnhof men's room.

DURING HIS JOURNEY BACK, Dimitri had worried about how Oktober would react when he told him he hadn't shot Lyubimov, but had liquidated him with his bare hands. Oktober, however, didn't seem upset by Dimitri's transgression of the rules. He had received Dimitri in his dark lair, made him sit in the single visitor's chair, then paced in circles around him, listening to his report. His questions weren't hostile; on the contrary, Dimitri had the impression that his chief was not at all shocked by his brutal impulse.

"What did you feel when you killed him?" Oktober asked, studying Dimitri closely. Dimitri stared back without answering, and a sardonic smile briefly lit Oktober's wan face. "You loved it," he said. "That's good. That's really good."

But the real surprise for Dimitri was what Oktober now told him about his victim.

Lyubimov had never been a defector, Oktober disclosed in a conspiratorial tone, his dark eyes twinkling oddly. His defection had been staged by Moscow Center. Lyubimov had been planted in the West as a double agent, and the intelligence he had provided to the CIA was, of course, a well-concocted feast of disinformation.

"Then we had a hitch," Oktober said. He was pacing again, restless, long-limbed, a spider weaving his deadly web. "The Americans smelled a rat. Somebody at Langley said Lyubimov was a phony and labeled his defection 'a Chekist plot.' "

"Did they have any proof against him?" Dimitri asked.

"None, but they started doubting his word and wanted to run a check on all the reports he had provided. The Lyubimov affair was one of our most difficult and costly operations. We had been preparing the ground for years, and now all our efforts were about to go down the drain."

He paused. "To save the project, we had to convince Langley that Lyubimov was genuine, that everything he had told them was gospel. What better proof that he was a genuine defector than having him assassinated by KGB agents?"

A sudden chill spread through Dimitri's body. "You mean to tell me," he said, "that I killed one of our men? A fellow Chekist?"

Oktober stared back, motionless. "Yes, and now they believe every word he said." His crooked grin was blood-chilling. "Do you feel sorry for him?"

Not for him, Dimitri wanted to say, for me, for all the others you might use in your game. "Oktober," he said slowly, "you deliberately ordered one of our best men killed."

The older man nodded.

"How do I know," Dimitri continued, "that tomorrow, or in a year, you won't sacrifice me too in one of your games?"

Oktober chuckled, a sly look infiltrating his face. "That's exactly the point, my boy. You'll never know."

When Dimitri was at the door, about to leave, Oktober called after him, "I was joking, of course."

"Of course," Dimitri said.

Oktober's hoarse cackle rang in his ears as he went out and closed the door behind him.

* * *

IN THE FOLLOWING YEARS, Dimitri assassinated four more people, two in Munich, one in New York, and one in Madrid. Three of them were well-known dissidents; one, an American agent about to infiltrate the Soviet Union posing as a Spanish communist, a hero of the civil war.

Dimitri quickly became familiar with the Western way of life. No member of the widely publicized jet-set crowd travelled as much in Europe and North America as Dimitri Morozov. But he always observed an austere, almost monastic way of life. Europe oozed pleasures and temptations that could have easily turned the head of a Russian like himself, burdened with memories of hunger and cold. But he couldn't afford any deviation from his strict rules. He was risking his life daily, and he knew that the smallest mistake could mean his death. It might start with returning twice to the same gourmet restaurant, the same nightclub, or the same hotel suite in a European capital; it might end with his bullet-ridden body lying in a side-street gutter. Any breech of department rules could be fatal.

He knew it from his Lisbon experience, in April of 1972. He had been sent to the Portuguese capital to liquidate a Latvian refugee leader who intended to establish a government in exile. But as he sneaked into the Latvian's room, he found himself facing his target's bodyguard, who wasn't supposed to be on the scene. He barely escaped with a bullet wound in his shoulder. On Dimitri's return to Moscow, Oktober told him he could never travel to Lisbon again. It had been an unfortunate accident, Oktober said.

But Dimitri knew better. If he had more thoroughly investigated his target's habits, instead of enjoying a lobster dinner at Cascais on the night of his arrival, he wouldn't still be carrying a 7.65 slug embedded in his left shoulder, six inches from the heart.

His other operations were successful. He always used his bare hands; he never felt any pity for his targets. Nobody had ever felt pity for him. Dimitri's most recent victim, a statuesque Estonian woman, had briefly stirred his desire, and he had held her firm body against his just a second longer before he snapped her neck.

Dimitri also carried out the kidnapping of Dr. Ernst Muller, the deputy director of West Germany's secret service, and his transfer to East Germany. Muller turned out to be a treasure trove for the East

German Stasi. Before he was liquidated, he delivered priceless information about the joint Pullach and Langley operations in the Warsaw pact countries.

Following the success crowned by Muller's abduction, Oktober promoted Dimitri to the key position of chief operations officer in Western Europe. He was posted in Paris under the cover of a senior Sovtorg representative.

It was in his Paris office late one evening, that he heard a knock on his door, and raising his eyes from the report he was reading, saw before him the tall, handsome man he remembered so well, GRU colonel Oleg Kalinin.

Chapter 10

LA GUARDIA AIRPORT was buried in snow, but the runways had been swept clean and the landing was smooth. "The captain, the crew, and the thirty-three thousand shareholders of North American Airways do thank you for flying with us," a flight attendant intoned on the loudspeaker system. Alex slipped a bookmark between the pages of Dylan Thomas's *Collected Poems* and dropped the fiery Welshman's book in his bag. Lately, after so many years of studying Russian poetry, he had discovered the English and American romantic masters. He was mesmerized by Thomas's talent, which had come to such a tragic end. One of the verses made him think of his mother: "Though lovers be lost love shall not; and death shall have no dominion."

Claudia was waiting for him at the arrival gate, waving happily. "Some guys get all the fun," the man walking behind Alex muttered. Claudia was wearing an embroidered white sheepskin jacket over a flimsy blouse of blue silk, white jeans, and high-heeled boots.

"God, I always forget how gorgeous you are," Alex murmured as she slipped into his arms.

"How could you remember," she quipped, "with all those little sex-pots crawling all over you in Providence?" She kissed him passionately, then took his hand. "Come," she said, her tiny dimple budding on her left cheek. She brushed a few strands of hair from her face. It had started snowing again outside, soft flakes that briefly blossomed like daisies on the wavy blackness of her hair.

"We'll take a taxi, I'm paying," she announced.

In the cab, he wanted to ask why this sudden generosity, but she assailed him with questions. Was he going to stay in Providence after he got his doctorate? Perhaps he could teach at Brown? What about Columbia? And the offer from Stanford, was it still valid? No, he didn't want to teach at Brown, he said, nor Columbia. Yes, Stanford was still open, but it depended.

"On what?" she asked.

"On you," he replied. "What about you?"

This was the question she apparently had been waiting for. Curling comfortably at the edge of the seat, draping her sheepskin like an ermine around her shoulders, she plunged into a breathless account of her adventures. She had called everybody, absolutely everybody in the fashion business during these last three weeks. Nobody had agreed to give her an interview, nobody was interested in her sketches or her résumé or her arts degree. They weren't hiring, everybody had said, they were overstaffed; actually they were firing; no, thank you, Miss Benevento, we don't need new fashion designers, our old fashion designers are very good, thank you. Don't call us, we won't call you.

On the front seat the bearded cab driver was shaking his head dejectedly; he seemed distressed by Claudia's ordeal.

Alex couldn't take his eyes off her. She was totally immersed in her story, illustrating it with spontaneous hand gestures and facial expressions. Her vitality was irresistible. While talking, she imitated the different voices on the phone, the French accents, the Italian intonation, the southern drawls. When quoting the negative answers, her face assumed a mask of contempt and her eyes shot deadly lightning.

So, she continued, nobody, absolutely nobody, wanted her. But — and there was of course a but; in every Claudia story told with such gusto, there was always a but — at the end she had said to herself, *Basta!* Enough! You're young, Claudia, you're talented — what am I saying? you're unique — and you're not so bad-looking on top of that (I'm so modest, Alex, you know), so don't just stand in your Brooklyn kitchen holding your mama's hand and begging those sharks over the phone, this is something any fat, ugly, dumb broad could do. Go to them, show them who you are and what you are and what you can do.

He looked at her sideways, half amused and half intrigued. Her style so closely resembled the Italian girl portrayed in any number of second-rate Hollywood movies. He had the feeling that she was talking like that just to amuse him. She was much too clever to think the way she talked. But with Claudia one could never tell.

This decided, Claudia was saying, she had set out on the conquest of Manhattan, armed with her résumé and her sketches — the summer collection, I showed you in New Haven, remember, Alex? And he said yes, he remembered; but now he was really worried, because the cab driver was getting too interested in Claudia — nodding his head to her story, sighing in compassion for her vicissitudes, clicking his tongue sympathetically, throwing longing glances at her — to watch the snowbound road ahead.

To cut a long story short, Claudia said, she had been shamefully thrown out of Oleg Cassini and Anne Klein and Halston by a few aging dragons who had stared at her hatefully and announced she wouldn't get even one step past them without an appointment. But finally she had landed at Havermeyer's, and walked out of the elevator at the very moment old Mr. Havermeyer was trying to get in. Such a nice old gentleman, Alex, exactly the opposite of what those poison pens are writing in the papers. "So I got hold of his sleeve and didn't let go till he heard my little speech. And guess what, Alex?"

"He hired you," he ventured.

"How did you guess?"

"Bravo!" the driver said, triumphant.

Alex leaned forward to ask Claudia's new friend to keep his eyes on the road. The sights unfolding before the car were unfamiliar. They whizzed past a sign saying Forty-ninth Street. "Hey, what the hell is this?" he said to the driver. "This isn't Brooklyn. Where are you going?"

But Claudia's soft laughter made him turn back. Her eyes were sparkling. "Easy, professor," she suggested, "easy."

He sighed. "I should have guessed it was you. What did you tell the driver?"

But the cab had already turned onto Park Avenue and sailed to a stop. A generalissimo in parade uniform opened the cab door. "Welcome to the Waldorf-Astoria, sir. Welcome, miss."

Smiling mysteriously, Claudia stepped smartly up the marble staircase of the sumptuous hotel and across the blue-and-white art deco lobby. People were turning their heads at her passage, and she didn't seem to dislike it. An old gentleman in a velvet smoking jacket, sitting under the ornate clock, rose and smiled hopefully at Claudia. Alex followed her, carrying his overnight bag, puzzled but enchanted at the same time. Every moment with Claudia was an adventure, he thought, a new lesson in the pleasures life can offer a young, vivacious person. She was unique, indeed. "Thirty-one," Claudia whispered with a conspiratorial wink to the liveried operator of the carpeted elevator, and the poor man nervously fidgeted with his buttons all the way up, apparently debating if he should call the house detective.

When they arrived at their floor, Claudia took Alex by the hand, dragged him to a double door and unlocked it. "Welcome to my place," she said, brushing disobedient wisps of hair from her face. Then, stepping aside, she let him enter first.

Alex was dismayed by the elegance of the suite. It was softly lit, furnished in light gray and vivid plum colors. The walls, covered with beige wallpaper, were decorated with colorful sketches of Parisian scenes — the Sacre Coeur, the Arc de Triomphe, a crowd on the Champs-Elysées. The living room was a showroom of exquisite chests and cupboards in turn-of-the-century style. The desk by the window, lit by a brass table lamp, was covered with green Italian marble. Alex liked the sketch that hung over it, of a barge on the Seine. It sailed under a bridge, with Notre Dame Cathedral looming in the background. The beige carpet was deep and soft under his feet. Two Oriental vases stood by the door. On a round table, set between two old-fashioned chairs with padded armrests, an assortment of canapés was artfully spread. A golden box of Godiva, his favorite chocolates, stood beside the hors d'oeuvres, tied with a crisp golden ribbon. A bottle of champagne peeked out of a silver ice bucket.

"Right on time," Claudia announced, carelessly throwing her coat on a sofa and scooping up a salmon sandwich.

"Claudia," he said, still holding his bag, "I must call Nina."

"I called her myself," Claudia said, planting a languorous kiss on his cheek. "She knows you won't be home before tomorrow." She nibbled on her salmon. "Divine!" she gasped, fluttering her eyelids. "Darling, will you pour the champagne?"

"I'd be delighted," Alex said, struggling with the cork, "if you'd just tell me what all this is about." The cork popped out of the bottle, hit the ceiling and landed on a plum-colored armchair. Alex wiped the foam from his sleeve and reached for the slender champagne glasses.

Claudia sank contentedly into a deep armchair, stretching her legs. "This is a celebration, Alex. I got an advance today. We're celebrating my first salary, and the forthcoming graduation of Alex Gordon, Ph.D."

"Good Lord, Claudia, you spent your entire salary on one night at the Waldorf?"

She frowned, plunging into a mental calculation. "Yes, that's about it." She brightened up and the delicious dimple bloomed in her cheek again. "So what? It's my money, and this is how I want to spend it. I bought us a memory. A night of outrageous decadence. Will you make love to me, big boy?"

She fell silent, and when she spoke again, her voice was lower, softer. "Can you think of anything better to spend our money on, Alessandro?"

HE WATCHED HER SLEEP lying on her back on the double bed, her head resting in a curved arm, the soft contours of her face barely visible under the stray mass of black hair. Her other arm was stretched out beside her, resting on the pillows with carefree abandon.

The bedroom was very still, very peaceful. He turned off the lights. In the window, the view of the New York skyline became even more dramatic, the Chrysler Building cutting its jagged profile against the dark background. A few brightly lit windows glowed forlornly in the night. His eyes shifted back to Claudia's nude body and he listened to her quiet breathing.

His life, he thought, had been molded by three women: Tonya, whose intense romanticism flowed in his blood; Nina, who had instilled in him the love of Russia; and Claudia, who had quenched his teenage yearnings and dispelled his solitude — but who also had taught him that life could be fun, not just an endless procession of slogans, red flags, and faceless crowds marching somberly toward the future.

He knew that Nina resented Claudia and thought she had stolen his love from her. She probably blamed Claudia for the change in his political opinions as well.

He loved Nina dearly. Still, her fanatical devotion to her communist gods had turned into a formidable wall between them. Every time he came home, he would fight with Nina over Kremlin policy. His former admiration of the Soviet Union had been shattered; he now regarded Brezhnev as a cynical dictator who oppressed with an iron fist a beautiful country and a great nation.

He wasn't the little Russian boy anymore, lost in a faraway country. He considered himself American. He had been intensely involved in the major issues: the Vietnam War and the struggle for equal rights, which revived his dreams of social justice. But his main interest was in his studies. His deep knowledge of Russia, its society and history, gave him an advantage over his fellow students; he was by far the best Sovietology student at Brown, easily scooping up scholarships and awards. His disappointment with communism had turned him from an unconditional admirer of Soviet Russia into a sober and unbiased critic. An article on the power struggle at the Kremlin that he wrote in the students' magazine was quoted in several national newspapers, and he was described as "a Brown scholar."

Still, he failed in his efforts to obtain a visa to the Soviet Union. A few months ago twenty-two postgraduate students had applied for Russian visas, to participate in a student-exchange program. Twenty-one were approved; Alex Gordon stayed home.

Beside him Claudia stirred and her hand came to rest on his thigh. Thank God for Claudia, he thought. The peppy teenager had grown into a smart young woman. A year after they met, she had graduated from high school, and there had never been a prettier prom queen. Her proud parents sent her to the University of Hartford, in Connecticut. Since then, Claudia had spent every other weekend with him, in Providence, or at some little country inn. They explored the forgotten forests and mountains of New England, driving along country roads, discovering quaint inns and lodges. When in the city, they would go to a movie, and to a disco late at night; Claudia adored dancing. Claudia's family, after a few halfhearted protests — her brothers were very close to her former boyfriend — had finally accepted Alex. Mama Benevento desperately tried to tame her rebellious daughter, but finally capitulated and let her be. Claudia was too independent to be bridled by a family that had spoiled her for eighteen years. There was nothing they could do to keep Claudia away from Alex.

But this beautiful period in their lives was coming to an end. Claudia had majored in arts, and returned home. He was about to get his doctorate and start a new chapter in his life. And he wanted Claudia to be part of it.

In a surge of tenderness, he leaned over the sleeping girl and kissed her exposed neck, breathing her perfume. He gently shook her shoulder. "Claudia? Claudia, wake up."

She stretched lazily, her eyes slowly opening. He again thought of a Dylan Thomas verse. ". . . the opening of her nightlong eyes." It had been written for Claudia.

"What is it?" she murmured. "What time is it?"

"Claudia," he said again. "Are you awake? Do you hear me?"

"Yes," she groaned. "What happened, Alex?"

"Marry me," he said.

"What?"

"Marry me. Please."

She was wide awake now, staring at him in astonishment. "What are you talking about? Go to bed, you need some sleep."

"Claudia, I'm serious. We love each other, we're good together, let's get married."

"You are serious," she decided, regarding him gravely with a look he'd never seen in her eyes before.

"What?" he said, feeling suddenly defeated.

She got up, put on a white bathrobe embroidered with the hotel logo, and carried her bag to the window. She took out a package of cigarettes and lit one with unsteady, nervous gestures. "No," she finally said, "I don't want to get married."

"You don't want to get married?" he repeated stupidly. He had been sure she would be thrilled by his proposal. "Why? Don't you love me?" He felt uncomfortable, sitting naked in front of her, so he went into the bathroom and wrapped a towel around his waist.

"I love you more than anything in the world," Claudia was saying. "But I don't want to get married. Not now."

"Why, Claudia, what's the matter?"

"Why? Because I want to become a fashion designer," she said, pensively exhaling a long puff of smoke. "It's a tremendous challenge, Alex. I want to give it my best shot."

"But nobody asked you to give it up." He sat back down on the bed.

"Oh yes. You did." She sat beside him and softly caressed his shoulder. "If we get married now, I'll have to live with you, all the time, perhaps at Brown, perhaps at Stanford. But I can't, Alex, don't you see? I have to be in New York most of the time. New York is the fashion capital. Besides, Havermeyer wants me to travel around the country for the next year or so and organize his fashion shows. He said that if I'm good at that, he might take a couple of my designs for his collection. This is going to be an exhausting year, I can't just get married and stay home."

"You're going to travel with him?" Alex asked suspiciously.

"With a team that he's putting together now. His son is going to be in charge."

"Oh, him," Alex muttered angrily. Ronnie Havermeyer was a frequent name in the gossip columns. A handsome man, he had a reputation as a hedonist and a womanizer. Alex suddenly had the feeling that he might lose Claudia. "We can get married and you can travel wherever you want," he suggested eagerly.

She shook her head. "You know, while I was looking for work, I even thought of modeling for a while. I went to this agency on Fifty-ninth and Sixth . . . Cosmopolitan Models, that's the name. I met a middle-aged guy who sat in an office with his feet on his desk, smoking a big cigar. He just glanced at my hips and shook his head. 'Lady,' this guy says to me, 'you're made to be a mother, not a model.' "

"Don't you want to be a mother?"

"Of course I do. And that's what will happen if we get married now." She saw him shaking his head. "Yes, yes, believe me. In two years I'll have two kids, and all my travels will be between the kitchen and the nursery, with a hop to the supermarket once in a while. I want to have children, but in my own time. I'll get married, but not right now." Trying to soften it, she adopted an exaggerated Italian accent. "I'll make you a lot of bambinos, okay, Alessandro? But in a couple of years, *capice?*"

"No, no *capice,*" he said testily, annoyed by her cool-headed attitude and her determination that her career came first. What the hell, he thought, if she was really in love, she should have agreed to marry him right away. He had always thought she was as romantic and impulsive as he. Three years ago it was Claudia who had raised the subject of marriage. She had wanted to get married then, but he had cooled her enthusiasm, saying that he had to get his Ph.D. first.

She had been deeply disappointed, and had said so. Since then, he'd assumed that she was counting the days until his graduation, eager to get married. But tonight she was behaving differently. If she started traveling — and with Havermeyer's son — they might drift apart. A year was a lot of time.

"So what is this?" he lashed out at her, making a sweeping gesture with his hand. "A farewell night?"

"Alex, I love you," she said returning to the bed. "Nothing has changed." Her hand slipped under his towel. "Let's go to bed, let's make love."

"No," he said, seething. "I don't want to make love now." He pulled away and left the bedroom. She called after him, but he didn't answer. He groped his way in the dark sitting room, banging his knee against the table where the food had been set. He pulled the drapes aside. The window glass was ice cold against his burning forehead. He glanced at the empty street below. A lonely figure was scurrying in the snow. What am I going to do if I lose her? Alex thought. How can I live without Claudia?

THE INSISTENT RINGING of the telephone tore Grimaldi out of a bad dream. He recalled only darkness and piercing screams, or perhaps these had been the strident summons of the telephone. He was bathed in sweat and gasping for air as he picked up the receiver. "Yes," he mumbled, "hello." The first spring rain rapped furiously on the windows, which were tinged in an eerie gray light.

"Is this the Evdokiev Hospital?" a deep voice asked in Russian. "My wife is about to have a baby and — "

"Wrong number," he muttered. "Always the same mistake." He slammed down the phone and wiped his moist forehead. The modular red figures on his digital clock spelled 6:50 A.M. In the grayness outside, skeletal boughs were swaying before his window, whipped by the Moscow wind.

Grimaldi got up, showered and dressed quickly. He cut himself shaving, and his skin burned as he splashed some Missoni aftershave on his face. His fingers were trembling, fumbling over his shirt buttons. What happened, he thought, what's the emergency? If it had been something really serious, Kalinin would have given him the code signal to leave the country, but he hadn't. His voice had sounded confident. Calm down, he said to himself, don't panic. Kalinin had been away for two weeks, on some assignment to Paris and Amsterdam. He was supposed to be back at the end of this week. He had evidently returned earlier: perhaps he had something urgent to report.

Grimaldi made himself a cup of black coffee, with no sugar, and slowly sipped it by the kitchen window. He looked out on a drab courtyard, flooded by the rain; the carcass of an ancient motorcycle with a sidecar was rotting by a rusty iron gate adorned with broken spikes. Nobody could suspect that the phone call was an emergency signal. The Evdokiev Hospital's number was almost identical with his own; only the last digit was different. Kalinin had worked hard to find a number close to his own for the "wrong number" routine; the hospital was ideal, because it permitted emergency calls around the clock without raising the suspicions of the KGB, which no doubt tapped Grimaldi's telephone.

He picked up his coat and went out. There was nobody outside the apartment, and the staircase was dark; somebody — probably the janitor — had again stolen the light bulbs. The lobby was deserted. The rain was pouring down furiously, drops ricocheting on the pavement. The militiaman who watched his building had found refuge in the next doorway. The streetlamps were still on, looming behind the wavering curtain of water like smoky globes of pale fire. He opened his umbrella. There was a public phone on the corner of Chapayevski, but he didn't use it. With all the foreigners living in his building, Grimaldi had no doubt that the booth was more heavily bugged than his own apartment.

Scurrying toward Balteiskaya, he stepped into a puddle and felt the cold water trickle into his shoe. He threw a look over his shoulder but didn't notice anything suspicious. At the corner of Balteiskaya there was a small workers' buffet that opened at six A.M. Twice a week he came over and ate their disgusting breakfast, only to justify the occasional use of the phone booth outside.

As he opened the door, warm air bathed his face, thick with the smells of stale tobacco, sweat, and frying oil. *"Dobroye utro,"* he said, squeezing in among the construction workers, metro employees, and police officers who crowded the narrow buffet. Wisps of cigarette smoke hovered in the air, and crushed butts littered the floor. The woman behind the counter, a middle-aged Siberian wearing a soiled white apron on her fat body and an angry scowl on her lined face, knew him well. "Good morning, Mr. Saint-Clair," she said formally, a steel tooth gleaming in her mouth.

Several looks converged upon him, focusing on his expensive coat and tailored suit. He had gotten used to the envious stares of the Muscovites; he could understand how the poor devils felt. He ordered some black bread, a cube of butter, a piece of salted herring, and a cup of tea, and carried his chipped tray to a table in the back.

After a moment the Russians stopped staring at him and resumed their conversations. He carefully studied the people clustered by the counter. He vaguely knew most of them, and their behavior seemed normal. His fears subsided; he could tell he wasn't being watched. He took his time munching the tasteless food; then, at 7:45, he went back to the counter. There were only a few people left; the morning crowd had already dispersed. The Siberian woman was washing dishes in a sink half full of greasy, soapy water. "I'll be late for the office," he said in stilted Russian. "Would you have ten kopecks for the telephone?"

The woman wiped her red hands on her apron and handed him a coin, then slid two red beads and one yellow one on the abacus that stood beside the cash register. Russians could live without computers and calculators, he thought, but without an abacus they would be lost.

He stepped into the phone booth. His first call was to his driver, Nikita, to come and pick him up at the buffet, and not at home as usual. The second, at exactly seven-fifty, was to another phone booth, a couple of miles away. The numbers of the public phones he could call changed every week, according to a prearranged schedule.

On the other end of the line the receiver was picked up; Grimaldi didn't say a word. "Tomorrow, at seven A.M., at the Gastronom entrance on Tchaikovskaya," a voice calmly said.

Grimaldi knew the code by heart. Tomorrow was today, seven A.M. was eight P.M., the Gastronom was the parking lot of the Ukraina Hotel. He felt reassured by Kalinin's serene voice. He was pleased he would see him tonight.

He went back to the buffet and paid his bill, ignoring the change the Siberian handed him. Tipping was forbidden in Russia, but nobody really cared. His Mercedes stopped outside and he hurried out, wondering why Kalinin had requested a crash meeting.

AT THE END of the day, as Nikita steered the Mercedes through the evening traffic, Grimaldi sank back in his seat. Lately he had been getting restless. His seventh year in Moscow was drawing to its end, and he wasn't thrilled anymore by the secret knowledge that he was running the top CIA agent in the Kremlin. His days at the office, buying caviar and salmon for his bogus Canadian company, were boring; his meetings with the stolid bureaucrats of the ministries of Fisheries and Foreign Trade were maddening. He rarely mixed with the foreign community, had no friends, and found little interest in the limited pleasures Moscow could offer.

He never approached a man, although he had run into some very attractive boys, and by their looks and gestures had understood they belonged to his own breed. But accosting one of them would be equivalent to suicide. Oleg, too, was out of bounds, of course; besides, the man was married and had children now.

For lack of choice Grimaldi tried, once in a while, to satisfy his sexual fantasies with a female, and picked up a woman who was probably a KGB swallow anyway, instructed to sleep with him as part of the routine surveillance of foreigners. In the morning she would leave, thrilled by his presents — a tin of Nescafé, some sticks of chewing gum, a couple of bathing soaps. He was tired of this ritual, too. Russian women had no imagination, he decided; they had no feeling for kinky sex, brutal and juicy the way he liked it. Poor things, with the life they were leading, all they could think about was survival, not pleasure.

Even his mission in Moscow had slipped into a routine pattern — communications with Kalinin, servicing dead-letter drops, coding the information, then dispatching the innocuous-looking letters to a cover address in Montreal. During his first months in Moscow he would read with bated breath the top-secret documents Kalinin supplied: minutes of the Politburo, military production reports, position papers for the disarmament talks, intelligence assessments. But after a while he had gotten used to handling the top-notch product; now he coded the reports mechanically, like a robot, and dispatched them to Langley via Montreal.

He didn't even enjoy his yearly home leave — the flight to Montreal, the sneaking to Buffalo, the switch of identities from Saint-Clair to Grimaldi, then his trip to New York for debriefing and some decent food and games. Washington was out of bounds, the risk of exposure too great. All this had become routine, and he knew how dangerous routine could be for a secret agent.

He had panicked only once, in 1970, when a young Russian had tailed him from his office to the National Hotel. If it had happened today, he might not have noticed the bastard — he wasn't as alert anymore. But that was almost four years ago; he had rushed to a phone and called Kalinin for help. His fear had soared when the young man had popped up at the Bolshoi minutes before his crash meeting with Oleg. He had barely overcome his impulse to run away during the intermission. He had good reasons to worry. As a Canadian businessman, he didn't have diplomatic status. If he were caught, he was bound to rot in the Lubyanka for the rest of his life.

Thank God it turned out to be a false alarm. The young man was just a KGB trainee who had been assigned, like a couple of hundred other students, to tail a foreigner around Moscow. Kalinin had brought him the good news a couple of days later; it appeared that the young man hadn't even filed a report, since he'd been transferred to another department. Perhaps Oleg had something to do with that; he never offered a full explanation.

When he'd accepted the Moscow job, Grimaldi had hoped it would catapult him to a top position in the Company. His prospects still looked promising: he knew that at Langley they spoke of him with awe, regarding him as the perfect spy, the CIA Scarlet Pimpernel. But even a legend couldn't last forever. He should quit while he was still on top, he thought, and return to headquarters to reap all the glory. The CIA was changing, a younger generation taking over. He should have packed and left already, gone back to Langley and claimed his portion of the spoils.

But he didn't want to leave without taking Kalinin with him; this would give the operation a dazzling climax. The greatest American spy since World War II, and his master, returning unscathed from the lion's den! Oleg wasn't ready yet, though. Grimaldi suspected he enjoyed his cozy position at the Kremlin and his personal privileges. His friend seemed to fear the challenge of resettling in an alien country under a false identity.

Grimaldi didn't have to wait forever; he could ask to be relieved, and his request would be granted. But his relationship with Kalinin kept him in Moscow. They met very rarely, for brief, practical conversations. Still, he felt he was Oleg's only support, and that pleased him; their intimacy was something far beyond their common endeavor. One day, when they were back in the States, they might become lovers again, like in those glorious days in Berlin.

"Here we are," Nikita said. The car stopped by the brightly lit entrance to the Ukraina. Two tourist buses waited outside, one carrying the sign MOSCOW CIRCUS, the other FOLKLORE. The Western tourists were about to start their night of fun, Russian style. He glanced at his watch. It was seven-fifty. He figured that the meeting with Kalinin would last five or ten minutes, then he would dine at the Ukraina to justify his visit to the hotel. "Pick me up at nine-thirty," he said to Nikita. "And be good."

"*Khorosho.*" The driver grinned. In ten minutes, Grimaldi thought, Nikita would be screwing his little girlfriend who lived off Kropotkinskaya. She wanted to leave him, but Nikita was always tempting her with American cigarettes he stole from Grimaldi's office. Well, at least he had something to think about other than his boss's nightly outings.

Grimaldi entered the Ukraina, nervously looking for something unusual, somebody waiting by the entrance, reading a newspaper, a couple hanging out by the phone booths or strolling by the duty-free shops. He didn't spot anybody except the two uniformed officers who checked the foreigners' papers and kept local swindlers, whores, and black marketeers out of the hotel. The front desk looked normal, too, with a couple of girls bent over large ledgers, and a squat concierge suppressing a bored yawn. When the KGB laid a trap, the front desk was the first place they planted a couple of agents, in hotel uniforms.

Grimaldi had a couple of vodkas at the foreign currency bar. He was getting jumpy again. Perhaps he wasn't so brave after all, he thought. He had been ashamed of his behavior back there in the Alps, and he had refused to admit that he was a coward. Clever, cunning, smart, but a coward all the same. It was time for him to settle down in a cozy office back home and let somebody else play games with the KGB.

At 8:02 he left the hotel by the lower entrance and casually strolled to the parking lot.

Kalinin's car wasn't there.

HE STOOD SHIVERING on the dark Kutuzovsky Prospect, and it wasn't the cold. Cabs were rare in Moscow at this hour, but he raised his hand, holding a package of Marlboro cigarettes, and three taxis stopped with a screeching of brakes. He took the second. On the way to Gorky Park, he slumped down in the backseat, wiping his perspiring face with a linen handkerchief. Emergency rules, he thought, God, I never expected I'd use them. Never wait for me if I'm late, Kalinin had said, never come to the parking lot again. Call me at the current pay phone number three times, at five minute intervals. If there's no answer, check our dead drop. Twelve hours after the missed appointment, call me at the pay phone again. If there's no answer, take a cab to Sheremetyevo and leave the bloody country before they get you, too.

He had called from the Ukraina. The first time the number had been busy, but the second and third there had been no answer. That left him with the dead-letter drop at Gorky Park. His thoughts were confused. He had an open Air France ticket to Montreal, via Paris, but it was too late to make a reservation tonight. His papers were in order, he had nothing to fear on that score. But he couldn't just walk into the airport tomorrow and catch the plane, that would seem too suspicious. He might have to use the emergency procedure, reserved only for cases of extreme danger.

What could have happened to Kalinin? He had spoken to him twice this morning, which meant he was probably free — unless he had been arrested already and been forced by the KGB to establish contact. They had some quite persuasive methods at the Lubyanka. But if Oleg had been forced to call him, why hadn't the Russkies arrested him at the Ukraina parking lot?

"Gorky Park," the driver announced. He smiled happily when Grimaldi handed him the cigarettes, and gunned his Zhiguli like a racing car. It was raining again, a fine, steady drizzle. Grimaldi stood for a moment at the park entrance, then doubled back toward the Moskva River. The riverfront was deserted; the nasty weather had chased away even the occasional pair of lovers. He stopped several times, looking back. But there were no shadows sneaking behind him, no sound of footsteps but his own. He raised his eyes. Ahead of him loomed the massive shape of Krimsky Bridge.

As he reached the near pillar of the bridge, sunk deep in the soaked ground, he knelt as if to tie his shoelaces. His fingers were trembling, and a hollow had formed in the pit of his stomach. If they were after him, now was the time. He cursed under his breath. This cloak and dagger stuff wasn't for him anymore. There should be a chain of agents servicing Kalinin and collecting his product. But Oleg had been adamant: no other agents, he had said, no cutouts, no intermediaries. Just you and me.

In the concrete support of the pillar there was a deep fissure a foot above the ground. He removed the chunk of concrete blocking the opening, then probed deeper. His fingers almost missed the single sheet of thick paper, folded several times. He grasped it, stuck it in his shoe, then got up. His knees were shaking.

The drizzle enveloped him; he walked, as if in a cloud of spray, across the bridge and caught another cab outside the golden-domed church of St. Nicholas. He was back at the Ukraina long before Nikita had completed his amorous exploit.

THE MESSAGE was blunt and concise, stunning as a death sentence. It was printed in block letters and numerals on a thick sheet of paper. He decoded it in the locked privacy of his apartment, checking the groups of numbers against his 1965 edition of *Anna Karenina*. His astonishment grew with every new word he jotted on the notepad lying on his desk, beside Kalinin's message.

> 1720 hours. Can't contact you, too late. Am leaving this message in case something happens to me and our meeting is aborted. Incidentally met at Paris Sovtorg office young officer KGB Department Thirteen violent operations. Turned out to be the one who tailed you to the National and the Bolshoi four years ago. Knew me, remembered seeing me in theater, asked if I knew you. I denied, he didn't believe me. I flew home earlier to warn you. Border police advised me at 1705 hours he had just landed. I believe he flew in to investigate our ties. If you don't meet me tonight get out please get out. Your devoted friend.

Your devoted friend. He rubbed his eyes. The room was entirely dark, except for the yellow circle the desk lamp cast on the papers before him. A cold tremor shook his body. His devoted friend hadn't come. His devoted friend was certainly under arrest, probably tortured, possibly dead.

Perhaps they were watching the apartment now, perhaps they had planted microphones while he wasn't there. It was too late to start looking for them, though. His devoted friend might have told them everything by now. Very few people could withstand torture.

He looked at Kalinin's letter again. There was another phrase, hastily scribbled at the bottom of the page, and he decoded it, already considering it a message from the grave.

"Officer's name Dimitri Morozov," were Kalinin's last words.

Dimitri Morozov. Did he know that name? He tried to concentrate, but he was too agitated by Kalinin's message. Relax, he said to himself, calm down, try to think, try to remember. Every detail might be crucial. Who is Dimitri Morozov? He probed backward into his memory. Where had he stumbled upon this name? It wasn't in Moscow, he was certain of that. It must have been years ago, back in Washington or New York, when he worked in the Soviet Division. Who the hell was Morozov?

A befuddled memory slowly surfaced. There had been a Morozov in Stalin's time. But it wasn't Dimitri, it was Nikolai . . . no, Boris, Colonel Boris Morozov. KGB, Second Chief Directorate. The image began to come clear. There was something odd connected with him. Of course, his wife! Tonya Gordon, the Jewish poet. She had been shot in 1953. She had two children: Alexander was her first husband's son; the second was Morozov's little boy.

He sat still, his eyes glued to Oleg's message. Dimitri Morozov. He had to be the son of Boris Morozov. The father had disappeared twenty years ago, but not before whisking his stepson, Alexander Gordon, to the United States. He remembered seeing an FBI report about the child, who lived with relatives in Brooklyn.

Two brothers, he thought, the son and the stepson of a KGB spymaster, one in Moscow, one in New York. One of them was a spy already. He wondered what had happened to the other. He went to the window and looked outside. The militiaman was walking back and forth in front of the house. A light blue car passed by, an old Zis, its muffler growling, and turned the corner at Chapayevski. He pulled the shades. He tore Kalinin's message and the top page of his pad to pieces, piled them in the ashtray and lit them with his gold lighter. He watched them burn, stirring the ashes.

So Dimitri had become a KGB officer, and a dangerous one. Moscow Center placed only the most trustworthy personnel in Western Europe. Department Thirteen sent to the West only accomplished killers. Morozov had trapped Kalinin, perhaps murdered him, the only friend Grimaldi ever had. He felt a sudden surge of hatred. Perhaps at this very moment Dimitri Morozov was torturing Oleg; perhaps he was laying a trap for him, too. But if he succeeded in getting out of here, he would hit back. He would crush the dirty bastard.

Grimaldi took a deep breath, feeling energy and resolve flood through his body. He'd make the young sonofabitch pay. He went to the kitchen and took an ice-cold bottle of vodka from the freezer. He broke the seal and poured himself a generous drink, then returned to his desk. He lit a thin black cigar and exhaled the thick smoke, gazing at a lithograph of two entangled nude girls on the wall across the room.

First, he had to get out of here. He had to give the Russians a plausible reason for his sudden departure. Therefore, he had to resort to the emergency procedure.

He leafed through the foreign diplomats' register until he found the home number of Oscar Housman, the economic attaché at the Canadian embassy. He knew the man superficially, had met him only a couple of times before. They had never exchanged anything but banalities. Housman was the only one who knew of his existence, but his knowledge was limited. He had been told there was an undercover agent in Moscow who might contact him in case of emergency; he hadn't been told under what name Grimaldi operated.

Grimaldi lit a new cigar and dialed the number. His fingers were trembling slightly. A woman's voice, low and reserved, flowed into the receiver. "Housman," she said.

"Good evening," he said, "this is Charles Saint-Clair. We met at the ambassador's New Year's reception."

"Oh yes," she lied, "of course. How are you?"

"I hope I am not calling too late. May I speak to Oscar?"

"Just a moment."

He took a sip of his vodka and spilled a couple of drops on his sleeve. Oscar Housman picked up the phone immediately; he must have been standing beside his wife. He had a tired, gravelly voice. "Good evening," he said.

"Charles Saint-Clair here." He carefully planted the code words into his question, as he had been instructed back home. "Excuse me for disturbing you at this late hour, but do you perhaps have the last commercial agreement between Canada and the Soviet Union?" He waited a moment for the first code word to sink in.

"Yes?" Housman said cautiously.

"I heard a rumor," Grimaldi went on, "that the Russians might sign a new contract for fish exports with France, and that might allow them to dump Canada and the U.S. via the Common Market."

There was a short silence on the other end of the line. Housman had understood his message, now he had to acknowledge. "I have no information about such a contract," Housman said calmly. "But if you wish, I can check that for you. As for the agreement, I have it in my office."

"I'd be very grateful if — "

"I'll look it up first thing in the morning. But I'm almost sure we benefit from the most-favored-nation clause, which means that if they lower their prices for the Europeans, they must do it for us, too. I'll check that and call you tomorrow."

Grimaldi hung up, relieved. Housman had used the "most-favored-nation" and "Europeans" key words, meaning he had gotten the message. Grimaldi had nothing to do now but pack and await the telegram. He gulped down his drink, thinking of Morozov again. Then he pulled the ashtray toward him and viciously killed his cigar.

THE TELEGRAM was delivered to his flat at seven-fifteen in the morning by a young mailman with red hair and black nails. "Come back at once, Mother very ill," his alleged sister had cabled from Montreal.

Two hours later he arrived at Sheremetyevo in a fierce rain. His flight was already boarding. He had called earlier, and his boarding pass was waiting at the Air France counter. He went through customs without a hitch; he was carrying only one bag. He was tieless and wore sunglasses, in spite of the darkness outside. He kept waving his telegram at everybody, and it helped; the customs officers and the KGB representative at the Air France counter mournfully shook their heads, spoke to him in low voices and looked at him with compassion. The telegram had apparently quelled any doubts they might have had about his sudden departure.

At the immigration booth, he handed his papers to the uniformed officer, a heavy gray-haired man with a permanent frown and suspicious eyes. The officer unhurriedly studied his documents, wetting his sturdy thumb on his tongue. He diligently compared the passport with the Russian visa form, casting long, speculative looks at Grimaldi. A shadow fell on his open passport, and Grimaldi turned around.

Mean black eyes, shaded by thick eyebrows, stared at him from a lean bloodless face. There was ruthless, almost savage power in the sharp jaw and the aggressive chin. Yet, it was a handsome young face, crowned by wavy brown hair, the nose and lips delicately carved in the waxen skin; the lined forehead and the sensitive mouth suggested inner torment.

The odd contrast in the young man's features made Grimaldi think of a Robespierre or a Dzerzhinsky, a fanatic revolutionary so utterly dedicated to men's freedom that he would readily chop off their heads to achieve it.

Dimitri Morozov hadn't changed much, except for the hair, which had been cropped short when Grimaldi had seen him four years ago. He recalled his shabby clothes at the Bolshoi. Today Morozov was wearing a foreign-made charcoal woolen suit that fitted him well, a smart blue shirt, and a striped tie. He shifted his eyes to the immigration officer.

"Charles Saint-Clair," the KGB officer said to the young civilian. "Canadian."

A chill ran up Grimaldi's spine. Morozov reached for the passport and picked it up. Grimaldi looked around for Morozov's team. They never came alone. He focused on four men in raincoats and hats, clustered by the main customs counter. They were smoking and conversing in low voices. Stinging sweat pricked his skin and soaked his underclothes. Morozov was playing a cat and mouse game with him. In a moment he would ask him, very politely, to step into the next room on a formality, and there they would arrest him, far from the crowd. A closed van with blackened windows would rush him to the Lubyanka, where the investigators would be waiting in their underground domain. They might have already done their job on Kalinin.

Morozov thoughtfully leafed through the passport, then raised his eyes, studying Grimaldi's face. His expression didn't change, but there was stark fury burning in the deep-set eyes. He leaned toward the booth and handed the passport, with a nod, to the immigration officer. He was letting him go! Grimaldi stared in disbelief at the uniformed clerk, who laboriously stamped his papers, then turned to the next passenger.

Grimaldi felt Morozov's eyes boring into his back, but he didn't turn around. He feared another trick. He stepped into the departure hall, looking straight ahead, and walked stiffly to the gate. The place was full of uniformed officers armed with handguns. Everybody seemed to be watching him. He mentally assessed the distance between himself and the gate. Twenty yards, ten, five. The ground hostess was nervously smiling at him; he was the last passenger.

"Monsieur Saint-Clair!"

He winced. The voice that lashed at him was firm and controlled.

He turned back. Morozov faced him, his arms crossed. His face was impassive. "I wish your mother a prompt recovery," he said.

ONLY AFTER GULPING down the third double vodka served by a skinny Air France hostess did Grimaldi begin to recover his senses. Out the window he could see the carpet of murky clouds they had sliced through, as they soared into a blue, sunny sky. He was safe now, out of Morozov's reach.

He felt a tremendous surge of hatred for the black-eyed devil who had debased him a few minutes ago, just for fun; he could swear that Morozov had enjoyed scaring the living daylights out of him. Grimaldi had never felt more humiliated. The Russian bastard had almost made him shit in his pants, deliberately ridiculing him. Just you wait, Morozov, he thought. We'll meet again, and you'll be the one who bites the dust.

Last night, reading Oleg's last message, he had dreamed of revenge. Now it was turning into an obsession, he could feel it in his bones. Not only revenge for what Morozov did to him and Kalinin, but for the damage to his career. Grimaldi ground his teeth, thinking of the debriefing in Langley that would probably start tomorrow. The Company experts would be cruel, merciless, suspicious, and he would have to endure all their insinuations. "Did you have to escape in such a hurry?" someone would ask. "Wasn't there any way to rescue Top Hat?" Someone else would pick up from there: "Perhaps, if you had waited another twenty-four hours, he would have established contact. Did you seriously consider a different solution? How did you escape so easily, with Morozov breathing down your neck?"

Even if he emerged from the debriefing unscathed, his hasty escape would tarnish his reputation. The story would trail in his wake, like the rumor of an incurable disease. Why did he stay in Moscow so long? officials would ask in conference rooms. If he had left a year ago, he might have saved the operation and Top Hat as well. Now the Russkies would be able to assess the damage — knowing what subjects Top Hat had dealt with — and in a year or two all the material he gave us would be obsolete.

Grimaldi had to prove he was still valuable. If he wanted to survive, he had to offer his superiors something new, something that wouldn't depend on the Top Hat fiasco. And he could think of nothing else but

Morozov. Morozov was with Department Thirteen, the most secret unit of Moscow Center. He was stationed in Paris, under the cover of a Sovtorg employee. If Grimaldi presented the Company the means to destroy him, he could kill two birds with one stone: defeat Department Thirteen and settle his personal account with Morozov.

For that, he could use Alexander Gordon. He would serve one brother to the other on a platter, and watch from behind the scenes, lending a helping hand if needed.

Yes, that could be done. He smiled back at the hostess who brought him a plate of food. The prospect of his revenge definitely made him feel better.

IT WAS LIKE hunting the wolverine, Dimitri thought, when you spend hours painstakingly trying to outwit the cunning, furry predator. And when you finally succeed in cornering the animal, bringing it within your power, and begin squeezing the trigger, you wait just a split second too long and the little beast suddenly darts between your feet and makes it to safety. He had hunted the wolverine in Siberia during a two-week endurance exercise with the untouchables. He remembered the trapped look in the animal's mean eyes. It trembled before him, crouching, waiting for its death. Dimitri had felt the intoxicating sensation of power as he stood in the snow, foretasting the pleasure of the kill. The trigger had slowly yielded to his steady pressure. He didn't want to fire yet, he was enjoying the moment, he didn't want the chase to end. But the shot had been too late coming, and the wolverine had suddenly darted beside him, into the low bushes and out of view.

Saint-Clair had made it this time, he thought, as he stood on the tarmac, hatless in the heavy rain, watching the Air France Boeing head for the low sky. Saint-Clair had escaped because he, Dimitri, had waited, that night at the Bolshoi, and last night at the Ukraina. There was nothing he could do now to prevent Saint-Clair from leaving. "Do you have any evidence against him?" Oktober had asked him yesterday. "Without evidence, you cannot arrest an eminent Canadian business-man."

Damn you, Oktober, he thought. Evidence or no evidence, he should have whisked Saint-Clair away last night; he could have wrenched a confession from the perfumed playboy in no time. He had missed his moment. To arrest the Canadian at the airport, Oktober said, he needed evidence. But the only man who could incriminate Saint-Clair was Colonel Oleg Kalinin. And Kalinin had vanished.

Fuck your mother, Kalinin, Dimitri cursed to himself. As soon as he had confronted him in Paris, he had realized the GRU colonel was guilty. He hadn't expected Kalinin's visit, and Kalinin hadn't expected to find him there. They had met late at night, at the Sovtorg office on Boulevard Pereire, and while they were discussing operational matters — the kidnapping of a NATO courier on his way to Brussels — Dimitri had suddenly asked about that night at the Bolshoi, four years ago. Kalinin had been caught off guard and denied everything. They both knew he was lying.

Dimitri had picked up the phone as soon as Kalinin left. He was sure Kalinin was going to defect, to save his neck; therefore he had blocked all his escape routes. Kalinin was a damned traitor, he was dead meat. Dimitri assumed he would run for his life. But Kalinin hadn't tried to escape, he had chosen the one route Dimitri hadn't thought of — back to Russia. By the time Dimitri had landed in Moscow, Kalinin had gone to ground.

He stepped back under the gate marquee and lit a cigarette, watching the black smoke left by the Boeing. He'd had no choice, actually. If he had phoned Moscow Center from Paris and accused Kalinin of treason, nobody would have believed him. He would have been brought back sedated and tied to a stretcher. From the airport they would have taken him straight to a nuthouse. Kalinin, after all, was the GRU man at the Kremlin, and no Moscow Center official would dare accuse him without an ironclad case.

There was one man, though, whom Dimitri trusted: Oktober. On his arrival in Moscow he had rushed to Oktober's headquarters. But Oktober had shaken his head. "You can't go near Kalinin without proof, my boy," he had croaked. "And you don't have a case against Saint-Clair."

Dimitri could guess what had happened. Back in Moscow, Kalinin had probably established contact with Saint-Clair, by a crash meeting or a dead-letter drop. Dimitri had followed Saint-Clair last night, but had lost him for an hour, at the Ukraina. Saint-Clair had vanished from the hotel lobby at 8:02 and returned at 9:10. Soon after, his driver had taken him home. During that one hour, he must have received Kalinin's message.

He mused wryly about the irony of the situation. Saint-Clair's hurried departure was the very proof against Kalinin he so badly needed. He shrugged. He would find Kalinin sooner or later; and if he handled the traitor wisely, he might even use him as bait to trap Saint-Clair.

IT TOOK HIS MEN three months to capture Kalinin, when, wearing an elaborate disguise and carrying a Czech passport, he tried to cross the Czech-Austrian frontier. By then Dimitri was already back in France, and the Saint-Clair affair had been taken out of his hands. In different circumstances he would have flown to Moscow and asked to resume the investigation. But the hunt for Kalinin had meanwhile become of limited interest to him; during that same week Dimitri had come across an amazing revelation that made other matters pale in comparison.

One of Dimitri's major functions was to keep an eye on the various emigré associations that swarmed in Paris like bees on a honeycomb. He had informers in some of the groups, consisting mostly of elderly Ukrainians, Balts, and Armenians meeting in drab, unheated halls, saluting dead flags, singing forgotten anthems and reciting pathetic speeches; at times they dressed in ludicrous uniforms, weighted with rusty medals, and solemnly announced the forthcoming liberation of their motherland.

Among all these lunatics could be found precious few dangerous leaders capable of organizing a serious resistance movement. But Department Thirteen was efficiently disposing of all enemies of the Soviet nation, gladly using any it could find to test its latest weapons, electric pistols, poison bullets and untraceable chemical potions.

Dimitri's most amusing occupation was reading the pamphlets and magazines the emigrés expended their meager revenues to publish. One of them, cheerfully christened *Victory Is Near,* had a section called "Soviet Crimes." It always carried the same stories — the gulags, the great purges, the massacre of the kulaks. The dodos who wrote the articles raised the numbers of communism's victims from one issue to the next, as if another couple of zeros in the death toll could send the world on a crusade against Russia. Dimitri's colleagues joked that at this inflation rate, the entire Soviet population would be dead on paper in a couple of years. Perhaps that was why the old gagas called their magazine *Victory Is Near.*

In the June issue of the magazine, Dimitri found an article about

Stalin's massacre of the Jewish writers. He absently perused the paragraph about his mother's execution in the Lubyanka; it was a rehash of old newspaper reports, and revealed nothing new.

But in a box on the article's second page there was an interview with Tonya Gordon's son.

Dr. Alexander Gordon, the article said, was a brilliant young professor at Brown University, in Providence, Rhode Island.

Dr. Alexander Gordon, smiling from a grainy photograph, spoke of his deep love for his mother and his unsuccessful search, over the last twelve years, for his brother Dimitri.

Dimitri read every word in the article several times, then turned to the picture. He picked up a magnifying glass and meticulously studied the smiling blond man who looked confidently at the camera. He was wearing a shirt with an open collar. A heavy Star of David hung on a chain around his brother's neck, and Dimitri clenched his teeth. Another Jew. Still, Jew or no Jew, he was his brother.

He didn't budge from his seat for an hour, mesmerized by his brother's face. Alexander was alive and well. Alexander had been looking for him since he was a child. His brother cared about him.

It was a strange feeling. For the first time in his life Dimitri discovered he was important to somebody. Alexander was his family, they had the same blood. He wondered what kind of man his brother was. Another big-mouthed Jewish activist? An American reactionary? In the interview he expressed no opinion about the Soviet regime, only spoke of his deep love for Russia.

Keep away from him, Dimitri's instincts screamed. A Jewish-American brother is the last thing you need. Lesser connections have put an end to many promising careers. You killed a man, back at Panfilov, because you feared he would expose you. Forget about Alexander Gordon. Don't meet him, don't call him, don't write to him. Burn this magazine.

Dimitri slowly emerged from his stupor and reached for the phone. His voice was unsteady, and must have sounded strange; he had to repeat his orders twice to make himself understood.

Chapter 11

THE LETTER FROM PARIS arrived on a Friday in August, in the middle of a violent summer storm. Nina wasn't home, and Alex trod downstairs to the building's front door still unshaven, wearing an old bathrobe. Angry thunder roared outside, and white lightning exploded in the hallway windows.

"Sign here, please, it's registered," the mailman said, studying him critically, and handed him an air-mail envelope. He was wearing a plastic yellow raincoat, and his cap dripped water on the foreign stamps. Alex scribbled his name, glancing at the letter; it had been sent to Brown and forwarded to his home address. "Institut de l'Europe de l'Est — Centre de Recherches," said the heading on the envelope. Alex took the letter back to the apartment, to the kitchen, where he was having his morning coffee, although it was almost noon.

The howling winds and the gray atmosphere of the rainy day reflected his morose mood. For the first time he could recall, he was idle and listless; his future looked uncertain. He had graduated in June; Nina had proudly framed his Ph.D. diploma and hung it over his desk. But his satisfaction had soon degenerated into apathy. Teaching at a prestigious university suddenly seemed to him dull and unappealing. The clash with Claudia that night at the Waldorf-Astoria had affected him deeply.

Their life together had been the cornerstone of his plans for the future. Without her, he didn't want to go to Stanford; he didn't want to teach at Brown, either. And if he took a job at Columbia or in Boston, his life would turn into endless waiting for the occasional weekend she would throw his way, like a bone to a starving dog.

Perhaps the best thing for him was to take a break, go away for a while. But where could he go? His renewed demands for a Soviet visa weren't even being answered. He had written to several French and English universities, but the replies had been disappointing. At the peak of the dog days, he had left Brown and come home, hoping to see Claudia. But Claudia was on the road, calling from faraway places like Gainesville, Florida, or Great Falls, Montana. She reported excitedly how successful she was, what superb collections she was presenting, what she had said to Ronnie Havermeyer and what Ronnie Havermeyer had said to her. She didn't seem to care much about Alex's plans. Anyway, she was due back today; they were going away for the weekend. Perhaps a trip to one of their old haunts in New England would be good for them.

He ripped open the envelope. It contained a letter and a glossy color brochure. The cover of the brochure showed a beautiful eighteenth-century mansion with a steep, slate roof, sturdy chimneys, and a cobbled courtyard. Inside there were photographs of libraries, seminars in spacious classrooms, a small lecture hall, and a garden with big shady trees. The caption on the front page was in French, the same as on the envelope. It was easy to understand: Institute of Eastern Europe — Research Center. An address in the Fourth Arrondisement of Paris was printed underneath.

The letter was written in English.

Dear Dr. Gordon:

Allow me to congratulate you on your brilliant academic success at the prestigious Brown University. I hope you are familiar with our research center, which has a reputation as one of the best institutions specializing in Eastern Europe and the Soviet Union.

We maintain constant contact with Brown University, and we have requested and read your Ph.D. thesis, "Stalin's Obsession — the Writers' and Doctors' Trials." It is an outstanding piece of research on a most important subject. We have added your thesis to our distinguished library collection.

Besides our 25,000 volume library, we are very proud of our archives, which contain a vast array of documents, many of them unique. I believe that you may find a great deal of original material in our archives, if you're interested in some additional research. We have succeeded in obtaining many unpublished documents on Stalin's secret projects to deport and resettle Soviet Jews after the Writers' Trials. As you know, these projects were scuttled by Stalin's death in 1953.

Currently we have twelve scholars in residence, most of them from European countries, and one from Canada. I have the pleasure of offering you a one-year fellowship in our center, starting October 1, 1974. We cannot, unfortunately, offer you an American salary, but our visiting scholars claim that our stipend of 7,500 francs (roughly 1,500 U.S. dollars) a month, plus a participation of 75 percent in housing expenses, is quite adequate. The airfare will also be covered by the center. You will have no obligations except for a weekly seminar of two hours and a monthly lecture.

If you accept our offer, please let us know by the end of August. I do hope your answer will be affirmative.

> Yours sincerely,
> Rene Martineau, Director General

Alex put down the letter, then picked it up and read it again. He couldn't believe it. He reached for the phone, but there was nobody he could call. Nina had gone to see her doctor; Joey was in Washington, striving to become a reporter; Claudia was on her way back from Georgia. Besides, she wouldn't be very happy to hear about this letter. Outside, the wind was wailing; a volley of heavy raindrops clattered on the windows like buckshot. He peeled the wrapping off a chocolate bar, and chewing slowly, read the brochure about the Paris center.

It was not a dream, it was for real! Written down, in black and white, a wonderful scholarship offer addressed to Dr. Gordon, and the timing couldn't have been better. A wave of elation gradually peaked inside him, and he leaned back, clasping his hands behind his neck. A year in Paris! He caught his reflection in the window, which overlooked the dark wall of the neighboring building. He was grinning. Life wasn't so bad after all; his luck was turning. A year in Paris was the best thing that could happen to him now. This letter was a godsend, exactly what he had prayed for.

* * *

"THIS LETTER is exactly what I prayed for," Grimaldi said, glancing again at the photocopy of the Paris letter before passing it to the chief of the Soviet Division.

"Really?" Grimaldi's lunch companion at Fernand's wasn't very talkative. Vince Morton was a bearlike man with a fair-skinned wrestler's face framed by some vestiges of limp blond hair pasted over his bald skull. A big-boned Texan, he had been a defector hunter in Vienna in his younger years, and regarded the KGB as the bad guys in a corpse-strewn western movie. He had liked Grimaldi's plan of using Alexander Gordon to ensnare Morozov. He now studied the letter, and finally raised his head. "That's good, Napoleone."

"The institute has been a KGB front for years," Grimaldi pointed out, relishing the taste of baked escargot as he dipped a crust of bread in the garlic butter. He sighed with delight. "You know, Vince, the whole time in Moscow, I had this dream of eating at Fernand's again."

Vince raised his head from his T-bone steak. "What do they use the center for?"

Grimaldi shrugged. "To provide cover for people they bring to Paris, maintain a permanent safehouse for their agents, funnel funds into Europe. It's an important operation. The director, Martineau, is an old-timer. Fought in Spain, spent two years in the First Directorate school at Sverdlovsk."

"How did you hook Morozov?"

"I planted an article about the Jewish writers in the *Victory Is Near* magazine; it's financed by us anyway." A black-haired young man with a sleek, graceful body slipped into a booth across the room, and Grimaldi followed him with his eyes.

"Most emigré publications are," Vince said, laboriously chewing his steak. "You also planted the Gordon interview?" His voice dropped as an elderly couple passed by their table.

"More or less. The guy who interviewed him is a free-lance journalist; we paid him."

"How did you know that Morozov would read the article?"

"He was bound to read it." A dapper older man joined the black-haired beauty. Why him and not me? Grimaldi thought. He stared at the boy, who responded with a brief, demure smile. He went on: "The Thirteenth keeps an eye on emigré organizations. Morozov is their representative in Paris; he had to read the article. And if he hadn't" —

Grimaldi refilled his glass of Muscadet — "I would have found some other way to make him meet his brother."

"You're sure he's behind this scholarship offer?"

"Positive," Grimaldi said, looking up. "Ah, my main course."

"A sole meuniere for monsieur," Fernand announced, placing the dish before Grimaldi. He had aged considerably since Grimaldi had seen him last, but he looked as phony as ever. He fussed around Grimaldi and tried to pour some Muscadet into Morton's glass. Vince grabbed his arm, shaking his head. "Another beer," he muttered, and Fernand retreated, his face a mixture of disdain and despair.

Grimaldi picked up his knife and attacked the golden sole with gusto. He was in an ebullient mood. The black premonitions that had tormented him during his flight from Moscow had turned out to be unfounded. On his arrival in Washington, he had received a hero's welcome; nobody had blamed him for the Moscow mishap, and there was talk of a promotion to a key position in the Soviet Division. In the meantime he had rented an elegant apartment in the Watergate. A car with a driver from the Langley pool was put at his disposal, and he was given a most liberal expense account.

The very night of his arrival, he had requested Alex Gordon's file from the Company archives. Page by page he read the material that had accumulated since the boy arrived in New York, more than twenty years ago. He leafed through old FBI surveillance reports and memos on Nina's communist activities. Some press clippings described the deaths of Tonya and Victor Wolf. The clippings were from 1962; the child must have been about thirteen.

The file also contained a photocopy of a letter the boy had written shortly afterward, to his brother Dimitri, in Russia. The letter had been returned by the Russian authorities and intercepted by the FBI. Another envelope contained a few glossy photographs of Alex Gordon taken at different periods. The first photograph was of a meager boy of seven or eight; the last of a handsome young man, tall and broad-shouldered, with fair hair, clear eyes, and a serious mouth. He was wearing an open shirt and looked very American.

The file also contained records of Gordon's studies at Brown, the rallies he had organized against the Soviet invasion of Czechoslovakia, his excellent grades. Grimaldi was particularly impressed with a paper Gordon had written, in his senior year, about "the KGB mentality."

Americans don't always understand that the Russians, party leaders in particular, have a different way of thinking. They are haunted by a paranoid fear of conspiracy. They see conspiracy everywhere — among enemies of the regime, ethnic minorities, Balts, Muslims, Armenians, Georgians. They fear dissidents, intellectuals, writers, emigrés. They attribute tremendous powers to these tiny groups. That is why they fill their gulags with intellectuals and dispatch assassination teams all over the globe to murder old, toothless emigrés who print ridiculous brochures and swear allegiance to phony Anastasias.

Most of all, the Russians dread a Western conspiracy. They see a diabolical plot behind every newspaper article or political declaration; they believe Western intelligence might poison the food exported to Russia, or introduce hallucinatory drugs into their water. They don't trust the free press, and employ armies of spies to check and double check any trivial item of information published in Western newspapers. A press release about a new bridge over the Rhine, for instance, would send every KGB agent running.

They still suspect Germany, fearing it would attack them again, on America's orders. Their resident agents in London, Paris, and Bonn have standing orders to check the reserves in hospital blood banks. If the reserves rise, it would be an indication the West is about to launch World War III. They fear Israel, and believe American policy is conducted by a secret Zionist-capitalist conspiracy. . . .

Grimaldi lit a cigar and exhaled smoke toward the ceiling. Alex Gordon was the man he needed. Morozov probably wanted to meet his brother as intensely as Alex yearned to find him. Dimitri must feel affection or at least a blood bond to Alexander. Such a feeling would be a weakness — it might cloud the Russian's judgment and make him react with his guts instead of his brains. Family ties could be a deadly weapon, if properly used. If Grimaldi succeeded in turning Gordon into his tool, he would destroy Morozov and avenge Oleg.

But where was Oleg? Could he possibly still be alive? If he was, why hadn't he used the tiny radio transceiver Grimaldi had given him, or any other means to establish contact? Grimaldi spent long nights at the Operations room in Langley, alerting the East European stations, listening to Soviet security forces' transmissions, perusing intelligence reports from the Soviet bloc. He doggedly explored any avenue that could lead to Top Hat.

Oleg Kalinin had taken a tremendous risk by coming back to Moscow to warn him. The least Grimaldi could do was try to reciprocate. Until now, though, all his efforts had failed. The only piece of news that could be connected to his friend's fate had been a vague item about a middle-aged man forcibly removed from a train by plainclothes security officers on the Czech-Austrian border. This could be anybody, but . . .

Grimaldi couldn't get Kalinin off his mind. What had happened to his friend? In the middle of the night, when the Operations room was in half darkness and the late-shift operators dozed in their seats, he would bend over the powerful electronic instruments, lined up along a light gray wall and watch the green hue of the computer screens, the bluish haze of the radar monitors, the transmitters' blinking red lights that signified that the coded radio call to Oleg Kalinin was being incessantly repeated. A short message on a secret wavelength, too brief to be intercepted, too smart to be decoded. "Top Hat contact base," the message said.

Grimaldi could imagine the electromagnetic wave traveling across the Berlin wall and the bleak plains of Eastern Europe, the wheatfields of the Ukraine and the green hills of Byelorussia, the forests surrounding Moscow, the peaks of the Urals, the Siberian *taigas* and frozen tundras. He hoped that somewhere beyond the Iron Curtain Oleg Kalinin was still alive, a free man, eluding the evil force that pursued him. He hoped Oleg would finally hear the voice whispering into his tiny receiver: Top Hat contact base.

Call base, Top Hat, he prayed in his heart, stay alive, my Oleg; don't give in, don't let them beat you, my friend. We'll find you, we'll take you out, we'll bring you home.

CLAUDIA'S REACTION to his decision to go to Paris surprised Alex. He hadn't expected her to be so possessive. "I love you, Claudia, but I have to go away for a while," he said to her, explaining his reasons. "I feel lousy sitting on my butt all week with nothing to do, hoping you'll come home for the weekend."

She didn't want to listen. Since he had told her about the scholarship, she kept hurling the same accusation at him. "If you love me, why do you want to leave me?" she said that Friday night, in the dining room of the small Connecticut inn where they were spending the weekend.

"Jesus H, Claudia," he protested, lowering his voice, "you're leaving me every other weekend."

"This is different," she flared. The only other couple in the dining room, a tanned, handsome athlete and a lovely black girl, turned back and stared at them. "I'm with you all the time, I'm calling you, I'm writing to you, I'm coming back."

"I'll be with you too," he said. The black girl smiled at him. "I'll call you, and I'll write to you, and in a year we'll be back together."

"Don't count on it," she snapped, her eyes burning. "Don't take me for granted." She shook her head. "And stop staring at that woman or else."

They finally reached a cease-fire and agreed that in nine months, next June, Claudia would join him in Paris and spend the summer with him. They would then have a serious discussion about the future. But Alex could tell this discussion would never take place. Claudia was drifting away, becoming immersed in her own life, becoming easily distracted when in his company. A few times, when she had come back from a trip, they had gone out with some of her model friends and their dates. The girls were indeed stunning, but he soon got fed up with their incessant chirping about divine dresses, divine makeup, and divine designers named Lorenzo, Vittorio, or Angelo. Not to mention the divine hairdressers, makeup artists, and photographers bearing similar names.

"You don't like my friends," Claudia said that night in Connecticut, planting her fists on her waist with the same sweet, disturbing gesture he remembered so well from the night they first met. But tonight she wasn't smiling.

"No," he countered, "I don't like them."

"You'd better get used to them, Professor, because I like them and I'm going to spend a lot of time with them."

"Suit yourself," he shot back. "I'm not going to spend any time with them, or with you, either, because I'm going away."

"That's true," she said, suddenly reflective. "You're going away. And you have no idea how far away you're going."

The fight ended in bed, sex having become a temporary panacea for their bitterness. But even sex wasn't fun anymore for two people exhausted from hurting each other.

They clashed and argued every weekend they spent together, until the summer heat was blown away by the chilly winds of September.

The day after their last fight, Nina and Claudia drove Alex to Kennedy Airport. At the security checkpoint in TWA's new terminal, Alex turned back and hugged Nina. The old woman tried to smile through her tears.

She looked awful, he thought, as he tightly held her frail, brittle body. Her hair had turned completely white, her cheeks had hollowed, and an opaque hue dulled her irises. She hadn't been well lately; her ulcer tormented her all day long. Since her retirement, she rarely left the apartment, except to see Dr. Sapirstein. But today she had insisted on accompanying him to the airport, although she had to share him with Claudia, a partnership she intensely disliked.

"I am happy for you, *golubchek*, really, you'll have a wonderful time in Paris. You did the right thing." She kissed him on both cheeks and repeated forcefully: "The right thing." The old girl was happy he was getting away from Claudia. The rivalry between the two women had erupted again recently, when Nina realized how deeply Claudia had hurt Alex.

He turned to Claudia. She was pale and upset. Her anger showed in her face. She had cut her hair short this morning, and he was sure she had done it to spite him, for she knew he loved her hair long and soft. Perhaps she was trying to tell him something by erasing the image of the Claudia who had existed for him until now. He held her tight, but her body was stiff and hostile.

"I love you," he whispered in her ear. Nina had tactfully taken a few steps back, displaying sudden interest in a long line of magazines on the newsstand rack.

"If you do, you shouldn't go away," Claudia said stubbornly.

He kissed her again and waved at Nina. He went through security, then proceeded to his gate without looking back. His throat was constricted, and he felt tremendous loss. He tried not to think about Claudia, and to concentrate instead on what lay ahead. His flight was already being paged. Alex boarded the 707 and took his aisle seat. He flipped through the in-flight magazine, but Claudia was on his mind, and he had to read the same phrase several times to grasp its meaning. Today he had lost Claudia, he thought.

He looked around. There were very few passengers on the flight, but the seat beside him was occupied. His neighbor was a man in his fifties, dressed like a dandy in a blue blazer over a flowered vest, a silk shirt, and a polka-dot bow tie. He was liberally sprayed with cologne. His tanned face, adorned by a Clark Gable mustache, was lit by a pair of cunning green eyes. He wore heavy gold rings on his manicured fingers.

"I guess we're going to travel together," the stranger said suavely. "My name is Grimaldi, Franco Grimaldi."

DURING THE LONG FLIGHT to Paris, Alex discovered that in spite of his flamboyant looks, Grimaldi was a fascinating man. Over dinner his new acquaintance told him about his life. He was with the United States Information Service and had traveled a lot. He had lived in Berlin, London, and Paris, and not long ago had returned from a tour of duty in Moscow.

The mention of the city of his birth aroused Alex's curiosity, and he assailed his companion with questions. Grimaldi answered with good grace, slipping in a question of his own now and then. Only when their plane started its descent toward Charles de Gaulle Airport did Alex realize that he had talked even more than Grimaldi, telling him everything about his parents, his lost brother, his scholarship, even about Nina and Claudia. He attributed this gregarious behavior to the unusual number of drinks he'd consumed. Grimaldi had repeatedly ordered double vodkas for both of them, and swallowed his in single gulps, the Russian way. Alex had soon joined him in shouting *"Nazdorovye!"* and slapping his back. That had lasted throughout the flight. A fine fellow, Grimaldi, a real man of the world, and he even spoke some Russian!

They parted at the airport, but not before Grimaldi had given him the address of his hotel, the Intercontinental at Place Vendôme, and his telephone number at the embassy. Grimaldi then wrote in his diary the phone numbers of the Institute of East European Studies. Yes, he had heard of it; a fine institution indeed.

Grimaldi offered to share a taxi to Paris, but Alex politely declined. He had heard so much about the City of Lights, he wanted to enter it alone and enjoy his first sight of it to the fullest. He hailed a cab, a Peugeot that looked very small on the outside but was surprisingly spacious once he got in. It was early morning, the sky was clear, and the first sunbeams cast a golden hue on the fabulous city. Alex's cab was driven by a stout Parisian with a red face and bleary eyes, who kept growling and lamenting all during their trip. The Frenchman addressed his irate complaints to his huge German shepherd, who sat enthroned on the passenger seat, suspiciously eyeing Alex and ominously licking his flews.

They entered Paris by the Porte de la Chapelle. Alex stared in wonder at the massive old houses, the lively markets set on small squares or branching off into side streets. The fall was at the peak of its beauty. It had painted the foliage of the trees lining the boulevards in yellow, brown, and magenta. The wind blew the autumn leaves onto the sidewalks, where they covered the asphalt with a golden carpet. The Parisians didn't look very cheerful. The men were grave-faced, conservatively dressed; the women, slim and graceful, wore fashionable clothes and seemed disdainful of everything.

As the cab progressed into Paris, the architecture improved. Brass, glass, and lights gleamed from crowded cafés and brasseries; he saw some opulent furniture shops, and a few exquisite boutiques. Small cars, mostly Peugeots, Renaults, and Citroëns, darted swiftly beside them, displaying a Gallic indifference to the traffic laws. Choleric drivers stuck their heads out of car windows, glowered at each other, and exchanged saucy opinions about their respective mothers and sisters, accompanied by eloquent gestures.

A beautiful immaculate church, crowned with domes and turrets, was perched on top of a hill. He had seen it on postcards; it was the Sacre Coeur, and the hill was Montmartre, the famous artists' colony. In front of them the Eiffel Tower sailed through the morning haze. They passed by the Madeleine, a gray-stone church modeled after a Greek temple, and crossed a huge square in the middle of which stood a sleek Egyptian obelisk covered with gold-painted hieroglyphs. On his right he caught a brief glimpse of the Champs-Elysées and the Arc de Triomphe.

They turned left along the Seine. The muddy waters of the river were spanned by a succession of beautiful bridges built in different styles. A couple was kissing by the riverfront. A long barge emerged under a vaulted bridge on their right, and Alex remembered with a pang that night with Claudia at the Waldorf-Astoria. There had been a watercolor painting of a Seine barge hanging in their suite.

The cab turned into a maze of narrow streets lined with very old houses and unusual monuments, churches, and small palaces. He was shocked to see a golden horse's head, the trademark of a horsemeat butchery. The cab entered the courtyard of a sprawling mansion whose stone walls had been restored to their original whiteness. A large veranda paved with rectangular flagstones led to a double-winged wooden door, painted light brown. Alex knew the place from the brochure he had read countless times back in Brooklyn. This was the Institute of East European Studies.

He carried his suitcase into the building. In the lobby he passed two young men in polo shirts and neatly pressed jeans who were heatedly discussing, in French, Lenin's relationship with his wife, Krupskaya. The director's office was on the ground floor, guarded by two secretaries busy torturing their typewriters. He introduced himself, and the older of the two, a silver-haired woman with a receding chin, stared at him stonily.

He repeated his name.

"Oh, Monsieur Gordon," she finally said, "we didn't expect you so early."

She disappeared through an inner door and he overheard a quick exchange; besides the secretary's voice, there were the sounds of two men speaking urgently. A door creaked open and slammed shut — apparently a second door to the director's office — and the secretary was back.

"Mr. Martineau will see you now," she said coldly. There were beads of sweat on her upper lip.

Alex knocked and walked into the inner office. Even before shaking Martineau's hand, he cast a quick look about the room. There was indeed another door in the far wall. In the ashtray on the director's desk there were two crushed cigarettes of different brands. One was "blonde," American-made, and the other a stinking Gauloise, which the French called "brune." A package of Kent cigarettes and a lighter lay beside the ashtray. The Gauloise, therefore, belonged to the visitor who had left in such a hurry.

"Monsieur Gordon, welcome to Paris and to our institute."

Martineau was a thin man with a pale, narrow face and limp black hair. His brown eyes, magnified by wire-rimmed glasses, blinked repeatedly, betraying an odd nervousness. The double-breasted jacket of his suit hung loosely on his spare frame. He shook Alex's hand, and a smile fluttered on his mouth. "We didn't expect you so early," he said apologetically and blinked again.

"I took the night flight," Alex said.

"Yes, yes, I understand."

Martineau sat down behind his desk, ramrod stiff. Papers, files, and magazines were stacked on the large desk in tidy piles. A narrow wooden tray contained sharpened pencils; another was full of paper clips. A large map of Eastern Europe and the Soviet Union hung behind Martineau's chair.

The director gradually relaxed as their conversation progressed. He explained the institute rules to Alex, and briefed him on the technical aspects of his stay in Paris. He suggested that Alex rent one of the apartments the institute's former guests had used, as they were all in nice surroundings and were kept in excellent condition. Alex agreed, and departed after promising to have lunch with Martineau by the end of the week.

Half an hour later he was in a cab again, house hunting through Paris. He looked at a few apartments in different parts of the city, one not far from the Opéra, a couple of others off the Champs-Elysées. He picked the fourth for two reasons: it was on the Left Bank, in the very heart of the students' quarter; and it was perched on top of a seven-story building, its windows offering a breathtaking view of Notre Dame and the turrets, ramparts, and needle-sharp spires of the Ile de la Cité.

He had lunch at the famous Brasserie Lipp, on the Boulevard Saint-Germain. He got a table on the covered terrace, which commanded a good view of the old church and the crowd of writers, models, and movie stars clustered around the Café des Deux Magots, across the street.

He ordered choucroute — hot sauerkraut with cold cuts — which was the house specialty. The waiter ushered two elderly gentlemen — he estimated their ages at between sixty-five and seventy — to the table next to his. He couldn't help overhearing their conversation. His graduate studies had required a decent knowledge of French, and had no trouble following the grandfathers' dialogue.

"Cher ami," one of them was saying to the other, his handsome, leonine face glowing, "I am in love."

His friend, florid-faced and white-haired, leaned forward. "Tell me about her," he said.

The happy lover described the way his beloved looked, the way her eyes sparkled in the morning, the color of her hair, the velvety feel of her skin. He talked with passion of the way she spoke, the colors she liked to wear, her taste in books and poems. He painted the sunlight in her face, the play of the wind in her hair as they strolled in the park, the softness of her voice, the magic of her touch. "She reminds me at times of that verse of Baudelaire," he said, quoting from memory. His friend countered by quoting another famous poet. The old man — and young lover — spoke for more than an hour, his friend listening, enraptured, interrupting the passionate account with an occasional question.

This is Paris, Alex thought, as he watched the two old men talking with such passion about a love affair. He recalled another conversation he had overheard in a Manhattan restaurant a couple of weeks before; his neighbors were two young men, no older than thirty. "Listen," one of them had said. He was dressed in an expensive suit and a silk tie. "Last night I picked up a girl at the Rendezvous bar. She was something, I tell you."

"Was she a good lay?" his friend asked. They both brayed in laughter, then switched the subject to the stock market.

This must be the difference between the French and the Americans, Alex decided, sipping his espresso. The French remain incurably romantic till their last breath, while we get cynical, or perhaps ashamed of our feelings, even before we come of age.

Alex paid his check, adding a tip that apparently was too generous, and left, escorted to the door by a very grateful waiter who desperately sought reassurance that he would come again. The air was crisp and invigorating. He felt good on this first day in Paris. He had arrived in the best of seasons, had found a great apartment, and had witnessed the French cult of love, brilliantly displayed by two old and forever young Parisians.

Back at the institute, an antique elevator panted and moaned all the way up to the library on the top floor. Here he felt at home. He wandered between the overloaded racks, relishing the dusty smell of old books, leafing through rare volumes of Russian history. The library was outstanding indeed, a very fine collection.

On a side rack he found a book he didn't know existed: the minutes of the Writers' Trial in 1949. His father's trial. He picked up the heavy volume and was about to take it to one of the desks when a rustling sound behind him made him turn. He took a sharp breath. Before him stood one of the most beautiful girls he had ever seen.

He drank in her beauty, nailed to his place. He couldn't take his eyes off her face, so lovely and yet so full of sadness. The face could have belonged to a Greek goddess, with its clear forehead, high cheekbones, and chiseled, passionate mouth. Her upper lip was slightly drawn up in an oval line. It was the mouth of the ravishing little Princess Bolkonsky, as Tolstoy had described it in *War and Peace*. Her skin was white, luminous, bestowing an ethereal glow upon the oval face and the gracious throat.

From that pure face stared huge, deep blue eyes imbued with innocence and unfathomable grief. They made her look so vulnerable, so forlorn, that Alex felt an instinctive craving to do all he could to dispel that profound sorrow. Yet, there was something enigmatic in the expression of her eyes, some secret knowledge that made her distant and unreachable.

Her blond hair was woven on top of her head like a crown of ancient gold. Her slim, small-breasted body and her delicate limbs made him think of an elf. Her black shirt and pants clung to her skin. The combined traits of ripe beauty, innocence and vulnerability produced a strange spell.

This was how his mother might have looked, he suddenly thought. Blond, blue-eyed, and pure at heart; romantic and innocent, a dream child lost in a cruel, cynical world.

"Bonjour," he said, and smiled. His voice was unsteady.

She looked at him gravely. "Bonjour."

"I am Alex Gordon," he said. "I arrived this morning from New York. I'm going to do some research here as a visiting scholar."

She nodded earnestly, like a little girl. A bearded student passed them holding an open book, and greeted her with a smile.

"And you?" Alex asked, desperately racking his brains for a clever remark, and failing. "Who are you?"

"My name is Tatiana." Her voice was clear and pleasant.

"Russian? I am Russian, too."

Her brief smile transformed her face. "I was born in Paris. My parents were Russian immigrants."

"What's your last name?"

"Romanov."

He raised his eyebrows. "You're connected with the czar's family?" The Romanovs were the dynasty that had ruled Russia until the revolution, when the royal family was massacred.

"We are distantly related," she said, her mouth tightening. She apparently didn't want to talk about that subject.

"So you really are a princess!" he exclaimed, so spontaneously that she couldn't help smiling. A student wearing glasses and a checkered sweater tried to squeeze by them, and she stepped aside, and gestured to Alex to follow her to one of the windows that overlooked the back garden. She walked with a slight limp, and this made her even more endearing, enhancing her vulnerability.

He switched to Russian. "You work at the institute?"

She shook her head, holding her books against her bosom. "I am writing a thesis on the Russian civil war for my degree, at the École des Langues Orientales. I only use the library."

She told him her research dealt with the White armies, financed by the West, that had tried to smother the October revolution after 1917. She worked at the library daily, from four P.M. until it closed at eight. She had a part-time job as an interpreter for several Soviet companies that had offices in Paris.

"And the Soviets employ a Romanov?" Alex asked. "They don't mind your being related to the czar's family?"

She shrugged, with a brief smile. "On the contrary, they seem to be very pleased to tell everybody that a Russian . . ."

"Aristocrat?" he suggested.

". . . Well," — She didn't seem to like the word — "that a grand-cousin of Czar Nikolai is working for them now. This is the best proof that they won, isn't it?"

Her voice was sarcastic, and he chose to change the subject. "I just found a nice apartment in the Latin Quarter," he said. "Where do you live?"

"Not far," she said cryptically.

"I would like — " he began, but was interrupted by the library clerk, who popped up beside them. "Will you please keep quiet?" he said angrily. He was a small, mousy man with bad teeth. "This is a library, not a café."

"Excuse me," Alex said, then turned back to the girl. Her face had turned red. "Will you have a cup of coffee with me?"

"I'd like that," she said seriously.

They found a corner table in the old-fashioned bistro across the street from the institute. An elderly waiter served them two café crèmes. Tatiana spoke very little. Alex did most of the talking, narrating his life story, describing his quest for his lost brother. When he mentioned his parents' deaths, she paled. "Many of my relatives were shot by the communists," she said.

The old waiter placed cutlery, wineglasses, and paper napkins on the tables. Alex glanced at his watch. It was almost eight. "Let's have dinner together," he suggested.

Odd anguish flashed in her eyes. "I can't," she said. "I've got to go." She vanished so silently that later he wondered if he had really seen her or if it had all been a dream.

In his new home that night, he tossed in his bed, bathed in sweat, and threw the long French pillow on the floor. Tomorrow he'd buy a normal pillow, he thought. Tomorrow he might see Tatiana again. He recalled those nights years ago when he was only seventeen and couldn't sleep, thinking of Claudia. Tatiana was the opposite of Claudia in every way — her coloring, her slight build, her vulnerability. Claudia had always been a streetwise kid, aware of her sensuality, exuding an animal attraction. She was cheerful and relaxed, able to take care of herself and have her own way in any situation. She didn't need a man's protection.

Tatiana did. She seemed as innocent as a child. It made him want to rescue her from real or imaginary dangers. He tried to imagine how Claudia's face would look if he told her his head had been turned by a Russian girl with golden hair. But Claudia's features faded out of his mind. In the Parisian night the face of the beguiling, tormented Tatiana floated before him.

WHEN TATIANA entered the library the following afternoon, he was waiting for her. It was raining outside, a typical Paris drizzle, and she wore a black military-style raincoat over a loose white blouse and a tight black skirt. She seemed pleased to see him, but when he mentioned dinner, she declined again. "Perhaps tomorrow," she finally said, "when the library closes."

The following day, which was a Wednesday, he came to the library again. He saw Tatiana at a desk by the window and waved at her, but chose a seat at the far side of the room. He didn't want to make a nuisance of himself. He decided to pass by her desk only after the attendant announced that the library was closing.

At five minutes before eight she suddenly appeared at his side. "Somebody offered me dinner," she said cheerfully. "Does the offer still stand?"

He looked at Tatiana in surprise. Her gaiety seemed artificial, her smile forced. But he was overwhelmed by her accepting his invitation.

"The offer is still good," he announced. "Where would you like to go?"

"If you don't mind, I would like to walk a little," she said. "It's a beautiful evening."

Outside, he looked at the starry sky. Yesterday's rain was gone; the air was cool and dry.

"I bet you haven't strolled through Paris yet," she said softly. "It's the most enchanting place in the world."

"Do you think . . ." he began, involuntarily glancing at her left foot, which she almost imperceptibly dragged.

"You mean my limp?" she asked.

His face flushed with embarrassment. Damn your big mouth, Alex Gordon, he thought.

But she wasn't embarrassed. "I'm all right," she said, "I can walk for hours. I was born with a deformed left foot. A doctor told me that all I need is a simple operation to fix it up."

"So why don't you do it?" he said, trying to sound casual. They started to walk down the street. Two nuns passed them, their heads bowed.

"Money," she said. "It costs money, you know, and even a Romanova can be very poor nowadays."

They walked side by side in the quiet streets, and he imagined they looked like a couple of Parisian lovers, he in a woolen shirt and casual jacket, she in tight jeans and flat-heeled boots. They stopped briefly at the magnificent Place des Vosges. He gazed in wonderment at the thirty-six ancient mansions that surrounded the garden and its four fountains. They stood under the statue of King Louis XIII, and she explained the history of the square.

"This way," she said, after describing the famous duel between two groups of French noblemen, fought under the windows of Cardinal Richelieu's house in the seventeenth century. They passed by the house of Victor Hugo, the author of *Les Misérables*. They reached the Seine and crossed the river on a narrow bridge. Underneath, the water gleamed dully, and the dark shadow of a barge silently slid upon its wavering surface.

"We are on the Ile Saint Louis now," Tatiana said, leading him through a labyrinth of picturesque lanes. They passed by several restaurants with large picture windows; young people were sitting around massive wooden tables laden with cold meats, raw vegetables, and bottles of wine. One of the diners raised his glass to Tatiana. A couple was kissing beside a poster of Jacques Brel.

He took her by the hand. She didn't object, but her fingers remained limp in his, unresponsive to his touch. Still, Alex was overjoyed. Here he was, on a beautiful Paris night, walking hand in hand with this stunning girl. Tatiana spoke Russian with a soft French accent that made his native tongue sound like music. She told him that she was twenty-two, the only daughter of Vladimir Romanov, and the grandchild of the Grand Duke Evgenyi Romanov, who as a young man had escaped the Royal Palace and his cousin Nikolai's fate. Her mother was ill and had spent most of the last year at the American Hospital in Neuilly.

Suddenly she fell silent. He turned back to her, but she had stopped in her tracks, staring fixedly ahead. They were in a dark, cobbled street that ran along the river. There were no shops or cafés as far as he could see, and the place was very quiet, very peaceful. Still, Alex felt vaguely alarmed. What were they doing here? he wondered. There was nothing to see here but darkness.

"Tatiana . . ." he began, but she kept gazing into the dark. Abruptly, she pressed his fingers, very hard, as if trying to convey a message; then she pulled her hand away and took a step back, her eyes still focused on the same spot.

He followed her look. Out of the black shadow of a doorway a man stepped forward and stood facing him. At that moment a bateau-mouche — a sight-seeing boat, loaded with tourists — passed on the river and its powerful floodlight swept the street, briefly painting the stranger in a ghastly white light. He was about the same height as Alex, with a shock of dark hair, and burning black eyes sunk deep in a very pale, sharply lined face. He was dressed in a dark suit, and a black coat was thrown over his shoulders. Could he be a mugger, a thief? Alex wondered. Had Tatiana lured him into a trap? Ridiculous, he thought, he had nothing worth robbing; she could have landed fatter prey if she'd wanted to.

Alex stood undecided in the middle of the street. He glanced back at Tatiana; she was leaning on a wall, her arms hugging her shoulders, her head bent. In the building on Alex's left a woman shouted loudly and a man answered. Quite close, a car passed by, its engine coughing hoarsely. Then there was silence.

The stranger approached slowly, his steps echoing on the pavement, until he stood before Alex, face tense, eyes searching, fisted hands trembling slightly.

"I am your brother," he said.

Chapter 12

ALEX STARED at the shadowed figure facing him, his stunned mind barely able to comprehend the single phrase spoken in a clear, crisp Russian voice: I am your brother. A strange chill made him shiver, and he tried to speak, but couldn't. The pale young man before him also seemed deeply disturbed. He took a package of Gauloises from his pocket and spent a few matches trying to light one. His fingers were trembling in the flickering light of the flames. The man offered the package to Alex, but he shook his head.

"Dimitri?" he managed at last, swallowing painfully.

The young man nodded. "I am Dimitri Morozov," he said.

"Dimitri . . . I don't believe it."

Emerging from his stupor, Alex took a couple of steps forward and clumsily hugged Dimitri. It didn't seem right, though; it was an artificial gesture, like embracing a total stranger. His brother's torso was stiff, unyielding. Dimitri looked embarrassed, and his hands feebly patted Alex's shoulders. Alex had seen this moment in his dreams endless times. He had played and replayed in his mind the reunion with his brother; he had visualized their smothering hug and their brotherly kiss, the surge of wild, overwhelming joy. It didn't happen exactly as he had fantasized it; nevertheless, his quest was over. He had a brother, he had found Dimitri! Or actually, Dimitri had found him.

"How did you find me?" Alex asked. The last few minutes resurfaced in his memory, and he turned, looking for Tatiana. She had disappeared. He turned back to Dimitri.

"Through Tatiana Romanova," Dimitri said. "We work together." He drew on his cigarette. "Yesterday she told me about you. I was amazed, I couldn't believe my ears. I didn't sleep all night. I finally asked her to set up a meeting between us. I wanted it to be a surprise." He emitted a short, dry laugh.

"Where is she? Where did she go?"

Dimitri shrugged, exhaling white, acrid smoke. "I guess she wanted to leave us alone. We have a lot to talk about, Alexander."

"What are you doing in Paris?" Alex asked. "Why didn't you answer my letters?" Now that he had recovered his faculty of speech, all his questions were flowing. He clasped his brother's arms. "Do you know you have an aunt in New York? Nina, our mother's sister? Did you hear that I was refused an entry visa to Russia?" He paused, shaking his head in wonderment. "I don't believe it. I arrived here three days ago, and now I'm standing in the middle of the street, with . . . with my brother. Do you know that I've been trying to find you for fifteen years?"

Tonya Gordon should have seen her sons now, he thought, alive, safe, meeting after so many years. What would she have said? And his father? He recalled a verse from his father's poem, dedicated to the heroes of Stalingrad. Brothers, Victor Wolf had called the Red Army soldiers.

> Each ready to die for his brother,
> Each willing to give him his life,
> With his body to stop the enemy's bullet
> That seeks to destroy his brother's heart.
> For brotherly life is unselfish and pure,
> And brothers forever are one.

Oh, Father, Alex thought, if only you could be by my side. You would have understood my feelings. *For brothers forever are one.*

A car turned the corner into the street and roared toward them. They hurriedly stepped aside.

"Let's go someplace where we can talk," Dimitri said.

"Do you know that they killed our mother?"

Dimitri nodded. "They killed my father, too."

Alex winced. "I didn't know. How did it happen?"

"Let's go somewhere," Dimitri said. "We have so much to talk about." He dropped his cigarette on the pavement and crushed it with his heel. "I want a place with lights, and food, and people. This is a great day. A reunion after more than twenty years. I want to get drunk. Let's celebrate."

"Yes, let's drink to it," Alex said. He felt a little uneasy. His brother's words sounded fine, but the reserved tone in which they were uttered didn't quite match the excitement they conveyed.

They hailed a taxi at the Pont de Sully. In the fuzzy light of the passing lamp posts Alex studied his brother. Dimitri was about his own height with powerful shoulders and strong arms that even the well-cut suit couldn't conceal. His handsome profile, crowned with a thick mass of hair, had a romantic air, but the eyes and mouth were hard, even mean. Bitter lines bracketed Dimitri's carved lips. He had a small mole over his upper lip. But there was something else in his brother's face that bothered Alex. It was a controlled face, its expressions carefully composed, the mouth sealed, the eyes guarded, refusing to betray any spontaneous feeling.

"You still live in Russia?" Alex asked.

Dimitri nodded, casting a quick glance at the cab driver. "I represent a Soviet company in Paris," he said.

"Which company?"

Again the short pause. "Sovtorg, foreign trade."

"You spend a lot of time in Paris then."

"Yes. And you?"

The taxi double-parked on the bustling Boulevard Montparnasse. Dimitri paid the driver with a hundred-franc bill he peeled from a thick wad of money. The restaurant was a huge, brightly lit hall packed with people, most of them young. It droned with laughter and animated talk, like a giant beehive. People constantly walked in and out, casually dressed students and unshaven artists mixing with bejeweled women in fur coats and men in expensive suits and bow ties. Overwhelmed waiters in black vests and long white aprons carried trays laden with food, leaving wakes of tantalizing smells. Wine corks popped all over the place. Dimitri led the way in past the bar, whose walls were covered with posters of paintings and prints by Picasso, Toulouse-Lautrec, and Magritte.

"I like this," Alex said as they sat down at a table by the far wall. "Let's have some champagne."

Dimitri hesitated a second, looking around with a fixed smile; his eyes were watchful, alert. Across the aisle a waiter uncorked a champagne bottle that spurted white foam, and two long-legged girls in short skirts squealed in delight.

"Champagne it is!" Dimitri announced. They ordered their dinner and turned back to face each other. In the bright light, Alex drank in every detail of his brother's face. He had a handsome brother, no doubt, although rather stiff and high-strung. He was well-dressed, in a blue suit, snow-white shirt, and silk tie. And there were some similar facial features — the large, clear forehead, the full mouth, the straight nose. There was also something familiar in the shape of Dimitri's eyes. Otherwise, they didn't look very much alike; their coloring was different, and so was their style of dress. Alex was casually attired in baggy, light gray tweeds and a comfortable navy-blue shirt with an open collar.

The waiter opened the champagne bottle. They raised their glasses. "To my dear, dear brother," Alex said impulsively, reaching across the table and squeezing Dimitri's shoulder. "I feel like I'm in a dream." He took a sip of the champagne.

"To you, Alexander."

"Everybody calls me Alex," he said.

"To Alex, then," Dimitri announced. His brief smile made him look absurdly young and mischievous. A group of black men, elegantly dressed and speaking a soft African language, settled beside them. Across the aisle sat a middle-aged couple: a woman in glasses and shabby clothes, and a broad-shouldered, balding man with a beer gut. He was struggling with the crust of melted cheese and croutons that sealed a bowl of onion soup. A stout woman with a red face and plump forearms was passing between the tables, selling cellophane-wrapped roses.

Alex leaned toward his brother. "Now, Dimitri, I want to hear everything that happened to you since we were separated."

"What do you want to know?" Dimitri asked, watching Alex with a crooked smile over the rim of his glass.

"Everything," Alex said eagerly. "You can't remember me, you were too little when we were separated. What is your earliest memory?"

"A stinking orphanage," Dimitri said viciously, just to test his brother's reaction.

Alex seemed shocked. "An orphanage," he repeated. "Good Lord, Dimitri, it must have been hell."

So this is my brother, Dimitri thought, studying the tall blond man who watched him with trust and compassion. He had never seen such vivid gray eyes, sparkling with intelligence and curiosity. His brother's smile was frank and engaging, yet the strong jaw and the dimpled chin revealed a stubborn streak. Alex had an athletic body and looked good even in his old, crumpled jacket. The most striking thing about him, however, was not his good looks, but the warmth and candor he exuded. His smile lit up his entire face; his eyes at times assumed a dreamy look. My brother is a poet, Dimitri thought with amusement, one of those innocent well-meaning suckers I eat for breakfast.

"Do you ever write poetry?" he asked abruptly.

Alex smiled. "Once in a while, in my spare time. I think it's hereditary."

For a moment Dimitri felt a pang of black anger. The bloody sissy can afford to be nice and innocent, he thought, and write poems in his spare time; he's had a cozy, sheltered life since he was a baby. He grew up in America, rich and comfortable, while I was starving in my freezing stable.

The thing he really hated about Alex, though, was his late father's attachment to him. Boris Morozov had taken an enormous risk, back in 1953, to smuggle Alex out of Russia and send him to America. It could have cost him his life. Perhaps it did. Why did he do it? Because he loved Tonya Gordon? So the little Jew landed in New York, Dimitri mused, and I was thrown to the dogs. Watching the handsome, confident man in front of him, Dimitri felt a surge of jealousy.

But his resentment soon simmered down, melted by Alex's disarming warmth. In a way, it was much better to have a nice guy for a brother, Dimitri thought, than to confront a scheming bastard like himself. With Alex, he could let down his guard, he had nothing to fear. He had been embarrassed by Alex's attempt to hug him when they met by the Seine, but it was only natural. Nobody, except for Tatiana and a few other women, had ever shown him any outward affection.

He resumed his narrative. He briefly spoke of his father's execution, without revealing that it had been caused by Tonya's crimes. Alex seemed genuinely shocked. He spontaneously squeezed Dimitri's hand. "I'm so sorry, Dimitri. I think I remember him, a tall, dark-haired man."

Dimitri spoke for a long time, through the champagne, the dinner, and the coffee, carefully editing his story, omitting the thefts and the murder in the quarry, substituting a well-rehearsed yarn about university studies and official missions abroad for the chapter about his KGB training and his operations throughout Europe.

He didn't tell Alex, either, that he had read about him in *Victory Is Near* and had hurried back to Moscow, where, after pulling some strings, he had finally discovered his brother's KGB file, containing some of his letters, his visa applications, and reports of agents who had occasionally checked on him in New York. The file was the best proof that Alex was sincere; he had been trying for years to come to Russia and find him. "I thought you were dead," Dimitri said to Alex, draining his glass. "I never received a letter from you, and nobody knew what had happened to you after Mother's death."

"Somebody must have destroyed my letters," Alex remarked. "Somebody very powerful."

"They didn't want us to meet," Dimitri agreed.

"Who is 'they'?"

Dimitri didn't answer.

It was a pleasant dinner, and he gradually unwound. They burst into laughter when they both ordered the chocolate mousse and discovered that they shared an addiction to chocolate. "This comes from Mother," Alex said knowingly. Nina had told him.

When the ancient clock hanging on the wall chimed three times, and the waiters, glancing at them with beseeching eyes, began piling the chairs upon the tables, they realized they were the last diners left in the restaurant. By that time Dimitri had started to enjoy their conversation. It was Alex's turn now, and he was telling his life story with such passion that Dimitri wanted to hear more.

Besides, for the first time in his life he felt he could relax and talk to someone without fearing his real intentions. He could turn his back on Alex — what a luxury! — without risking getting stabbed. Everybody else he knew was a potential enemy. The agents of the Western services would riddle him with bullets if they knew he was the assassin who had left behind a trail of bodies with broken necks. His colleagues at Department Thirteen would tread on his corpse without thinking twice, to climb higher in the KGB hierarchy. His mentor, Oktober, could send him to his death with no more remorse than if he were stepping on a cockroach.

Alex was different. With him Dimitri felt even safer than with Tatiana. With Tatiana he had to be careful and watch his mouth; after all, she was from an emigré family, and on top of that, a Romanov.

Alex, he knew, wouldn't plot behind his back; he didn't want anything from him; wished him well. He was family; he was his brother. It was a strange feeling, which both confused and pleased Dimitri: a reassuring feeling, because it was safe, and yet upsetting because it was a secret he had to conceal from the KGB; a feeling tempting and scary, soothing and disturbing, like a secret sin, forbidden and yet delightful.

When they left the restaurant, he turned to Alex. "If you meet other Soviet citizens, don't tell them you're my brother."

Alex frowned. "But I mentioned you in all my letters and my visa applications."

"I know. That must be the reason why you didn't get a visa. Anyway, they might know I have a brother in America, but they shouldn't know I met him in Paris. In our foreign service, fraternization with non-Russians isn't recommended, and you are an American now. I could be recalled home for less than that."

"Fine," Alex said. "Let's say that I needed some figures for my research, I called Sovtorg, and we met."

Dimitri nodded. They crossed the street and turned left.

"But what about Tatiana?" Alex said.

"I'll take care of her."

Dimitri took Alex to a small all-night bar in the Rue Vavin, where they continued their conversation over a bottle of cognac. In the background concealed loudspeakers diffused cool jazz arrangements by Gerry Mulligan.

Of course, Dimitri didn't mention his hatred for the Jews, and most of all for Tonya Gordon. Still, when the liquor had slightly eroded his defenses, he pointed at the Star of David that hung on a chain from his brother's neck. "You wear that all the time?"

Alex seemed surprised. "Of course," he said. "It's Mother's. We are Jews, aren't we?"

"My father was Russian," Dimitri said quickly.

"It doesn't make any difference," Alex said. "According to the Jewish faith, it is the mother who counts."

Dimitri clenched his teeth. He was aware of the Jewish tradition, although he had been trying to bury that infuriating knowledge in the deepest recesses of his mind. Before leaving Moscow, he had formed a secret KGB cell of the Pamyat anti-Semitic group. Quite a few officers had joined the group. He could imagine what his comrades would say if they knew his mother was Jewish. He would be kicked out of the organization he had founded! He swallowed his glass of cognac in a single gulp. "If you know so much about being Jewish," he slurred, "why don't you grow a beard and sidelocks, too? And wear a soft hat, like a . . . a . . ."

"A Hasid?" Alex smiled cheerfully. "Oh, but I did," he said, "for a while."

"What?" Dimitri eyed his brother incredulously.

"Yes." Laughing softly, Alex told him about a summer when he had gotten fed up with the waspy ambience of Brown. He'd set out on a search for his roots, which led him to a building in Brooklyn's Crown Heights neighborhood that housed the headquarters of the Lubavitcher Hasidim. "They taught me to pray, and took me to the yeshiva — their religious school — across the street. I even started wearing a skullcap, and tried to grow a beard."

"You've got no beard now," Dimitri pointed out.

Alex shrugged. "I didn't last very long. I regard every religion as a burden. I saw the abandon of the Hasidim when they prayed, and I got scared. I was afraid that if I got hooked, I could turn into a fanatic." He paused. "They weren't really fanatics, though. They were very kind, they had wonderful songs and dances, and a simple love of life. But it was too late for me. If they had gotten to me ten years earlier, you might have been talking to a guy with sidelocks and a fur hat, wearing a long silk caftan."

"Thank Jehovah for that," Dimitri snapped sarcastically.

They parted at dawn, exchanging promises to meet again the same time the following evening for a drink, and perhaps dinner.

Dimitri was living on the fifth floor of a massive eighteenth-century building overlooking the Parc de Monceau. He took a cab straight home. At least in Paris he didn't have to go through the routine of sanctuaries, changing cabs, and living in hideouts. He had an official position, he represented a Soviet company, and his status was perfectly legal. The French Sûreté guessed, of course, that he hadn't been sent over to promote the sales of Russian *matrioshka* dolls, but as long as they hadn't caught him red-handed, he was free to carry out his clandestine operations.

He unlocked the apartment door and walked into the small vestibule.

The scent he knew so well lingered in the dark apartment, and he was suddenly fully awake. He didn't turn on the lights. He took off his clothes, then stepped into the bedroom, approached the large bed, and with a sharp movement pulled the covers aside.

Tatiana woke up with a start and peered at him in the dark. Then she lay back on the pillows and opened her arms, her naked body offered to him, belonging to him, eager to satisfy all his desires.

WHEN ALEX RETURNED HOME, dawn was breaking. He picked up the phone and dictated a telegram to Nina in New York.

"Wonderful news. Dimitri is in Paris. Met him tonight. You have another good-looking nephew. Letter follows. Love Alex."

He hung up, opened the high French windows and stepped onto the narrow balcony of his rooftop flat. The air was fresh, and the black, twin-towered mass of Notre Dame hovered ominously over the slated roofs. A narrow strip of sky, low over the horizon, was slowly turning from gray to purple, with a touch of gold. It was a magnificent sight, but his thoughts were elsewhere. Dimitri's striking, passionate face was vividly etched in his mind. After so many years, he thought, he had found his brother. His brother was a winner; a self-made man, he had climbed out of poverty and hunger to a high position in the Soviet hierarchy. His brother was handsome and intelligent.

And a damned liar.

He sat behind his desk and wrote a long letter to Nina, narrating in detail his reunion with Dimitri. "Ninochka, dearest," he then added, "there is something else, not so pleasant, that I must tell you. I don't buy a word of what my brother told me."

> You taught me, Nina, never to believe in coincidences. When I recovered from the shock of meeting Dimitri on the Seine embankment, I started to think. I can't believe that it was just by coincidence that I got a scholarship to the Institute of East European Studies in Paris, where by pure coincidence I met Tatiana Romanova, who by sheer coincidence happens to work for my brother, who by a wonderful coincidence happens to be posted in Paris. It seems to me that everything was planned from the start: the grant, the Paris letter, the meeting at the library. Apparently Dimitri found out about me — perhaps from my visa applications — and conceived a clever scheme to lure me to Paris. *Not that I care, as long as it was for a good cause.*

He underlined the last sentence.

The sunshine painted the growing pile of written onionskin pages a bright yellow. He put down his pen, ran the back of his hand over his unshaven face, and went to the kitchen to brew some coffee. He was thinking of his conversation with Dimitri.

"Have you been to the Institute of East European Studies?" he had innocently asked his brother.

Dimitri had shrugged. "I only heard about it from Tatiana. She told me she was doing some research there."

Thinking about it left Alex angry. What does he take me for, he wondered, an idiot? I devoted seven long years to the study of the Soviet Union. I know enough about my native country to recognize a KGB operation when I see one.

He carried his mug of coffee to his desk, sat down, and stared absently out the open window. The institute looked exactly like a front, like so many others that the KGB had established throughout the free world — cultural centers, peace movements, friendship leagues, travel bureaus — all of them providing cover for clandestine operations. He remembered that, on arriving at the institute, he had overheard a conversation in Russian at Martineau's office. And in an ashtray on his desk he had seen a crushed Gauloise cigarette, the brand his brother smoked. Could Dimitri have called on Martineau to make sure Alex would be properly manipulated?

He picked up his pen again.

I'm afraid, Ninochka, that my brother doesn't look kosher. In the cab, taking us to dinner, he admitted he was working for Sovtorg. But I know, and you know, that Sovtorg's envoys abroad are almost exclusively KGB agents.

At the restaurant I also noticed that Dimitri insisted on finding a table close to the exit, with his back to the wall; he carries neither credit cards nor checkbook, but pays for everything in cash; during dinner he kept checking and studying everyone who approached our table. He has traveled all over the world, which as you know is also unusual for a Russian.

And what do you think of Tatiana? Dimitri has on his payroll the daughter of notorious emigrés, a member of the czar's family! Now, Ninochka, you know that any bona fide Russian wouldn't touch a Romanov with a ten-foot pole. The most innocent contact with such a people's enemy could earn him a one-way ticket to a sub-Arctic gulag, unless he had been explicitly authorized to do it.

There can be no doubt, I'm afraid, that my brother has KGB written all over him.

He drained the last bitter drops from his cup and leaned back in his chair, rubbing his fingers over his chin stubble. KGB spy or not, Dimitri was his brother. Dimitri had gone through all this trouble, planning such an intricate operation, just to meet him. It meant that everything wasn't phony; Dimitri cared about him; perhaps he was even risking his career by bringing him over to Paris. Alex felt a renewed surge of warmth for his brother. He recalled his affectionate smile at the restaurant, and the way he raised his glass: "To you, Alex!"

Perhaps Dimitri had no choice, perhaps he had to lie to him, to protect himself. Nothing could change the fact that Tonya Gordon's two sons were together again.

TATIANA had first met Dimitri one Thursday, eighteen months before, when she was walking down the Rue de Lille after her evening seminar. She wasn't accustomed to walking the streets of Paris alone; she had recently broken up with her boyfriend, a fellow student named Louis. A black car stopped beside her, at the dark corner of the Rue de Beaune; two strong arms grabbed her from behind and threw her on the backseat, then the car sped off. She fought, and tried to scream, but someone clamped a hand over her mouth.

"Nobody will hear you, Tatiana Borisova," a cool voice said in Russian. "Besides, we mean you no harm, I just want to talk to you. If you misbehave, your relatives in the Soviet Union might be harmed."

She shook her head violently.

"Oh yes," the man said. "You do have relatives in Russia. They don't call themselves Romanov today. But I know all about the Golitzins in Moscow, the Zvetayevs in Kiev, and the Yulins and Daniloffs in Odessa. Now, may I take my hand off your mouth?"

She nodded, vanquished. What could she do? This man knew about her relatives, who had hesitated too long when her grandparents had fled Russia. Their children were still living, under assumed names, in the Soviet Union.

"Who are you?" she asked after he had removed his hand.

"We work for the Soviet government," was the answer, and she realized that her deepest fears had come true. This man belonged to the KGB.

The driver of the black car was a scrawny man with broken teeth. He dropped off his passengers in another dark street, and Dimitri led Tatiana to a café crowded with workers. They were in the commuter suburb of Bagnolet. After they had settled at a corner table and ordered coffee, Dimitri leaned toward her.

He spoke matter-of-factly. "We know all about you, Tatiana Borisova. We know that you're related to the grand duke Peter, that you play the piano, that you left your boyfriend a month ago. We know your mother is very ill and your father is an architect. We also know what he does after hours."

She listened in mounting panic to Dimitri's discourse; this tough man knew all their secrets! He mentioned her father's ties with the emigré organizations, and named a close friend of their family who had become a CIA expert. Then he brought up the most devastating secret of them all, the story of her cousin Igor, who had infiltrated the Soviet Union posing as an Austrian journalist.

"How do you think Mr. 'Egon Kunzle' " — he pronounced Igor's assumed name with disdain — "got his visa to the Soviet Union so easily? And found an apartment in Moscow so easily? We knew all about him from the very beginning. We actually planted the idea of his going to Russia."

"Why?"

"Because we wanted him in our power there, and you in our power here," Dimitri helpfully explained.

He told her all this in a low, casual voice, while sipping his coffee. He seemed certain that she wouldn't run away, and he was right. She knew she could escape, but for what purpose? The man who had kidnapped her could bring death upon her relatives in Russia, and tragedy upon her parents in France, with a snap of his fingers. So she stayed and listened to him.

She stood up to him only once, when he calmly threatened her father with death.

"Boris Romanov is a French citizen," she flared. "He came to this country at the age of three. He is protected by the French government."

"So were several others," Dimitri said placidly, throwing a batch of photographs on the table before her. "Emigré leaders," he added matter-of-factly, "prematurely deceased."

He pointed at each of the photographs, announcing the names of the assassinated dissidents. "You wouldn't want us to add your father's picture to this collection, would you?"

She stared in horror at the people in the photographs, some of whom she recognized, then raised her eyes. Morozov was watching her with a sarcastic grin. There was something so deadly and also triumphant in his eyes, that she guessed he'd been involved in some of those murders; perhaps he was even the murderer.

"So, Tatiana Borisova, what do you say?"

She couldn't believe their conversation was real. She had often participated in emigré meetings in her family's house at Saint-Germain, or accompanied her father to conferences out of town. Still, it had been nothing but vain talk, hollow declarations, pompous nonsense about the liberation of the motherland. She had taken none of it seriously, not even the departure of her cousin for Russia.

Now, all of a sudden, she awoke to the cruel reality of the secret war. The KGB had infiltrated their organization, it probably controlled the emigré societies all over Europe. Now she herself had no choice but to accept the crude barter Dimitri offered: the lives of her family and friends in exchange for the information she would provide. The cover chosen for her contacts with Dimitri was the position of an interpreter at Sovtorg. "And remember," he said later, when the black car was speeding back toward Paris, "if you speak a single word of this to your father, it will be his death sentence."

"And if I go to the police?" she asked. The car was crossing the Ile de la Cité.

Dimitri ordered the driver to stop the car. "Why don't you?" he said. "The police headquarters are right across the street. What will you tell them? Whatever it is, they won't believe you. In the unlikely case they do, they may expel me to Russia. I'll survive. But you — you'll start worrying about your family . . . and about your own life."

His laugh was short and dry as he left her on the sidewalk.

That was how she began to work for him. A month later she became his mistress.

*   *   *

IT WAS A RAINY SUNDAY and Morozov had summoned Tatiana to his apartment. After closing the door behind her, he steered her to his bedroom, undressed her with deliberate slowness, and threw her on the bed. She didn't lift a finger. He unbuckled his belt while she watched him, immobile, holding her breath. It wasn't rape; they both knew she wouldn't fight. He thought she feared him; he couldn't guess that she was fascinated by his raw power, and his absolute domination oddly excited her.

That first time, she had let him do as he wished. She'd been docile and passive, obeying him like a robot. Then, gradually, she reversed their roles. During the following weeks, she learned to satisfy his sexual urges, using her body, her mouth and hands, to guide him to new peaks of pleasure. And when this powerful man groaned and panted in abandon, when his body grew taut with passion or went slack in her arms, she felt she was in total control. She played him like her piano. And she loved the music.

She knew she belonged to him, and accepted that; but she didn't love him. In their bizarre relationship there was no place for her emotions. She enjoyed having sex with him, and didn't feel debased. She was far more affected by her role as a spy inside her father's organization. She came daily to the Sovtorg building, and went to Dimitri's office staring straight ahead, her shoulders hunched, avoiding the avid looks and the lewd smiles of middle-aged Russians in gray suits and brown shoes.

Once a week she would bring Dimitri her report. It contained the names of people who participated in emigré meetings, summaries of the topics discussed, details of future activities. Dimitri showed special interest in contacts between the emigrés and the CIA. She felt disgusted with herself. Even the knowledge that she had saved her relatives' lives didn't appease her sleepless nights.

The arrival of Dimitri's brother troubled her deeply. She had been ordered by Dimitri to strike up a conversation with him the day he arrived at the institute. She did as she was told; it was easy. But she didn't expect the brother of her sinister, brooding lover to be so charming. She wasn't ready to deal with a man she could like, a man she didn't fear.

The afternoon they had spent together had been delightful. She was drawn to the only natural, real person in the world of deceit in which she lately moved. Alex Gordon was so much like her, she thought; or rather, like what she had once been. He was an honest, candid young man who liked music and poetry, and cared about people. The poor guy had no chance if his ruthless brother turned against him. If Dimitri wanted to, he could destroy Alex. She had wanted to warn Alex, the night she led him to the meeting with Dimitri. Beware of your brother, she had wanted to scream, beware of his deadly hug, beware of his kiss.

But she had only dared to press his hand briefly. Then she ran back to Dimitri's apartment, to prepare herself for his pleasure.

SHE MET ALEX GORDON again the following evening at the Bofinger brasserie, an old Parisian eatery with a magnificent stained-glass ceiling. She came with Dimitri and watched Alex closely when Dimitri told him she was his girlfriend. Alex paled as he stared at both of them; finally he managed a smile. "Congratulations, Dimitri," he said. "Tatiana is a ravishing woman. I think Mother looked like her when she was young."

Tatiana could see that Dimitri didn't like the comparison; she was familiar with the tightening of his jaw, which indicated anger. But he didn't say a word. They spent the evening together; after dinner they went to an old Parisian nightclub, on the Montmartre hill, where young performers sang old French songs on a small stage. They ended the evening over an assortment of oysters in an all-night bistro at Place Clichy.

In the following months, they spent a lot of time together, eating out, going to movies, nightclubs, even driving to the countryside for an occasional weekend. Getting to know each other better, the two brothers also discovered the profound gap that separated them. Alex was infuriated with the trite communist slogans that seemed to dictate his brother's views, and he resented Dimitri's suspicious attitude toward the Western way of life.

As for Dimitri, he couldn't cope with the degree of personal freedom in America; for him it was a dangerous phenomenon, bordering on anarchy. In August, Nixon had resigned, following the Watergate scandal. The Americans must have gone crazy, Dimitri said, to kick their President out of the White House for such nonsense. He failed to understand the functioning of a society that was not tightly controlled from above.

Tatiana was fascinated by the development of the brothers' relationship. At first there was genuine affection and curiosity on both sides; she was surprised to discover how charming Dimitri could be. But after a few weeks the honeymoon turned sour; Dimitri raised his defenses. Tatiana had the feeling that her lover had grown scared of his own behavior. Alex had begun to influence him, and he'd become too carefree and spontaneous, obviously enjoying a different life from the one he had chosen.

Afterward, Alex's openness was countered by Dimitri's reserve. Whenever Alex made a political remark about the Soviet Union, Dimitri would clam up. Alex's attempts to bring up the deaths of their parents were also met by sullen silence. Finally, these subjects dropped completely out of their conversations. The brothers preferred to discuss food and movies, sports and international events. They debated the fall of Saigon, the French presidential election that brought Giscard d'Estaing to power, Gerald Ford's chances in 1976. Russia became a subject they tackled very rarely and very cautiously.

To Tatiana, their whole relationship seemed increasingly artificial. The only things that bound Alex and Dimitri together — their background, their family, their native land — had become taboo.

Several times Dimitri had to stay late at the office because of some last minute emergency; Tatiana and Alex were left alone. On these nights, they would go to a concert or a ballet performance, things which Dimitri intensely disliked.

Whenever she was alone with Alex, Tatiana felt an awkward tension rising between them. Their conversations were strained, interspersed with uneasy silences. When he touched her, helping her out of a cab or holding her coat, she felt a current shooting through her flesh. Later she would remember every smile, every look they exchanged. She caught herself watching Alex's mouth, the sparkle in his eyes, the lock of blond hair that so endearingly fell on his forehead; and she felt an overwhelming desire to reach out and touch him, feel the contour of his lips with her fingers; taste them, softly, with her mouth. It slowly dawned on her that she was being drawn into a dangerous infatuation with Alex Gordon.

She suspected Alex felt the same way about her. She could tell by the way he looked at her, by his metamorphosis into a happier person when they were alone. Yet it was an impossible situation. Dimitri inspired her with tremendous fear. If she ever cheated on him, he would kill her without thinking twice. He might even kill his brother. Therefore, she went out with Alex whenever Dimitri told her to, but was always on her guard. She never gave Alex the opportunity to hold her hand again.

She made sure to always be at home, lying naked in the large bed, before Dimitri returned. Like a modern Cinderella, she would leave Alex, wherever they were, at least a half hour before Dimitri's expected time of arrival; she would rush home, to undress and perfume herself for him. The last few times, she cried while combing her hair before the mirror, and watched the tears run down her face.

One night in the beginning of February, she found Dimitri waiting for her when she came home. He was fully dressed, sitting on the single armchair in the vestibule.

"I . . . I didn't expect you before midnight," she stammered.

He nodded, lighting a cigarette. "I know. How is my dear brother?" His tone was cynical, with no trace of any warmth.

"We went to a ballet. We saw *Romeo and Juliet* at the Opéra."

"Good," he said absently. "Look, I received an urgent phone call from home. I have to fly to Moscow, tonight. Something unexpected has come up."

"When will you be back?"

"I don't know." He went into the bedroom and was back in a moment, carrying a light suitcase and a black briefcase. He put on his heavy overcoat. "In two or three weeks, I suppose."

He pulled her to him and kissed her hard on the mouth. "Wait for me," he said, his hand moving over her breasts, slipping down her body. "Keep this for me. And don't make mistakes."

The black eyes were intense.

Romeo and Juliet, performed by the Corps de Ballet de l'Opéra, had been magnificent. After the performance, Alex helped Tatiana into a taxi, then walked down the Rue de la Paix, crossed the opulent Place Vendôme, and strolled along the riverbank toward the Pont des Arts. The streets were almost empty, and the fierce cold had driven away even the lovers and the bums who roamed the Seine embankment. A light snow started falling. He shivered in his light coat, so he raised his collar and wrapped his woolen scarf more tightly around his throat; but he didn't want to go home yet. He knew he wouldn't be able to sleep, not after spending an evening with Tatiana. She had bewitched him completely, and he was desperately in love with her.

He had never felt this way before. He wasn't the same man who had arrived in Paris five months ago. His life had become a long wait for the few hours he would spend with Tatiana, mostly in Dimitri's company, sometimes alone. They were so good together, speaking the same language, sharing the same tastes. They could communicate by a look or a smile. And she was irresistible, vibrant, exciting — she could change in a flash from a mischievous youngster to an inquisitive scholar, a sensitive art lover, or a stunning young woman.

He thought of nothing but Tatiana, ate badly, slept little, dressed carelessly. He knew he was being unfair to Claudia by courting another woman; but had she been fair to him? They could have been married by now. He felt a deep resentment toward Claudia for her refusal to go along with him when he'd needed her. Tatiana was more sensitive, she wouldn't have refused to marry him if they had been so deeply in love. He stopped writing to Claudia; compared to his obsession with Tatiana, his love for Claudia now seemed nothing more than a mild affection.

Tatiana had enticed him to the point that nothing else mattered — not his research, not his relationship with Dimitri. He courted Tatiana assiduously, but very subtly, letting his eyes speak, refraining from any straightforward word or gesture. He knew he was breaking a moral code and abusing Dimitri's confidence; coveting his brother's woman was wrong, but he couldn't help it. His affection for his brother had given way to a blinding jealousy. He couldn't stand the way Dimitri was treating the girl, as if she were his property. He couldn't stand watching Dimitri touch her, stroke her hair, or kiss her possessively.

Tatiana wasn't the only reason for his drifting away from Dimitri. The suspicions Alex had when they first met were now confirmed. He noticed the strange rendezvous places his brother would propose — mostly street corners where he would be picked up by a chauffeur-driven car. He noticed Dimitri's unusual hours, his use of public phones only, his sudden disappearances. His brother seemed involved in something very fishy indeed.

Meanwhile, Dimitri had become increasingly prone to sudden outbursts of anger and embarrassing, stubborn silences. Alex knew that he was also to blame; still, being with his brother wasn't fun anymore.

Alex had mentioned Dimitri to Grimaldi, whom he had met again a week after their arrival in Paris, when Grimaldi had left him a message at the institute. Alex had called back, and his flamboyant friend took him out to lunch in an exquisite seafood restaurant off the Champs-Elysées. Since then, he and Grimaldi had met often, mostly for lunch or dinner. Grimaldi knew the best gourmet restaurants in Paris, was a personal friend of the chefs, and always picked up the tab. "Uncle Sam is paying," he said once. "The USIS is very generous, so don't worry."

Grimaldi always appeared in different attire; he was a strutting peacock in his flowery vests, silk ties and kerchiefs, his lively eyes shining from a deeply tanned face. Alex suspected a sun lamp was responsible for his friend's healthy complexion. He liked Grimaldi's animated way of speaking, and enjoyed watching the sparkle of golden rings as his bejeweled hands accompanied his fascinating stories. Grimaldi was a great storyteller, an amusing bon vivant, and Alex liked his company. Besides, he was a perpetual source of information about life in Russia.

Alex had told Grimaldi about Dimitri, but didn't share with him his suspicions that his brother was a KGB employee; he didn't want to endanger Dimitri. Besides, Grimaldi didn't seem to care much about Dimitri's line of work; he was fascinated by the human angle of the story, which he regarded as a triumph of poetic justice. "You and your brother are Tonya's revenge on the system that murdered her," he once said. Alex wanted the three of them to have dinner together; he thought Dimitri would be amused by Grimaldi's extravagance. But Grimaldi didn't think it was a good idea.

He and Grimaldi were going to have lunch tomorrow, Alex remembered. He crossed the Seine by the Pont des Arts and plunged into the picturesque Latin Quarter. As he passed by the King's Club disco, a couple came out, kissing passionately. The girl was blond and slender; Alex clenched his teeth. A group of black musicians was leaving the Bilboquet, and he thought of his favorite jazz club in Greenwich Village. At the corner of Saint-Germain the wind was whipping an old poster from the presidential campaign, showing Giscard d'Estaing confidently looking to the future. A street vendor was selling hot grilled chestnuts, and Alex yielded to the temptation.

The entrance to his building was dark. He took the tiny elevator to the seventh floor. As he stepped out, chewing a chestnut, he saw a woman's figure huddled by his door. His heart missed a beat as he recognized the silken mass of blond hair and the soft sheepskin Dimitri had brought her from Moscow.

"Tatiana!"

She stood up. Her face was chalk-white.

"What happened? What are you doing here?"

She stared at him, suddenly so close, so accessible. "I came — " she began, then bit her lip. "Dimitri left for Moscow tonight, he won't be back for two or three weeks."

He wanted to say something, but couldn't find the right words. The paper bag with the chestnuts slipped from his fingers. They looked at each other for another moment, then he stepped forward and collected her in his arms. Her face was cold, but her lips were soft and burning, feverishly trembling under his mouth.

"I love you, Tatiana," he said. Her eyes lit up with happiness, but almost immediately melted into something else — fear.

OKTOBER was a night person, Dimitri thought, as he climbed the dark, winding stairs to his office. It was past two A.M., on the second night after his return to Moscow. He had spent most of the day sleeping in his apartment on Pushkinskaya Street. In the afternoon he had dropped in at the office and read a few reports. He had dinner at the KGB club with a couple of friends from the department. Nobody knew why Oktober had called him back. There was a lot of talk of the Italian Brigate Rosse and the French Action Directe, two left-wing guerrilla organizations that had lately been infiltrated by the department. But nothing unusual had happened these last few days that could have required Dimitri's presence.

He returned home and browsed through John Barron's book about the KGB, which had just been published in New York. At one-thirty a car picked him up and took him to the old mansion that Oktober had turned into the Wet Affairs headquarters.

"Come in, Dimitri," Oktober's cracked voice called when he knocked on his door. What would Oktober say, Dimitri wondered, if he knew that Dimitri had just left his brother in Paris? Could Alex be the reason for his sudden recall? Dimitri felt a pang of anxiety.

He walked into Oktober's tiny den. The files were stacked in neat piles all over the place — on the desk, on most of the chairs, even on the floor. Oktober himself was seated on a straight-backed wooden chair behind his massive desk. Oktober hated armchairs.

"Take off your coat," Oktober croaked again. "Sit down. What's new in Paris?" Dimitri peered at him through the thick cigarette smoke that hung like a veil in the gloomy, cold room. Oktober had grown even more skeletal since he had seen him last. The sharp nose curved down like the beak of a bird of prey; the cheekbones bulged, tautening the wizened skin. Oktober's burning eyes had sunk deeper in their dark sockets, and his scrawny neck couldn't fill the collar of his black sweater. His long white hair was getting yellow, and curled at the edges.

"In Paris — " he began, and shut up, realizing that Oktober had asked his question as a means of introduction. He didn't seem to want a report of Dimitri's activities.

"I called you back, my boy," Oktober was saying, lighting a fresh cigarette with the stub of another, "because a year ago you carried out, almost single-handedly, a very important operation. Time has come for the next stage."

Dimitri watched him in puzzlement.

"I want you to meet somebody," Oktober rasped. "Right here."

He went to the door connecting his den with his secretary's office and opened it. "He's here," he said to somebody in the office. "You can come in now." He stepped aside.

"Good evening, Dimitri," a pleasant voice said.

A man in an elegant suit appeared in the open doorway, his body outlined against the dim light coming from behind. Dimitri squinted. The man stepped inside and turned toward him. He was smiling.

Dimitri recognized the handsome, scarred face of Oleg Kalinin.

Chapter 13

IN HER FANTASIES, Tatiana had countless times imagined the moment when Alex took her in his arms. She had anticipated the softness of his full lips against hers, the blond head snuggling in the hollow of her neck, his voice saying, I love you, Tatiana. And she would murmur, I am yours, Alex. Since the first moment I saw you, there was nobody else, life was just an illusion. She had visualized him carrying her to his bed, feverishly undressing her, then sinking into her as she clung to him with her trembling body. It could have been like that, it almost was like that, except for the terror Dimitri had instilled in her, a blood-chilling presence that stuck to her even when she pulled Alex inside her and whispered her love into his ears.

Even in these moments of an absolute love like nothing she had ever known before, she remembered Dimitri's warning. "Don't make mistakes." The image of his face never left her eyes, his hinted menace rang in her ears, the fear of his revenge clung to her skin like a cold, wet shroud. "Keep them for me," he had said, as his hand had touched her breasts and thighs, "and don't make mistakes." An hour later she had made the worst mistake, for which she might pay with her life. But she couldn't help it. The thought of Alex had driven her mad. He was so close, alone, yearning for her; she had gone to him, knowing she might be sentencing herself to death. And Alex as well. She shuddered.

"What's wrong, my love?" Alex asked, raising his head.

"Nothing," she said, stroking his hair. "Nothing. Hold me, Alex, *lyubimi*, make love to me."

The fear of Dimitri's revenge haunted her throughout the following week, which otherwise was the happiest of her life. She spent every single moment with Alex. She needed him beside her, had to be sure that whenever she reached for him, he would be there. She didn't go to Sovtorg; they probably didn't expect her to come when Dimitri was away. Alex didn't go to the institute, either. He didn't return phone calls and didn't open the letters that came from a woman in America named Claudia Benevento. "She used to be my girlfriend," Alex said to Tatiana. "It was ages ago."

They explored Paris the way only lovers could, and she was amazed to discover how people and places, sights and sounds, smells and tastes she knew so well, seemed so different to a person in love. The Parc de Monceau and the Luxembourg Gardens, the gravel paths of the Tuileries, the forests of Fontainebleau and Rambouillet, the stone-paved banks of the Seine, all of it looked as if conceived for the two of them, and them only.

Even the occasional *clochard* under a Seine bridge, the wildly kissing couple under a tree in the middle of a furious rain, a love song of Piaf or Brel played on the radio — everything seemed as if it had been staged for them by a brilliant theatrical director.

Theirs were the crooked streets of the Latin Quarter and the Marais, Montmartre and the Bastille, the little cafés of the Place de la Contrescarpe, the *chansonniers* and the literary nightclubs, the small Vietnamese and Italian restaurants behind the Saint Sulpice church; theirs were the crisp, starry Parisian nights and the dreamy dawns, sung by generations of poets, when an immaculate mist rose from the Seine and invaded the adjoining streets, slipping into the doorway where Tatiana stood with Alex, passionately kissing.

"I want to marry you," he said to her one cool, cloudy afternoon. They had spent the night in a small inn at the Vallée de la Chevreuse, and walked hand in hand beside a lazy, narrow stream. He was wearing a white turtleneck sweater.

"No, it can never happen," she said, oddly disturbed. A family was having a picnic by the water, the children were chasing each other in the grove. A tiny black dog barked furiously at their approach, then scurried to safety, its tail between its legs.

Alex looked at her. The wind was blowing her hair across her face.

"We love each other, Tatiana. I want to marry you and take you with me to America."

She stubbornly shook her head. When she spoke again, despair had infected her voice. "Dimitri will never let this happen."

"Dimitri is out of your life for good," he said, "It's just you and me."

But Dimitri was with them all the time, an unwanted but persistent companion. They avoided speaking about him, but Tatiana could tell Alex was deeply troubled; he couldn't forgive himself for having stolen his brother's girl. Their love, however, was so deep, so consuming, that nothing else seemed to matter.

But one night she awoke in terror. In her nightmare she had seen Dimitri, coming for her with a rope, calmly tying the noose around her neck. A cold fire was burning in his eyes, and his mouth was bitterly drawn. "I warned you," he said softly, before strangling her, "no mistakes." She awoke suffocating, gasping for air.

"It's all right, my love," Alex whispered to her, gently stroking her forehead. "It was only a dream. Calm down, all right? Look at me. Tatiana, look at me."

She lay on her back, staring at the fluttering curtains.

"What's the matter, my love?"

"He'll kill us," she whispered. "Dimitri will come back from Moscow and kill us both."

He stared at her in dismay, then shook his head. "What are you talking about?"

"Alex," she murmured in despair. "We must leave, before he comes back. If he finds us, we're as good as dead."

In the soft light of dawn she saw he was smiling. "Don't be silly," he said. "He's my brother. I'll talk to him and — "

"You don't know your brother," she said. "You don't know what he can do. You don't know who he is."

Alex rolled away and sat up on the bed, looking at her closely. His face grew serious, and he softly touched her cheek with his fingertips. "Who is my brother? Tell me."

And she did.

*   *   *

HIS PHONE CALL awakened Grimaldi. "You must be out of your mind," his friend groaned into the receiver. "It's not seven yet. What happened, the Russkies attacked?"

"I'm sorry," Alex said, his eyes glued to Tatiana's chalk-white face. She sat across the table, huddled in his bathrobe. "It's urgent."

They had spoken of Dimitri until daybreak. Tatiana seemed scared to death. He will kill us, she kept repeating. If you go to him, he'll kill you, and then he'll find me and kill me, too.

Alex had proposed that she fly to America and stay with Nina. Tatiana refused again. Dimitri's thugs would find her, she said.

"Alex! Hey, Alex!" Grimaldi's voice brought him back to reality. "What's wrong? Can't it wait until lunch?"

"Something came up, and I need your help." Alex was speaking like a robot, disjointed thoughts flashing through his mind. A murderer, Tatiana had said, his brother was a murderer. He had guessed Dimitri was a spy, but hadn't suspected him of any violent acts. Not his brother, not Tonya Gordon's son.

"What kind of help?" Grimaldi sounded reserved.

"I told you about my brother? Meeting him in Paris, I mean."

"Yes."

Alex felt disgusted with himself, as if he were betraying Dimitri. Let's hope it's a false alarm, he thought. Let's hope Tatiana is imagining things, that he's just a second-rate spy, paying for his stay in Paris with some chicken feed about imaginary emigré conspiracies.

"Alex? Are you there?"

"Listen, you work with the embassy, you know quite a lot of people. My friend Tatiana — "

"Your friend?" Grimaldi sounded amused. "You told me she was your brother's girl."

"My friend Tatiana," Alex repeated, irritated, "is afraid Dimitri might try to hurt her, and I thought she might need protection." She stared at him from across the table, her eyes wide with fear. Somewhere, far away, a church bell was ringing.

"Tell her to go to the police," Grimaldi said impatiently. "This has nothing to do with the embassy."

I must not incriminate Dimitri in any way, Alex thought. He phrased his words very cautiously. "Tatiana thinks Dimitri might try to hurt her, with the help of the Soviet . . . services. I'm sure she's wrong, I don't believe he's involved in anything illegal. But just to be on the safe side, I'd like you to' find out if your embassy friends suspect Dimitri of any unusual activities."

"If we have a file on him, you mean? As a Russian agent?"

Alex didn't answer.

"His last name is Morozov, isn't it?"

"Yes," Alex murmured. "Dimitri Morozov."

"I'll see what I can do," Grimaldi said. "Let's make lunch at one-thirty, the Closerie des Lilas." He paused. "And another thing. Come alone, don't bring the lady along."

GRIMALDI ENTERED the famous Parisian restaurant fifteen minutes before the agreed-upon time.

"Ah, Monsieur Grimaldi, vous êtes déjà là!" The owner of the Closerie ceremoniously shook hands with him and motioned to the maître d', who led him to a secluded corner table. "La table de Monsieur Ernest Hemingway," he disclosed conspiratorially, fussing with the gleaming cutlery.

Grimaldi chuckled. Each table at the Closerie became Monsieur Hemingway's when the patron was an American tourist. The truth was that Hemingway had mostly sat on the terrace, but who cared about the truth, anyway? He settled on the soft bench, ordered a champagne kir, and contemplated his progress. His plan was moving along nicely. Alex was coming to him, to ask for help against his brother. Grimaldi hadn't taken into account the appearance of the Russian girl and her infatuation with Alex. But if both brothers were involved with Tatiana, it was a welcome development; the girl could unwittingly help him turn Alex Gordon into his tool against Morozov.

"Hi, Franco."

Grimaldi raised his eyes. Alex stood before him in a pair of freshly pressed jeans, a snow-white shirt, and a smart, light gray jacket. His face was pale; he had cut himself shaving.

"You look worried," Grimaldi said. "How's Tatiana?"

Alex hesitated a moment. "Scared," he said. A striking, Spanish-looking woman sitting at the next table turned and stared at him with smoldering black eyes, smiling slightly.

"Sit down before the señora rapes you," Grimaldi grunted. "Let's order, and then we'll talk."

After their order had been taken and he had tasted the Nuits Saint Georges, Grimaldi leaned forward. His eyes carefully swept the restaurant, then he concentrated on Alex.

"Did you — " Alex began impatiently.

"Let me tell you something first. You didn't call me because I work at the U.S. Information Service, right?"

Alex hesitated, then nodded.

"From the very beginning you suspected I was more involved with intelligence gathering than I cared to admit."

Alex nodded again. "Yes. You spoke to me about your life in Moscow, London, Bonn . . . You seemed too knowledgeable, and too smart, to have spent your life mailing out pamphlets about the American dream. But I preferred not to ask. Besides, I didn't care."

"I accept that. But I want to be frank with you." He clammed up abruptly when a silver-haired waiter deferentially placed a plate of smoked salmon before Alex, and half a dozen sizzling snails in garlic butter before Grimaldi. *"Attention, c'est chaud,"* the waiter chanted, poured some wine in their glasses and vanished.

"I have been a CIA agent since the Company was established," Grimaldi said, intently watching Alex, who winced. His fork froze in mid air, then returned to rest on the plate.

"And our meeting on the plane — "

". . . wasn't fortuitous, no. We knew who you were, and we knew that the Institute for East European Studies was a KGB cover organization. We wanted to find out if you were working for them."

Alex stared at him reflectively. "Very smart."

"You know why?" Grimaldi said. It was the moment to plant the first seed. "Because we wanted to make you an offer. We wanted to ask you to join the Company. We think very highly of you, Alex; you're a top Soviet expert."

Alex ignored the cue. "You wanted to check me out, you said. And what did you find?"

Grimaldi gave a short laugh. "We found out you were a bona fide scholar who had nothing to do with their clandestine activities. So we asked ourselves, why did they bring Boris Morozov's stepson over here? You see," he lied, "we didn't know Dimitri was your brother. Only when you told me about your meeting him here did I understand that he had masterminded the scholarship affair."

"So you came over to spy on me," Alex summed up.

Grimaldi spread his hands, palms up. "Yes, I flew here to spy on you, and found out you were clean."

"I thought you were my friend."

"We became friends, but that's another matter."

"Sure," Alex said and looked away. It had started raining outside, and the first drops made sinuous patterns on the terrace windows. A cozy darkness crept into the restaurant.

Grimaldi deftly extracted a reluctant snail from its purple-brown shell and leaned back. "Still, I haven't found out what Dimitri's real intentions were. Perhaps he wanted to recruit you."

Alex shook his head.

"Not yet," Grimaldi said, chewing with pleasure. "I'm sure he would have approached you sooner or later."

"He's my brother, for Christ's sake," Alex said stubbornly. "He wanted to meet me."

Grimaldi reached for his briefcase and took out a pale yellow file. "Do you want to meet him?" he asked gently.

A HALF HOUR LATER Alex raised his eyes from the file. He hadn't touched his food, and the waiter, after returning several times, had finally taken away his plate. On Grimaldi's whispered orders, he had brought them two double glasses of Hennessy cognac.

"This — " Alex began, and his voice broke. Grimaldi handed him the brandy, and Alex gulped it down. His eyes were out of focus. Grimaldi signaled the waiter for another drink.

"Is all this true?" Alex asked, his fingers nervously plowing through his hair. A vein was throbbing at the base of his throat. He started to get up, then sat down again, his left hand fidgeting with his shirt buttons.

"As far as I can tell, yes," Grimaldi said.

"So Tatiana was right," Alex said in a low, almost inaudible voice. "According to this file, my brother is a cold-blooded murderer. He has killed at least three people, perhaps more."

Grimaldi lit a cigarillo with deliberately slow gestures, and blew out the match. "You know about Department Thirteen."

"Of course I do. I've read everything published about the KGB. But it says here that Dimitri kills with his bare hands. That's not KGB procedure."

The waiter brought another cognac and placed it beside Alex.

Alex was staring fixedly at a glossy photograph of a woman's body, her head twisted in an impossible angle. Her skirt was torn, revealing her white thighs. "If all this is true, how come he moves freely throughout Europe and even enjoys special privileges?"

Grimaldi exhaled a long whiff of smoke. "These are only conjectures, Alex, we have not a shred of solid proof."

"So you might be wrong!" He downed his second glass.

Grimaldi shrugged. "I know how you feel. You want us so badly to be wrong." He drew on his cigar. "But I trust our sources." He suddenly felt he had beaten around the bush too long. He leaned forward. "What do you want, Alex?"

"I want to take Tatiana to the States and marry her. I want her to be safe."

"All right. Listen to me, and listen to me good. Tatiana's life is in danger, and yours may be, too."

Alex made a deprecatory gesture with his hand.

"I know you're a big hero," Grimaldi said acidly. "But Tatiana is right. If Dimitri comes back and finds out about you two, he might kill both of you. Do you understand?"

He went on. "We can offer Tatiana safe passage to America, and a new identity. We'll guarantee her protection. But" — he raised his hand as Alex was about to say something — "first, she must be debriefed by us, here, in Europe. She has worked for Morozov for eighteen months; she must know a lot about his operations."

"No," Alex said, "no debriefing." He fell silent, then seemed to change his mind. "Where do you want to debrief her?"

"Not here," Grimaldi said. "Paris is too risky. In Brussels, or London, perhaps Frankfurt. We have safehouses in those cities."

"How long will it take?"

"About two weeks. That's also the time it will take to prepare her papers."

Alex was slowly coming back to himself. "I want to talk it over with

Tatiana." He slid back his chair and stood up. "I'll call you in a couple of days."

"No way," Grimaldi said. "It's yes or no, and it's now. If you leave, you leave tonight."

"Why, what's the hurry?"

"The hurry is" — Grimaldi picked up the murdered woman's photograph — "that if your brother returns from Moscow before you call me, your precious Tatiana will look like this. You understand this, *tovarich? Ponimayesh?*"

Alex stared back at him, his jaw locked in fury, then turned back and bolted out of the restaurant.

Just you wait, golden boy, Grimaldi thought, sipping his cognac, one day I'll make you dance to my tune. I'll make you destroy your brother for what he did to me. And to Oleg.

IN OKTOBER'S OFFICE Dimitri Morozov and Oleg Kalinin faced each other as their black-clothed host paced restlessly, telling them a strange story of deceit. Dimitri was bent over a lukewarm glass of tea, which he held between his palms; he still hadn't recovered from the shock he had experienced when he saw Kalinin's silhouette fill the doorway of Oktober's office.

The stunned silence that followed Kalinin's appearance had been broken by Oktober's rasping voice. "You didn't expect to see this one here did you? You expected to meet him at the Lubyanka, in chains, or facing a firing squad. Well, Dimitri, don't you remember what I told you? Never trust what you see and what you hear. Deceit, deceit, deceit" — he emphasized the words by thumping his fist on his desk, a white-haired conjurer wickedly grinning through the smoke — "that's the essence of the secret war. Remember that, Dimitri!"

Kalinin settled in one of the chairs while Oktober, waving his cigarette like a conductor's baton, his predator's eyes glued to Dimitri's, revealed to him the secret of Operation Top Hat.

It had started shortly after the war, when Oktober was stationed in Berlin, charged with infiltrating American OSS circles. He had detected a certain weakness in an American officer, Franco Grimaldi, and concluded he was ripe for establishing emotional contact with another man. Captain Kalinin had been chosen for the job and performed brilliantly.

He had succeeded in winning Grimaldi's total devotion.

Dimitri's eyes shifted from Oktober to Kalinin and back. Kalinin seemed ill at ease; he scowled at Oktober, then crushed his cigarette in the ashtray and lit a new one. He avoided Dimitri's look. What is Oktober trying to tell me? Dimitri wondered. Does he mean that the American was a homosexual and Kalinin was ordered to screw him and get screwed just to gain his confidence? Dimitri knew his chief wouldn't hesitate to assign an agent such a task.

Kalinin's friendship with Grimaldi was very helpful for a while, Oktober's narrative continued, but it was cut short by Kalinin getting himself shot and wounded in the Austrian Alps.

"That's where I got my scar," Kalinin said, almost shyly, and wiped his bald forehead with a light blue handkerchief.

By the time Oleg recovered, Oktober said, Grimaldi had been posted at Pullach, with Gehlen.

"Grimaldi's new job made him even more valuable to us," Oktober said. "I tried the same approach again. On three different occasions my men tried to seduce Grimaldi. We had quite a few people on the job. But Grimaldi was very careful; he knew that if he was caught, he would be immediately thrown out of the service."

Dimitri nodded. The CIA didn't employ homosexuals, for fear of just the kind of thing Oktober was planning.

Indeed, Grimaldi's sexual urge had finally vanquished his caution. The American had slipped, and gotten involved in a homosexual affair. He had been caught and immediately kicked out of Pullach. Ironically, he hadn't been seduced by Oktober's commando squad of irresistible queers, but by a local boy, absolutely innocent, unaware of the tragic consequences of his short-lived affair with the swashbuckling American officer.

Grimaldi had been recalled to America and disappeared. "We thought he had been forced to resign from the CIA, and we closed his file," Oktober said. "Oleg Kalinin, as you might know, came back home, and made a fine career in the GRU."

Then, in 1966, Grimaldi suddenly resurfaced. A local KGB stringer identified him in London, where he was posted as CIA liaison officer with the British SIS. He had somehow survived the Pullach scandal, and was still on active duty. Oktober decided to revive the wartime operation.

Dimitri grimaced skeptically. "The real liaison between the two services is carried out in Washington," he said. "What could you get from the man? Grimaldi couldn't sell you anything."

"Yes, but he could buy! We could turn the tables, and use him to feed the CIA with first-class disinformation." He emitted a rasping laugh. "A man in love is ideal for that purpose. They say that love is blind. Have you ever been in love, Dimitri?"

Oleg Kalinin had been recalled to active duty. He had contacted the CIA representative in Vienna and offered the Americans their best deal since the war: a high-ranking agent in the Kremlin. At first Kalinin had pretended that he wanted to defect, but had let the Americans convince him to stay in Moscow and spy for them. On one condition, though: that his case officer would be his old friend from the Berlin days, Franco Grimaldi.

It had worked perfectly. Grimaldi had come to Moscow, under cover, and for seven years had been fed a cautiously blended cocktail of true and false information.

"In Moscow it was a totally platonic relationship," Kalinin said quickly, and Dimitri nodded, amused by the man's misery.

"I wanted Grimaldi here because of his ties with Oleg," Oktober said coldly. "When somebody feels, he doesn't think; when he is emotionally involved, his judgment is muddled. He disregards the occasional inconsistency; he feels he has to protect his agent, not control him. Grimaldi blindly believed Kalinin, and guaranteed the authenticity of his material. Anybody else would have checked and double-checked the product. Not Grimaldi. He was in love with Kalinin. He still is."

That was how Top Hat had become the best American agent in Russia since the war, even more trusted and respected than Colonel Penkovski. The American assessment of Soviet missile and nuclear power, submarine deployment, active tank divisions, was based mostly on Kalinin's phony reports.

"It could have continued for many years to come," Oktober said, "if, during a routine surveillance exercise, a KGB trainee named Dimitri Morozov hadn't followed Grimaldi and seen him meet Kalinin at the Bolshoi."

"Saint-Clair," Dimitri whispered.

Oktober nodded. "That's right, Saint-Clair."

"But why didn't you tell me?" Dimitri shouted angrily, rising from his seat. He turned to Kalinin: "Why didn't you tell me when we met in Paris?"

"Sit down," Oktober snapped. "Kalinin had no right to tell anything to anybody. He was a double agent in deep cover. By the time he contacted me, you had taken action, and the hunt for Kalinin and Saint-Clair was on. I tried to stop you, remember?"

"I thought our men had captured him on the Austrian border."

Oktober shrugged. "I planted that item, so the Americans would stop looking for him. I didn't want them to find out that Top Hat was our mole, not theirs." He sighed. "You unwittingly blew the best operation I ever conceived, Dimitri."

WHEN DIMITRI WAS SUMMONED again to Oktober's lair, a few days later, Kalinin wasn't there. It was late evening. Oktober was seated behind his desk, the table lamp casting bright light on the papers that lay before him. His face was in shadow.

"I called you because we have to decide what to do with Kalinin," he said quietly.

Dimitri raised his head. "What to do with him?" he repeated.

"Yes. Operation Top Hat is over. Kalinin's face is known to the Americans. One of their agents might identify him in the street or . . . in a cinema, a restaurant. If they find out he's alive, they'll start asking questions. How come this most dangerous spy is walking free in Moscow?" His long white fingers drummed lightly on the rough surface of the desk. "We must decide if we should keep him alive, or kill him."

Dimitri slowly sat down and lit a Gauloise. "Why do you ask me?" he said. "Can't you decide alone?"

"I can never decide alone." Oktober went into a bout of coughing. "Any decision to kill a man should get the approval of the Politburo, you know that."

"Yes, but you are the one who advises the Politburo what should be done." Dimitri smiled wanly. "Except if it is an accident. If it so happens that Kalinin is run over by a car, or falls from his balcony, the Politburo will not need your advice."

There was a short silence. Oktober's hands moved closer together in the circle of yellow light. "What do you think?"

It was not a game, Dimitri realized. In this room, tonight, Kalinin's fate would be decided. But why him? Dimitri had the strange feeling he was being tested. Not for his operational capacity. If he were ordered to kill Kalinin, he could do it easily. But he was being asked to think, to think and advise. Oktober didn't need his advice, yet he was asking for it. Why?

He remembered that day at Panfilov, when he had seen Kalinin for the first time with the KGB committee. Kalinin had spoken for him, and Dimitri had known he was a friend. The next time he'd seen Kalinin was at the Bolshoi, then in Paris, and finally in this room. Kalinin had quietly swallowed the humiliation imposed upon him by Oktober. He had been forced to divulge a most intimate secret, his homosexual experience, to a perfect stranger. All of a sudden, Dimitri wanted to save Kalinin's life.

"You want to kill Kalinin, to remove the danger of the Americans discovering they have been deceived," he slowly summed up. "We had a case like this in Frankfurt, when you sent me to kill one of our men. He died because he had done a good job."

"Killing Lyubimov paid off," Oktober pointed out.

"Perhaps it did, but Kalinin's case is not the same."

"Oh really?" Oktober's voice was skeptical. "Tell me why."

"We can kill Kalinin," Dimitri said, trying to sound indifferent. "The news will reach the West."

Oktober nodded. "Of course."

"They'll deduce that we killed him because he passed secrets to Saint-Clair. Therefore, they'll assume that everything he reported is worthless now. They'll assume we are going to modify our strategic deployment, knowing that they've had access to our plans. All our efforts during the last six years, Operation Top Hat, will go down the drain."

"Go on," Oktober said.

"We have some other options. We can put him on trial, sentence him as a spy, and throw him in prison. The result will be the same. On the other hand, we can reinstate him at his old position. But then the CIA will get suspicious. Saint-Clair will not — "

"Grimaldi," Oktober corrected.

". . . Grimaldi. He won't forget our meeting at the airport, the day he escaped. He won't believe it was a false alarm."

"So, what's your conclusion?"

"Leave them in the dark. Let them guess what happened to him. Make Kalinin disappear. Send him to a place where no one will recognize him. Baikonur, or Kazan, Tashkent. We have facilities there. But keep him alive. We might still need him."

"What for?"

"Grimaldi," Dimitri said. "We used Kalinin twice to bait Grimaldi, we might use him another time."

For a long time Oktober didn't speak. Somewhere in the dark, silent mansion, a clock chimed nine times. Oktober bent forward, his predator's profile invading the circle of yellow light. His eyes were narrow slits, gleaming dully. "Good," he finally said. "Very good, Dimitri."

Dimitri got up. "Wait," Oktober said. "There is another matter I want to talk to you about."

There was a knock on the door. "Come in," Oktober said.

Tamara Fedorova, Oktober's stout, middle-aged secretary, peeked inside. "There is an urgent phone call for Tovarich Morozov," she said. "From Paris."

He left Oktober's room, closing the door behind him. The receiver on Tamara's desk was off the hook, lying on a heap of files. "Morozov," he said. He immediately recognized the voice of his deputy, Nikita Srebrov. He sounded unhappy. "It's about Tatiana Romanova, Comrade Morozov."

"What about her?"

"She's left your apartment." Srebrov fell silent.

"Where did she go?" he roared, and Tamara jumped from her seat. He sharply waved his hand at her, then put his hand on the mouthpiece. "Get out!" he hissed at the woman, who ran from the office, her face livid.

"Where did she go?" he shouted again into the mouthpiece. "Speak, man, speak!"

"She was followed to the apartment of a man you know, Alex Gordon, where she spent the last few nights."

The cruel words hit him harder than a physical blow; his body swayed. The bitch! Fury formed in the pit of his stomach, swelled in his chest, and his hands clawed with hatred. She was cheating on him! With his brother. His own brother, the American Jew-boy. I trusted him, and he stole my woman. If only I could lay my hands on you, brother, if only I could get hold of your throat . . .

"I'm flying back," he said. "Tell everybody I'm taking tomorrow's afternoon flight and I'll be there in the evening."

"Yes, Comrade Morozov."

"And stick to her, wherever she goes. I want a full report."

"Yes, comrade."

He slammed the receiver on its cradle. "Tamara!" he yelled.

Oktober's secretary darted in immediately; she must have been listening by the door. "I have to fly to Paris, tonight. Find me a flight, I don't care how many connections I have to make."

"I thought I heard you say you were flying tomorrow."

"You'll reserve a seat for me on Aeroflot for tomorrow, and inform everybody about it, understand? Then, very quietly, you'll put me on the first flight that leaves tonight. Use an alias, if you want. I'm flying back right away."

Deceit, he thought, always deceit. Tatiana has a couple of woman friends at Sovtorg. Through them, she'll hear that I'm coming back tomorrow. Let her think she has one more day.

He stepped back into Oktober's office. His knees wobbled as if they were made of cotton.

Oktober stood by his window, looking out at Bichevski Park and smoking one of his pestilent cigarettes.

"I have to fly back to Paris," Dimitri said casually. "Some minor problems."

Oktober nodded. "Fine. But there's something I want you to do for me."

"Of course."

"I want you back here," Oktober said, without turning. "We are in a difficult period, and I need somebody beside me. I want you here, as my deputy. You've been in Paris long enough."

So this had been Oktober's motive in calling him home. Not only to tell him about Top Hat, but to test him, and prepare him for his return. In a different situation he would have been overwhelmed. Oktober was making him his right-hand man. It meant he would become department chief in a few years. It was a good reason for rejoicing.

But tonight Oktober's words seemed to concern somebody else, not him. Right now Dimitri was obsessed with the maddening thought of Alex and Tatiana. He could picture the two of them in bed, naked, Tatiana licking and sucking Alex's body as she did his. He could hear her panting and screaming with abandon. He wanted to kill her, kill Alex, see the horror in their eyes as he snuffed out their lives with his hands! He didn't care about Oktober or the promotion. His brother had stolen the only woman he had ever loved! Alex had all the women he wanted, in America, but he had chosen to steal his Tatiana. All that mattered now was getting back to Paris.

"I'll finish my business in Paris as soon as possible," he heard himself saying.

"Good," Oktober said as he reached for the door. "That's good, Dimitri. Do whatever you have to do, and come back."

TATIANA AND ALEX strolled hand in hand by the pond of Parc Montsouris and watched a few children shove their toy sailboats away from the shore, screaming gleefully. Several grandmothers were sitting on white-painted iron chairs, huddled in the morning chill. A young mother in corduroy pants and high heels clumsily chased a toddler who scurried too close to the water.

"I'd like to have your child," Tatiana said, offering her mouth to Alex, who bent over and lightly kissed her cool lips.

"So why don't we go to the bushes," he suggested, "and make one?"

She started to speak, but the words froze in her mouth as her eyes shifted to a point beyond Alex's shoulder. He turned around. Two men were striding toward them, followed by a sturdy young woman. She was wearing a navy-blue windbreaker, jeans, and flat-heeled shoes. The men were more conservatively dressed, one in a black overcoat, the other in a tan mackintosh. The man in black was in his forties, while his burly friend seemed at least ten years younger.

"Mr. Gordon, we must talk to you," the older man said in American English, softened by a southern accent. He had drooping eyes, a thick blond mustache, and a pointed chin.

They could be Dimitri's men, Alex thought. He took a step back, grasping Tatiana by the arm. The woman was trying to approach her from the other side.

"We are friends of Grimaldi," the younger man added.

"Prove it," Alex said, pulling Tatiana toward the group of French-women who stared at them suspiciously. He threw a look over his shoulder. No one was approaching from behind, except for an elderly couple, feeding a flock of plump Parisian doves.

"It's true, believe me," the young man insisted, while his friend raised his lapel and whispered something in a tiny microphone.

"Don't come any closer," Alex said, "or we'll start a commotion. You don't want that." If the strangers were armed, they would have the upper hand anyway, Alex thought. The old women, smelling trouble, were already beating a disorderly retreat. Even if we yell, nobody will help us, Alex realized, but he didn't feel fear. He coldly assessed their chances to escape.

"Look!" The man in black pointed toward the park entrance, where Grimaldi had materialized. He stood there, cool and elegant in his dandyish camel's-hair coat, nonchalantly smoking his cigar.

Thank God, Alex thought. "That's Grimaldi," he said to Tatiana, whose eyes frantically darted about, "my American friend. It's all right."

They walked toward Grimaldi, the three strangers forming a compact group around them. The stout woman fell in step with Tatiana and smiled at her. "My name is Jane," she said.

"Leave her alone," Alex said fiercely. He was seething with anger now. "How did you find me?" he asked Grimaldi as they reached the CIA agent. "How did you know we were here?"

Grimaldi's face was drawn. "We must leave immediately," he said. "There's no time to waste."

"I asked how you found us," Alex repeated. "You've been spying on us, since we parted at the Closerie."

"Yes, and so have your Russian friends." Grimaldi gestured toward an ivory Fiat parked by a billboard praising Dim panty hose. The old people who had been feeding the pigeons in the park were hurrying toward the Fiat, not looking so old anymore.

"I told you — " Alex began.

"We have no time to argue," Grimaldi said, cutting him off impatiently. "Dimitri is back and he's looking for you."

"That is not true," Tatiana interjected in her French-accented English. "My friend Natalie said that he's coming back tomorrow."

"Yes," Grimaldi said. "That's what he wanted you to believe. Thank God I had people posted at both airports. They spotted him at Orly passport control. Now let's move!" He pointed at two cars, a tan Citroën and a silvery Mercedes, parked by the curb.

"Will you come with me, please?" Jane said to Tatiana, who shot an anguished look at Alex.

"She's coming with me," Alex said.

Grimaldi shrugged. "Burt, you and Jane take them," he said, nodding toward the Fiat; then he ran to the Mercedes. They crowded into the silver-colored car, Grimaldi, Tatiana, and Alex in the back, the man in black beside the driver. The two younger agents headed to the Citroën, the woman to the passenger side. As she bent to enter the car, Jane's windbreaker opened and Alex glimpsed the butt of a handgun protruding from her belt.

"Where are we going?" Alex said as the Mercedes darted forward up the narrow street. The Citroën was next, followed by the Russians' Fiat. As they reached the intersection, the driver of the Citroën following them braked suddenly and spun into a sideways skid, tires screeching. It finally came to a stop, blocking the street. The Fiat, trapped behind it skidded to a stop and began honking furiously.

"Good," Grimaldi said as the Mercedes turned the corner and sped down the Boulevard Jourdan. "If there's no car ahead, we're home free."

"Where are we going?" Alex asked.

The driver, a young man with an acne-ravaged face and a rebellious red forelock, changed lanes a couple of times, plunged into a side street, made two right turns, and emerged on the avenue again, going in the opposite direction. "No car ahead of us," he said confidently. "We've lost them."

Grimaldi leaned back. "Do you have your papers on you?"

"My passport," Alex said, and turned to Tatiana.

She fumbled in her bag. "I have my carte d'identité."

"That's all you need to cross the border," Grimaldi said.

"Wait a minute," Alex said. "Wait. I want to stay here and talk to Dimitri. I think he'll listen to me."

"Sure," Grimaldi chortled, "and then he'll wring your neck." Tatiana pressed Alex's arm, shaking her head. The Mercedes turned onto the Boulevard Peripherique, the ringlike highway circling Paris.

"You said we're crossing a border. What border? Where are we going?" Alex asked.

"You're in danger, we're taking you out of the country."

"What are you talking about?" Alex said. "First take us home, then — "

Grimaldi's voice was hard. "There's no going home," he said. "Dimitri is probably there, waiting for you. There's no place in Paris where you'll be safe. If you're hungry, we'll buy you lunch later. If you need clothes and cosmetics, we'll provide them. But if you want to save your girl's life, Alex, please shut up, relax, and enjoy the ride."

They changed cars at a discreet garage in Le Bourget, where a black Peugeot was waiting. At the border, Belgian immigration officers waved them through without even glancing at their papers. They drove into Brussels in the late afternoon.

TEN DAYS LATER, chased by a furious rain, Alex barged into the Café du Brabant, on the Grand Place in Brussels. He took off his new rain-coat — another present from Uncle Sam — and sat down by the large bay window overlooking the magnificent square. His eyes swept the tall houses with their gabled roofs and exquisite turrets. Alfred, an obsequi-ous waiter wearing a short white jacket with golden epaulets, bowed his narrow head. *"La même chose pour monsieur?"*

"Yes, Alfred. A large café crème, and two croissants."

"La même chose, then. Right away, monsieur."

La même chose, the usual, as for a regular customer. How quickly his life had entered a new routine, he thought with wonder. Every morning, at nine o'clock sharp, a Company car would pick up Tatiana at their apartment and take her for her debriefing session, which lasted until six P.M. Their apartment was in the Rue Gaspard, one of the narrow streets behind the Grand Place. It was a large, cold flat with standard furniture, and they hated it.

They hated the new clothes and toiletries they had to buy to replace what had been left in Paris. They also hated the constant presence of armed agents: the woman, Jane, who stayed in the apartment all day and all night, sleeping on a cot in the sitting room; and the younger male agent, Burt, positioned in a car parked across the street. Their guardian angels stuck to them even on the rare evenings they went out, to a restaurant or a cinema. Last night Grimaldi had agreed to ease off on the security measures and leave them alone in the apartment. Jane had left, after hugging Tatiana; in spite of everything, they had grown accus-tomed to each other. Only Burt remained in the car outside, still watch-ing the house entrance.

At this hour the Café du Brabant was almost empty, except for a couple of elderly ladies, who were devouring slices of moist chocolate cake. Alex ordered another coffee and sank back into his thoughts.

Thank God, the damned flat and the bodyguards were only temporary. In two days Tatiana's debriefing would be over, her papers would be ready, and they would fly back to the States. He had already written to Brown, accepting the offer of a teaching position for the following year.

He had phoned Nina — from a long distance phone booth at the post office, since Grimaldi had forbidden any use of the phone in their apartment — and told her of his plans. "I am bringing you a bride, Ninochka. A *krassavitza,* a beauty." He didn't tell her, of course, that Tatiana was a Romanov princess. He said that he was going to marry Tatiana and settle in Providence. "You'll live with us; we might need a babysitter soon." Nina had sounded stunned, but pleased.

He put down his empty cup, thinking of Claudia. He had never imagined that their love affair would end like this, with him running away, not answering her letters. But what could he do? Bewitched by his new love for Tatiana, he could do nothing but pursue her.

Most of all, he felt lousy for what he had done to Dimitri. It was difficult to face the fact that he could so despicably betray his brother. For a betrayal it was, an abuse of his brother's trust. All my life I've looked for Dimitri, he thought miserably, and when I finally found him, I seduced his woman. Now I will feel guilty for the rest of my life.

Not that Dimitri was a saint; quite the contrary. His brother was a spy and a ruthless killer. While reading Dimitri's file, Alex had instinctively felt that the accusations against him were true. During the months they had spent together, he had realized that his brother was very cunning, and had a violent streak. One night, at the ancient Brasserie Flo, they had discussed Kim Philby, the notorious Soviet mole inside the British intelligence service. Alex had spoken of the frustration of Philby's colleagues, who had suspected him for years but didn't have any proof against him. "Proof, no proof," Dimitri had said. "If I were in their place, I would have killed him long ago."

Alex indignantly objected. "But perhaps he was innocent."

Dimitri chuckled. "So what?" he said.

The rain turned into a downpour, and the antique square all but disappeared behind a swaying gray curtain. Alex thought of the life he would have with Tatiana. He could get a nice house in Providence; perhaps Tatiana could teach as well; they would have a couple of kids. Not a lot of excitement, but a happy, pleasant life. If he wanted excitement, he thought, he should have accepted Grimaldi's offer. The CIA man had been lunching with him almost every day, pressuring him to join the Company. He was the top Soviet expert in America, he was bright, smart — that kind of flattery. At first Alex had been tempted by the offer, but Grimaldi's insistence had finally gotten on his nerves. Yesterday he had turned down the offer in the bluntest possible way.

"All I want," he'd said to Grimaldi, who watched him, unusually pale, "is to live with my lovely wife in a quiet neighborhood, raise her lovely children, and teach at a good university. That's final, Franco, so leave me in peace, okay?"

"And Dimitri?" Grimaldi blurted. "Will he leave you in peace?"

"If he doesn't find me, he will," Alex said. "Anyway, that's another reason why I don't want to join your organization. Dimitri is my family, we have the same blood. We're brothers, dammit. And I don't want, ever, to have to fight my brother!"

He had bolted angrily out of the restaurant, leaving his steak untouched. Once back in the States, he swore, he would never go near Grimaldi or any other CIA agent again. And perhaps, in time, Dimitri would forgive him.

Gazing out the window, he saw two young kids·scurrying in the rain, protecting their heads with a soaked newspaper. They had their arms around each other's shoulders and were laughing. As they passed by the Café du Brabant, they turned for a second and he saw the physical likeness between them. Brothers, he thought.

"For brothers forever are one," his father had written. If Victor Wolf were alive, he thought, he wouldn't have forgiven him. Lately, he thought quite often of his father, and tried to guess how he would have reacted to his behavior. But this time he didn't have to guess. Victor Wolf was a pillar of morality; he could never have condoned what Alex did to his brother.

He suddenly had an idea. It was crazy, true, but perhaps it could work. He got up and descended the steps to the lower level of the café. He stepped into a phone booth bearing the sign INTERURBAIN. He knew it meant long distance. He had enough coins to call Paris. He took his notebook out of his pocket and dialed.

"Sovtorg," a sweet Russian voice chirped in the receiver.

"Dimitri Morozov, *pojalost*," he said, his throat suddenly dry. He knew they wouldn't ask him for his name; KGB standing instructions were to let anyone from the outside establish direct contact with resident officers.

"Morozov," he heard his brother's voice.

He took a deep breath. "Dimitri, it's me," he said.

There was silence on the other end of the line.

"I must talk to you, please, don't hang up."

Dimitri didn't speak.

"Dimitri, I wanted . . . . I wanted to tell you how sorry I am." He was suddenly at a loss. What could he say to him? That he was sorry he stole his girl? "I am sorry, very sorry, for what happened with Tatiana. I didn't want this to happen. I was the happiest man on earth when I met you. I have no family but Nina and you. I thought, perhaps, we could meet and talk things over. I didn't want to hurt you. I don't want to lose you."

Silence again, that same hostile silence. But Dimitri was listening; Alex could hear his hushed breathing.

"Dimitri, that night, on the bank of the Seine, I — "

"I wish I'd never met you." Dimitri's voice, hoarse, hateful, filled the receiver, uttering a final curse before severing the last link between them.

"For me you're dead," Dimitri Morozov said.

WHILE ALEX WAS SPEAKING to Dimitri, Grimaldi was sipping a bitter espresso barely a hundred yards away, in the elegant Café des Anglais. He didn't know that Alex was so close, but Alex was the subject of his thoughts and the reason for his ill temper.

Grimaldi's plans for Alex Gordon had turned sour. Everything had worked to perfection, including the disclosure of the ugly truth about Morozov at the Closerie des Lilas and the timely escape to Brussels. Gordon had every reason to join the CIA and the battle against his brother. But the bastard had refused. He liked Dimitri, in spite of everything, and didn't want to fight him. He wasn't looking for excitement in life. All he wanted was a middle-class existence, with his little house, his little wife, his little mortgage, and his little babies. And probably a new little car every two years, lace doilies on the television set, and a barbecue brunch in the backyard on Sunday, wearing a stupid smile and a pink apron adorned with embroidered little piggies.

The entire operation was a failure. Gordon wouldn't join the CIA and wouldn't fight his brother. This man, who understood the Soviet Union so well, who was familiar with Dimitri Morozov's way of thinking, refused to assume the role he had been assigned. Grimaldi now knew he had misjudged Alex Gordon. The man was much weaker than he had thought. He wouldn't hurt a fly unless he had a very good reason. He would fight Dimitri only if he felt overwhelming hatred toward him, only if he was motivated by a blinding lust for revenge.

Revenge, he thought, but for what? Dimitri had done him no wrong. Alex had no reason to be bitter. In a couple of days Alex would fly back to the States and live happily ever after with his Tatiana. Nothing could prevent him from building his own paradise. Except . . . except if it didn't happen, if he lost Tatiana forever and the reason for that loss was Dimitri.

He put down his cup. The idea swiftly budding in his mind was appalling, but it had its inner logic. If he only knew how to play it right! If it worked, Alex would be on his knees, begging Grimaldi to help him tear Dimitri to pieces.

Grimaldi got up and walked out in the rain, feeling as if he were in a dream. He took a cab to the main Brussels post office. The place was teeming with people. That was good. He entered a phone booth, wrapped his handkerchief around the mouthpiece, and dialed long distance. The line was busy. He waited a moment and dialed again.

"Sovtorg," a voice said.

"Dimitri Morozov," he grunted into the mouthpiece. A moment later he heard Morozov's voice. It sounded disturbed.

Grimaldi assumed a low, strained tone. He spoke French. "Tatiana Romanova," he rasped. "Tomorrow, nine o'clock. Thirty-seven, Rue Gaspard, Brussels, apartment seventeen."

"Hello? Hello?" Dimitri's voice roared in the receiver.

Grimaldi hung up and walked out, using his handkerchief to wipe the cold sweat off his forehead. There was no reason for remorse, he thought. The girl's debriefing was over, she was expendable anyway.

FROM HIS RENTED TAURUS parked on the corner, Dimitri watched Alex leave the building and get into a black Peugeot. Nikita Srebrov, who sat beside him, had seen the car earlier and reported there was someone inside, waiting. For a moment Dimitri had thought it might be a trap, but he quickly dismissed the idea. If somebody wanted to kill or kidnap him, they would most likely do it in Paris, where his address was known and his routine was no secret. They didn't have to lure him to Brussels for that. He had no idea who had telephoned him, but the tip had been worth exploring. As he saw Alex now, his heart leapt with savage joy. The driver of the Peugeot kicked the engine into life, and the car drove away.

"Wait for me," he said to Nikita, then crossed the street and entered the building. The entrance lobby was cold and somber. He didn't take the elevator — elevators could turn into deathtraps. Instead, he stealthily climbed the staircase. There were four apartments on each floor, and apartment 17 was on the fifth.

Moving in the dark, he felt the pounding of his own heart. In a moment he would be facing Tatiana. What would he say to her? That he loved her more than anything in the world? That he had never loved anybody else and she had betrayed him? He suspected that she didn't love him, only feared him, but it didn't make much difference. She was his woman, he had trusted her and taken care of her, and she had stabbed him in the back.

He reached the fifth floor. Apartment 17 was on the right. His fingers caressed the lock on the door. It was a child's play for a KGB agent. He fished in his pocket for his tiny kit of tools. It took him less than a minute to let himself in. He stepped inside, softly closing the door behind him.

"Alex?" It was Tatiana's voice.

He stopped in the middle of the sitting room, breathing heavily. His heart painfully leapt in his chest. It was unreal, he couldn't take one more step.

"Alex?"

She appeared in the doorway, breathtakingly beautiful, a virginal elf in a white skirt and a loose white shirt, a smile dancing on her lovely mouth. He was frozen where he stood. She could have walked past him and he wouldn't have been able to stop her. She could have pulled a gun on him, and he wouldn't have defended himself. She could have talked to him, and he would have talked back, and done anything in his power to bring her back to him.

But she cried in horror and ran back into the bedroom, helplessly limping. That shook him out of his torpor, and he darted after her. The sight of the bed made his blood boil. The bitch had fucked his brother here, perhaps minutes ago. She had pulled his cock inside her, she had scratched his back, she had whispered that she loved him. He turned toward her, his hands clawed.

Tatiana stood by the bed, trembling. Her face was livid and tears streamed down her cheeks. She was trapped, she had nowhere to hide. As he approached her, she didn't even raise her arms to protect herself. She stared at him with dull eyes, in which he read deep despair and listless resignation. She realized it was all over, there was no hope left. She was waiting to die.

He took another step toward her. She didn't move. Now she was crying bitterly, biting her lips. Impulsively he reached for her, hugged her with all his force and pulled her toward him, burying his face in her hair. He breathed her fresh smell and held the frail, beloved body, which shivered in his arms. He raised her face toward his. She closed her eyes.

The telephone rang, a shrill, loud scream that filled the apartment. She winced, but he held her tight. The phone rang a few times, stopped, then began ringing again. The noise of running steps suddenly rose from the stairway, and he felt her body tense with hope. It could be Alex, coming back to rescue her.

But the ringing stopped and the steps faded away. He bent toward the face, so defenseless, and kissed the trembling mouth. Tears were welling in his own eyes. "I loved you so much, Tatiana," he gasped. His eyes swept the whiteness of the bed behind her, and black fury heaved in his chest. His hands closed on the slender, milky neck, and he pressed, his thumbs digging deep into the yielding flesh, feeling the girl's frantic convulsions, hearing the gurgling sound escaping from her throat. And then she went limp in his arms and he let her collapse at his feet.

He fell on his knees and gathered the girl's corpse in his arms. He rocked her gently, kissing the still face, wailing in agony.

Chapter 14

ALEX UNLOCKED THE DOOR and stepped into the apartment. "Tatiana," he called. "Where are you? I've got your passport." He threw his coat on an armchair. The U.S. consul had been less efficient than he had expected; it took Alex more than a hour to get Tatiana's papers. Anyway, the formalities were over now. Tatiana's debriefing had been completed yesterday, so they could spend the day at their leisure. Tomorrow they would fly to Washington aboard a U.S. Air Force plane. He hoped they would never see Grimaldi again.

"Tatiana?" The apartment was absolutely still. Tatiana never turned on the radio or played a record; she loved the silence. He crossed the living room and entered the bedroom. She wasn't there. "Tatiana?" Getting no answer, he turned toward the bathroom and, from the corner of his eye, saw a strange white heap on the left side of the bed. A silent scream of terror rang in his ears. Something was terribly wrong.

Her inert body lay before him, her head oddly twisted and her huge eyes wide open, frozen in dread. At first he couldn't grasp the meaning of the gruesome sight and stood awkwardly by the bed, staring down. No, she couldn't have fainted. She had been happy and healthy when he'd left her only an hour ago. But now her body lay utterly motionless at his feet. Hopeless comprehension gradually seeped into his benumbed brain. She was dead.

He crouched beside her and his throat contracted, his breath bursting in short, painful gasps. He was shaking uncontrollably, and he had a horrible feeling of déjà vu. Her corpse was spread on the floor the way he had seen it in his nightmares. She was dead, Tatiana was gone.

He bent over and touched her face. Her skin was cold. Incoherent ideas rushed through his head. He shouldn't have left her alone, it was his fault, they shouldn't have come to Brussels, what would he do with her passport, where was Grimaldi, for God's sake! Tatiana had known she would die like this, she had warned him. . . . Still, from all this confusion one clear thought emerged and gained total control over him. "Dimitri," he murmured. He stood up, and turned away from the body. Dimitri.

He ran down the stairs and into the street. Burt was sprawled luxuriously on the driver's seat of the Peugeot, smoking. A bossa nova blared from the car radio. Alex yanked the door open. "Get out," he managed. "Out!"

"What's the matter with you, man?" Burt said, showing no intention of complying.

Alex grabbed him by the lapels of his jacket and dragged him out of the car. "The keys," he snapped. "Where are the keys?"

"What the hell — " Burt began, and Alex hit him viciously in the stomach. Burt doubled over in pain, then raised his fists. "Hey, you wanna fight?" he muttered. He was a big man, and he towered over Alex, but Alex hit him in the face with such savage power that Burt fell next to the car, blood trickling from his mouth. Alex kicked him like a madman, and Burt tried to protect his face with his hands.

"The keys!" Alex yelled. A couple of elderly men stopped on the sidewalk, watching them in horror. "Police!" one of them shouted. "*Au secours!*"

Burt shakily pointed toward the car, and Alex looked inside. The keys were dangling in the ignition.

"Papers," he breathed.

"In the glove . . . compartment," Burt gasped, struggling up from his knees. Alex shoved him aside, jumped into the car, started it, and drove off, the tires screeching on the asphalt.

He gunned the car through the city center, ignoring red lights and approaching vehicles, chased by the shrill whistles of police officers. Following the signs posted at the major intersections, he soon reached the international highway heading toward the French border and, beyond it, Paris. His mind was blank, except for one thought. Find Dimitri and kill him.

Later he couldn't remember how long it took him to drive to Paris, nor much of what happened on that eerie voyage, except the long columns of cars along the road, the fog rolling down the slopes of the Belgian hills, then the torrential rain as he approached Roissy. He must have shown his papers at the border, but he remembered nothing. He emerged from his trance only when, having parked his car on Boulevard Pereire, he barged into Sovtorg and was beaten senseless by two Russian guards. He regained consciousness lying in a gutter, soaking in the ice-cold water that quietly flows at night in the deserted streets of Paris.

DURING THE NEXT FEW DAYS — or was it weeks? he never kept count — Alex searched for Dimitri. He was determined to avenge Tatiana's death. He didn't shave, he barely slept, he drank heavily in the neighborhood bars. He occasionally collapsed from fatigue on the back-seat of the black Peugeot.

Most of the time, he wandered like a ghost in the streets, or lay in wait outside the Sovtorg offices. At night he hid in a hallway facing Dimitri's building, his eyes glued to Dimitri's black windows. Twice he sneaked into the building, climbed the staircase and pounded on Dimitri's door, but there was no answer. He haunted Dimitri's usual hangouts, the restaurants and bars where they had spent so many nights with Tatiana. No, *monsieur*, we haven't seen the gentleman who had dinner with you. Yes, we remember him perfectly, a handsome young man. How is the lovely lady who came with him? *Une beauté*, quite exceptional, don't you think?

Nothing mattered anymore, nothing but finding and killing Tatiana's murderer. He didn't know how he would do it, he had no weapon; nevertheless, there was nobody on the face of the earth who could stop him once he found his brother. But his brother had vanished.

One night he tried to climb the wall surrounding the Sovtorg building, and was beaten up again by the guards. One of them was a tall, bitter-looking man with a widow's peak crowning his narrow, expressionless face; the other was blond, good-looking, with a bull neck and wrestler's shoulders. The blond man was wearing a black polo shirt and a leather jacket; he punched and kicked Alex with a lopsided grin on his face. They didn't call the police, though; perhaps Dimitri had ordered them to avoid any contact with the authorities.

A few times Alex glimpsed Soviet officials walking in and out of the building. One foggy afternoon he thought he saw his brother at an office window, staring down at him. But he couldn't be sure he wasn't hallucinating. When he went into a bar for a drink, the barman refused to serve him, and two waiters threw him out. While struggling with them, wriggling in their arms, he slipped and staggered against a wall mirror. It reflected a filthy, bleary-eyed wreck, face covered with bristle and caked blood, lips parched, hands trembling.

That night, as he was lurking again by the wall surrounding the Sovtorg building, he was startled by the roar of a powerful engine. A black sedan, headlights blazing, darted toward him at full speed. He tried to run, but he was too slow. He hurled himself toward the wall, lost his balance and fell heavily on the pavement. The car climbed onto the sidewalk and rumbled toward him. The sedan's left side hit him with tremendous power, throwing him against the concrete. He felt the swish of hot air and the smell of rubber when the car wheels hissed by his side; then everything went black.

He woke up in his apartment, lying on his bed. He couldn't move; he was in terrible pain. Somebody was applying a cold towel to his forehead. He opened his eyes, but everything was blurred. He tried to speak, but no sound came out of his mouth.

"Don't move," a woman said softly, and he recognized the warm, musical voice of Claudia Benevento.

DURING THE LAST FEW WEEKS, Claudia had become deeply worried. Alex had stopped writing and didn't return her calls, despite the messages she left on his answering machine. She didn't know why he was ignoring her. She longed to hear his voice, and see his smile as he said, "Hi, Claudia" in that breezy way of his. Now that he was inaccessible, she realized how much she missed him.

Claudia had reached a stage in her life when she could look in the mirror and see herself the way she really was. She knew she was proud, possessive, and fiercely independent. She was a one-man woman, and the man was Alex Gordon. There had been nobody else in her life since that balmy evening when the sixteen-year-old brat that she was had fallen for the boy who helped her carry her load of skirts and petticoats. True, she had experienced a couple of inconsequential flirtations while she was away — a disastrous dinner with a basketball star in Dallas; a violent evening with Ronnie Havermeyer in Indianapolis, when she had to kick the oversexed brute out of her suite; a brief kiss with a handsome designer who turned out to be gay — but they had nothing to do with the passionate attachment she felt for Alex.

She was deeply hurt when he left for France. It was partly her fault, she conceded. She had been intoxicated with her budding career as a designer, and instead of making Alex a part of it, had chosen to show him how successful she could become on her own. Refusing to marry him had been a mistake; they could have decided not to have children for the first few years, and she could have traveled as much as she wanted.

When Alex vanished behind a wall of silence, Claudia sensed something was wrong. Alex was a handsome, romantic young man, neglected by his sweetheart, alone in Paris, enjoying a new freedom in the world's love capital; it was a dangerous combination, whose bottom line spelled another woman. On a Sunday afternoon she went to see Nina Kramer.

"Oh, it's you, Claudia," the white-haired woman said dryly. "Come in." She led the way into the living room. On the wall hung a large photograph taken on the Champs-Elysées in Paris. There was Alex, his arm thrown around the shoulder of a dark-haired young man. They were both smiling at the camera. The dark-haired man hugged, with his other arm, a lovely blond girl with huge, sad eyes and an expressive mouth. She was dressed in white.

"That's Dimitri?" Claudia asked.

"Yes, and the young lady is girlfriend of Dimitri. He is also my nephew, you know." Nina sat on the edge of a chair, very erect, her gnarled hands on her knees. "Sit down, please. Anything the matter?" She didn't even offer her a cup of coffee, but Claudia was immune to her hostility.

"I see you're reading," Claudia said, by way of small talk. On the small table beside Nina's chair lay a new book. It was entitled *The Chief — the Real Story of Sasha Kolodny, the Greatest Spy in World War II.*

Beside the book lay an old English-Russian dictionary. Claudia had seen lots of Russian books in the house, but only once before had she seen Nina reading something in English. That was when the old woman had painstakingly gone through Alex's doctoral thesis, word by word. That time, too, she had used a dictionary.

Claudia nodded toward the book. "Is it good?"

"Yes, yes, very good," Nina said, her face coloring slightly.

"I didn't know you read spy stories," Claudia said.

"This is not story," Nina said severely, "this is true." A brief smile flashed on her face. The old girl was behaving very strangely, Claudia thought; she seemed almost happy.

Nina pushed the book aside and became her old self again, cold and humorless. "Please tell me how are you, Claudia," she said, her tone a total contradiction of her kind words.

"I wanted to ask you," Claudia said, taking out her package of ciga-rettes, "if — "

"I ask you not to smoke here," Nina said sternly.

"Sorry. I wanted to know, Nina, is Alex okay?"

Nina looked at her strangely. "Okay? Of course Alex is okay. Why not?"

She spread her hands. "Well, he doesn't write to me, he doesn't answer my calls."

"He answers mine calls," Nina said. "Did you have a fight?"

"No, it's just that I don't know what's going on."

"Perhaps he is very busy," Nina said coldly. "He is writing an impor-tant work on the trial of his father."

"I know, but he never calls me."

"I thought you were never in New York." There was a note of rebuke in Nina's voice.

Claudia stood up. "Well, if you write to him, tell him I miss him."

Nina got up, too. As the apartment door closed behind her, Claudia had the impression that Nina knew much more than she cared to reveal. Anyway, she wasn't worried, and Alex was writing to her; that confirmed Claudia's suspicions.

She didn't give up, though. In the evening, she called a friend of hers who was a flight attendant with TWA and flew to Paris regularly. "Karen, would you do me a favor? When are you flying to Paris again?"

"On Tuesday night. Why?"

"I'd like you to take Alex a small present, okay? He had his birthday a couple of weeks ago." It was a lie, but what the hell.

"Sure, if it's not too heavy."

"Of course not, it's a cashmere scarf."

Claudia didn't hear from Karen for two weeks. When she finally called she apologized profusely. On arriving in Paris, she had been offered a chance to take her vacation right away, and there was this French guy with a chalet at Avoriaz, in the French Alps, you know, those snowbound peaks and valleys, and the fur carpet in front of the fireplace, and that delicious champagne . . .

"Did you see Alex?"

Karen seemed embarrassed. "All men are pigs, you know."

"You mean your Frenchman?"

There was a long silence. "Well, honey, don't get upset. I went to see Alex before leaving for Avoriaz. But just as I was getting out of the cab, he came out of his building with a girl. A stunning blonde. They seemed very . . . very friendly, I'd say." She paused. "I'm sorry, Claudia, I really am."

A stunning blonde. She could be the girl in the photograph. But Nina had said she was Dimitri's girlfriend. Claudia angrily slammed down the phone. She had taken the call in her office at Havermeyer's. The entire floor was in turmoil. People were running in and out of her office, spreading sketches, colorful fabrics, belts, and jewelry on her desk. She was in the middle of preparing her fall collection, the first "Claudia" collection that Havermeyer was to present to the chain-store buyers in a couple of weeks.

Launching her own collection was the realization of all her dreams. Still, Claudia didn't hesitate for a moment. She wasn't the kind to give up easily; she wouldn't sit miserably in her room, wringing her hands and daubing her tearful eyes while the man she loved was being stolen from her. Life was a perpetual fight, and she was going to fight for Alex. There was nothing she could do in New York. For a moment she considered calling Nina; the old woman had phoned three times during the last week, leaving messages. But she finally dropped the idea. The conversation she'd had with Nina when she visited three weeks before was all the humiliation she could take. Let her stew, Claudia decided. She picked up the phone and reserved a seat on the evening flight to Paris. The hell with the collection, she thought, there would be other fall seasons, but there was only this opportunity to win back her man.

The Boeing jet landed in Paris in the early morning. On her way from the airport, she stared out of the cab window. In different circumstances she would have been thrilled; she'd been looking forward to the summer she was going to spend here with Alex. But now she felt indifferent to the views that unfolded before her. She thought of her upcoming confrontation with Alex. Her future, she reflected, depended on the next few hours.

The cab brought her directly to Alex's building. It was eight-fifteen in the morning; he was probably still home. She picked up her overnight bag — she had no intention of staying in Paris more than a couple of days — and walked into the building. The entrance was neat, the floor covered with black and white tiles. The names and apartment numbers of the tenants were inscribed on a plan of the building that hung on the concierge's door.

She took the elevator to the seventh floor and pressed the brass button by Alex's door. Her breath was shallow, and she was very tense. The blond girl in the photograph was constantly on her mind. That was ridiculous, she thought, there were other blondes in Paris. But Dimitri had a blond girlfriend, and Alex was seen with a blond girl. Several times during the flight she had rehearsed the things she would say to him — or to them, if the girl was here — but they had faded away and her mind was now totally blank.

Nobody came to the door. She pounded on it, with the same result. "Alex, are you there?" she called. There was no answer. What should she do? She was alone, in a faraway city, unable to speak the language. Suddenly another door opened, on the opposite side of the landing. A small old woman stared at her. She was wearing a brown woolen nightgown and padded felt slippers. "I'm looking for Alex Gordon," Claudia said.

The old woman shook her head and said something in quick French, from which Claudia picked up only the word "concierge." Claudia took the elevator back to the ground floor and knocked on the concierge's door. She expected an old, choleric woman, hissing and puffing, like in all those novels about Paris; therefore she was surprised when the door was opened by a plump but pretty young woman with red cheeks, who held a baby in her arms. "I am looking for Alex Gordon," Claudia said slowly. "Perhaps you could help me."

The girl's face turned somber. *"Oh, madame,"* she said, *"Monsieur Gordon a ète blesse dans un accident. Il est a l'hôpital!"*

She missed a heartbeat. "Hospital?"

The girl nodded miserably.

An hour later she was at the American hospital in Neuilly, staring at the unconscious, heavily bandaged young man who was burning with fever, tossing on the narrow bed, babbling incoherently about a girl named Tatiana.

ALEX STIRRED, opened his eyes, and gazed fixedly at the crimson window curtains in the bedroom of his apartment. Claudia bent toward him. "Are you awake, Alex? Can you hear me? It's Claudia."

She saw him moving his lips; recognition flickered in his bloodshot eyes.

"Don't try to speak," she said. "You're too weak. Just nod, if you understand what I'm saying."

For a long moment there was no response, then he painfully moved his head a bare fraction of an inch.

"You were at the hospital," Claudia said. "The police found you in the street. You were hit by a car. Do you hear me?"

A slight nod again.

"You remember the accident?"

There was no reaction.

"You remember the car that hit you?"

He stared at Claudia's face and with great difficulty moved his left hand toward her. He looked terrible, an emaciated man with sunken yellow-tinged cheeks, cracked lips, saliva running down his chin; his face was covered with a two-week-old beard. Her eyes filled with tears when she recalled the handsome young man he used to be.

"When you were brought to the hospital, you had three broken ribs and a broken arm. Don't try to move your right arm, it's in a cast. Your whole body was cut and lacerated. You lost a lot of blood, and you were very weak. You spent a week in a coma, and the doctors thought you would never make it. Wait, don't move."

From the kitchen, Claudia brought a bowl of chicken soup, which she'd been keeping warm since Alex had started shifting in his bed. She slipped a pillow behind his back and carefully pulled him up. He was light as a child, a bag of loose skin hanging from a heap of bones. She started spoon-feeding him, like a baby.

"I brought you home from the hospital five days ago. You were still unconscious, and you're under very strong medication. We only disconnected the I.V. this morning. I've been injecting you six times a day, a nurse taught me how to do it." She patiently fed him the soup, although most of it dribbled down his chin.

"You must sleep now, and I'll feed you more when you wake up. The worst is over now."

He nodded, this time more distinctly, and closed his eyes. For the first time in five days she let out a sigh of relief. Now she could perhaps take a shower, and even doze a little bit. She hadn't had a moment to herself until now. She had spent ten days and nights at the hospital, drowsing once in a while on a bench in the corridor; since their return to the apartment, she hadn't left his bedside, except when the nurse came.

But her troubles were not over yet. In the ensuing nights, Alex kept waking up, screaming hoarsely in spite of the heavy sedation. He was bathed in cold sweat, and his body shook as an eerie fire burned in his eyes. In the muddled stream of words and hacked phrases erupting from his mouth, Claudia again discerned the girl's name, Tatiana. Each time he pronounced it, in infinite love or in intense pain, she felt as if he were plunging a knife in her heart. Alex also repeated "Dimitri," his brother's name. His torment reached its peak when he uttered the word "murder," then wildly thrashed on the bed, kicking away the covers, crying, choking, his good hand fiercely clawing at something in the dark.

As those fits seized him, Claudia would gather him in her arms and rock him gently, until his convulsions subsided and he sank again into an agitated sleep.

When he was asleep, she wandered restlessly through the apartment. Everywhere, she found traces left by the other woman. The toothpaste, the comb, and the cosmetics in the bathroom; the clothes hanging in the closet, between his suits, or mixed in with his shirts and underwear; a couple of books, a handbag, some blond hairs sticking to his clothes. She often stood in the dark, gazing at the bed where he now lay, and couldn't help imagining him with Tatiana, naked, making love, moaning hoarsely. She tried to escape these obsessive thoughts, and would seek refuge on the narrow balcony, where she stared out at the sleeping city, letting the cold wind lash her face. But the image of Tatiana wouldn't fade away.

When she washed him, and changed his sheets, she thought of Tatiana's hands, lovingly stroking his naked body. Jealousy and anger churned inside her. She felt she was loosing her mind. He had been a part of her life for years, and he had betrayed her so willingly. My God, Alex, she thought, looking at his pitiful figure, how could you do this to me?

From the bits and pieces she could put together, she roughly figured out what had happened. He had become infatuated with Tatiana, and they had become lovers; the girl had been murdered afterward. Alex held Dimitri responsible for the murder. Nina, whom she phoned from the apartment, broke down and admitted that Alex had indeed spoken to her a few weeks before and announced he was coming back to New York with Tatiana, whom he was about to marry. Yes, Tatiana was the blond girl in the photograph; she used to be Dimitri's girlfriend. Alex had said she was the love of his life, Nina added. He had called from Brussels.

Brussels, Claudia thought, what was he doing in Brussels? And how did he get into the car accident in Paris? Nina didn't know, and there was nobody Claudia could ask. Alex had been found in the street by the police and brought to the hospital unconscious. She had called the Institute of East European Studies, but a woman's sour voice answered that Mr. Gordon hadn't been seen for several weeks. No, they didn't know that Mr. Gordon had been involved in an accident. How terrible indeed.

The riddles that haunted her were solved by a swarthy man with a trim mustache and green eyes. "My name is Franco Grimaldi," he said, introducing himself when he came to see her one morning. He was in his fifties, ostentatiously dressed in a blue cashmere blazer and bow tie, velvet vest and gray trousers. Massive gold rings glimmered on his fingers. "Alex told me a lot about you."

"You know him well?" They were sitting in the living room, with the door to Alex's bedroom closed.

"Very well." Grimaldi lapsed into uneasy silence, then frankly admitted: "I work for American intelligence. I flew over to Paris on the same plane as Alex."

She eyed him suspiciously. He didn't exactly fit her image of a secret agent.

Grimaldi told Claudia a harrowing story about Alex's brother, a killer in the service of the KGB; he described Alex's infatuation with a girl of Russian origin, Tatiana Romanov, and their flight to Brussels, for fear of Dimitri, her former lover. Grimaldi had made arrangements for their return to America in a few days.

"Dimitri tracked them down. He followed them to Brussels. He broke into the safe flat where Tatiana was hiding, and he strangled her."

Claudia winced. The image of Dimitri hugging Tatiana on the Champs-Elysées flashed before her eyes.

"I shall never forgive myself," Grimaldi said, looking away. "I was in charge of her safety, and I failed to protect her. She died because of my negligence."

Claudia clenched her teeth. The story was tragic, indeed, but she couldn't forget, for a single second, that the man was speaking of Alex's mistress. The one who had taken him away from her.

Grimaldi then told her how Alex had jumped into a car and driven to Paris, seeking revenge. He had tried to force his way into Dimitri's office, determined to kill him. "What happened to him on that street was not a car accident," he said, his eyes holding Claudia's in bleak focus. "The Russians tried to do away with him, and he was lucky to survive."

"Where were you when the car hit Alex? You had promised to protect him too."

"We tried," Grimaldi said, "but there was no way to control him, he acted like a madman. Besides, our people are instructed to stay away from Russian compounds. That could create international complications."

Claudia frowned. The excuse sounded phony. She decided she didn't like Grimaldi; he was too sleazy for her taste.

Grimaldi told her that he was returning to Washington the following week, and he suggested that Claudia take Alex back home. "Paris is still too dangerous for him," he warned. "We think that Dimitri Morozov has gone back to Moscow, but we can't be sure. Even if he has, I'm certain he would send his agents to assassinate Alex. This apartment is being kept under our surveillance, but so was the flat in Brussels that Alex shared with Tatiana." Grimaldi offered his help for Alex's safe transfer to New York.

Claudia listened in stunned silence. Here was this green-eyed dandy, telling her of the wild passion of her lover for another woman, describing how he had almost died because of her. He would never have done that for me, Claudia thought; he never fought for me, he always took me for granted. She had never been so humiliated, but she was not going to show it. She stared defiantly back at Grimaldi when he spoke about her lover's betrayal. She didn't need anybody's pity.

"Thank you," she finally said, and got up. Grimaldi hesitated a moment, then stood up as well. "I'll stay here with Alex until he recovers, then I'll take him back home. Thank you for your help, but I'll manage by myself."

Three weeks later a cab took Claudia and Alex to Charles de Gaulle Airport, where they boarded an Air France flight to New York. Alex was still very weak. He kept silent most of the time, answering Claudia's questions with monosyllables. He had behaved like that since he'd started to recover. He was entrenched behind his ramparts, refusing to communicate with her; their former closeness had vanished. She avoided any mention of Dimitri and Tatiana; nevertheless, his answers were cryptic. He had changed, she thought. His spontaneity, his infectious laughter, had faded away. There was no more warmth in his smile. His eyes had acquired a hard look; two bitter lines framed his mouth.

This is the end of our love, Claudia thought. Watching the stranger beside her, she realized they had nothing left in common. He had hurt her and humiliated her. True, she had also been to blame, for the way she had treated him before. But she'd done everything in her power to redeem her mistake and bring him back. She had left her work, jeopardizing her career, and flown to Paris to find him. She'd saved his life, but she couldn't save their love. There was no use trying to resuscitate something that was dead. He didn't belong to her anymore; even now, his feelings were with the dead Tatiana. As soon as they were home, she would turn a page and spend the rest of her life trying to forget Alex Gordon.

From Kennedy Airport, Claudia took Alex to Nina's house. When they arrived in Brooklyn, she had the cab driver unload Alex's luggage on the sidewalk, then she kissed him lightly on the cheek and drove away. He made no effort to stop her. She watched his immobile figure until he disappeared from her sight. From her life as well, she thought, and clenched her teeth, holding back the tears.

* * *

"GOLUBCHEK MOI, LYUBIMI!" Nina received him with hugs and tears, but he was reserved, remote. Something had broken inside him, and he recoiled from any sentimental effusions. She had prepared a real feast for his return, but he barely touched the food, skipping even his favorite, chocolate mousse.

After the coffee, Alex retreated to his room. He heard her pacing restlessly behind his closed door. Poor girl, she loved him so much. But he couldn't talk to her now, all he wanted was to be left alone.

For the next few months he rarely left the building, mostly sitting by his bedroom window, staring at the blank gray wall across the yard. He spoke very little; Nina's attempts at conversation shattered against his silence. He didn't react even when she brought the book about Sasha Kolodny from her bedroom, and showed him several passages. "He is alive, you know, perhaps I meet him some day," she said.

He only nodded and mumbled some niceties, as in all their conversations. She was deeply hurt by his apathy, but he couldn't help it. Nothing mattered now, nothing had any meaning. He was at his home in Brooklyn, but his thoughts were far away, the grisly scenes from Brussels and Paris flashing through his mind like an endless tape of horror, perpetually replayed.

As time passed, though, nature gradually took over. Alex started eating, and slowly recovered his health. When he emerged from his torpor, he threw himself into physical activity with an intense determination. He jogged every morning, worked out at home, then exercised at the Atlantic Fitness Club. He began visiting Jack Macmillan's Gym again, although Jack was long dead, and mercilessly tortured the punching bag night after ferocious night. His body recovered before his mind; he regained weight, which turned into taut sinew and stone-hard muscle, powerful arms and tapered legs.

It was weird — a kind of escape, or perhaps his own way of regaining his sanity. Yet, it took him a long time until he could read newspapers, make phone calls, or open letters. The only letters he wrote were returned unopened; the only phone calls he placed were unanswered. All were directed to Claudia Benevento.

Four months after his return, in the early fall of 1975, Alex flew to Washington. He was slowly surfacing from the nightmare. He could think of Tatiana without breaking into a cold sweat or starting to shiver.

His obsession with revenge wasn't gone, but it had metamorphosed into a cold, ruthless determination.

He landed at Washington National, rented a car, and drove to the CIA headquarters at Langley Woods. He had called ahead, and was expected. At the main gate he got a visitor's tag and was ushered to a conference room in the main building. Grimaldi was waiting for him, smoking a black Swiss cheroot. Alex took a chair, facing the peacockish agent, and impatiently brushed off Grimaldi's attempts at small talk. "You're still fighting the KGB?" he asked.

Grimaldi nodded. "Somebody has to do it." he said, tilting his head. "What about you? First they killed your mother and father, then your girl. Do you still want to hide on some goddamn campus and let others avenge your dead?"

Alex quietly said: "That's why I came. I wanted to find out if your offer still stands. If the Company wants me, I'll join."

"We want you, all right," Grimaldi said.

FROM LANGLEY WOODS Alex drove to Baltimore. He swallowed a tasteless hamburger and a beer at a diner, then parked his car behind the Excelsior Hotel. He crossed the lobby and went down the stairs to the grand ballroom. Rhythmic pop music filtered through the closed ballroom doors. He found a chair and patiently waited until the doors opened, and a group of thin, long-legged models emerged, chirping and laughing, swinging their large handbags. Claudia was the last to come out. She had lost weight, and looked slim and elegant in a blue pantsuit. She was laughing, a throaty, carefree laughter. "Tomorrow at five," she called after the departing girls, then she saw Alex and stood still.

He got up and approached her.

"What are you doing here?" she breathed, nervously running her fingers through her hair.

He ignored the question. "How was the rehearsal?"

She hesitated. "Fine. The fashion show is tomorrow."

"I know. I checked with your office." He paused. The silence was tense. "Will you have a drink with me?"

She looked at her watch and nodded indifferently.

The hotel bar was polished mahogany, leather, gleaming copper, and subdued lights. In the background Johnny Cash lamented a lost love. A middle-aged couple was holding hands in one of the booths, the woman throwing anxious glances over the man's shoulder.

Alex ordered a chilled vodka. Claudia asked for a glass of champagne, then changed her mind. "White wine will be better," she said.

"I came to talk to you," Alex said. "I can't go on like this, Claudia. You don't answer my calls and my letters, but we have to talk."

She shrugged. She was perched on the edge of her chair, her back ramrod stiff.

"You saved my life in Paris. I'll never forget that. But I didn't come here out of gratitude. I love you. I don't think I can live without you."

"I thought you couldn't live without Tatiana," she said scornfully.

"I became obsessed with Tatiana, that's true. I don't deny it. But you're the love of my life."

"Don't give me that bull!" she said angrily. Looking over her shoulder, Alex saw the bartender, who was polishing glasses, turn his head toward them.

"It's true, though," he said patiently. "We had a wonderful relationship, you and I. Then I went away, and had a dream. That was Tatiana, a dream that turned into a nightmare. Now I'm waking up, and it's not always easy."

She lit a cigarette with angry, disjointed gestures, without looking at him. "What do you want, Alex?"

"I want to marry you."

"What for?" she asked sharply, leaning forward over the table. "To hold your hand? You lost her, so you remembered your fall-back girl? What do you think I am, a consolation prize?"

"No, you're not," he said. "I told you, Claudia, I love you, and I want to marry you."

She shook her head. "It's too late."

"Why? Is there someone else?"

She shook her head again. "I am seeing somebody, but that's not the point." She drew on her cigarette and slowly exhaled the smoke. He had the feeling she was making a tremendous effort to control each of her movements. "By the way," she said, "before I came to Paris, I was faithful to you, I never cheated on you."

"Which isn't the case now," he said, completing her thought. "I understand. But it's not cheating — you left me after I left you."

"You wrecked my life," she said forlornly, suddenly off guard.

"I know. And I don't know if I can help you rebuild it again. I've changed. My whole outlook on life has changed. I don't want to teach anymore. I'm going to work for the CIA."

She smiled bitterly. "So you're still seeking revenge. You're still after your brother."

"I guess so. I don't want to lie to you. And I'll tell you something else. I still think quite often of Tatiana. I can't get her out of my mind. But I don't think of her as I did before. It's like something from another life. I don't know if we would have been happy together."

She raised her eyes and looked at him skeptically. Her mouth was bitter. On the jukebox, Johnny Cash had ended his ballad, and now "Killing Me Softly" by Roberta Flack was playing.

"I told you," Alex went on, "I was obsessed with Tatiana, it was an infatuation." Memories flooded his mind and muffled his voice. "A terrible infatuation, it brought only misery and death."

"You're telling me that you want to marry me, but Tatiana will always be between us."

"No," he said, leaning forward and taking her hand. It was cold. "I love you, I dream of you, and I want to make a life with you. I'm ready to beg your forgiveness, if it would help. I hurt you terribly, I know. You're extremely beautiful, you're a proud woman, and" — he smiled wanly — "you're Italian. You must have gone through hell because of what I did to you. I can't think of a worse humiliation."

"Well, I was also to blame, at the beginning," she admitted spontaneously, softening a bit.

"You mean my leaving for Paris? Yes, it was your fault. But I don't want to talk about it. I want to talk about the future, not the past."

She leaned back and crossed her legs, exhaling a long puff of smoke. "Did you tell Nina that you were coming to propose to me?"

He nodded. "She was very pleased. She's sitting now in her old chair by the stove, praying that you say yes."

Claudia frowned. "That's new."

"She thinks you're a saint. She knows you saved my life. She says what you did was very Russian." He beckoned to the waitress for another round of drinks. "The reason she didn't want you before was because she knew you would take me away from her. She was right. Now she knows that I'll be unhappy for the rest of my life without you. And she knows I'll never meet anybody like you again. Anyway, Nina's opinion doesn't matter."

"Alex . . ."

"You're going to say no, aren't you?"

She nodded gravely. She was more relaxed now, the old, confident Claudia. "Alex, we've changed, both of us. You're not the same boy I was in love with when I was sixteen. You betrayed my trust. And I'm not the same, either. I was cheerful then, I was a happy person. I grew up in a warm family, with great friends and lots of love. You opened a new world for me, and our love was a great adventure. But that adventure ended badly. I've become cynical now, even bitter. I don't trust declarations of love anymore, Alex, even yours." She looked into her empty glass. "I don't want to get hurt again."

"Please don't say no. Think it over. Remember, Claudia, I love you. It's a different love now, deeper, more mature. It's not a teenage passion anymore." He let out a deep breath. "And don't forget — I'm yours and I'll always be. Even if you reject me, you can never forget what we had together. We can't get away from each other. We can still be very happy. You loved me once. Don't you love me now? Tell me, I must know. Don't you?"

She bit her lips and stubbed her cigarette with abrupt, angry gestures.

"Why are you so upset?"

"Because you make me hesitate," she said frankly, "and I hate it. I had everything organized and decided. You were out of my life for good. I had made up my mind. And here you come and buy me a glass of cheap wine, and there's this music and the lights, which make me sentimental, and things aren't so clear and final anymore. I don't want to melt again, Alex, I'm still hurting."

"Perhaps I'll stay here and we'll meet for breakfast, to talk it over again?"

She stood up. She was so lovely, he thought, with the shadows nestling along her high cheekbones, and her head proudly raised. Her voice was calm. "No. Go back to New York. I can't answer you now, Alex, and I won't answer you tomorrow. If you insist on an answer right now, it will be no. I hated you when . . . when all this happened. I don't hate you now, but I still feel betrayed. Humiliated. Leave me alone, let me be with myself for a while." She refused the second glass of wine that the waitress brought. "They say," she said, turning to Alex and picking up her purse, "that time heals all wounds. Do you believe that?"

* * *

Claudia gave him her answer on New Year's Eve. She called him long distance from Seattle, and they laughed and cried over the phone.

Six weeks later, in a modest ceremony in Washington, Alex and Claudia were married. Only a few friends and relatives were at the wedding.

A year after their marriage, shortly after Alex completed his training course at the CIA, their first child was born. The baby was a blond, blue-eyed little girl, and they named her Tonya.

But deep in his heart, and never aloud, he called her Tatiana.

PART THREE

War

1977–1991

Chapter 15

A NEW SURGE OF RAIN splashed on the glass panes as Dimitri, standing by the high window, gazed at the morose grayness of Boulevard Pereire. He was in his old dusty office at the Sovtorg building in Paris. It was March 15, 1977. Exactly two years ago he had hurriedly escaped from Paris, after his return from Brussels; today was the second anniversary of Tatiana's death.

He had stubbornly avoided Paris since, though not because he feared the authorities. The Belgian services had failed to establish any link between him and the dead girl; the French had no grounds to accuse him of the hit-and-run accident that had almost killed his brother. Actually, the man who had hit Alex was Evgeni Zaitzev, one of Dimitri's agents in Paris. The accident had occurred almost a week after Dimitri had returned to Russia. The French Sûreté couldn't know, of course, that he had cabled the instructions in code to Zaitzev, from Oktober's black mansion in Moscow.

No, his reason for avoiding Paris was different: for him Paris was Tatiana. Everything in this city — the rainswept streets, the parks, the restaurants and cafés, the language, even the people — reminded him of her. It was a tormenting memory, which he vainly tried to chase away. He had loved Tatiana with a savage passion that he had never experienced before. No other woman had excited him as she had, no other woman had driven him to the same peaks of ecstasy. And no other woman had awakened in him such intense feelings of love, such a desire to share his life.

During the past two years, since leaving Paris, he had slept with lots of women. It was rough, mean sex, always on the verge of violence; it left him spent, but angry and dissatisfied. It was an attempt to overcome the haunting memory of Tatiana, but the attempt always failed. The sad, slender girl with the golden hair was the only woman he had ever cared for. Her death left an open wound that still burned inside him with fierce, intense pain. Just like his hatred for Alex Gordon.

He had made a mistake about him, though. Revenge didn't necessarily mean murder. If Zaitzev had succeeded in killing Alex that night, his brother would have suffered for a split second and given up the ghost. That was not sufficient punishment for what he had done. He would make Alex Gordon suffer for years, Dimitri thought, make him live in torment and fear, turn his days into a nightmare and his nights into hell. "Revenge means hitting your enemy where it hurts most," Oktober had croaked one night, "making him wish he never saw the light of day."

Vengeance, however, was a double-edged sword. For the avenger it could become an ugly, overwhelming obsession. Alex Gordon was constantly on Dimitri's mind, surfacing in his memories, a hated, yet constant companion. Standing now in his old Paris office, Dimitri tried to discard Alex's image from his thoughts and to concentrate on his present mission.

When he had left Moscow a couple of weeks before, he hadn't intended to come to Paris. His destination had been Oslo. Since becoming Oktober's deputy, he was on the road most of the time, supervising Department Thirteen's operations. He had gone to the Norwegian capital to set up the assassination of a KGB mole, code name Greta, a Foreign Ministry secretary who had been supplying Moscow Center with secret documents for the last twenty-five years. Greta had recently drawn the suspicion of the Norwegian services, and had to be silenced before revealing the tremendous scope of her betrayal. Dimitri's plan was to kill the woman at home and dress up her murder as a heart attack. But an urgent message from Oktober had cut short his preparations and summoned him to Paris.

Two Russian dissidents living in Switzerland, and a CIA team dispatched from Langley, were about to meet in Paris, Oktober's cable said. The purpose of the meeting was to establish an overall plan of dissident activities inside the Soviet Union. Oktober wanted all those who assisted at the meeting dead, Americans and Russians alike. It was the first time in years that Dimitri had been ordered to kill American agents.

Since Jimmy Carter's inauguration, America was becoming an active enemy again. The weakling President who kept blabbering about world peace was openly scorned by Moscow Center; but his quixotic crusade for human rights was alarming. He had just exchanged letters with the notorious dissident Andrei Sakharov, and he welcomed another dissident, Vladimir Bukovski, at the White House. This had to be stopped. A good juicy hit would warn the CIA to leave the dissidents alone.

The phone on Dimitri's desk buzzed discreetly, and he picked up the receiver. It was Monsieur Doriot, the owner of the antique firearms shop Le Mousquetaire, on Quai Voltaire. He had been Dimitri's main supplier when he had lived in Paris, and was the first he had called upon his arrival.

"I've got what you want, Monsieur Morozov," Doriot happily chirped. "Two dueling pistols from the early seventeenth century. They belonged to the Marquis Bussy d'Amboise, who was killed in a duel under Cardinal Richelieu's windows in 1627."

"Very good, Doriot," Dimitri said. He was proud of his ancient firearms collection, which occupied an entire room in his Moscow apartment. He spent hours, a few times a week, dismounting and cleaning his guns, pistols, and ornate muskets. "They're certified authentic?"

"Of course, monsieur. When can I expect you?"

Dimitri glanced at his watch. It was 10:35 A.M., and he had nothing to do before lunch, when his agents would report at his office. "Why not right now?" he said.

"I'll be delighted. À tout de suite, Monsieur Morozov."

Dimitri's car, a black Citroën, was waiting by the main entrance, driven by Murad Islamkulov, a Turkman with a broad, fleshy face. The use of drivers as cover for high-ranking operatives was a routine KGB practice. Islamkulov was one of Dimitri's top agents. "Quai Voltaire, Murad," Dimitri said.

The car emerged from the driveway, its roof battered by the fierce rain. In front of them the outer gate began opening. As the Citroën reached the gate, a blinding white light suddenly flashed in the car windows. Lightning, Dimitri thought, but then a tremendous force heaved the car off the ground and tossed it toward the wall. Its left side was crushed against the gatepost and it turned over heavily and landed on its roof, as deafening thunder rumbled from behind.

Islamkulov slumped over him, his arms limp, his liquid black eyes wide open.

DIMITRI CRAWLED OUT of the wrecked car through the shattered windshield; fine debris had rained all over the place. His left thigh hurt terribly, and he leaned against the wall. His trouser leg was torn and he had lost his shoe. He felt a stinging pain along his jaw, and ran his hand over his face. There was blood on his fingers. A familiar odor wafted about, but he couldn't place it. The Citroën lay on its roof with its wheels in the air, like some giant beetle flipped on its back. Dimitri still didn't understand what had happened; then he turned around and gasped in astonishment.

The Sovtorg building had vanished. In its place he saw a heap of rubble, stones, broken beams, and pieces of furniture. A couple of human figures crawled painstakingly beside the ruins like giant, gawky crabs. Of the entire building, only one wall was still standing, crisscrossed with fat gray lines that marked the former connections of walls, floors, and a staircase. A bidet and a toilet seat, miraculously intact, hung at the wall's upper left corner; they made the ruins look oddly obscene.

Dimitri took a couple of steps toward the building, the rain furiously whipping his face. The wail of sirens rose behind him, and suddenly the place was full of cars, police, ambulances, firemen. A few medics carrying stretchers darted past him, heading for the ruins. A woman was screaming shrilly. Somebody threw a blanket on his shoulders. *"Monsieur, vous êtes blesse!* You're wounded!" a concerned voice called to him, but he shook his head and kept trudging toward the ruins.

His numb mind started to clear, and he figured out what had happened. An explosion had blown the building to pieces; the blast had overturned his car, killing Islamkulov. Still, his life had been saved because he was in the car. If Doriot hadn't called, and he hadn't decided to leave unexpectedly, he would also be buried under the ruins now, like so many of his men.

A police officer was bent over a heap of torn papers. Dimitri winced.

"The archives!" he called, and beckoned to one of the Sovtorg guards, a blond man who wandered about, eyes wild, jaw slack, but apparently unscathed. "You, are you all right?" He had to repeat his question for the guard to understand.

"Yes, I'm looking for Grisha."

"Forget about Grisha," Dimitri hissed. "The French will take care of him. You go and find all our people who are able to walk, and collect all the papers scattered around, understand?" The man showed no intention of complying, a dumb expression painted on his face. Dimitri yelled at him: "The papers, the documents, you idiot! The French mustn't get their hands on our papers."

"But Grisha — "

"I am Lieutenant Colonel Dimitri Morozov, and I am ordering you to collect all the papers from these ruins, you half-wit! Now go and do it, on the double!"

"Yes, comrade," the guard mumbled, still dazed, and scurried toward the ruins.

Dimitri's head was spinning, and he slumped down on a block of masonry. A sharp pain repeatedly pierced his chest; every time he took a breath, he felt as if a dagger were ripping his lungs. He must have been flung against the dashboard when the car overturned, he thought. People were running beside him, carrying immobile bodies on stretchers. He heard moans, and one of the bodies stirred; the man was alive. Most of the people inside the building had probably been killed; thank God, some of his men were out on assignment, looking for the dissidents and their CIA contacts.

A couple of firemen half carried him to a café across the street, where he was laid on a bench. His clothes were soaked with rain, and he shivered violently, but the pain in his chest subsided, turning into a dull throbbing. He struggled to a sitting position. The owner served him a bowl of beef bouillon laced with brandy. The warmth spread throughout his body. He gazed dully at a Toulouse-Lautrec poster of the Moulin Rouge hanging on the wall. Tatiana loved Toulouse-Lautrec. Once she said to him that he looked like Lautrec's portrait of a poet called Aristide Bruant.

After a while a police officer came to him and asked for his address. He gave the name of his hotel, the huge Concorde-Lafayette at Porte Maillot. Foreigners were less conspicuous in large hotels; operational units never stayed at small hotels, where they were easily remembered. A police car took him to the hotel, where a doctor dressed his wounds and sedated him.

He woke up in the late evening to an insistent pounding on his door. He got up. He was still dizzy, but he was not in pain. He limped to the door. A police officer had come to interview him. Dimitri ignored his questions. "What caused the explosion?" he asked. "A bomb?"

The Frenchman was surprised. "No, of course not," he said. "It was a gas leak. A ruptured gas conduit leaked a huge amount of gas that accumulated in the basement. Then some electric spark, or a match" — he shrugged, spreading his hands and comically puckering his brow — "triggered the explosion. A tragic accident, monsieur."

Dimitri recalled the sharp odor he had sniffed after the explosion. It was indeed gas.

"Do you have some other information?" the officer asked.

Dimitri stared at the Frenchman's face. "Oh no," he said finally. "I'm sure it was an accident as you said, a gas leak."

Suddenly, unable to control himself, Dimitri laughed bitterly. The officer stared at him in bewilderment. No, they'll find nothing else, Dimitri thought, no bomb, no explosives, no dynamite. Just a gas leak. A tragic accident. That's what they would diligently write in their reports before closing the file.

But he knew it was not an accident. Not on the anniversary of Tatiana's death. Not on a morning when Dimitri Morozov had been cunningly lured back to Paris, his own base of operations. Now he was sure that there would be no meeting between dissidents and CIA agents; it was a red herring. The story had been cooked up and leaked to Oktober, just to bring Dimitri to Paris and set him up for the kill.

The killers had meticulously planned everything, except for a small detail: Doriot's call, which saved his life. Dimitri was sure that the French would find no clue as to the identity of the men who had ruptured the gas pipe after sealing the basement. It might have been somebody wearing the uniform of Gaz de France, or the electrical company. Whoever it was would never be found.

But Dimitri could identify fingerprints all over the operation, the unmistakable fingerprints of the man who had volunteered to join the CIA in October 1975, completed his training last winter, and right away — according to the reports that were piled on Dimitri's desk in

Moscow — had joined the Soviet Division of Clandestine Services. The man who knew that the Soviet obsession with subversion was so intense that the report about CIA agents meeting dissidents in Paris would send Dimitri running. The man who had sworn to destroy him. This had been his first blow, and others would certainly follow as soon as his enemy found out that he had survived.

Alex, you stinking carcass, he thought, you're behind this, I know it. This is a declaration of war, my brother. Now it's my turn. You'll live to regret the moment Tonya Gordon brought you into this world. If I don't kill you first, that is.

ON THE PLANE, on his way back, Alex felt strangely elated. The plan had worked smoothly — the uniforms of the Électricité de France had been a perfect cover for the team of three agents that had infiltrated the Sovtorg building under his orders. He should keep using uniforms and official papers in the future; people respected them, especially the Russians. And he should always act as swiftly. The entire operation — the puncturing of the rusty gas pipe, the sealing of the basement, the installation of the plastic timer which would be pulverized by the explosion — it all had taken less than fifteen minutes. It had been easy, almost too easy.

But his brother had escaped again. He clenched his teeth. He had been so close, dammit! Dimitri had no reason to leave the building, he was supposed to be there when it blew up. The sonofabitch won't be so lucky next time. He thought of the bodies they had dug from the rubble. The fact that he had killed so many people didn't bother him. Why should it? After all, nobody had forced them to join the KGB. Two years ago he would have been appalled to think that he had caused the death of nineteen people. But that was in another life, before Tatiana's murder. He was a different person then, a romantic, he thought, in a surge of self-contempt. Still, the pictures of the maimed corpses he had seen in the newspapers kept flashing before his eyes.

Grimaldi picked him up at Dulles International, drove him to Langley and proudly paraded him in the seventh floor executive lounge where all the Clandestine Services chiefs came "for their pint of blood," as he used to say.

"We're very proud of you," he beamed, sticking his thumbs in the pockets of his paisley vest. "It was a superb hit. And what counts most — it's untraceable. They can never prove it wasn't a gas leak." He ordered a double vodka for Alex, a cognac for himself, then savored the odor of the Churchill cigar he'd lit. "That was a beaut, Alex. You've got a great future ahead of you. You go on your first operation abroad — and wipe out the entire Department Thirteen headquarters in Western Europe. It will take them ages to recover. All their archives gone, nineteen agents blown up — "

"Except the one I wanted," Alex said bitterly.

"You'll get him next time," Grimaldi replied, and blew a whiff of smoke at the ceiling. "You've just started."

Alex nodded. He had just started, indeed. He had gone through a preparatory course in Washington, and an abbreviated physical training course at the Farm. He was a few years older than the other trainees, but he had an edge over them — his burning motivation. The sessions in Washington had been routine — espionage techniques, coding, transmitting, decrypting; the seminars on geopolitical questions and foreign services were disappointing. At the Farm, on the other hand, he had enjoyed the physical exercises, the firearms practice, and most of all, the hand-to-hand combat.

On the completion of his training, Alex had joined the discreet Redwood unit where Grimaldi served. Redwood was a part of S/D — the Soviet Division of Clandestine Services, operating against Soviet targets. Alex had been offered a higher position as an analyst with the Office of Current Intelligence, but had turned it down. He was determined to go after Dimitri Morozov, and could only do it as a field agent. Dimitri's face didn't leave his mind for a single moment. At night he would often wake up bathed in sweat, gripped by murderous, black hatred.

His appointment as an operational agent so early in his career was an achievement by itself, but he had nobody to share it with. Claudia wasn't happy with his career at the CIA; she suspected he had embarked on a vendetta. She was right, of course. They had a tacit agreement not to discuss his job, and that put a chill on their relationship. Nevertheless, their marriage was successful. Claudia wasn't traveling as much as before; she had taken a couple of years off, to be with the child. She was painting now, mostly delicate aquarelles that reminded him of the French artist Marie Laurencin.

Nina, on the other hand, had become overtly hostile. She told Alex she couldn't understand how he could ever raise his hand against the land of his birth. He hadn't admitted that he worked for the CIA. He had told her a vague cover story about a research section at the State Department, but she had seen through his bluff. She often telephoned Claudia; they got along well, at last, and sometimes he felt they had created a common front against him.

He felt very lonely, in spite of his love for Claudia. He couldn't mourn his lost love on his wife's shoulder. The only person with whom he could share his agony was Nina, and Nina was drifting away from him.

Since joining the Company, he had lost his peace of mind. He couldn't concentrate on reading; he rarely listened to music. His only relaxation, when he returned to his Chevy Chase home, was the time he spent with little Tonya, making faces and clowning for her, changing her diapers, feeding her, and impulsively seeking Tatiana's poignant vulnerability in her clear blue eyes.

"Congratulations, Napoleone," a slim black man said, and his voice brought Alex back to reality.

"Thank you," Grimaldi said. "It's not official yet, Ned, but thanks anyway."

"What's not official?" Alex asked. Ned chuckled, moving away.

"Well," Grimaldi said with studied indifference, "old Vince Morton is leaving the Soviet Division, and I am going to succeed him. I guess it's partly because of you, Alex. There was another candidate, Ralph Rusk, you know him?"

Alex nodded.

"But after Paris they didn't want to consider anyone but me. So I'm taking the skipper's seat, thanks to your gas leak. And you" — he pointed his cigar at Alex like a king's scepter, his green eyes glowing — "as soon as you complete your first year in the division, you're going to become my deputy. Which will give you all the power you need to crush your beloved brother."

"I've got another plan," Alex said, staring intently at Grimaldi. "I want to bring Dimitri to Bonn in a couple of months. I already know what the bait will be, and this time he won't escape."

Grimaldi stared at him, his smile slowly fading. "You don't waste time, do you?" he said. "Did you ever think that while you're planning Dimitri's funeral, he might be preparing yours?"

*   *   *

THE TELEPHONE in the living room rang at midnight. She had just fallen asleep. She woke up with a start and hurried in the dark, shivering in her nightgown. Even before picking up the receiver, she had a presentiment that something unusual was going to happen. A faraway woman's voice asked: "Nina? Nina Alexandrova?"

"Da," she said in Russian, her body shaking. Alexander was her father's name in Russian. Nobody had called her Nina Alexandrova for more than fifty years.

"Somebody wants to speak to you," the woman said, also in Russian. "A friend of yours. One moment, please."

A man's voice, old and cracked, filled the receiver. "Nina? Ninochka, is that you?"

Her knees buckled and she collapsed in the nearby chair. The voice was old, but she would recognize it always, she had been waiting so long to hear that voice again.

"Sasha?" she whispered. "Sasha?"

"Yes, it's me, Sasha. *Lyubimaya,* how are you?"

"Sasha, my God, I don't believe it, you're alive." He had called her *lyubimaya,* his beloved. "Where are you?"

"In Moscow, and I feel fine. Are you all right?"

"Oh yes," she managed, crying and laughing at the same time. "Yes, I feel fine, too. How did you find me?"

She could swear, by his voice, that he was crying as well. He said something she didn't understand.

"Who is that woman?" she asked, bracing herself for bad news.

"What woman?"

"The one who called me."

He laughed. "Oh, she is my neighbor. I was afraid to cause you a shock — we are not very young anymore, so I asked Maria Fedorova to speak to you first. She's gone now."

"Thank her for me," she blurted, laughing with relief. "Can you speak, or do you want me to call you back? International calls are expensive, you know."

"No, it's all right, I don't mind spending all my savings on this call."

"Tell me, Sasha, my dear, what happened to you?"

He would tell her everything, he said, but not over the phone. He had finally received the book about him, almost three years after it had been published in England, and found her name. He had gotten her telephone number from the writer; yes, he had spoken to London; actually London had phoned him. The publishers were very excited that they had found him at last. They were going to produce a special program about him on British television, and they were flying him over to London. And — brace yourself, he said, brace yourself and don't say no — the publishers wanted to bring her, too, from New York, so they could meet, almost sixty years after they had been separated.

She was dumbfounded. "They'll pay for my trip to London?" He said yes, they would pay for her trip and her stay, a whole week in January. They wanted her to appear with him on television and be interviewed about their youth together, is that all right? And she said yes, she would come to London in January, she wanted so much to see him, she was pinching herself, she thought it was a dream, and she expected to wake up any moment.

He laughed, then asked her to be discreet about their plan. The English publisher wanted their appearance on television to be a surprise to the viewers. She agreed, it made sense indeed. "They'll sell the book all over the world after they see you on TV." She giggled. "You'll become famous, rich, a capitalist." After exchanging some more words of affection, they hung up.

She didn't sleep that night, and she didn't want to. She sat by the window, in the dark, thinking of him. Their conversation had filled her with tremendous joy, an overflowing happiness she hadn't believed could exist. Everything seemed different, life was beautiful, she felt young again, she even softly intoned a few measures of "Ochi Chornaya," a love ballad about a pretty black-eyed girl, which Sasha used to sing to her. "It's a bourgeois song, but that's the way I feel about you," he used to say.

Stop that nonsense, Nina, she humorously scolded herself, you're an old woman, you're almost seventy-five years old, and he's eighty! But for her he was still the young, handsome Red cavalryman with the shock of blond hair and the mischievous eyes. The years that had passed since their separation, her life with Samuel, her miserable times in Russia, Palestine, and America — suddenly all that didn't matter anymore. What counted was that she was going to be with Sasha again, her Sasha.

Was he married? A widower? Did he have children? He hadn't said.

But it didn't really matter. They had each lived their own lives. What counted was that after all those years he had called her "my love." And he had cried — they had both cried — with happiness.

She felt an urge to call and tell somebody the great news. She started dialing Alex, then, on second thought, replaced the phone on its cradle. No, she thought, she shouldn't tell him. He was with the CIA, he might make a fuss over the whole thing and spoil her wonderful adventure. She decided not to tell anyone; it could reach the newspapers and harm Sasha. She would only tell Alex and Claudia that she had decided to go on vacation to Europe, just once in her life. After all, she had the right to such a small luxury.

Her plan worked perfectly. Alex didn't suspect anything when she told him she was going to Europe for a week or two; on the contrary, he and Claudia encouraged her. "That's wonderful, Ninochka," Alex said over the phone, behaving nicely for the first time in more than a year. "Take a vacation, enjoy yourself!" He offered to give her some money for expenses, but she proudly refused. Claudia also seemed very happy for her; she was a sweet girl indeed. They had become very close after she had saved Alex's life; the past was forgotten. Besides, Claudia had given them little Tonya, a cute little devil. Nina adored her.

In mid-December Nina got a phone call from British Airways. Her ticket had arrived, the nice girl said, it was a roundtrip ticket to London, departing on January 21, return open, could she come and pick it up at the office?

Their office was on Fifth Avenue, in Manhattan. A few days before Christmas, dressed in her best clothes — her new patent leather shoes and the new beige coat she had bought for the trip — Nina took the subway into Manhattan, walked into the British Airways office, and picked up the plastic pouch they had ready for her. Later she had lunch at a nice Chinese place, off Fifth Avenue, where she examined her ticket thoroughly.

Sasha called once again, to make sure everything was all right, and on January 21 she took a cab to the international terminal at Kennedy Airport. "I feel million dollars," she happily confided in Alex, who had flown from Washington to say good-bye.

"Take care, Ninochka," he said, kissing her warmly. "And beware of the men in London, they are dangerous, they crave older women."

Oh boy, have I got news for you, she thought.

*   *   *

THE FIRST HITCH occurred on her arrival at Heathrow Airport. She was tremendously excited by the thought that she would meet Sasha in a few minutes. Would he like her? Yesterday she had gone, for the first time in her life, to a beauty parlor. The girls at the parlor had told her she looked great. Still, when Sasha had left her, she was a young girl, with soft white skin and long, abundant hair. Today she was an old woman. Would he remember the girl who had given him her love?

She couldn't wait to see him, her patience had run out. The line before the immigration counters seemed to be the longest in the world, as was the wait for her bag, which a nice young man loaded on her cart. But when she finally reached the arrival hall, Sasha was nowhere to be seen.

She stood, undecided, in the middle of a crowd of harried passengers, welcoming parties, drivers, porters, and airline employees. Over the loudspeakers a mellifluous voice announced an Alitalia flight to Rome, departing from gate 27, then repeated the announcement in musical Italian. On the newspaper rack before her, fat headlines announced the forthcoming meeting between Presidents Carter and Sadat, and Israel's Prime Minister Begin.

"Madame Nina Kramer?"

She turned sharply. Before her stood a florid-faced British gentleman in a dark suit, stiff-collared shirt, and striped tie. He held *The Chief*, Sasha's biography, in his left hand.

"Yes, I am Nina Kramer."

He bowed slightly. "Derek Sloane, from Graham and Dickinson. We published the book about Mr. Kolodny."

"Oh yes, how are you?" She ceremoniously shook his hand.

"I hope you had a pleasant flight," he inquired.

"Yes," she said mechanically, "yes, thank you." She looked over his shoulder, a dark foreboding invading her thoughts.

"I'm awfully sorry," Sloane said, "but Mr. Kolodny has been delayed. He has been a little indisposed the last few days."

"He is ill?" she asked anxiously.

"No, not really." Sloane took hold of her cart and pushed it toward the exit. "He is supposed to arrive today, on the late Aeroflot flight from

Moscow. I'll take you to your hotel, so you can eat something and rest. You must be very tired."

"Yes," she said, "thank you, sir."

In the funny cab, the kind she had seen in English movies, she sat silent and erect during the long drive to London. She stared with curiosity at the double-decker buses, the police officers with their unusual helmets, and the House of Commons, which she glimpsed from a distance when they crossed the Thames. The hotel in Hampstead Heath was a neat establishment called the Tudor Arms. Her room was small but pleasant, decorated in light colors. She hesitated for a long while, then finally gathered all her courage and called room service for a couple of sandwiches and a glass of milk. Then she turned on the television and watched school programs for a couple of hours. She was just about to lie down for a nap when somebody knocked on her door.

It was Derek Sloane again. "A small problem, I'm afraid," he said. "Mr. Kolodny cannot come, he is too weak to travel."

Her disappointment was immense. She wasn't going to see Sasha after all! "So . . . so I come for nothing?" she stammered.

"Not necessarily." There was another possibility, Mr. Sloane pointed out, that was perhaps even better than the one they had planned. If Mrs. Kramer agreed, they could arrange for her to fly to Moscow tomorrow, and meet Mr. Kolodny there. The BBC had some local TV crews in Russia, and they could film Mrs. Kramer and Mr. Kolodny in Moscow. "Just imagine," he said, "you two talking to the camera with the Kremlin as a backdrop." If she agreed, they could arrange everything; they had good connections with the Soviet consulate and could get her a visa in a matter of hours.

"I don't know," she said. But her imagination was already galloping wildly, and she knew she would give anything to be there, to fulfill the dream that had been burning inside her for the last fifty years. The temptation was tremendous: walk in the streets of Moscow, stroll in Red Square, see the Kremlin, Lenin's mausoleum! She suddenly had a golden opportunity to visit Russia before she died. Yes, she thought, she wanted to go, but would Sasha agree? "I want to speak with Sasha first," she said, "on the telephone."

"Very wise," Sloane said. "We'll make the arrangements." He left fifteen minutes later with her passport, "to get you a visa in any case," and she stayed in her room, waiting for Sasha's call. It came in the early evening. Sasha's voice was tired and rasping, but he was very enthusiastic about her coming to Moscow. "It's only a three-hour flight, Ninochka. I'll be delighted to show you Moscow. Come, come quickly!"

The next afternoon, exhilarated, yet gripped by profound trepidation, she landed at Sheremetyevo Airport. The sun was setting, its last beams painting the snowbound fields on both sides of the runway in pale gold. She was in Russia, on Soviet soil! The terminal was a huge, modern building surrounded by scores of airliners from many countries. She felt like she'd come home; or rather, like an aging mother meeting her child after years of separation, amazed at the way the child has grown up. Walking along the vast concourses, she stared with wonder at the show-cases full of Russian artifacts, the colorful posters of Ostankino and the Lenin Museum, the bust of Brezhnev carved in black stone. She smiled at the handsome officers, clad in green uniforms and shining boots, who stood guard in the arrivals hall; she spoke in Russian to the immigration clerk, who seemed pleased and said to her, grinning: *"Dobro pojalovat, tovaricha."* Welcome, comrade.

He was waiting for her at the exit of the customs hall, a very old man, not so stocky anymore but still erect, broad-shouldered, dressed in an old dark suit, a white shirt, and a tie; his leonine head proudly raised, his mane of white hair neatly combed, the sharp eyes nestled under thick eyebrows. He was holding a bunch of fragrant red roses. And she started crying even before he collected her in his arms. She smiled through her tears. "Roses in January," she said, and burst out crying again.

"Nu, nu, Ninochka," he said gently, softly caressing her hair.

"It was black when you left me, remember?" she said.

"What?" He smiled. His teeth were stained by nicotine.

"My hair, it was jet-black. And you had these blond curls."

"Well, we're both of the same color now," he said. "White. Let me look at you."

She stepped back, blushing like a little girl, feeling the warmth rising on her skin, setting her cheeks on fire. She stared back at him. His jaw was still strong, though split by age on both sides of the chin, and his mouth was full, determined, like in the picture the English writer had brought to her.

He reached over and took off her glasses. "Wonderful," he said, "you look wonderful. I would have recognized you anywhere, my Nina."

She wiped her tears, but they kept coming. "I should have gone with you to Palestine when you asked me," she said. "Our lives would have been so different."

He nodded.

"Oh, Sasha, how childish I was. How foolish."

"Come on, now, don't cry. We can't change the past. Let's go." He took her by the hand. She held his roses close to her face, breathing their perfume.

"Where are we going?"

"We'll leave your bag at your hotel, we'll have dinner, we'll drink a little, and we'll talk."

"You're not married?" she blurted. "There was nothing in the book about your marriage."

He smiled a wistful smile. "I was, and it's a sad story. I didn't want them to print it."

Later, when they were seated at the Kiev Restaurant, in her hotel, they spoke a little and drank a little and cried a lot, over the years they had wasted, over their going their separate ways, which no reunion could ever bridge. She knew a lot about him from what she had read in the book, and he filled in the gaps. Yes, he had gotten married, in Spain, during the civil war, to a Russian girl named Irina. They had returned to France together, where their two daughters, Katya and Nina, were born. "Yes, Ninochka, I named her after you. I told Irina that was my way of remembering you."

When the World War broke out, Irina and the children had returned to Russia, and he had been left behind to direct the Soviet espionage network in occupied Europe. "I guess you know all about that," he said, lighting a black cigarette. "It's all in the book." But when he returned to Russia after the war and was thrown into the Lubyanka Prison, Irina had divorced him and taken the children away. She had even testified against him, had denounced him to the KGB as an English spy. The KGB inquisitors who tortured him in prison had shown him her declaration, in neat proper handwriting on four pages of a child's copybook. "Well, I was in prison, and she wanted to save her hide, so she signed all they told her to."

When he was released, she hadn't even called, and his letters to her were returned. She was dead now, and he didn't mind. But his daughters were both married, one in Orel, the other in Kazan, and he had four grandchildren whom he loved dearly. "Nina might come to Moscow while you're here," he said. "She wants to meet the other Nina." When he smiled, his eyes became slanted slits surrounded by tiny wrinkles; his mouth stretched; and he looked like an old, kindhearted Chinaman.

But when the smile vanished from his face and he stuck his chin up aggressively, his forehead somber, his eyes burning with cold fire, he suddenly became a formidable, brutal man, and she could feel the power that he had once exuded. Here was the Chief, the man who had ridiculed the Gestapo, broken the Nazi codes, and scared the KGB so much that they threw him into an underground cell for eleven long years.

After his release, he said, he had been reinstated in the KGB, but a few years ago he had retired. He lived now on his pension. "I was also decorated," he said with undisguised pride. "Better late than never. Order of Lenin, the highest decoration of the country. I am a hero of the Soviet Union."

"Hero of the Soviet Union," she repeated, transported, then raised her glass. She couldn't believe she was doing this. "Let's drink to the hero."

He swallowed his vodka in a single gulp, then put his hand over hers. "Now let's hear about you, *lyubimaya,*" he said.

She leaned forward and clasped both his hands. "I don't want this to end, Sasha, I don't want to wake up from this dream."

A BEAUTIFUL DREAM it was. For a full week, they spent practically all their time together, strolling in the streets of Moscow and on the banks of the Moskva River, touring the city monuments, visiting the Bolshoi and the Maly Theater, sitting on a bench in the park, or in some ancient café before an order of *blinis* and *kvas*, and talking. They had a whole lifetime to talk about.

They also spent their nights together. "I am an old man," he admitted to her the first evening, with his disarming smile. "I am too old for lovemaking. But at least let me sleep beside you and hold your hand." She had blushed and said yes, she wanted that very much. This is not you, Nina, she told herself when she undressed in the bathroom, put on her nightgown, and slipped under the covers at his side; this is another woman. You would never do this. And, as he turned off the light and reached for her, she smiled to herself. Yes, indeed, she was another woman.

She had never been happier. If they could only stay together, she thought, if they could only finish their lives together. But she knew this was impossible, each of them was going his own way.

It was a wonderful week, although there were a few distressing moments. One afternoon they crossed Dzerzhinski Square and she almost fainted, staring at the Lubyanka, where her sister had been shot. She said that to Sasha, who shook his head sadly. Yes, he knew about Tonya and Victor, and all the others. Stalin, he said, Stalin was the tragedy of the revolution.

Nina also got upset during the television interview, which was very strange, with three stone-faced Russians filming them in front of the Kremlin and St. Basil's Church, while a fourth man asked them stupid questions in high school English. She had seen interviews on television; this wasn't an interview. But Sasha said the questions didn't matter, actually — the BBC people would edit the film and leave the questions out.

There was also the matter of Sasha's morose mood, which she perceived after sobering up from her initial elation. Most of the time he was rather sullen and ill at ease, although he was very gentle and loving toward her. At times, when she caught him off guard, his eyes had a grim, almost desperate look. She asked him if something was worrying him, and he denied it with unusual vehemence.

On their last night together, he cried when she told him about their little boy who had died. At the airport he hugged her strongly and kissed her very softly, very lovingly, on the mouth. "Ninochka," he murmured, "dearest, I love you, I've loved you all my life." He added cryptically: "Remember that, come what may."

She remembered that on arriving in New York, when two FBI agents who had been waiting for her at the airport arrested her for espionage and assistance to a foreign agent.

"IT'S QUITE CONCLUSIVE, I'd say," FBI Special Agent Norman Neave muttered, spreading the contents of the thick file on the desk, placing documents and photographs in neat rows, as if he were playing a game of patience with oversized cards.

"Conclusive my foot," Alex Gordon grunted, bending over the desk. They were in the headquarters of the CI-3 counterintelligence squad, on the eleventh floor of the FBI's Washington field office. It was late at night, and the large agents' room with its thirty metal desks was all but deserted. A lonely agent sat by the window, reading some material under a bulletin board covered with postcards of girls in bikinis. The odor of stale tobacco hung in the air. Agent Neave had his own office, separated from the squad room by a glass partition.

"See for yourself," he said, pointing at the tidy rows of glossy photographs. "Photos of Nina Kramer and a KGB officer, Sasha Kolodny, known as the Chief." He repeatedly struck the glossy photographs with the back of his hand. "Here they are by the Kremlin, in Red Square, at Gorky Park, in Sheremetyevo Airport."

"The man was her former lover, for Christ's sake!" Alex snapped angrily.

"When? Sixty years ago?" Neave glowered at him, picking up a report. He had plump, pink hands. "Did she tell you that she was going to Moscow when she left the country?"

"No," Alex said. "So what?"

"What did she tell you?"

"She said she was going to London for her vacation," he admitted reluctantly.

"And what is she saying now? Did you see her?"

Yes, he thought, he'd seen her. His Nina — broken and humiliated — was being held in the women's detention center on Eleventh Avenue, with the junkies and whores of New York's West Side. "She says she went to London to tape a joint television interview with Sasha Kolodny, who had phoned her from Moscow. But in London she found out the man was sick — he's eighty years old, he couldn't travel. So the publishers flew her to Moscow, and the interview was taped there."

"Oh really?" Neave countered, smoothing his brown mustache. He stuck his round paunch forward. "I know those answers by heart. I questioned her, remember? Well, let me tell you, there's not a word of truth in what she says. First of all, there was no television interview, not in London and not in Moscow."

"But she said . . ." Alex began, then fell silent.

"The BBC never planned such an interview. ITV never planned such an interview, either. The publishers of the book about Kolodny are a very respectable London firm. They never invited him or Nina Kramer to London. No representative of theirs ever met Nina Kramer at the airport. She didn't pay for her flight ticket. It had been prepaid in London and cabled to New York. We traced the source — the check came from the Russian trade mission there."

"Sovtorg," Alex murmured, feeling a chill.

"The same with her hotel," Neave went on triumphantly. "Sovtorg paid for it. And for her flight to Moscow. She had a Russian visa waiting for her in London. Nobody gets a visa for Russia the same day — it takes a least two weeks to process an application."

Alex took a deep breath and paced around the desk. On the wall was a photograph of a thinner Neave and three other men, looking elated, surrounding two terrified young boys. Under the photograph was an inscription in handwriting. "Boyce and Lee. The Falcon and the Snowman, January 1977."

"And what does your aunt say about this?" Neave asked, handing him a batch of photostats. Alex shuffled through them. They were sequences of letters in unintelligible groups of four and five. He looked questioningly at the CI-3 agent.

"Microdots," Neave said. "We removed them from a guidebook of the Kremlin, in Russian, that she was carrying in her suitcase. We haven't decoded them yet, but it's only a question of time."

"The book was a present from Sasha," he muttered.

"Of course," Neave sneered. "What more do you want? She's a communist, she was investigated in the fifties, she secretly flew to Moscow and met with one of the greatest spymasters of the KGB, she came back carrying a book full of coded instructions, she lied every inch of the way, and you say she's innocent?"

Alex shook his head. "I say she was framed."

Neave eyed him skeptically. "By whom?"

Alex walked to the window and looked outside. Before him stretched the dull water of the Anacostia River. Between a large junkyard and an empty field, their ugliness mellowed by a thick layer of snow, rose the stark bulk of an electric power plant, spewing thick smoke. A train passed close by, hooting sadly.

The last days had been tough. He was in Bonn, working with the West German service on a scam intended to entrap Morozov. A high German official, known for his ties with exiled minority leaders, was to approach the Stasi, East German intelligence, and offer secret documents about the Armenian underground in Russia. It was bait Dimitri couldn't ignore; a few months before, three Armenians had bombed the Moscow subway. They had been arrested, tortured, and shot, but hadn't revealed the names of their accomplices.

In the middle of a meeting, Alex was called to the telephone. It was Claudia, and she sounded hysterical. Nina had been arrested the night before, on her return from Europe. All the New York papers carried her photograph on their front pages. They described Nina as a Russian mole planted in America fifty years ago. One headline proclaimed: RED NINA WAS RED SPY.

Flabbergasted, Alex cut the meeting short and flew back home. Claudia met him at Kennedy; she had left Tonya with her mother. She told him on their way into the city that bail had been denied. Nina had been judged a danger to the security of the United States.

In the women's jail they met Nina, who looked like a ghost. Because of his position with the CIA, they were allowed to talk in a separate room. Nine cried continuously and wrung her hands. Claudia hugged her closely, and Nina gradually regained control over herself. Bit by bit she described her trip to London and Moscow, but in the middle of the story she broke down and doubled up in a fetal position, weeping and mumbling unintelligible words in Russian, her eyes glassy, her clenched fists trembling. When Alex tried to hug her, she screamed and turned to the wall. Leaving Claudia with Nina, Alex flew back to Washington to meet the man who had arrested her.

Sovtorg had paid for her ticket, Neave had said, and for her hotel. Alex knew it had to be Dimitri. His devious brother could easily have made the payment untraceable, of course, by paying cash and leaving a phony address. But he had chosen to leave Sovtorg's fingerprints. Dimitri had wanted him to know who had done this. Nina's ticket was Dimitri's signature. The damned snake had chosen to attack him by destroying Nina.

Alex turned back to Neave. "Let me ask you a few questions," he said, making an effort to control himself.

Neave was stuffing a big meerschaum pipe. "Shoot," he said. Too many action movies, Alex thought.

"How did you get all these pictures from Moscow?"

"That's classified information."

In two steps Alex was upon him, shaking him by his lapels. "Don't give me that shit, do you hear me?" Neave's pipe fell on the floor, the tobacco spilling on the brown carpet.

The FBI agent grabbed his wrists. His face had turned white. "Let me go! You crazy or what?" His eyes darted toward the telephone.

Alex grabbed the phone and stuck it in Neave's face. "Go ahead, call your boss, ask him if you should answer my questions. Ask him! Tell him I threatened to bust your face, before he kicks you out of the service."

"Me? Why me?"

"Because, brother, you're in big trouble. This little old lady has been set up, with your active cooperation. This is a KGB scam, and you've fallen for it. When the truth is revealed, they'll need a scapegoat for that blunder. You."

Neave glowered at him hatefully, then stepped back. "Okay, okay," he muttered with wounded dignity, "don't get excited. I can't disclose the modus operandi — "

"I don't give a damn about your modus operandi," Alex snapped. "I want to know if your people took the pictures, and why."

Neave kept dallying, denying, eluding the issue, but finally, cornered, he admitted that yes, the FBI had been tipped before Nina Kramer's departure that her destination was Moscow; and yes, she had been under FBI surveillance since she left Kennedy. He had alerted the security people at the American embassy, and they were waiting for her in Moscow; they took the pictures of the couple. He didn't know who had tipped the FBI. Nor did he know who had furnished the newspapers with the details of Nina's past.

It all figured. "As I told you," Alex said, "it's a frame-up." Dimitri, you scum, he thought, did you have to involve her in this? This poor old woman, your mother's sister. Did you have to pillage her last dream? Her one moment of happiness?

"Frame-up?" Neave had regained some of his confidence. "Why would they frame a harmless old lady?"

"Because they wanted to get at me."

"Who's 'they'?"

Oh hell, Alex thought, what should I say? My brother? My brother, who is a KGB man, wanted to hurt me? By framing his aunt? He shrugged in silence and turned to leave. He was by the door when the telephone on Neave's desk rang. The agent picked it up. "Neave," he said. He listened for a moment, then turned toward Alex, glaring malevolently. "It's for you."

It was Grimaldi. "I knew I'd find you there," he said. "We just received a flash from Moscow. Sasha Kolodny committed suicide today in front of the Lubyanka. He shot himself in the head. Hundreds of people saw him do it; your brother won't be able to cover it up. Kolodny is a hero of the Soviet Union, you know."

Alex quietly replaced the receiver and stared at the dark window. Dimitri's plot was falling apart. He had apparently forced Kolodny to play that despicable farce with Nina. The old man, probably remorse-stricken, had cracked and killed himself. Good for you, Dimitri, he thought. At least the suicide proved Nina had been framed. He suddenly realized that he would have to break the news to his aunt. How can I tell her? he thought in anguish. It will kill the old girl.

But when he arrived at the detention center, Nina wasn't there. She had been taken to the hospital during the night. A stroke, the warden said. He found her at Bellevue, lying motionless on her bed, a small, gaunt woman, her white hair spread on the pillow, looking like death. There was, though, a strange tranquility about her, as if she had quietly waited for her hour to strike, and parted from the world of the living without regret. She didn't recognize him. Massive brain damage, the doctors said.

Two weeks after she suffered her stroke, a letter arrived at her home. It had been posted in Vienna. The address had been written in block letters on an old air-mail envelope. Alex opened it. The letter was in Russian. It was signed by Sasha Kolodny.

My Nina,

When you receive this letter I won't be alive anymore. I cannot live after what I did to you. And what use is there in staying alive? I had my greatest moments of happiness when you were here, in my arms. I'll never experience such happiness again, even if I live to be a hundred.

Before you left I told you that come what may, you should always remember that I love you. This is the truth, but not the whole truth. I was blackmailed into framing you, by the classic old method that, I must admit, I also used to practice in the past. I was threatened that if I didn't take part in the plot to incriminate you, I would never see my daughters and my grandchildren again. I'm an old man, my love. Katya and Nina, and their children, are all I've got. I couldn't allow any harm to come to them. I had no choice but to comply.

I lied to you. About the British publisher inviting us to London, and about the television interview. But I didn't lie to you about my deep love for you. Ninochka, we both made a tremendous mistake in our youth, in choosing our new religion, in parting from each other. We should have gone to Palestine, together, and built a new life for ourselves. But we can't change the past, and we paid for our stupidity. I will die a sad and disillusioned man. I hope this letter will at least bring you some solace, by letting you know you were the only woman I ever loved.

The last line, scratched and twisted, reflected Sasha's terrible agony. "I didn't betray you," he wrote.

Alex rushed to the hospital and broke into Nina's room. Perhaps, he prayed, the letter would shatter the blank wall her disrupted brain had erected around her. He squatted by her bed and read the letter aloud, several times, stroking the old woman's forehead. But Nina stared fixedly into space, seeing and hearing nothing, a dead soul in a dwindling body.

She died two days later, without surfacing from her coma.

Chapter 16

SHORTLY BEFORE DAWN on December 27, 1979, Dimitri Morozov landed at Kabul International Airport, in Afghanistan, aboard a military Ilyushin aircraft. With him were twelve agents from his department and sixty KGB commandos, trained at the special operations school at Balashikha. They were all dressed in uniforms of the Afghan army. They immediately boarded Afghan jeeps and trucks, which had been prepared beforehand, and headed toward the presidential palace. At the palace gate the convoy was stopped by an Afghan roadblock. As the sentries approached the vehicles, Morozov's men opened fire on them, riddling them with bullets.

Dimitri led the assault on the palace, firing his submachine gun at anything that moved. In the splendid lobby, furnished with crystal chandeliers and precious silk carpets, three Afghan officers barred his way. They were apparently amazed to see soldiers in Afghan uniforms attacking the palace. After a brief hesitation, one of the officers pointed his pistol at Dimitri. He was a colonel, burly and balding, with a thick black mustache. Dimitri mowed him down. The other two raised their hands in surrender. He shot them as well. Oktober's orders had been precise and merciless: no witnesses should survive.

More Afghan soldiers appeared in the doorways, and his men hurled themselves upon them, shooting and throwing hand grenades. Out of the corner of his eye he saw two Russians slump to the floor. He was enraged. They hadn't expected so much resistance. Firing madly, Dimitri ran up the marble staircase to the president's living quarters. Frightened screams, thuds, and bursts of machine-gun fire echoed throughout the palace. Scared servants scattered before him, trying to hide in bathrooms, closets, under the beds. He fired at them in short, accurate bursts, and dashed through the long succession of rooms, reloading his weapon.

He heard his soldiers running behind him. He hesitated in a narrow, dark passage, then crouched by an open doorway, spraying the room before him with bullets. It was the presidential bedroom. Parade uniforms, civilian clothes, and women's silk robes were strewn on the large bed and on the white carpets. A bottle of perfume had overturned, spilling a golden liquid that spread a sweet, musky odor.

Dimitri darted up the steps to the top floor, kicked in a locked, lacquered door and entered a room. It was something unexpected — a barroom, with mirrors, round stools, a rosewood counter. Behind the counter several racks were loaded with bottles of imported liquor. Glasses of various sizes and shapes stood in two cupboards. This is how a Muslim president breaks the Islamic ban on alcohol, he realized. Hearing a muffled sob on his left, Dimitri swerved and simultaneously squeezed the trigger of his Kalaschnikov. Two fingers, closely entwined, collapsed on the floor. He bent over. Before him lay President Amin and a young, dark-skinned woman, probably his mistress.

Dimitri straightened up, his breath shallow. His face was on fire, his forehead covered with sweat. He stepped behind the bar and poured himself a tall glass of cognac. He had accomplished his mission.

The next morning, the Soviet protégé, Babrak Karmal, was sworn in as president of Afghanistan and asked the Soviet Union for the assistance of her troops.

At a modest ceremony in Moscow, Dimitri Morozov was promoted to full colonel.

AFTER THE AFGHAN COUP, Dimitri was assigned to train PLO guerrillas at Balashikha. He disliked Arabs, but was pleased that by training the Palestinians, he would be indirectly fighting Israel and the Jews. He loathed the state of Israel, although he had to concede it had a fine army and an excellent intelligence organization. But Jews had always been good spies, he thought, because of their sly, treacherous nature.

In early fall he was back in department headquarters. On Oktober's orders he reluctantly showed the department's poison research laboratory to four Bulgarian visitors, members of their secret service. When he'd taken over Department Thirteen, Oktober had transferred the poison laboratory to his department.

Dimitri led the Bulgarians to the cellar, where the research facilities were located. The scientists moved silently between the visitors; they were not allowed to talk to foreigners. Dimitri knew several of them, including an old, bald gnome with a wizened face and bright blue eyes; Oktober claimed that he had worked in the notorious poison chamber of the Stalin era.

When the tour was over, the Bulgarians specified what they wanted. Dimitri had to comply; these were Oktober's orders. He regretfully parted with the laboratory's latest invention, half a dozen tiny poisoned pellets that could be noiselessly fired from the tip of an ordinary-looking umbrella. The Bulgarians later used the weapons to murder two of their dissidents in Western Europe.

In 1981 Dimitri was in Warsaw, advising the Polish army on techniques for seizing power and imposing martial law; the Kremlin thought this was the best way to contain the dangerous Solidarity movement. Dimitri had a different opinion. He thought the Polish services should assassinate Lech Walesa and the other Solidarity leaders. The movement would be decapitated and fall apart. But the Poles feared that such a step might lead to a revolt.

On his return to Moscow, he clashed with Oktober; it was their most violent confrontation ever. Oktober wanted Dimitri's operational team to assassinate Pope John Paul II, whose Polish origins and explicit declarations had become a threat to the Polish regime. Dimitri refused. "We can do it," he said, "but if it ever became known that Soviet Russia assassinated the Pope, the political consequences would be devastating."

They brought their opposing views before a secret Politburo board, which ruled in favor of Dimitri. The attempt on the Pope's life was taken out of KGB hands and entrusted to Mehmet Ali Agca, a Turkish terrorist who was manipulated by the Bulgarians. All connections with the KGB were carefully severed.

That summer, in Rome, Agca managed to approach the Pope's open car in St. Peter's Square, fire and wound him in the stomach. But John Paul II survived. The identity of the assassin was eventually exposed. Former KGB chairman Yuri Andropov, now an eminent member of the Politburo, invited Dimitri to his Kremlin office and thanked him warmly for his foresight. Oktober's disgrace was only a matter of time, Dimitri realized.

With Brezhnev's death, in November 1982, Andropov was crowned the new Soviet leader. A few weeks later Oktober was ordered to resign. At thirty-two, Dimitri Morozov became the youngest chief ever of Department Thirteen.

Dimitri stuck to Oktober's tradition of keeping his department separate from the rest of Moscow Center. He refused to move his headquarters to the new complex at Yasenevo, where all the other branches of the First Chief Directorate were grouped. Department Thirteen stayed in its black mansion, impregnable to the outside world, an entrenched maverick princedom.

Dimitri's new position bestowed upon him a bundle of privileges. He was offered a large apartment on Kutuzovsky prospect, complete with a well-stocked pantry and bar, and a full-time cook and housekeeper. The apartment was in the same luxurious building where Andropov lived. With his new job came a dacha at Porech'ye for weekends out of town. A shiny Volga limousine with a driver was assigned to him. He gained admittance to several exclusive stores and clubs, reserved only for the upper ranks of the Soviet *nomenklatura*. The orphan from Panfilov, who once stole food in order to survive, had made his way to the top.

But the orphan from Panfilov didn't want this kind of life. He turned down the dacha and the new apartment, for Dimitri's tastes had by now grown ascetic, utterly rigorous. He disliked people's company, and never attended official dinners and receptions. He dressed only in black: a rough *rubashka* with tight, buttoned collar, black belt, and boots; he carried a gun at all times under his jacket. He looked more and more like his tutor, the austere Oktober. Like Oktober, he worked mostly at night.

He took no interest in art or music; he rarely visited his apartment, and transformed Oktober's former den into his dwelling. He ate little, and preferred simple, basic food. His body became very lean, his cheeks sunken, his full shock of hair prematurely gray. His features were now sharper, more angular, the nose beaked and jutting forward, the lips thinner, the skin colorless; only his eyes burned with a restless, flickering fire.

Women were attracted by his tormented good looks; his brusque manner and his indifference didn't discourage them. He used them to satisfy his sexual needs, then retreated into his black shell. He was unable to develop a deeper relationship with a woman; something had died inside him, together with Tatiana. Besides, what could he give a woman? Nothing but a stern life with a cold man dedicated to his secret schemes. The only luxuries he afforded himself were the occasional glass of cognac and cheap cigarettes, the soldiers' brand. And, of course, his collection of ancient weapons, to which he dedicated special attention.

Dimitri's colleagues could criticize and even ridicule his unusual behavior and strange tastes. They could guffaw behind his back, calling him Oktober's bastard. But nobody could deny that Oktober's bastard was the most dedicated of the center's department chiefs.

Dimitri became the Wet Affairs chief when alarming winds of war were blowing in the Kremlin. Ronald Reagan's ascension to power in Washington had plunged the KGB into fear — paranoia in Dimitri's opinion — of a sudden nuclear attack. Reagan's speeches about "the evil empire" and his decision to embark upon the Star Wars project enhanced the KGB's suspicion. The entire KGB was mobilized to carry out a huge operation, code-named RYAN. It was an acronym for *raketno yadernoye napadenie* — nuclear missile attack. Dimitri was charged with violent operations against American scientists involved in the Star Wars project.

Dimitri thought it a risky, challenging undertaking. But RYAN, Afghanistan, Poland, and Star Wars were for him nothing but counters in the only contest he really cared about: the deadly game he played against his brother.

A YEAR AFTER assuming his duties as chief of Department Thirteen, Dimitri drove to the small farm Oktober had chosen for his retirement. Oktober's house was an old, low structure of rough brown wood, on the high bank of the Kliazma River, northeast of Vladimir. It was a cold, windy day, with a gray sky and the tang of rain hanging in the air. Oktober was in the backyard, tilling the soil. He was wearing a faded brown tunic over his baggy pants, and old cracked boots. With his frail body, bent over from the waist and his long, limp hair falling across his face, he reminded Dimitri of a Russian serf from the pre-revolutionary era. The resignation in his body, bowed to the ground, symbolized the eternal submission of the Russian peasant to the rule of Mother Earth and the whims of his masters in Moscow and Petrograd. Nothing had changed, after all.

"Growing your own cabbage now, Oktober?" he inquired dryly.

Oktober glowered at him and continued to hoe the moist soil.

"I want you to come back to Moscow with me," Dimitri said, "as my personal adviser."

Oktober straightened up and leaned on his hoe. "You don't need me!" he lashed out. "You've taken away my department, what more do you want?"

"To tell you the truth," Dimitri admitted, "I don't think highly of your political judgment. But I can still use the devious brain of a crazy old Chekist."

Oktober stared at him shrewdly. "You need me for your brother, don't you?"

I need you for myself, Dimitri thought. You're my only friend. I've got nobody else but you.

He shrugged and looked away. To the south, beyond the immense cornfields, the antique Church of the Intercession towered over the village of Bogolyubovo.

"I was born there, you know," Oktober suddenly said. Dimitri stared at him with surprise. He knew nothing about Oktober, except for the rumors that were always wafting through Moscow Center. In his youth, some rumors said, Oktober had been a fanatic inquisitor. He'd had his own wife shot for deviationism, and his entire family had perished in Stalin's gulags. There were other rumors that Oktober was a priest's son and had massacred his family to protect himself from exposure. The communist regime had always considered religion its vilest enemy, and Oktober's link to the Church could have cost him his life.

"You had a big family?" Dimitri asked cautiously.

Oktober reached down, picked up a lump of dirt, and crushed it between his fingers. "They're all gone. There's nobody left."

"Did you have a wife, children?" Dimitri pressed on.

"They're all gone," Oktober repeated.

"What happened to them? Were they killed?"

Oktober wiped his pale forehead with his sleeve. "Let's go eat," he said.

They lunched silently on black bread, potatoes, and smoked sausage.

There was a half bottle of vodka on the table, but they didn't touch it. After the meal they walked on the riverbank overlooking the muddy waters of the Kliazma. The current carried branches and logs. The spring rains had caused a few floods in the area. The cornstalks on their right were still green. A few heavy drops of rain splashed on Dimitri's face, and he glanced at Oktober. The old man's face reminded him of the sharp profile of an Indian chief he had seen once in the *Ogonyak* magazine. He had the same leathery, sucked-up cheeks, a predator's cruel mouth, and long wispy hair. We are quite similar, Dimitri realized. We are both lonely men, with nothing left but our work.

"He's got under your skin, I see," Oktober said.

"Who?"

"Your brother. You can't live without him. You know, hate is very similar to love. It's a bond between you, maybe even stronger than love. Your war makes you inseparable." A thin, defiant smile lingered on the old man's lips.

"His wife had another baby last month," Dimitri said. "A boy. They called him Victor."

Oktober picked up a blade of grass and chewed it thoughtfully. "What do you think about Gorbachev?" he asked abruptly. Mikhail Gorbachev had become Russia's leader a few months before.

Dimitri stared at him for a moment, then said bluntly: "He is a disaster. He must be removed."

Oktober glanced at him with raised eyebrows. "Who will remove him? The party? The KGB?"

"Some people you know at the KGB, perhaps," Dimitri cautiously said. "Will you come back, Oktober? I need you."

The rain caught up with them by the river bend. They walked back in the furious deluge, the water streaming upon their faces and soaking their clothes; there was no use running, they were too far from the house. When they had sloshed through the mud and reached the house, Dimitri repeated his question. Darkness was imminent, the last diffuse light filtering through the murky clouds in the west. "Well," Oktober finally said, gesturing at the open spaces around him, "I always had a dream of living in the country. Perhaps I should keep it like that. A dream."

They left, together, the following morning.

* * *

OKTOBER was the only one to share Dimitri's secret and take an active part in the planning of his actions against Alex Gordon. He seemed to delight in devising ever more ruthless, more diabolical tactics in the brothers' war. It had been Oktober who advised Dimitri to hit Alex by setting up Nina Kramer.

"Your brother is emotional, he's a family man," Oktober had said. "He loves his wife, his child, his aunt. Perhaps he has relatives in Russia. Hurt them — and you'll hurt him. Each time you stab one of them — he'll scream as if you were sticking pins in a voodoo doll."

Oktober had been right. The Nina Kramer scandal and her death had dealt an agonizing blow to Alex Gordon. His emotional link to his family was definitely the chink in his armor. Yet, there was another reason for Dimitri to go after Alex's family. The bloody bastard had one.

For most of his life he'd had Nina, who loved nobody but him; he had his wife, Claudia, who looked very striking in the pictures Dimitri's agents had dispatched from Washington. He had his lovely little daughter, and now a small boy. Dimitri never said it to Oktober, but he secretly envied his brother for being surrounded by a loving family. Dimitri was a lone wolf, he had nobody. Alex had stolen the only person who had been dear to him. Well, now it was his turn to hit back. Nina Kramer's death was a foretaste of his revenge. Other hits like that would come in the future.

It was a very complicated task, however. Alex would surely have guessed, after Nina's death, that Dimitri might go after Claudia and the children; therefore, Alex kept them under constant protection. Dimitri's men reported from Washington that Claudia, her daughter, and her son were always escorted by armed bodyguards.

Dimitri tried to find other members of Alex's family in Russia. Tonya had a brother, Professor Gordon, who once lived in Leningrad, but he had died. Dimitri recalled how insistently Alex had questioned him, back in Paris, about Victor Wolf's family. Alex had seemed so eager then to find all his father's relatives.

Fine, Dimitri thought. He would be delighted to help his brother locate his bunch of Jewish aunts and cousins. He knew how to take good care of them. He instructed Ivan Sereda, his orderly, to find Victor Wolf's file in the KGB archives. If he had relatives, their names would be there. The KGB always used relatives as tools to blackmail its targets.

In the meantime, Dimitri had chosen more traditional weapons for their duel. After failing to kill Alex in Paris, he embarked, with equal resolve, on a secret offensive intended to outwit his brother, sabotage his operations and sap his credibility.

Which was exactly what Alex was trying to do to him. Since Nina's death, he had been preparing his counterattack. He finally hit back at Dimitri by exposing a KGB plot to assassinate Mexico's president, Gomez y Diaz. The assassination was thwarted at the last moment, and the rumors said that one of the conspirators had switched allegiances shortly before the attempt on the president's life.

Alex found out that Dimitri had visited Mexico a week before the coup was to take place. He then worked out a plan for setting Dimitri up as the Russian agent who had betrayed the KGB. The scheming Jew, Oktober reported, had deposited sizable sums of money in Morozov's name in several Swiss banks; then he planted doctored evidence that pointed at Morozov as the CIA's informer. Two KGB networks in Mexico City were destroyed, their members arrested, and the role of the Soviet embassy was exposed in the world press, with a lot of embellishment, of course. All the clues indicated that the chief of Department Thirteen was the turncoat.

The KGB established an internal board of inquiry, to investigate Dimitri. For the first two weeks the evidence against him, planted by Alex, piled up on the board's desk. Dimitri felt his life was hanging by a thread. But then the tide turned. The board couldn't ignore Dimitri's immaculate record and his solid position inside Moscow Center. The testimony of Oktober, who had come back from retirement to work with him, helped convince the board of inquiry that Dimitri had been framed by the CIA.

"Your brother is trying to pay you back for Nina's death," Oktober told him that night, "All right, let's play the game by his rules."

"How, Oktober?"

"Don't come to your office for a while. Don't go home, either. Hide somewhere, disappear. Let him assume that he scored, that you're in jail, perhaps even dead. And while he rests on his laurels, we'll hit back."

So Morozov's name disappeared from all CIA reports out of Moscow. By suddenly vanishing, Dimitri gave his brother a reason to believe that he had won. Alex Gordon was now deeply involved in supplying operational intelligence to the anti-Soviet rebels in Afghanistan. "Fine," Oktober said, "let's give him a victory there, if that's what he wants."

On March 15, 1985, in a rocky gorge in Afghanistan, Mujaheddin rebels pillaged the wreck of a Soviet Antonov aircraft that another guerrilla unit had shot down with a Stinger missile. In the wreckage they discovered a briefcase full of documents which soon reached Alex Gordon's desk in Washington. Most of the papers dealt with the supply lines for a summer offensive against the rebels. The detailed plans described a two-prong attack in the semidesert region of Kandahar, in the southwest. Alex flew personally to Karachi, crossed the border into Afghanistan, and passed the information to the chiefs of the Mujaheddin, who prepared to repel the offensive.

Suddenly, a month before D day, the Russians attacked in force, following a totally different plan. Instead of Kandahar, they stormed Zebak, in the rocky mountains three hundred kilometers to the north, by the Pakistani border. The rebels suffered a tremendous defeat. Alex was devastated. A week after the offensive began, he received a postcard from Brussels bearing the photograph of the Manneken Piss — a tiny statue of a naked boy, which was the city's symbol. The postcard carried a single phrase: "Never believe good news on a March 15."

March 15 was the day of Tatiana's death.

"I'd love to have seen Alex's face," Dimitri said to Oktober, "when he realized I was the one who served him the phony plans."

"I'd love to see your face right now," Oktober retorted, and took a rectangular envelope out of his briefcase.

Dimitri looked at him sharply.

Oktober spread a few photographs on the desk. "These arrived with the diplomatic pouch from Washington."

Dimitri shuffled through the photographs. He recognized his brother in a crowded restaurant, in the company of a corpulent man who seemed vaguely familiar. He looked questioningly at the old man.

"Remember Saint-Clair?" Oktober said.

"Saint-Clair? You mean . . . Grimaldi? This is Grimaldi? I can't believe it."

Oktober nodded. "He vanished after he escaped from Moscow twelve years ago. We thought he had retired from the service. We were wrong. He is the director of the Soviet Division."

"The director?" Dimitri repeated.

Oktober nodded. "Actually, he's Alex Gordon's mentor."

"Good God," Dimitri rasped. A smile spread on his face. "This seems to be my lucky day, Oktober. We can use him for our plan." '

He buzzed Ivan Sereda. His voice was hoarse, charged with contained triumph. "Vanya," he said to the short, wiry Ukrainian, "get the GRU electronic intelligence center in Alma-Ata on the phone. I want to speak to its commander."

GRIMALDI, holding his glass of champagne in his left hand, worked his way through the crowd. The Gordon party had attracted about fifty spooks, mostly from the Company, the rest from the other branches of the intelligence community and the State Department. He bumped into Claudia beside one of her paintings, a water color of two women on a beach, the outlines of their graceful bodies barely suggested by light, gentle strokes in gray, black, and pale blue. Claudia was dressed in a low-cut, bottle-green dress that enhanced her dark beauty. With her left hand she held little Victor, and with her right, a glass of whiskey, while explaining something about the painting to Rudy Sullivan from DDP/ CA — the Covert Action staff — and his fat, white-haired wife, who looked five years his senior.

"Hi, Claudia," Grimaldi said.

Her smile lacked warmth. "Hello Franco."

She had never liked him. He supposed she couldn't forgive him for the role he had played in Alex's affair with Tatiana. Grimaldi had seen Alex both with her and with Tatiana; he knew that she had come in second. Claudia couldn't forget that; she was a jealous, proud woman. But what a woman! She reminded him of a tigress, a graceful, fierce animal devoted to her mate and determined to use her claws to defend what was hers.

Rudy and the old lady mumbled something about how great a party it was and congratulated Claudia again, then disappeared into the crowd. Claudia turned toward him.

"You look absolutely smashing," he said.

"You look very well, too. I like the velvet jacket. Nobody would guess that you're retiring." He read a hint of triumph in the dark eyes. She was glad he was stepping out of their lives.

"Well, I'm not exactly retiring. I'll stay with the division as a consultant."

"Says who?" she asked. At least she wasn't a hypocrite, he thought, amused.

"Says Alex," he answered. "He claims he can't run the place without me. Which, of course, is absolutely true."

"The same old modest Franco," she said sarcastically.

"Mommy, Mommy!" Tonya appeared beside them, her lovely face flushed. She had fair skin and a rosy, pouting mouth. "May we have some ice cream, Ronnie and I?" A mischievous little face peered over her shoulder.

"Ronnie is my brother's son," Claudia explained. "Okay," she said, "it's in the freezer. But take Victor with you to the kitchen, he has nothing to do here with all these grown-ups."

"Mommy, he'll spoil everything," Tonya wailed.

"I don't want to hear you speak like that about your brother," Claudia said quietly, placing Victor's little hand in Tonya's. "Off you go." The little girl shrugged and dragged her brother to the kitchen. Victor followed obediently, then turned back, smiled and waved at his mother.

"I still have to congratulate you officially." Grimaldi raised his glass and assumed a solemn intonation. "A toast to the new chief of the Soviet Division, and to his gorgeous lady! Cheers."

"Cheers," she said absently, and drained her glass.

"I hope you're pleased with the promotion," he said. "I was fifty-eight when I got the division, Alex is barely thirty-seven."

"Yes," she said without enthusiasm, "I am pleased. I'll see him even less than before. Great, isn't it?"

Her bitterness surprised him. "Perhaps you'll have more time for your painting," he said.

She shook her head. "It's not the time I need, it's the peace of mind." She picked up another scotch from the tray of a passing waiter. "I'm going back into fashion design."

A silver-haired man, possessively holding a stunning blonde by the waist, passed by, raising his glass. "Congratulations, Claudia," he said. "The right man in the right place."

"Thank you, Irv," she chirped, with the same fake smile.

Grimaldi was watching her closely. "Back to fashion design?" he repeated. "So you'll start traveling again?"

"Probably. It won't make any difference to Alex. He doesn't see much of me anyway." Her lips twitched slightly.

Before moving away, Grimaldi noticed that her glass was empty again, and she was looking for another. She would be drunk as a skunk before the party was over. Claudia was in bad shape, and her marriage was definitely on the rocks. It was rumored at Langley that Alex and Claudia had hoped a second child might save their marriage; but it hadn't worked.

He couldn't blame her. She was a passionate woman who needed a lot of attention. But Alex was almost never at home, and when he was, his mind wasn't there. He was so obsessed by his schemes, so enthralled by his crusade against Morozov, that nothing else mattered. Grimaldi wouldn't have been surprised if Claudia was seeing somebody on the side. A sexy, desirable woman, she could have any man she wanted. She would be driven crazy by the thought of wasting her youth and her beauty, waiting for a husband who didn't even care for her.

He waved at Alex, who was earnestly talking to the deputy director of Plans. Alex looked very cool and self-possessed in a dark suit, striped shirt, and Lanvin tie. The warm, gentle boy Grimaldi had met on the Paris-bound plane had grown into a confident, ruggedly handsome man. Somewhere along the way he had discarded the warmth and the gentleness.

Grimaldi gave his unfinished glass to a waiter and made his way to the back porch. He needed a smoke, but smokers had lately become the lepers of the free world. He preferred to catch a cold outside rather than light a cigar in the Gordons' living room and provoke an enraged assault by some health nut, screaming bloody murder.

There was nobody on the porch. He lit a Corona and stared into the darkness. So this is it, Frankie, he thought. You're sixty-six, and you're retired. You can stop pretending. You're out, in spite of all this crap about being a consultant.

Grimaldi sighed and exhaled a long plume of smoke. He knew Alex wouldn't need his services; perhaps he would reluctantly throw him a bone once in a while. Alex didn't like him; he probably blamed him for Tatiana's death, although he never spoke about it. At least Alex didn't suspect that he was the one who had delivered the girl to Morozov. Morozov, too, would never learn that he had been the informer. That call from the phone booth in Brussels was a secret he would take to the grave.

He had no regrets, though. The girl's death had caused Alex to fall into his hands like a ripe fruit. The phone call had been a brilliant move: it had triggered the brothers' war, which gave him eleven more years of this thrilling life and a promotion to the top slot. He had been right to bet on Alex Gordon. Setting him against his brother had been an idea of genius.

A cold wind was rising from the nearby creek. What would he do now, he wondered in sudden panic. What would he do tomorrow, next week? He had no life outside the Company. He had nobody to share his anguish, his pain, his feelings. Or his bed. He'd had a few lovers during the last few years, very brief affairs, mostly one-night stands in New York, where he could pick up a boy in a gay bar. But with the AIDS scare, he couldn't risk even that anymore. Besides, his sexual powers were dwindling; he was really getting old, despite his dyed hair and mustache.

He shuddered at the thought of the bleak years ahead, alone in his apartment, waiting for a phone call from Langley that would never come. He would be forced to give in and buy a condo in Florida with the inevitable trimmings — shuffleboard in the afternoon, early-bird dinners, shaky swims in the oceanside pool. And foolish conversations with brown, dried-up old people in bright clothes, obsessed with their bowel movements and warming their ancient bones in the sun, waiting for death. It was maddening.

Grimaldi threw away his cigar, went inside, crossed the crowded living room and left without saying good-bye to his hosts. He walked quickly to his car, shivering in the chilly autumn air.

He unlocked his door and opened it, but the light didn't come on. He bent down to look in. A fuse, perhaps? Then he saw the immobile figure on the passenger seat.

"Hello, Franco," the dear, familiar voice said, and his heart leapt in his chest. "Don't turn on the light. You know my penchant for dark and cozy cars."

"Oleg?" he gasped. "Oleg, is that you?"

SHORTLY AFTER MIDNIGHT there was a discreet knock on the door of unit 132 at the Skyways Motel in Rockville, Maryland. Grimaldi turned off the lights and opened the door, letting Oleg Kalinin sneak into the room. He bolted and chained the door, checked the window drapes, then turned the lights on. He affectionately patted Kalinin's shoulder; he still couldn't believe he wasn't dreaming. His friend, whom he had believed dead for more than twelve years, was here, alive and apparently well.

Alex Gordon rose from his armchair by the coil-shaped radiator. He was wearing a pair of jeans and a heavy woolen sweater.

"Oleg Kalinin," — Grimaldi gestured — "Alex Gordon." He anxiously watched the two men. It had been his idea for Oleg to meet the new chief of the Soviet Division.

Alex shook Kalinin's hand. "Grimaldi told me a lot about you," he said in Russian, "and I know what you did for us. But I didn't expect that I would ever meet you. We thought you were dead."

"Whiskey?" Grimaldi said, smiling at his friend. "You like it straight, on the rocks."

Kalinin smiled back and nodded.

"And an iced vodka for you," Grimaldi said to Alex. He opened the minibar and fixed the drinks, choosing a Bailey's cream for himself. He opened a cellophane bag of roasted peanuts, and placed a chocolate bar beside Alex; he knew his weaknesses.

"Cheers!" he said, raising his glass.

"*Na zdorovya,*" Oleg echoed.

Alex picked up his glass, his eyes glued to Oleg's face. His reserve made Grimaldi feel uneasy, and he fidgeted nervously with his bow tie.

"Grimaldi told me," Alex said slowly, "that you arrived last week with the Soviet delegation to the space congress."

"The Fourth International Congress of Astrophysics," Kalinin corrected. He hadn't changed much, Grimaldi thought. The same smile, the same confident voice. His skin had acquired a deep dark tan, though, and his waist had thickened. Still, he looked very distinguished in his elegant charcoal suit, light blue shirt, and dark blue silk tie.

"What is your position with the delegation?" Alex asked.

"Deputy administrative director."

"And your real functions?"

Kalinin shrugged. "I am a brigadier general in the GRU — "

"General? Well, Oleg, congratulations!" Grimaldi raised his glass, and Kalinin acknowledged the toast with a grin. Alex remained impassive.

"My field," Kalinin went on, "is electronic intelligence, and I am interested in all the lectures and papers concerning satellites. Surveillance, photographs from outer space, signals, telecommunications, that kind of stuff."

Grimaldi stared at him in surprise. Oleg hadn't told him anything about his functions when they met in his car. He had only asked for a meeting, later in the night. He was leaving Washington the following morning.

Alex was perched on the edge of his chair, very intense, his back stiff. "When Grimaldi escaped from Moscow twelve years ago, you were a wanted man, and the KGB hunted you all over the country. Now you're here, a general and an expert on electronic intelligence. Tell me about your comeback, Top Hat."

Kalinin smiled again, at the mention of his code name. "I was hunted, but not exactly by the KGB. There was this young officer, Morozov" — Grimaldi glanced at Alex and noticed the tightening of his jaw — "who had stumbled on my ties with Grimaldi. In Moscow, Franco called himself Saint-Clair, you know."

Alex nodded, sipping his drink.

"Morozov had nothing tangible against me, only suspicions. He confronted me in Paris, then went after Grimaldi in Moscow. I advised Franco to leave, then I decided to lay low until I could get in touch with Morozov's superiors. I finally succeeded in meeting with Morozov's boss, the chief of Department Thirteen — "

"Oktober?" Alex asked, writing diligently on a yellow pad.

"Oktober, yes." Oleg Kalinin leaned back in his armchair. "I had known him since the war. I found him and convinced him that I was innocent. He stood by me like a rock; he virtually saved my life. Morozov had me brought before a KGB inner court. I spent several months in prison during the investigation."

"Morozov tortured you?" Grimaldi asked quickly.

"It was not a picnic," Kalinin said coldly. "Morozov himself was abroad most of the time, but some of his cronies did the dirty work. Oktober testified on my behalf, however, and I was finally released and reinstated."

"When?" Alex watched him with his head thrown back, his eyes narrowed in suspicion.

"Franco left Moscow in February 'seventy-four. I was arrested in April, and released the following February."

"You spent ten months in prison? Lubyanka?"

"No, Morozov held me incommunicado at Lefortovo Prison. It is in the southwestern outskirts of Moscow."

"I know where Lefortovo is," Alex said, scrawling a note on his pad. He raised his head. "From what you're saying, I understand that Grimaldi — I mean Saint-Clair — was also cleared."

"Oh, yes, absolutely. He is not suspected of any wrongdoing. He represented a respectable Canadian company in Moscow. He had to leave in a hurry because of the unfortunate death of his mother, that's all."

"And you?" Alex persevered. "Were you totally cleared?"

"I was finally rehabilitated," Oleg said cautiously, "but there was, how shall I call it, a cloud of mistrust around me. Morozov had spread the word that I was a traitor. Oktober thought it would be better for me to get away from Moscow. That way nobody could accuse me of maintaining contact with American agents."

"Where did he send you?"

"Alma-Ata, in Kazakhstan. I was appointed commanding officer of the GRU electronic intelligence center there. On January first, this year, I was promoted to brigadier general. That meant I was completely rehabilitated. Last month I was transferred back to Moscow, to the Science and Technology Division. This is my first trip abroad. There are also three KGB people with us, besides the scientists."

Alex stepped to the minibar to pour himself another drink. "Why didn't you contact us during all these years? We've been looking for you since you disappeared."

A condescending smile flashed on Kalinin's face. "Do you really think that would have been the right thing to do? I was exiled, suspected, and watched, with Morozov still breathing down my neck. . . . You think I should have risked my life and gone looking for some American agent, who might also have been a decoy?" He shook his head. "Come on, Mr. Gordon."

Alex bowed his head. Good for you, Oleg, Grimaldi thought, that's the answer Alex deserved. He raised his glass to his lips. The Irish cream was smooth and velvety.

Alex picked up the chocolate bar, but on second thought put it back on the table beside him. "And on arriving in Washington, the first thing you thought of was finding Grimaldi?"

The sarcastic smile appeared again on Kalinin's face. "Something wrong with that, Mr. Gordon?"

"You can call me Alex," he said coldly, then began pacing about the room, his hands clasped behind his back. "You followed Grimaldi to my house and got into his car. How did you get in?"

"Waiting in dark cars is Oleg's specialty," Grimaldi said, and they both laughed.

Alex abruptly changed the subject. "What do you think of your General Secretary?" he asked Kalinin.

"Gorbachev? I like him. He's a dreamer."

"Do you know him?"

"I met him in the seventies, when he was in Moscow as a member of the Supreme Soviet, and later in Alma-Ata. He came with a Politburo mission. He is a maverick. He has some very naive ideas about rebuilding the Soviet Union, retreating from Afghanistan — "

"You think he means it? He'll abandon Afghanistan?"

"He means it, but he won't stay in power long enough to do it. He's losing his hold on the country."

"Seen from Washington, he doesn't seem so weak," Alex remarked. "Gorbachev has been General Secretary for almost two years now, and he seems quite popular."

"Do you know any Soviet leader who wasn't popular? Frankly, I am surprised Gorbachev has survived for so long. Take my word: the old guard in the party will kick him out very soon, perhaps before the end of this year."

"What does the KGB think of him?"

"At first they liked him. Now they loathe him. Morozov wants him dead. The KGB bosses think he wants to curtail their power. It's a belief shared by the army and the party machine."

Grimaldi lit a cigar and strolled over to the window. He parted the drapes slightly and looked outside. The street was calm and peaceful. The two company cars parked by the opposite sidewalk were dark, but he noticed the glowing tip of a cigarette in the closer one. There were two agents in each car, equipped with walkie-talkies and handguns, watching the motel entrance. His eyes swept the street and rested for a moment on the huge abstract mural painted on the exterior wall of the Savings and Loan building. It was the work of some Spanish artist, he vaguely recalled.

He turned back. Alex was pacing back and forth, frowning in thought. "You're in electronic intelligence," he said. "What do you know about the KGB bugging of the American embassy?"

"It's Moscow Center's greatest coup of the last decade," Kalinin said.

You bet, Grimaldi thought, sucking his black cigar. The embassy fiasco was one of the worst scandals in Langley's history. Two stupid Marines, serving in Moscow as embassy guards, had been sexually entrapped by KGB "skylarks." The bozos had begun by letting the girls in at night and screwing them all over the deserted embassy. The girls had then convinced the Marines to let in "some friends," who had bugged the embassy, planted a microphone in the ambassador's desk, and opened the CIA resident's safe. The KGB agents had photographed a list of American deep-cover agents in Moscow. Most of them had disappeared during the last two months; they had probably been tortured to death.

And the idiots called themselves Marines, Grimaldi bitterly thought. The Russian whores had only to pull off their panties for the Marines to lose their heads. The KGB penetration had been a tremendous blow to the CIA networks. At least three boards of inquiry were investigating the disaster, and the State Department had already rushed two assistant secretaries to Moscow. There was talk of replacing the ambassador.

"This will get Morozov his general's stars before his fortieth birthday," Kalinin was saying.

"Morozov?" Alex stopped in his tracks, his hands stuck in his pockets. "What has Morozov got to do with this?"

Kalinin grimaced indifferently. "Everything," he said. "This was a Morozov operation from start to finish, didn't you know?"

"I thought that the bugging . . ." Alex began. He still seemed stunned. Morozov's name always produced that effect on him, Grimaldi noted.

"He didn't give a damn about the bugging. All he cared about were the networks. And he got most of them. He knows how to make his prisoners sing, believe me. It's a matter of months before he rounds up all your remaining agents."

Alex stood with his back to the window, his face stamped with hatred. "So we're left with no agents in Moscow," he said hoarsely. "How can we restore our networks there?"

"Somebody must start again, from scratch," Kalinin said.

"You, for instance?" Alex looked at him suspiciously, but Kalinin shook his head.

"No, I am too well known for these cloak-and-dagger games."

Alex looked at Grimaldi. A mixture of fear and sweet anticipation flowed into Grimaldi's veins, for he knew what was going to happen. Even before Alex Gordon asked his question, he knew he was going to answer yes, Alex, definitely yes, I'll do it.

Alex was watching him closely. He said, "Franco, I know you're looking forward to your retirement. But we're in trouble. We can't let Morozov get away with this. You know Russia, you've served there for years. Will you go back to Moscow and rebuild our networks?" He paused. "I know it's risky. Kalinin can help you. Think it over, you don't have to answer me right now."

"No need to think, Alex," Grimaldi said. "I'll go, I'll do it." And he thought, Thank you, Oleg, God bless you, my friend. Thanks to you they won't get rid of me so easily, they still need me! A triumphant feeling swelled in him. Franco Grimaldi isn't finished, he said to himself, Franco Grimaldi is still in the game, alive and kicking. Florida can wait.

MOST OF THE ELATION he felt that night at the Skyways Motel had evaporated by the time he arrived in Moscow, three months later. Still, in spite of the jabs of fear that sporadically pierced his gut, he was confident that no harm would come to him. Moscow was not as sinister as before. Russia was becoming a free country; the press was drunk with the newly acquired glasnost; the KGB was no longer the evil power, lurking in every shadow. He had a few years of exciting life ahead of him, with the help, and perhaps the love, of Oleg.

The arrival in Moscow couldn't have been smoother. Using his old Saint-Clair passport, he had boarded the flight in Toronto. The plane was full of Canadian businessmen, reporters, and tourists who treated the employees of Sheremetyevo Airport with amused irreverence. He went quickly through customs and immigration, hailed a cab outside, and less than an hour later checked into the magnificent Cosmos Hotel. His room, which offered a beautiful view of Mir Avenue, was equipped with a color television, a radio, and a modern telephone. Russia had definitely changed since he'd left twelve years ago.

He took off his coat, turned on the radio, and heard the beautiful sounds of Tchaikovsky's *Evgenyi Onegin*. There was a knock on the door. His luggage had arrived. He took a few one-ruble notes out of his pocket and opened the door. He winced, then stood still.

Three men waited outside. He immediately recognized Morozov, an ominous gaunt figure dressed all in black. He didn't know the white-haired man who stood beside him, but he could guess he was the man he had feared all along: Oktober. The face of the third man was momentarily blocked by Morozov.

"Welcome to Moscow, Mr. Grimaldi," Morozov said.

He was panic-stricken. Morozov knew his real name! Then the Russian stepped inside, and behind him he saw the grim, unsmiling face of Oleg Kalinin.

Kalinin softly closed the door behind his back and leaned on it. He was wearing a long coat and a Russian fur hat. Grimaldi retreated to the window, his eyes shifting nervously from Morozov to Oktober. He couldn't look at Kalinin. Incoherent thoughts darted through his mind. Was Oleg on their side? Perhaps he had been captured? Had he betrayed their friendship? And these two men, Dimitri and Oktober, what would they do to him? He shuddered. He thought of the Lubyanka cellars, and of the KGB torturers. He couldn't withstand pain, he was an old man after all.

Morozov placed his briefcase on the bed. He opened it with swift, efficient movements and took out several files which he neatly arranged beside each other, on the bedspread. He put down one blue file, and beside it placed three brown ones marked with Roman numerals, I, II, III, and a black file fastened with two clasps.

"Let's see," he said in English, "what have we got here." He picked up the blue file and opened it. It was full of old, yellowing documents, printed by some ancient typewriter. He absently leafed through the brittle sheets. "These are the minutes of the conversations you had with Kalinin in Berlin, in 1948," Morozov said matter-of-factly. "All the information he fed you, and you passed to the OSS and the CIA. All false."

He threw the file on the bed and picked up the second one, which was bound in brown paper. "This file and the two others" — he gestured at them, then continued in his low, respectful tone — "contain copies of all the reports Kalinin delivered to you in Moscow, during the years 'sixty-seven to 'seventy-four, when you were here under the name of Charles Saint-Clair. A few of them — unimportant, of course — were accurate, and were given to you only to establish Kalinin's credibility. All the rest are fake. First-grade disinformation. For seven years you fed the CIA with lies, Mr. Grimaldi."

Grimaldi blinked as the stunning meaning of Morozov's words seeped into his mind. Everything was fake — all these reports, all these documents he had risked his life for. But how could that be? Kalinin was their best agent, he was Top Hat, for God's sake! Unless . . .

Morozov handed him the fourth file. "I don't think you want to open this one in our presence. Inside you'll find some explicit descriptions and photographs of your intimate activities with Oleg Kalinin."

Grimaldi stepped back, feverishly shaking his head, refusing the black file. His breath was shallow, and a nerve twitched uncontrollably in his left cheek. His eyes held Oleg in desperate focus. He tried to speak, but his throat was paralyzed. "Oleg," he finally managed, his voice rasping, "you were part of this? You betrayed me? Oleg, it was all a lie?"

Kalinin stared back at him, speechless. A sickly pallor had spread over his face. He didn't deny it, didn't proclaim his innocence. "You traitor!" Grimaldi cried out, and hurled himself at Kalinin. "You bloody, lying, fucking sonofabitch!"

Morozov blocked his way and clamped his arms, pushing Grimaldi back against the wall. A standing lamp fell, and the bulb shattered to smithereens. Stinging beads of sweat popped out on Grimaldi's forehead. Morozov's fingers were hard and sharp, like iron hooks. "Calm down!" he hissed. "This is not a lovers' quarrel, this is serious."

Morozov nodded to Kalinin, who turned and scurried out of the room. "Sit down!" he barked at Grimaldi, and he obeyed, staggering to the bed and sitting down heavily on it, between the files. His heart was beating unevenly, and his mouth was sticky.

"Now listen to me," Morozov said in the same firm, commanding voice. "We can arrest you for espionage. We have ample evidence against you, from 1948 until today. We can put you in prison for the rest of your life."

He paused. "Or we can shoot you and dispose of your body. Nobody will ever know what happened to you."

Morozov chose a sturdy cigarette from a soldier's cigarette case, made of battered metal sheets, and lit it. "We can also send you back to your country and release all these files to the newspapers. All these fake reports. If your bosses at the CIA take them seriously, you'll be accused of being a double agent who betrayed his country for years, in connivance with the KGB. If they have some sense of humor, you'll become the laughing stock of your intelligence community."

Morozov sucked on the cigarette and exhaled gray, acrid smoke. Oktober still hadn't said a word, he just watched Grimaldi with his narrow, evil eyes. The romantic music of Tchaikovsky had been flowing from the radio; now Oktober brusquely turned it off.

"You'll be portrayed by the world media," Morozov said, "as a gullible homosexual who misled the CIA for forty years, causing irreparable damage. And for what? For a piece of Russian ass."

He chuckled. "Even if they let you go, there would be no place you could hide. Look at him, all the secret services in the world will say, look at this stupid old queen. He was chief of the Soviet Division! What a joke, the CIA."

Grimaldi stared at Morozov.

"So," Morozov said, "which alternative would you prefer, Grimaldi?"

Grimaldi averted his eyes, which were welling with tears. His world had crumbled, there was nothing left. Nothing but shame and disgrace. What choice did he have? Rot in some stinking Lubyanka dungeon, or be covered with ridicule. How could he face the public humiliation? He was a proud man, he had dedicated his entire life to the Company, he had made a brilliant career. And now he would become the laughing-stock of America.

"Well?" Morozov lashed out coldly, looking at his watch. "I don't have all day."

Grimaldi swallowed and licked his dry lips. "What do you want?" he asked Morozov.

Alex's brother smiled thinly and sat down beside him.

Chapter 17

AS THE BALMY MAY NIGHT softly invaded the peaceful city
of Geneva, Nikita Srebrov sat, immobile, by his hotel room
window. The Grand Hotel Mondial faced the silvery lake,
and Srebrov's eyes were glued to the city symbol, a graceful plume of
water spurting high above Geneva's skyline. His clothes were hung in
the closet, his toilet articles neatly laid on the marble slab in the bathroom. Books and papers were neatly stacked on the small desk by the
telephone. He was already dressed in a conservative blue suit, a plain
cream-white shirt, and a paisley tie. He stole a look at his watch. It was
7:48. In twelve minutes exactly, abandoning all his belongings behind
him, he was to leave his room, sneak out of the hotel, and defect to the
United States.

He was forty-three years old, plump and balding, and he looked at the
world through huge, sad eyes of deep brown color, which some women
found utterly disarming. His English was excellent, his French adequate.
He had spent most of the last sixteen years as a close assistant to Dimitri
Morozov. He had been with him in Paris, then back in Moscow; he was
always close behind him when their Wet Affairs team carried out its
spectacular coups, in Helsinki, Kabul, Frankfurt, or Mexico. A resourceful chief of staff, he made the machinery work to perfection, smoothly

orchestrating the arrivals and departures of agents, the prompt supply of forged passports and documents, the timing of operations, the swift dispersal of escape vehicles. Pedantic as a German, and an excellent organizer, Srebrov saw himself as a contemporary Atlas, carrying the entire Department Thirteen on his shoulders. Morozov held him in high esteem, although he was a bad shot and a source of desperation for his karate instructors.

In his younger years Srebrov had enjoyed the adventure and the danger. He had relished the sensation of belonging to the upper crust of Soviet society. He drove a 1988 Volga, lived in a spacious apartment off Gorky Street, owned the traditional dacha south of Moscow, and his two boys went to a special school. His wife Katya was fat and plain, with a trace of mustache on her upper lip, but she was an able anesthesiologist and earned a fine salary of 220 rubles a month at Moscow's Lassov Hospital. He must have loved her once, he thought, but couldn't remember when and why. He didn't love her anymore; actually, he couldn't stand her — she was too vulgar and a constant nag. He found refuge in his fascinating work and his rare stamp collection. The love he denied Katya he wholeheartedly gave to his country. Even Gorbachev's reforms and the disintegration of the Soviet empire hadn't influenced his views, or so he had thought.

But all that was before his trip to America, in the early fall of 1989. Dimitri Morozov had sent him to Florida to supervise the assassination of a Cuban exile, Miguel Garcia. Garcia's extremist organization was apparently financed by the CIA. According to certain sources, it planned a coup against Fidel Castro.

Srebrov had arrived in Miami at the end of September, and for twelve days had done nothing but stalk Garcia and prepare the operation. He carried an Australian passport which identified him as a Czech-born engineer who had immigrated to the Down Under in 1982. He had brought over his hit team, briefed the agents on the operation, traced their escape routes, and equipped them with weapons which had been smuggled over by another unit. But on the eve of the coup a cryptic message had arrived, advising him to wait. The day after, a second message had ordered him to be ready for immediate action, but a third one canceled the previous orders and instructed him to stay put.

Srebrov understood that a power struggle was being waged at Moscow Center, perhaps even at the Kremlin. His suspicions were soon confirmed by a Department Thirteen courier, an old buddy of his with whom he held a crash meeting in the cocktail lounge of the Fort Lauderdale airport. "This motherfucker Gorbachev objects to your project," his friend the courier said bluntly. "He actually objects to all our projects. All he wants is détente with America. He thinks we should stop all wet operations against Americans. He'll sell us down the river without a second thought. There are rumors that he even wants to disband Department Thirteen."

Srebrov was angered, but not surprised. Gorbachev's betrayal had been the main topic of gloomy conversations at the department canteen. Morozov, who had supported Gorbachev initially, was now ready to wring his neck. Morozov had said it, in so many words, and even added that something should be done before it was too late.

Srebrov now leaned toward the courier, who was blissfully sipping a frozen margarita. "What's the bottom line?" he asked. "The men are waiting, what should I do?" Over the loudspeakers, an angel's voice was chirping something about Florida's clean air regulations.

"Wait," was the answer. "Until they decide what to do, wait. Stay in Orlando, Miami, Fort Lauderdale, but don't come back. As long as you're here, Dimitri can pressure Gorbachev into action. He can say that the team is in place and it's too late to call the project off. But if you come back to Moscow, Gorbachev will kill the entire operation. And kill Thirteen as well."

Srebrov, therefore, had waited. For three long weeks, which was the first vacation he'd ever had, and his first long stay in America. During those three weeks he fell desperately in love with America, with her sweet, tempting way of life, the beautiful beaches, the rustling palms, the happy hours, deep-sea fishing, cable TV, tequila sunrises, grass, football, Pontiac Trans Ams, Disney World, and a golden-haired and brown-skinned sex goddess who had been born in Indiana and was a waitress at a seafood place; her name was Heather, but everybody called her Cookie.

He never found out if Cookie had been served to him by some devious scheme of Department Thirteen's archenemy, Alex Gordon. As a matter of fact, he didn't care. He wasn't one of those famished sex maniacs who gladly discarded their principles and betrayed their country for a juicy young girl. He was a cool-headed, conscientious Soviet agent. Yet, Cookie's ravenous sexual appetite and her astounding expertise in bed amazed him; he hadn't suspected that women could be so inventive. He also had a great time discovering some of South Florida's hot spots with Cookie, and spending thick wads of Gorbachev's money on her.

But most of the time, wherever he went, he thought how wonderful his life could be in this warm, sunny paradise. He thought of weekends in the keys, and fishing expeditions to Bimini and the Grand Bahama, seafood dinners on the waterfront, wild nights in the glamorous discos and nightclubs. He visualized himself and Cookie, dressed to kill, being shown to their table in a gourmet Boca Raton restaurant by a pompous headwaiter wearing a tuxedo and a European accent. It didn't have to be Cookie, actually; South Florida was swarming with Cookies and other delights from all over America. He stared with tremendous envy at the young Americans, certainly less gifted than he, parking their shiny new cars in their driveways and entering their neat, beautiful houses facing the Intercoastal Waterway, the ocean, or just a limpid, shimmering blue pool. And at night, screwing their leggy, sexy American women.

What have they got that I haven't? he kept asking himself. Why can't I live the same kind of life? I can make a fortune from the publication of my memoirs, on top of a fat bonus from the CIA. I can spend the rest of my life working on my stamp collection. I can escape from Katya and never see her again. Communism is the only gospel, that's certain, but in communist Russia I will never have this kind of life. And besides, Russia is falling apart; anarchy and famine will invade the country in a matter of months.

He let himself indulge in the fantasy of so many unhappily married men entering middle age — to start everything over again, in a new world, with a new woman, and do all the things he had wanted but hadn't done in his life. For most men it was just a fantasy; but for him, a high priest of the KGB, a coveted prize for the CIA, it was within reach.

Obsessed by these thoughts, he almost felt relieved when he was approached by a friendly couple in a crowded North Miami bar. It was his last night in America. The Garcia project had been definitely shelved, and the following morning he was to return to Moscow via Mexico and Havana. After a couple of drinks, his new acquaintances began blabbering something about a friend of theirs, a magazine publisher, who wanted to print interesting stories in his magazines, and . . . "my goodness, you are such an interesting man!" He understood immediately what the nice Mr. and Mrs. Ozack wanted; they had CIA stamped all over them. He agreed to meet their friend in Europe in a few weeks. He had no doubt the publisher friend was one of Alex Gordon's men. When he went home to pack that night, he thought Mr. and Mrs. Ozack had saved him a phone call. If they hadn't contacted him, he would have called Alex Gordon himself. He had already memorized Langley's phone number.

It took another six months to prepare the operation. He didn't tell Katya, of course. He stealthily emptied his stamp albums into numbered glassine envelopes, which he stacked at the bottom of his suitcase, under his clothes; they were the only memento of his former life he was going to take with him, in a money belt he had prepared for his escape. He knew he would miss the kids, but as they grew up, they resembled their mother more and more, and this thought itself would dispel his longings. One day, perhaps, he would bring them over to America, just for a visit.

He had flown into Geneva last Monday for a routine meeting with the Department Thirteen *rezident.* The Americans made a final contact with him; their operational team was in place. Today, in his hotel room, he ranged the envelopes containing his stamps in his money belt and wrapped it around his flabby waist, under his body shirt. The first thing he would do in America, he thought, was go on a diet and start working out in a health club. That decision made, he shaved and combed his hair across his skull, to conceal the expanding bald spot. In America they had lotions against balding, and if those didn't help, there were hair transplants. A hair transplant was very expensive, but with the CIA money, he could afford it. Perhaps he could even require it as a part of his new identity. He sprayed his face with Gucci aftershave, took his time dressing, then lit a cigarette and sat by the window, waiting for H hour.

He glanced at his watch again. One minute before eight. He got up, put his key in his pocket and left the room. A film of sticky sweat formed on his palms, and nervous spasms squeezed his stomach. He took the elevator downstairs. His mouth was dry, and he almost jumped when the elevator stopped at the third floor and another man got in. The elegant lobby was full at this hour, with many guests clustering around the concierge desk and the main entrance, on their way to dinner, theater, or a concert.

He went to the newspaper stand and bought the *Journal de Genève.* Perhaps one of Dimitri's watchdogs was in the lobby, secretly stalking him. Dimitri often sent people from the inner security unit to shadow his own operatives, for fear of defection. But Srebrov couldn't attract anybody's suspicion. He was coatless, he wasn't going out, and he had made it a habit, the last four days, to buy the *Journal de Genève* before dining alone at the hotel's Alpine Restaurant.

He stepped behind the newsstand and turned the corner into the shopping arcade. It was deserted, and the shops were closed. He walked quickly toward the men's bathroom. The hotel barber shop faced the door marked HOMMES. It was dark. He boldly approached it and turned the handle. The door was unlocked. He breathed the smell of oils, shampoos, and lotions hanging in the air. In the dark, the two chrome and leather thrones resembled monsters from outer space. The second door, in the back of the shop, was also unlocked. He stepped into a narrow corridor, came down three steps, pushed another door, and found himself in an inner court. The cool evening air was a caress against his burning cheeks. A cab was waiting in the courtyard, its engine droning. He opened the back door and sat down, beside the immobile figure huddled across the seat.

The cab sailed smoothly into a narrow, quiet street. At the corner it turned right into a brightly lit avenue and merged into the stream of identical-looking Geneva cabs. A few minutes later they were on the highway leading to the French border.

All that time the passenger beside him didn't say a word. As they left the outskirts of Geneva, Srebov turned to him. He was blond, very handsome, with ice-cold, calculating eyes. "Good evening, Vladimir Ivanovich," he said in soft, impeccable Russian. His handshake was strong but brief. "My name is Alex Gordon."

ALEX WAS DETERMINED to start Srebrov's debriefing without delay. That same night, in a secluded farm south of Grenoble, he held the first session with the defector. Srebrov's name meant "silver" in Russian, yet Alex swiftly realized that the man was a gold mine. Gifted with the memory of a computer, Srebrov produced an endless string of facts about Department Thirteen's operations, assassinations, forgeries, blackmail, and agents abroad. He disgorged concise reports about methods and techniques — the weapons used, the poison labs, the three revolving hit teams, the bank accounts abroad — as well as the department's hierarchy and plans for the future.

But for Alex the most precious information was the detailed portrait of his brother that Srebrov drew, trait after intimate trait, starting with his taste in clothes and food, and ending with his strange friendship with the dying, cancer-ridden Oktober.

For two full weeks the defector spoke softly, soberly, to the delight of Alex and his interrogation team. Except for his repeated requests for a new identity and a new home in Florida, Srebrov performed flawlessly. But it wasn't until the last day that he disclosed his most explosive secret, which left Alex astounded.

They were sitting over coffee and chocolate cake in the dining room, sipping the steaming brew from earthenware mugs by the table made of black logs. At Alex's elbow a tape recorder was turning noiselessly. The lights were on, despite the early afternoon hour. Outside it was raining, a warm, late-spring rain that gently drummed on the window shutters while feeble gusts of wind wailed in the chimney shaft.

"So he hates Gorbachev," Alex was saying.

"Hates him? He wants to kill him," Srebrov snapped, munching a mouthful of the rich cake. Noticing the amused smile on Alex's lips, he added: "I'm serous, Alex, he is going to kill Gorbachev."

Alex squinted. "What are you talking about, Nikita?"

Srebrov wiped his mouth with the back of his hand. "I'm not part of this affair," he said cautiously, "and I don't know all the details. I've only put together some bits and pieces I happened to overhear during the last few weeks. What I've heard is, Dimitri is going to bump off Gorbachev."

In recent years, Srebrov's story went, a secret group headed by Dimitri Morozov had formed inside the KGB, then gathered support in the army, the party, and even among some stray intellectuals. The movement was named "Pamyat," which meant Memory, the memory of eternal Mother Russia. It was a hard-line, reactionary group whose tough communist ideology was laced with Russian nationalism and harsh anti-Semitic feelings. Their ideas were similar to Stalin's wartime blend of communism and nationalism, which he had used to stir patriotic feelings among his countrymen.

Alex nodded. "I've heard about Pamyat, but I didn't know it had anything to do with Morozov."

Srebrov chuckled. "Some say that Pamyat's black uniform was introduced by Morozov. He dresses only in black, you know."

Alex was intrigued. He had seen, in English and German newspapers, several stories about the black-clad Pamyat activists. Their interviews were full of confused gibberish about the purity of the Russian race. The interviews, interspersed with hard-core communist dogma, were accompanied by pictures of long-haired men with burning eyes, photographed on a background of ancient weapons, religious icons, Russian flags from the Napoleonic wars, and pictures of Lenin and Stalin.

The KGB inner circle of Pamyat leaders, Srebrov went on, was deeply worried by Gorbachev's reforms, and believed he was leading the Soviet Union toward a civil war. "They say communism and Western democracy cannot mix. A communist state and a communist economy cannot coexist with free political parties, free elections, and a free press."

Alex nodded. "They're right."

"But that's exactly what Gorbachev is trying to achieve. Morozov believes Gorbachev is a disaster for Russia. He has already lost Eastern Europe, Nicaragua, Angola, Ethiopia, and Iraq. He agreed to the reunification of Germany. He is responsible for the revolts in the Baltics, in Georgia and Armenia. Russia isn't a world power anymore, but a country on the verge of anarchy that begs food from the Germans and the Americans. That's Gorbachev's fault, and that's why Morozov thinks Gorbachev must be stopped."

"By assassination?" Alex was still skeptical. Srebrov's story seemed rather farfetched.

"Yes," Srebrov said gravely.

"Who knows about this?"

"Very few people. Even Morozov's closest assistants are kept out of this affair."

Alex tried to think objectively about the idea. In Gorbachev's Russia the KGB was indeed the great loser. If détente brought freedom, democracy, and friendship between Moscow and Washington, there would no longer be any need for KGB spies, assassins, and torturers. The KGB bosses blamed Gorbachev for all their troubles. From their point of view, the assassination plot made sense.

"What are their plans?" Alex asked Srebrov.

"As far as I know, Morozov intends to carry out the assassination on foreign territory, so that it won't be linked to the KGB. The murder will be disguised as an accident."

"Foreign territory, you say?" Alex walked over to the window and looked out through the slits in the shutters. Gray clouds were clustered around the Alpine peaks, a dark mass pressing against the whitecapped mountains. "Where? What country?"

"Your country, of course," Srebrov said mildly.

Alex turned around sharply. "What are you talking about?"

"Gorbachev will visit the United States in the spring of 'ninety-one. The assassination will take place during this trip."

Alex watched him over the rim of his mug. "That's ridiculous. Gorbachev will be under our protection from the moment he sets foot in America. The KGB can't operate in the States."

"Well . . ." Srebrov was apparently enjoying Alex's bewilderment. "Morozov, it seems, has a trick up his sleeve: a secret ally in the United States. A rich, very powerful American."

Alex frowned. "Who is he?"

"I don't know who he is. No name was ever mentioned, and I understand that Morozov has a private channel of communication with this man. The rumors say he is an industrial tycoon, heavily invested in the Star Wars project. He is going to lose billions if the détente between Moscow and Washington prevails. If the Americans keep disarming, they won't need Star Wars gadgets anymore."

Srebrov finished his chocolate cake and clicked his tongue, contemplating his clean plate. "You see," he chuckled, "our right wing and your right wing have a common interest. Get rid of Gorbachev. May I have some more of this cake, please?"

SREBROV'S REVELATIONS were still echoing in Alex's mind when he boarded the Air France flight from Paris to Washington. Srebrov himself was flown to the States on a Company jet, bound for the CIA airfield at Fort Leary, Virginia. He was to spend a couple of months there, for a detailed, in-depth debriefing.

But Alex doubted if Srebrov knew any more about the plot against Gorbachev. Srebrov had only heard a rumor. But if the rumor was true, it could change the history of the Soviet Union, and perhaps the world. If Gorbachev was assassinated, the hardliners would seize power in Moscow. The Soviet Union would fall into the hands of his brother and a ruthless junta. Détente would be drowned in blood, Russia would become an evil empire again, and cold war would break out anew.

There was no time to lose. Alex's mind, already in gear, was swiftly tracing a plan of action. He would cancel all existing operations. He would set up an emergency headquarters far from Langley, in Washington or New York. He wouldn't inform his superiors yet. He would work outside the framework of the CIA. Dimitri's mysterious ally was involved in the Star Wars project; therefore, he must be a leading figure in the aerospace industry. Alex's men would fan out over the country and screen owners and presidents of aerospace companies; then, when the search narrowed down to a few names, he would tap their phones and place them under surveillance. That would mean breaking the law, but he had an emergency on his hands, so the hell with the law.

He should also alert Grimaldi in Moscow and instruct him to find out more about Pamyat's intentions. Top Hat must have his own channels to KGB inner circles. On the other hand, Grimaldi shouldn't be informed of the plot against Gorbachev. Alex had never completely trusted Grimaldi. And that night, at the Rockville motel, he had felt strange vibes, watching the looks Grimaldi and Kalinin exchanged. There was something between those two he couldn't fathom.

The flight attendant brought him an iced vodka, and the thread of his thoughts was broken. He raised his eyes. Across the aisle sat a lovely blond girl in a white minidress, with long flaxen hair and graceful shoulders. She was tenderly embracing the young man who sat beside her. He had long, fair hair, the lean, sensitive face of a dreamer, and a passionate mouth. She was about Tatiana's age at the time of her death. They looked very much in love.

Alex was oddly perturbed; he stared insistently at the couple, unable to take his eyes off them. Feeling his intense stare, the girl turned toward him, then stiffened, smiling uncertainly, and averted her eyes. Alex felt a pang of raw envy. They were so happy, dammit, so much in love! They seemed to belong to another world, another life. What has happened to me? he thought. The young man across the aisle, that was me, not so long ago. Passionate, romantic, desperately in love. I liked music and poetry, I trusted people, life was fun for me. Now there's nothing left.

What kind of life do I have? It isn't mine, anyway, it belongs to my brother. He's the one who fills my thoughts and stirs my emotions. His picture hangs in my office, and the most intimate details of his life fill thick files that I keep in my safe. I know more about him than about myself; I know what he likes to eat, drink and smoke; I'm more interested in one of his casual paramours than in my own wife. I spend my days and nights with him, dogging his steps, striving to penetrate his mind and guess his thoughts. I'm with him when he confers with Oktober, when he brutally enters a woman's body, when he snaps an emigré's neck, pumps bullets into an Afghan president or a Ukrainian dissident.

He closed his eyes and pressed the cold vodka glass against his cheek. Tatiana was the cause of this blood feud. But Tatiana had departed from his life long ago. And his revenge, trailing in the wake of her memory, had become his unique purpose in life.

When he was a little boy, Nina had told him the story of the Taj Mahal. The beloved wife of an Indian prince had died, and he had decided to build around her coffin a splendid shrine. His architects and engineers toiled for many years and raised a most beautiful palace around the black coffin of his dead wife. But when he stepped inside the palace, the prince realized that the coffin didn't belong there; its small, grim shape offended the pure beauty of the marble dwelling. The prince turned to his slaves, pointing at the coffin. "Take this thing away," he said.

That's me, he conceded. I built a black Taj Mahal, a machine of revenge, around my lost love; I dedicated my life to avenging her death. But now it is the revenge and not Tatiana's memory that haunts my mind. Tatiana doesn't matter anymore. I removed her from my sinister Taj Mahal long ago. My feud with Dimitri has become an end in itself, the essence of my life. And it has already consumed my youth, and Claudia's love.

When he arrived home night had fallen, and the house was dark. The children were apparently with Sandra, a friend of Claudia's who lived two blocks away. They often spent the night there when Claudia was on a business trip. Sandra had two girls of approximately the same ages as his kids. But something was wrong, Claudia wasn't supposed to leave until the end of the week.

His bodyguard turned on the lights and began his routine tour of the ground floor, checking the rooms thoroughly. Alex entered the living room to fix himself a drink. He immediately saw the letter, lying on the silver tray beside the cognac decanter. And even before he tore open the envelope and unfolded the single plain sheet of paper, he had guessed the ominous news it concealed, a verdict long delayed but no less cruel for that.

"I am leaving you," Claudia wrote.

* * *

CLAUDIA HAD DONE HER BEST to make her marriage work. She had swallowed her pride after Alex betrayed her in Paris. She had given him another chance when he proposed to her that night in Baltimore. She had given up her career, had carried his children, had been at his side whenever he needed her.

But he hadn't needed her. Perhaps in the first year of their marriage, when he was still a trainee, he had. That was their best year, and she had naively believed that the nightmare was behind them. She met a lot of new friends, most of them young CIA wives. She and Alex spent a lot of time together. She had the baby and they moved into a pleasant house in Chevy Chase. They never spoke of Tatiana.

Then Alex completed his training, became an operational agent and started traveling. She didn't know where he went or what he did. He didn't tell her, for security reasons.

But Washington had other means of communication. It was the CIA wives' tom-tom, broadcasting with lightning speed any scrap of information concerning their husbands' dark trade. That way she learned that Sandra's husband was being transferred to Covert Operations; that Caroline's husband was involved in the Iran-contra affair; and that her own husband had tried to assassinate, in Paris, a top KGB man named Dimitri Morozov.

A surge of bitterness had swelled inside her. He hadn't forgotten. His first step, fresh out of the training center, had been to rekindle the strife with his brother. Because of Tatiana.

And her nightmare had started again.

"Time heals all wounds," she had said to Alex that night in the dark Baltimore bar. But time hadn't healed his wounds. Instead of trying to forget, he had embarked on a bloody quest for vengeance. He didn't care about her, he cared about Tatiana. She, Claudia, was the convenient wife tucked away in the house, cooking his meals, pressing his shirts, raising his children, while he traveled the globe, fighting his crazy brother for a woman they had both lost.

The maddening frustration didn't leave her for a single moment. Did he really love her? Or was she only a substitute for his Russian princess? When he smiled at her and talked to her, he was probably thinking of Tatiana. When he made love to her, his eyes closed, he must be making love to Tatiana. She was jealous even of Tonya. When he held the child against him, caressing her blond hair and touching her milky cheeks, he must be hugging Tatiana.

Her Alex went through an ugly metamorphosis before her eyes. The sensitive, decent young man for whom she had fought so desperately, gradually withdrew into himself. His natural curiosity faded away, his sense of humor dried up, his cheerful smile changed into a guarded expression. His casual clothes were replaced by strict, dark suits and ties. He turned into a cold master spy, fanatically dedicated to his private war. He raised a wall between them, and never let her get close. He traveled abroad often, and when he was in Washington, he came home late. He had little time for the children and no time for her. Her rival was dead, but her shadow still obsessed him.

For years she had suppressed her pain, avoiding a confrontation. It was her foolish pride, she thought. She couldn't go through another humiliation. She was afraid to talk things over with Alex; he might deny everything and accuse her of unfounded jealousy. She tried to develop other interests, started painting, returned to the fashion business. She smoked a lot, and began drinking in secret. Finally, after Nina's death, she couldn't play games anymore.

"Alex, what's happening to us?" she softly said one night after they had made love. He had performed mechanically, without passion; he now lay immobile beside her, his profile etched against the white window curtains. "Our marriage is falling apart, and you don't care. Does Dimitri matter more than your family?"

"I don't know." He didn't bother to deny he was fighting a private war against his brother. "I can't help it, Claudia; I won't have any peace until I destroy him. He's an evil man."

"I don't know if you'll destroy him," she said. "But you've already destroyed us. You don't care about me or the children. You're obsessed by your revenge. You're still fighting your brother over a dead woman." She averted her eyes, she felt so degraded.

"No," he said, "It's not her, it's him."

"This madness has already cost Nina's life," she went on. "Isn't that enough?"

"No!" He jumped out of bed, trembling with fury. "No, on the contrary! That's one more reason to get rid of him. You don't know what kind of man he is. He hates our mother, he hates my father's family, he is a compulsive murderer." She had never seen Alex like this, his eyes burning, his face distorted, the words spewing hatefully from his mouth. "There is nothing sacred to him — he would go for you and the kids if he only could. That's why I have people watching you all the time."

"But I can't live like that!" Claudia shouted. "All these bodyguards make me sick! I don't have one private moment." She tried to control herself. "Alex, let go, for God's sake! There's a wonderful life out there, and it's passing us by."

"Later," he said stubbornly. "We'll have a great life later, after I get rid of Dimitri."

"But you never will get rid of him," she said wearily. "You're two old, scarred fighters, circling around each other, staggering, bleeding, unable to win and unable to call it a draw."

"No," he said. "No." His eyes still burned with that strange fire. "I have a plan, trust me, I know what I'm doing."

She got out of bed and ran downstairs. She spent the night on the living room couch, smoking and getting drunk. She couldn't make him change his mind. She should have left him that very night, she thought later. But she still loved him. She couldn't bear the thought that their wonderful love had turned into torment.

Lately she would often stand before the mirror and look at herself. She was still very attractive; she could perhaps find someone to care about her. Men turned their heads to look at her, and she was often approached, in the supermarket, the department store, even in the street. A couple of days ago a handsome boy, much younger than she, had approached her at a Washington gallery, and she accepted his invitation for a drink the following afternoon. But at the last moment she decided not to go. She could guess what was bound to come afterward. Not that she didn't want it. She did. She yearned for a fervent embrace, for a body burning with passion, for someone making love to her hungrily, all night long, proving to her she was wanted. But she had decided that the day she wanted another man, she would leave her husband.

Actually, the episode with the young man had been the last straw. Time to move away, Claudia, she said to herself; time to start again, old girl. She packed a couple of suitcases, collected her paintings, and drove with the children to Sandra, to say good-bye. On the porch Sandra hugged her tight. She was crying. "Take care, Claudia," she said, "you deserve a little happiness."

She reached her mother's house in Brooklyn after midnight. Her insistent knocking woke up Mrs. Benevento, who appeared at the door, gray hair disheveled, an old dressing gown thrown over her shoulders. "Claudia," she gasped. "What happened?"

She hugged her mother. "Now, don't say anything. I left Alex. I'm here with the children. They're in the car, asleep. I want to leave them with you for a while, I have to find a small apartment in New York and a new job."

"The kids are in the car?" her mother repeated, her hand darting to her chest.

She nodded.

Her mother shook her head. "I saw this coming, as God is my witness. Didn't I tell you, Claudia, you should never have left Stevie."

"Mother, don't. Please." It was so humiliating.

The old woman stared at her with compassion, then nodded and sighed. "I'll help you with the kids."

Claudia left Brooklyn at dawn, after the children were sound asleep. She drove into the awakening streets of Manhattan. The city was peaceful at that early morning hour, the sidewalks empty, the asphalt deserted. The sky was pale blue, and the first rays of the rising sun painted the towers of the World Trade Center in liquid gold. She rolled down the window. The air was still cool and pure. Arriving in New York alone was a strange feeling for her, scary and yet thrilling, full of uncertainty, but also of promise. A new beginning, which she so deeply wanted to be, at last, a good one.

DIMITRI'S AGENT, who followed Claudia to New York, reported to him every move she had made since leaving Alex. After a couple of weeks in a small East Side hotel, he stated, Claudia Gordon had rented a loft in Soho and returned to work with Havermeyer. The press announced her comeback — a new collection would be presented the following spring. At the same time, she was approaching the Soho galleries, trying to exhibit her paintings, but without success.

A couple of months later Dimitri's agent witnessed another development in Claudia's life. At a party in the Village, Claudia met a handsome English businessman, Robin Westlake, who was a dedicated art collector. They were seen together at restaurants, Broadway shows, and mostly at art exhibits. One night Claudia was seen entering Westlake's apartment building in his company. She came out late the next morning. The same thing happened the following night, and the next.

"Claudia Gordon and Robin Westlake have become lovers," the agent's report solemnly concluded.

Dimitri couldn't help smiling.

Chapter 18

Alone in a black company sedan, unshaven, shivering with cold, Alex Gordon watched the entrance to Claudia's building in New York for the third night in a row. On the two previous nights she hadn't come home at all; now it was already two-forty A.M., and he had to face the inevitable conclusion: she was spending her nights with a lover. A stab of raw jealousy pierced his gut. Who was the man she had left him for? Who was the one who held her in his arms, kissed her mouth? Claudia was a part of him; they had grown up together, spent half of their lives together. She had saved his life once, and been at his side all through his adult years. How could she conceive the rest of her life without him? How could she now be intimate with someone else? He missed everything about her, her spontaneity, her stubbornness, her passion, even her jealous scenes. She had gotten under his skin much deeper than he had ever realized.

His throat constricted with a bitter feeling of loss. He tried to chase the maddening thoughts from his mind, but the distressing images kept parading before his eyes. He had been betrayed and humiliated. His Claudia was in bed right now with another man. Who was the man? He could put his team on her trail, of course, and in twenty-four hours find out all the lurid details. But he wouldn't use his official position to settle his private affairs. Besides, he couldn't bear the thought that his marital problems would become public knowledge.

The only person he had spoken to was Sandra, Claudia's friend. He had spent a long evening with her, a month after Claudia had left him. Sandra had been astounded by his distress. "I didn't suspect you loved her so much," she admitted.

"I didn't say that," he said defensively.

"You didn't have to."

After a long hesitation Sandra had agreed to give him Claudia's address, and he had called Claudia several times. She was very restrained, very civil, but cut short his hints at a reconciliation. "Don't even think about it," she said bluntly. They reached an agreement about the children, though; she would have them during their vacations, he during the school year. When they were with him, she would fly to Washington once a week to spend the afternoon with them. She made a point, then, of not seeing Alex, and when she called to speak to the children and Alex answered, she refused his pleas to meet with her. "It's no use," she said, "It's over, Alex."

Alex, meanwhile, had been surprised by the intensity of his own pain. Perhaps he wasn't as cynical as he thought, perhaps his family mattered much more to him than he had wanted to admit. He couldn't imagine his life without Claudia at his side. He kept replaying in his mind the scenes from their past, since the day he had met her in Brooklyn. It was a torment. He was unable to speak to the children about their mother, was at a loss before Tonya's frank, cruel questions. "Don't you love each other anymore, Daddy? Are you going to get a divorce? What will become of me and Victor?"

With Claudia gone, he had lost his peace of mind. He couldn't stay home nor could he carry on with his office routine. He hired the widow of a former agent, Brad Cunningham, to take care of the children, and escaped to New York.

His new project, the search for Morozov's secret American ally, had come at the right time, he thought; he would be so deeply immersed in the operation that he wouldn't have time to feel sorry for himself. He had a cot brought to the operational headquarters he had established at New York's Rockefeller Center. He slept there at night, while reports from all over the country arrived by fax, phone, and teleprinter. But he couldn't stop thinking of Claudia, of the danger of losing her for good.

That was why he had gone to beg Sandra for Claudia's address.

Now the radio in his car suddenly came to life in an outburst of static, and Angel Soltero's voice filled the receiver. Soltero was a young, irreverent agent of Puerto Rican origin, with a slight body, a birdlike face, and dark, veiled eyes. "Robocop to Rambo," he announced. "Robocop calling Rambo."

Soltero had a mania of using his own private code based on film heroes. Beside Robocop and Rambo, he had business dealings with Rocky, Batman, Ghost, the flatliners, and of course, Pretty Woman.

"Go ahead, Angel," Alex said wearily. He had instructed Soltero to put an end to his childish game, but he didn't intend to pursue his reeducation at three in the morning.

"Wherever you are, you'd better fly back to base," Soltero solemnly announced.

"Why, what's the matter?"

"We found your man, Rambo."

"You did." He was suddenly wide awake. "You personally?"

"With the help of the flatliners, of course." The flatliners were several FBI agents of the CI-3 counterintelligence squad that Alex had commandeered, thanks to his good relationship with their New York bureau.

"Who is he?"

"I give you three guesses, Rambo."

"Jesus, man, will you stop this stupid game?"

There was a short pause, for effect. "Devereaux," Soltero breathed finally.

"You're sure?" Bingo, he thought, my hunch was right.

"Positive."

"How did you find out?"

There was a silence.

"Angel? Angel, do you read me?"

Soltero's voice came over the radio again, strangely subdued. "I'm afraid you won't like the answer."

"I'm on my way," Alex grunted. He started the engine and gunned the car through the empty streets of New York. Soltero's message, if it was true, crowned months of strenuous work, which in the beginning seemed like looking for a needle in a haystack. Alex's men had spread across the country, vetting chairmen and owners of companies that specialized in space hardware, radar, lasers, rocket and missile research.

The first list consisted of more than a hundred names, but a couple of months later, after a thorough check of the tycoons' political opinions, it had been winnowed down to twenty-five.

The list was eventually narrowed to five names. Alex's suspicions had focused on an elderly Georgia millionaire, Alfred Devereaux, one of the major Star Wars contractors. He was a right-winger with murky Ku Klux Klan connections; he had declared several times that after Gorbachev, Russia would become America's worst enemy again. Therefore, the Star Wars project should be continued.

Alex had been ready to bet on Devereaux, but he had not a scrap of evidence to support his suspicions. Now here was Soltero, calmly announcing that he had positively identified him as the man conspiring to assassinate Gorbachev. He wondered how Soltero could be so sure.

Soltero was waiting for him by the skating rink at Rockefeller Center. He was wearing studded jeans, a leather jacket, high-heeled boots, and a mischievous smile. Alex suspected he consciously dressed to fit the stereotypical image of a Puerto Rican as seen by his colleagues. "Will you buy me a cup of coffee, gringo?" he asked. Thank God, he had put Rambo and Robocop to sleep.

Alex nodded. He was in no mood to enter his gloomy lair, up on the seventeenth floor, and start looking for a clean spoon and an unused plastic cup. They went around the corner to an all-night restaurant and ordered some coffee and chocolate cake. The aging waiter, who spoke only a few words of English, had trouble understanding them, and Alex repeated his order twice. He then turned to Soltero.

"I'm listening, Angel."

"Two weeks ago," Soltero started, "I had a long talk with Jack Caldwell of the flatliners. He thought we should look into the past schedules of our suspects — "

"Which suspects?"

"All of them." He passed his fingers through his hair. "We assumed there must be regular contacts, at least once a month, between Morozov and his buddy over here. We decided, therefore, to check the schedules of all our suspects during the last two months, looking for any unusual contacts. Which we did. It turned out to be" — he mirthfully swallowed the last piece of chocolate pastry — "a piece of cake."

"What is it I won't like?" Alex asked impatiently.

Soltero raised his hand. "Alex, let me tell it my own way."

"Okay, go ahead." He beckoned to the old waiter, who refilled their cups. "Where do you come from?" Alex asked.

The man smiled, revealing decaying teeth. "Odessa," he said, "Russia."

Angel raised his arms in mock despair. "The Russkies are here already," he said. "Why don't we just give in?"

But noticing Alex's cold stare, he hurriedly continued. "We verified the time employ of our suspects, as I said. And we found out that six weeks ago Devereaux made a three-day trip to New York. He had a few bona fide appointments, and one non–bona fide meal. He lunched at La Côte Basque with a stranger, a man the flatliners couldn't identify. But I have his description for you."

He took a sheaf of papers from his jeans pocket and leafed through it. "Here it is." His voice had suddenly acquired the same tone as before, on the radio — pained, and very serious. "The party who met Devereaux was a man of about sixty-five to seventy years of age. Deep tan, green eyes, dyed hair and mustache, striped shirt, silk tie, double-breasted blazer with two rows of gold buttons, gray twill trousers, Gucci loafers . . . wearing a lot of flashy gold jewelry, several rings, and a bracelet."

Alex took a sharp intake of breath. There was only one man he knew who fit that description. Grimaldi.

"When was that?" he managed, a wave of fury swelling inside him. He made a tremendous effort to control himself. Grimaldi had been here and met Devereaux. Devereaux was suspected of being Morozov's partner. Grimaldi was posted in Moscow, where he had ample opportunities to meet Morozov. He had all it took to be the ideal courier between Morozov and Devereaux. There was only one logical explanation for Grimaldi's meeting with Devereaux: he was Morozov's agent. Napoleone had crossed over.

He frantically racked his brain, trying to conceive of a different explanation, but to no avail. Grimaldi couldn't have met Devereaux by coincidence.

Soltero was looking at him oddly. "When was that lunch?" Alex repeated.

"Six weeks ago. We checked. It coincides with Grimaldi's last home leave. He had crossed the border by car from Montreal, flown from Buffalo to the Farm, and after debriefing, had returned to New York for two weeks."

Alex shook his head, his feelings a mixture of disbelief and resignation. "What's your source?" he asked.

"The maître d' and two of the waiters at La Côte Basque. He spoke to the maître d' in French. The man was a gourmet, knew his way around French cuisine."

"Did you show them pictures of Grimaldi?"

Soltero nodded. "We came back three days after the first interview, with a few photographs. The waiters picked Grimaldi's photograph out of the display. Sorry, Alex."

Alex was nodding mechanically. Yes, there could be no doubt who the rotten apple was. The dirty traitor, he thought. How could he betray his country at the end of such an impressive career? And Dimitri, how did he recruit Grimaldi? What had been Kalinin's game when he came to Washington?

His devious brother was playing a new game, he thought. But then he remembered Srebrov, and Cookie, and slumped back in his chair. He had stolen Dimitri's man, and Dimitri had stolen his own. He and his brother were back in the ring again, bleeding and exhausted, locked in absurd combat. What had Claudia said? Two old fighters, stumbling and staggering, but still punching each other, unable to win and unable to call it a draw.

"You, keep on with your work as usual." He pointed a finger at Soltero and got up, leaving a dollar bill on the table. "I'll have to double-check your report with Moscow."

"Why?"

"Perhaps Grimaldi has a logical explanation," he said. "Perhaps it was an innocent lunch."

"Innocent." Soltero's voice was heavy with sarcasm. "You've got a spy in Moscow who's been fooling these KGB dummies for years. Your own Scarlet Pimpernel. Your spy sails unscathed through all the KGB traps, he comes and goes from Moscow at will, without anybody even bothering him. What is his secret? Your answer is — the man is a hero. And your hero happens to come home on leave, and happens to know our prime suspect, and happens to have lunch with him. Innocent, my foot, Señor Alex."

"Perhaps he has a legitimate explanation," Alex stubbornly repeated.

"Do you believe that? Really?"

Alex stared blankly at him and turned to go.

* * *

Morozov was waiting for Grimaldi in the backseat of his Volga, at Tatarskaya, a gloomy street off Lenin Square. It was getting late, a dry wind was rising from the east, and people were hurrying home, chased by the fierce onslaughts of winter. A long line for vodka snaked around the block, the men shivering and stomping their feet. As he saw Morozov's profile in the car window, enveloped in the smoke of his soldiers' cigarette, Grimaldi clenched his teeth in disgust. He hated the young sonofabitch — his mannerisms, his black clothes, his ascetic habits. Morozov had made him admit his own weaknesses, and turned him into a traitor.

But what could he do? Refuse, that day at the Kosmos Hotel, and be exposed, kicked back to America and covered with ridicule? Admit before his peers that his sexual lust had blinded his senses, and that for the last forty-five years he had unwittingly served as a tool of the KGB? He'd rather die than face them, hear their cynical remarks and their mocking laughter, imagine what they were saying behind his back. The story would certainly have ended up in the papers. No, he had to lie low, keep passing Kalinin's phony reports to Washington, complete the present project with Morozov and Devereaux — then retire somewhere very far away, where they'd never find him.

What a mess, he thought. He was identified with Top Hat, the greatest American mole of the last fifty years. Some mole! For years Oleg had been feeding him first-rate rubbish, concocted in the Lubyanka disinformation workshops. And he had gullibly swallowed it, because he loved Oleg. He hadn't seen him since the Kosmos meeting. He clenched his fists. If he saw Kalinin again, he might strangle him with his bare hands; he had never suspected he could be so ignoble. They had been lovers, and Oleg had betrayed him. Perhaps Oleg had never loved him, only used his body to draw him into that sordid trap.

He opened the car door and slid into the back, beside Morozov. The chief of Department Thirteen touched the driver's shoulder, and the man started the engine. The car darted forward.

"Where are we going?" Grimaldi was very jumpy lately.

Morozov shrugged. "Nowhere. We'll cruise around town awhile, it's safer that way." His voice sounded tense.

"Why the precautions, Morozov?"

The younger man stared at him, his black eyes gleaming in the falling dusk. "Gordon is after you," Morozov said. "He is investigating your connections with us."

A chill descended upon Grimaldi, a terrible fear, and for a moment he was speechless. "What are you talking about?" he finally managed. His throat was dry. "Who told you that?"

Morozov didn't answer, just looked absently out the window.

"What is your source?" Grimaldi repeated.

"I have good sources," Morozov said. "Gordon must have smelled something. Srebrov, perhaps."

The interior of the car was suddenly hot and stuffy. Grimaldi wiped perspiration from his brow, then unbuttoned his collar and rolled down the window. The wind whipped his flushed face. He saw a long line of cars waiting outside a service station.

"I don't believe it," he mumbled. His tongue was thick and sticky. "Srebrov is a fool, and besides, he doesn't know a thing. You told me that yourself." There was no way Alex Gordon could have found out about him. Nobody in the KGB except Morozov knew about their connection. Still, if Alex discovered his role in the plot, he was a dead man.

"How do you know he's investigating?" he asked again.

Morozov continued to gaze out the window. "He's already sent three coded cables to the political officer at the embassy, to inquire about your contacts with Soviet officials."

The political officer was the CIA resident. He didn't know anything about Grimaldi's assignment. But if Alex had instructed him to investigate Grimaldi/Saint-Clair, it meant Alex suspected him of something fishy.

"How do you know? You broke the embassy code?"

Morozov said nothing. And Grimaldi understood. The man was as cunning as the devil; he still had access to the embassy. Even after the Marines' scandal, and the debugging of the entire building, Morozov still had ways to penetrate the embassy's secure rooms. Or perhaps he had planted new bugs in the political section.

"You must stop him," Grimaldi said, mopping his forehead with a silk handkerchief. "You must stop Gordon."

Morozov grimaced. "Easy to say. The man is well-protected, even better than your president."

"You have to smoke him out," Grimaldi said urgently. "Lure him to . . . Paris, to Havana, bring him here. You must get him under your control. If he really finds out about the Devereaux affair, it will be my funeral. And yours," he added viciously.

Morozov glanced at him slantwise, lighting another pestilent ciga-rette. "Any ideas?" he asked.

THE PURPLE CAB turned the corner and came to a stop before the house in Washington where Claudia used to live with Alex and the children. She caught a glimpse of her face in the cab's rearview mirror. She saw her eyes glowing with anticipation, her mouth harboring a secret, mis-chievous smile. She could barely contain her excitement. In a moment she would hug her children, and then it would be time for the big surprise that she had been planning for the last three weeks. She was as thrilled as a little girl about to receive the doll of her dreams.

It wasn't the first time she'd come back home. Since she had reached her agreement with Alex, the children lived with him most of the year. She flew in from New York every week to spend a few hours with Tonya and Victor, but had avoided seeing Alex. Recently, he'd been busy somewhere in New York. She preferred it that way; she didn't want to talk to him and reopen old wounds.

She loved the afternoons with the children. She would take them out, to the movies, a shopping mall, or a fast food restaurant. But she couldn't stand the sight of the CIA bodyguard who followed them everywhere. It was the same man most of the time, a bearlike middle-aged agent with heavy jowls, suspicious, beady eyes, and a brown hairpiece. A cigarette was always stuck in the corner of his mouth. Tonya claimed the bear's name was Babcock; she had once heard her father call him that. Claudia felt like Babcock's prisoner. Wherever they went, she could sense his stare boring into her back. It was infuriating. Another of Alex's manias, she thought, another result of the insane brothers' war.

The afternoons they spent together were too short, and the disgusting bodyguard was getting on her nerves. She dreamed of a relaxed, long weekend alone with the kids, in a place where no one could find them. She spoke to Robin about it, and he encouraged her. "If you feel like that, love," he drawled in that fabulous accent of his, "just do it! Go ahead, be a sport." So, with Robin's help, she had concocted a plan to give the slip to the bodyguard, then sneak away with the children for a weekend in the country. She told nobody about it; only Robin knew.

She prepared everything down to the last detail. It was exciting, like planning one of Alex's covert operations. She rented two rooms at the Chesapeake Inn for two nights. She bought warm clothes and presents for Tonya and Victor. It had been fun, choosing windbreakers, sweaters, and shoes, especially for Tonya, who was on the verge of becoming a young lady now. She loaded the clothes and her own stuff in a Thunderbird she rented at Washington National Airport, then drove to the city and parked the car behind the Savoy 3 Cinema, off Dupont Circle. She even wrote a letter to Alex, which she would leave with the housekeeper, explaining that she'd taken the children away for a weekend and they would be back on Sunday night. She also intended to call him from Baltimore or Chesapeake City and reassure him.

She then took a cab home. As they reached the house, she asked the cab driver to wait, ran up the steps, and rang the doorbell.

Her plan worked perfectly. The housekeeper, Mrs. Cunningham, was very nice, and promised to give the letter to Alex when he came back. Tonya looked ravishing in a new jeans outfit. She was wearing her hair long now and looked very feminine. She hugged Claudia lovingly. "Mommy, I have a boyfriend," she whispered excitedly in her ear. "His name is Jimmy, he is the coolest guy in our class." Jimmy, of course, was mad about her and was going to become a rock singer. But he was also interested in space travel.

Tonya's confidences were interrupted by Victor, who jumped on his mother, grinning toothlessly, screaming with delight. He was almost seven, a healthy, merry child who had inherited her complexion and her ardent black eyes. He insisted on examining the belly of the small toy robot she had brought him, and of course broke it in thirty seconds flat, which was an endurance record for a toy. She and Alex used to joke that they should buy Victor a hammer to go with every toy they brought him, so he could dispose of it faster.

They piled into the cab, then drove off, the CIA car trailing behind them. Only then did she tell the children about her plan. They were going to spend the weekend touring the Chesapeake Bay area. They would drive to Baltimore by country roads and spend the night at the Chesapeake Inn. The following morning they would board a round-the-bay cruise and visit the historic community of Havre de Grace. The next day they would take the car and explore the surrounding rivers, forests, and Civil War battlegrounds.

Victor was thrilled. "Will we see Indians?" he kept asking, clapping his pudgy hands and shooting imaginary arrows in the air. Tonya was very excited, too, but didn't calm down before securing her mother's promise that she could call Jimmy from the hotel. They all agreed it was going to be a fun weekend. But just before leaving the cab, Victor spoiled things a bit by asking if his daddy would join them. Claudia felt a throb of nostalgia, looked away, and stiffly walked to the cashier's booth of the Savoy 3 Cinema.

The movie was *The Gods Must Be Crazy*, which they'd already seen twice. The theater was full of kids and teenagers laden with popcorn and giant Cokes. Claudia and the children sat by an exit door. She noticed Babcock take a seat on the opposite side of the cinema. As soon as the lights went off, she prodded the children, and they smoothly sneaked out of the dark hall. They were in the Thunderbird and on their way in seconds. "We did it!" she announced happily. The children cheered, and Victor jumped excitedly on the front seat.

A half hour later they had left Interstate 95 and were on a deserted road that wound through the peaceful Maryland countryside. Claudia was lecturing the children about the name Chesapeake, derived from the "Chesepiook" — the great shellfish bay — of the Algonquin Indians, when she noticed two other automobiles in her rearview mirror. One of the cars gathered speed and came very near, tailgating her own and turning on its lights.

"Mommy, what does he want?" Tonya cried out in alarm. Victor turned back in his seat and merrily waved at the blazing headlights. Claudia, suddenly terrified, tried to accelerate, but the second car overtook them, cut sharply into their lane and braked, swerving slantwise and blocking the road. She hit the brakes and her car stopped with tires shrieking, inches from the other automobile.

Four men jumped out of the cars and converged upon Claudia's Thunderbird. Good God, she realized, they were carrying guns! She frantically fumbled with her seat belt. Tonya was screaming in fear, burying her face in her hands. Panicked, Claudia tried to lock the car doors, but she was too late. Two of the strangers, whose faces were covered with ski masks, yanked the right side doors open and pulled the children out of the car. Another man pointed a gun at Claudia. "Don't move!" he shouted.

Claudia hurled herself upon him, wildly clawing and kicking. The man seized her by the waist, then slipped, and they both fell on the asphalt. She tried to grab his gun, but he punched her in the belly, a tremendous blow that left her stunned. The other assailants dragged the wildly resisting children toward the first car. Tonya was screaming and pounding on her kidnapper's chest with her fists; Victor was twisting and kicking, yelling shrilly.

Claudia heard the roar of another car engine and turned. A third car appeared and braked beside them. Babcock, whom they had left in the Savoy Cinema, jumped out of it, pulling his gun. She hadn't fooled him after all.

With surprising speed for a man of his age, the burly agent fired several shots. The two men holding Tonya and Victor seemed confused. Tonya wriggled free and dashed toward the roadside ditch. Her captor feebly tried to raise his arm, then swayed and slowly collapsed, a dark stain expanding on his chest. The man holding Claudia threw her aside and aimed his gun at Babcock, but Claudia jumped on him and plunged her teeth into his hand. The man cried in pain, and his gun clattered on the road. He hesitated a moment, then ran toward the first car.

The man, who had Victor was holding him like a human shield and firing back at Babcock. Claudia let out a hoarse shout and darted toward him. She saw the gun's barrel pointed at her but didn't care. The masked man let Victor go and fired. "Mommy, Mommy!" the little boy cried out, scurrying toward her, his arms open, his little face wet with tears. He had almost made it when he suddenly lurched and crumpled, his arms spread wide. Claudia was beside him in two steps and collected him in her arms. The child was gurgling, breathing unevenly, and her open hand on his back, holding him against her bosom, felt the sticky touch of blood.

She heard shouts in a foreign language, and running steps, mixed with a few scattered shots. Their assailants dashed to the front car, carrying their wounded with them, then the car bolted forward and took off. "Mrs. Gordon!" somebody shouted hoarsely, probably Babcock. Tonya's voice was suddenly very close, and Claudia groped for her daughter, who knelt beside her, screaming hysterically. Then she heard more voices, and car engines, and the place was swept with lights. But she stayed there, squatting on the narrow road, and gently rocked her son's little body, feeling his spasms subside and the tremor of his limbs slowly fade away.

* * *

A COMPANY HELICOPTER waited for Alex at Baltimore-Washington Airport and flew him to First Memorial Hospital. It was almost midnight. From above he could see the lights of the hospital landing strip glowing in the shape of a cross. An icy shiver ran down his spine. The child was badly wounded, they had said to him in New York, but alive. Alive, that was what counted. He jumped on the tarmac, bending before the ferocious wind, and ran into the emergency entrance. God help him survive, he thought, help him through this war he should have had nothing to do with. Victor's toothless smile flashed before his eyes. What the hell were they doing in Maryland? he asked himself for the thousandth time.

A white-haired nurse was waiting for him outside the emergency room. "I am Nurse Gannett," she said. "The child is in surgery, Mr. Gordon. Will you come with me, please." They walked quickly past an old man in a wheelchair and two young nurses, softly giggling, their white shoes squeaking on the linoleum. A lovely blond woman with an inflated belly painfully trudged toward them, pushing a stand on wheels from which hung a plasma infusion. Behind a closed glass door a telephone was ringing forlornly.

A sign over two swinging doors said: SURGERY — AUTHORIZED PERSONNEL ONLY. The nurse led him into a spacious corridor with gleaming white walls. A heavy odor of antiseptic filled the air. White beds with green plastic mattresses were lined up along the wall. Against the opposite wall stood three chairs, and by them, leaning on the wall with a paper cup in her hand, he saw Claudia.

"Here you are," the nurse said, "Dr. Fuldheim will be with you shortly." She disappeared behind another door.

Alex's eyes were glued to his wife. He hadn't seen her since she'd left him. She wore a beige sailor's coat with large buttons, tan pants and brown boots. Her pants were covered with black and brown stains and were torn over her left knee. Her hair was a mess, falling limply on her shoulders. There were dark smudges under her eyes, and a fresh scratch across her left cheek, between her ear and the bridge of her nose.

"Hello, Claudia," he said.

She nodded.

"How is he?"

Before she could answer, the exit door opened and Nurse Gannett was back, followed by a tall, athletic man of about sixty, with grizzled hair and sharp features. He was dressed in a surgeon's green outfit. "Mr. Gordon?" His voice was weary. "I am Dr. Fuldheim. Your boy is still in surgery. We are doing all we can. I'm afraid his chances are very slim. He was hit by two bullets in the back. His lungs and some major blood vessels have been severely damaged."

Alex stared back at him. "But he's alive?" he asked.

Fuldheim looked at him oddly. "He is still alive, yes. But as I said, his condition is critical."

Alex turned to Claudia. "Where's Tonya? What happened to her?"

"We are taking care of your daughter," Nurse Gannett interjected. "She is in a state of shock. We've — "

"She was wounded, too?" Alex interrupted hoarsely, his eyes darting between the nurse and Claudia.

"No," Nurse Gannett said calmly. "She's okay, but she has suffered tremendous emotional stress. She was hysterical and we had to sedate her. She's asleep now, she'll be all right."

Alex turned to Dr. Fuldheim again. "What are my son's chances?"

Fuldheim laid his hand on Alex's shoulder. "Mr. Gordon," he said, shaking his head sadly, "you must face the truth. Only a miracle can save your little son."

The surgeon and the nurse hurried back to the operating room. Alex stared vacuously after them. His knees wobbled and he slumped in one of the chairs. His son was dying. Victor might not come out of the operation alive. He couldn't let that happen, he should do something. But what, good God? He had done something, indeed — for the last fifteen years he had been doing something, and in exchange he was about to get the dead body of his little boy.

He looked around. Claudia was speaking to him, but he didn't hear. Right now, his daughter was in some dark room, stuffed with drugs, haunted by a living nightmare that would mark her for life. Claudia stood before him, bruised, battered, lucky to be alive. He suddenly thought of Nina, remembering the glazed look in her eyes the day before she died.

All these people were dead or suffering because of him. Because of his war with Dimitri. Because of his vendetta, Nina had died, and Victor was about to die, too; Tonya was tormented by boundless fear. Claudia had run far away. But not far enough.

His grim thoughts were interrupted by Nurse Gannett. "An urgent phone call for you," she said.

He followed her to a small cubicle, where a telephone sat on a desk piled with papers. He picked up the receiver that lay beside the phone. "Yes," he said.

It was Babcock. "My findings confirm my initial report," he stated bluntly.

Alex took a deep breath. Right now he didn't give a damn about Babcock's findings.

"Your wife's car," Babcock went on, "wasn't followed by anybody except me. We found the two cars used for the attack, one on the scene of the shooting, the other outside the Baltimore airport. Both cars were rented in Baltimore this morning, long before Mrs. Gordon took her plane for Washington. It was an ambush, Alex."

His mind on Victor, he had trouble following the agent's report, so he asked him to repeat it twice. Only when Babcock started telling his story for the third time did he grasp the startling meaning of his words. "Wait," he said, leaving the receiver off the hook. He returned to the surgery ward. Claudia stood where he had left her, sipping from her paper cup.

"Claudia," he said. "I'm sorry to have to ask you these questions, but we must know. What were you doing with the kids on the road to Baltimore?"

"What difference does it make?" she asked, without looking at him.

"It's important. We must find out who attacked you."

She turned back to him, her face dejected. "I wanted to be alone with them," she began, then told him about her plan to spend the weekend with Victor and Tonya on Chesapeake Bay.

"Who else knew about this?"

She frowned. "What do you mean? Nobody knew."

"Nobody?"

The blood drained from her face. "Robin knew, of course, he helped me plan the entire thing. Are you trying to insinuate — "

"Robin is your friend?" Even at this moment, he couldn't pronounce the word boyfriend. "What's his last name?"

"Westlake, why?" She grabbed his arm. "Alex, what's going on?"

"Come with me," he said.

She hesitated, looking in anguish toward the operating room doors, then followed him to the small office. "Babcock? Check right away on a man called Robin Westlake. . . ." He paused. "You're right." He turned back to her. "His name doesn't sound American."

"He's a British citizen," she said stiffly.

"Address?" Alex asked, stifling his jealousy.

She hesitated, then gave an address on New York's Upper East Side and a telephone number.

Alex repeated the information. "The man is British," he said. "Check with immigration as well. Call me back." He hung up.

"What's all this about?" she flared, "Do you suspect Robin?"

He took her by the shoulders. "Believe me, Claudia, I pray to God that your Robin has nothing to do with this. Because if he has, I'll never forgive myself."

He leaned on the window, resting his forehead on the ice-cold glass. He did hope Claudia's lover wasn't involved in the plot. He already blamed himself for not having screened Westlake thoroughly. But he'd been held back by his foolish pride; he couldn't bear the thought he would be shadowing his rival in the streets of New York. Besides, he had feared that Claudia might accuse him of interfering with her private life. But this was exactly what Dimitri would have arranged: a lover for Claudia, then a deadly ambush for her and the children.

Alex took Babcock's second phone call an hour later. Claudia stood beside him when they spoke, waiting for the verdict.

It was a grim verdict indeed. Robin Westlake wasn't at home, Babcock announced. A search of his apartment had established that some of his clothes and toilet articles were missing. The doorman had seen him leave the building with a suitcase and take a cab to the airport shortly after six o'clock. Immigration reported that a Robin Westlake, British passport number 47592845, had left the country aboard a TWA flight to London. The ticket had been purchased four days before.

Claudia stood motionless, white as a sheet. Alex took a step toward her, but she turned and ran away. Her steps echoed in the long, empty corridor. He gave chase, and lost her for a moment at the brightly lit entrance, then discerned her shadow in the parking lot outside. He caught up with her only when she stopped, breathing shallowly, by the parking lot fence. She was distraught, casting frenzied glances about her.

He gently took her by the shoulders, but she struggled violently in his arms. "Let me go!" she muttered fiercely, her body trembling. "Don't touch me!"

The night was bitterly cold. The moan of the easterly winds was interrupted by the occasional wail of an ambulance siren. He stared at her, a broken, betrayed woman shivering from cold and humiliation. He could guess the feelings that were raging in her heart. She had left him, after fifteen years, and fallen in love with another man. Her lover had given her happiness, he had made her feel beautiful and attractive. And now she discovered that her lover had been a devious enemy, a man who didn't care for her, who had used her to destroy her family. The man she loved had planned the kidnapping, and probably the killing of her children.

"Claudia, listen to me," Alex said.

"Leave me alone."

"Don't blame yourself. You couldn't possibly have guessed." He looked away. "This is Dimitri's doing. I'm sure he sent Robin Westlake after you as soon as he learned that you'd left me."

She didn't answer, and he went on. "There is something I want you to know," he said. "I'm leaving the Company."

She didn't look at him.

"I'm in the middle of an operation," he said slowly. "It will take me two or three more months to complete. It's an important project that might influence the future of this country. As soon as it's over, I'm leaving the Company. I was a fool, I realize that. You were right all along."

She kept silent. Her mouth was sullen, her eyes hostile.

"Let's go in," he said. "They might have news about Victor."

The mention of Victor's name brought her back to reality. She turned and hurried back into the surgery area. There was nobody in the waiting room. She fumbled in her bag, lit a cigarette, then smashed it under her heel.

A nurse they hadn't met, a young black woman with a generous mouth, entered through the swinging doors. "You are Mr. and Mrs. Gordon? Your daughter wants you."

Tonya's room was dark. Alex made out her shape lying in the bed, and the blond hair spilling over her pillow. "Mommy?" she said. "Daddy?" Claudia stepped forward and grasped her right hand.

"Daddy?" Tonya said again. Her voice was slurred. "Where are you?"

"Right here, princess." He bent over her and kissed her cheek. "Give me your hand."

He took her left hand, facing Claudia across the bed.

"How's Victor?" Tonya asked.

"We don't know yet, sweetheart," Claudia managed. She was crying.

"Can we go home?" Tonya said. "Can we go home, please?"

VICTOR DIED at dawn. They had done everything possible, Dr. Fuldheim said, but the child was doomed from the start. Alex shook his hand. "Thank you, Doctor," he mumbled, then collapsed in a chair, wrapping his coat around him.

"My baby," Claudia murmured, her voice cracked. "He's gone, Alex."

He raised his face toward her, shaking his head. He couldn't speak. No, he hadn't realized that it could end like this. An innocent little boy had died because of his foolish games. It had all been his doing. A Russian gun had shot his son, but his own hand had pulled the trigger. A feeling of terrible guilt swelled in his chest.

"Claudia," he breathed, reaching for her. "Claudia!" But he couldn't utter the words that seared his gut like a red-hot iron. What have I done? Claudia, he wanted to say. What have I brought upon you and the children! What have I done to Victor, who bears my father's name!

Victor Wolf suddenly emerged in his mind, a powerful, faceless presence. I've failed you, Father, Alex thought. I wanted you beside me, that's why I gave your name to my child. But I gambled with his life and I betrayed your memory. If you only knew that your son's life is dedicated to his brother's destruction! You wrote that "brothers forever are one." But these two brothers want each other's blood. Now I've had to see my son die to realize what madmen we've turned into.

A hoarse moan escaped from his throat, and he burst out crying. He turned to the wall, his body torn by violent spasms, and buried his face in his trembling hands. He was unable to look into Claudia's eyes, as shrill sobs poured out of his chest.

Claudia's hands hesitantly touched his shoulders, his face; then she gently pulled him to her bosom, stroking his hair. Her whole body was trembling; he knew she was probably crying, too. She didn't speak, just held him tight, and he felt grateful to her, for not making him face alone the demons he had unleashed.

When he raised his head, she was still bent over him, looking at him gravely. "I — " he began, and bit his lip. "I want . . ."

She took his face between her hands. Her face was puffed and her eyes had a lifeless look. "Tonya is waiting," she said, her fingers softly stroking his skin. "Let's take her home, Alex."

Chapter 19

FAR AWAY, the Kremlin clock towering over Spasskaya Gate struck three times. In the darkness of his small office, Dimitri leaned back in his chair and lit a cigarette. He was used to the blackness of night, and loved its soothing, velvety silence. At these predawn hours, when nothing stirred, when even his night-shift orderly slumped, exhausted, in his seat, Dimitri's mind was sharp as a razor. Night was his realm, solitude his element, and these were the hours when he conceived his most devious intrigues.

His cigarette glowed faintly in the dark, and the smoke hovered before him like an old, thick spider's web, swirling in the air and slowly dissolving. He had learned the advantages of night, like so many of the secrets of his trade, from Oktober, who was a night predator, too. But Oktober had died a week ago in terrible pain, his skeletal body finally yielding to the cancer that devoured his flesh.

In Oktober's cold, monastic alcove, Dimitri had witnessed, appalled, the final phases of the old man's malady. Oktober was the only human being he felt attached to, the only man whose advice he valued. His only friend. He needed him badly. He wanted to help him, but didn't know how. Oktober had stubbornly refused to take medicine; his last wish had been to die at his farm, by the Kliazma River, and Dimitri had driven him there in a howling snowstorm. Death, however, hadn't waited. When they arrived at the farm, which was nearly buried in snow, Oktober was already a rigid corpse, his mouth gaping in horror, his glazed eyes fixedly staring into the raging tempest. He had been denied his final peace, and according to an old peasants' superstition, was doomed to haunt the bleak lands where he was born, till kingdom come.

Where are you, Oktober, when I need you so badly? he thought. When I can use your cunning, your intuition, your wicked mind? Dimitri had been so close to breaking his brother and making him his prisoner; yet his foolproof plan had failed because of an elderly bodyguard and Alex's crazy wife. And because of his incompetent field agents, who had blown their easiest assignment ever.

He hadn't wanted to kill little Victor Gordon, of course. He didn't kill children, and besides, he needed Victor and his sister as hostages. He wanted to kidnap them and use them to blackmail Alex into abandoning his investigation of Grimaldi and Devereaux. He couldn't let his brother interfere with his project.

Gorbachev was becoming more of a threat with every passing day. He had let this white-haired demagogue, Boris Yeltsin, usurp Russia, had let the Balts kick out the Soviet army and the Germans unite again. He had authorized Jewish emigration to Israel and groveled before Israeli cabinet ministers, receiving them with full honors at the Kremlin. Capitulating before the Americans, he had even joined their pack against Russia's longtime friend and ally, Iraq's Saddam Hussein. Instead of helping Saddam, as in the past, he had meekly agreed to an American offensive against Iraq, which was imminent. Gorbachev had to be done away with, and if the plot could be kept secret for just another six weeks, he would be.

This had been Dimitri's goal in kidnapping Alex's kids: a six-week reprieve, until Gorbachev came to Washington, where he was going to die. Dimitri knew his brother's sentimental side, and his wife's devotion to the children. He had no doubt that if the kidnapping had succeeded, Alex would have promptly abandoned the Devereaux investigation, to save Victor and Tonya.

But at the crucial moment his inept operators had panicked, killed the little boy, and escaped. The plan had failed.

Help me, Oktober, he thought. I need some other scheme to lure my brother into a trap. Every man has a secret lever that can make him act irrationally, risking everything, even his life. What's your secret, Alex? What's your lever?

He closed his eyes, summoning his conversations with Oktober from the depths of his memory. "Hit his family," Oktober had said to him in this very room, his sly eyes burning. "Hit his relatives, in Russia and abroad. He is obsessed with his family." That was true, his brother's foolish quest for family was his Achilles' heel. But Nina was dead, Claudia and Tonya well-protected, and he hadn't found any of Alex's relatives in Russia.

A memory surfaced in his mind, and he reached for the intercom button.

"Yes, Comrade General." The voice of Sereda, his orderly, was slurred with sleep.

"Come over." He leaned back, drew on his cigarette, and turned his desk lamp on.

Two minutes later there was a soft knock on the door. Sereda walked in with a steaming cup of tea and a Swiss milk chocolate bar, broken to pieces in a small dish.

He pushed the dish aside. "I asked you, quite a while ago, to get me the file on Victor Wolf." For years he had been requesting the file on Alex's father, hoping to find the names and addresses of his surviving relatives there. The last time had been about six months ago.

Sereda nodded. "Victor Wolf, Comrade General. I remember that. The Jewish writer, the 1949 trials. I asked for the file several times, I even went myself to Central Archives at the Lubyanka north wing. They say there's no such file. I asked them to check again, but I didn't get any answer."

"No such file?" Dimitri repeated. He had gotten the same response in the past. "How could that be, Sereda? The man was arrested, tried, and condemned. He must have not one, but half a dozen files."

"That's what I told them, Comrade General. The only explanation they could offer was that the documents might have been filed in some other section."

Dimitri took a sip of the strong, fragrant brew. That was Soviet Russia, he thought, his anger rising. Incompetence, bureaucracy, irresponsibility wherever you turned. "All right," he said. "Check under the Anti-Fascist Writers Committee records. The 1949 trials. The Seventh District

Tribunal records. The Vorkuta prisoners' records. The lists of prisoners who died at the camps."

Sereda was scribbling on his pad, licking his meaty lips.

"It's all computerized," Dimitri said. "It's a matter of minutes. You can access this information on our own computer. Do it, right away, and come back with the file."

Sereda came back the following night. He was nervous, fidgeting with his pads and pens. "I checked everything you told me, Comrade General," he said, and swallowed hard. "No file."

THE DIRECTOR of the KGB Central Archives was a mousy, middle-aged colonel, with a sallow triangular face tapering to a receding chin; he had a small, bitter mouth and shifty brown eyes. Apparently terrified by the summons before the formidable chief of Department Thirteen, he perched nervously on the edge of his chair, sweat popping on his forehead.

"I want to know what happened to that file, Sevliev," Dimitri said, exhaling a long plume of smoke toward the little officer.

"I have no explanation, General." Sevliev's shrill voice was trembling with implied apology. "We found no trace anywhere."

"What do you mean, no trace?" Dimitri exploded, and Sevliev winced as if he had been slapped in the face. "The man was tried and exiled. He most certainly died. He existed, didn't he?"

Sevliev helplessly spread his arms. "I could have told you that the file might have been misplaced. But it isn't just one file. There must be quite a few dealing with Victor Wolf. And if there's nothing left in our archives, that could mean somebody has done a very thorough job. I believe that all the records concerning Wolf have been removed."

"Removed by whom?"

Sevliev raised his small hands again. "Somebody very high up, Comrade General. There's no other way files can disappear. We destroy records very rarely, only on explicit orders of the Politburo. This might happen in matters of national security."

"Victor Wolf never threatened national security," Dimitri snapped, killing his cigarette in a pewter ashtray he had inherited from Oktober.

"But if I may, Comrade General . . ." Sevliev raised his finger, like a schoolchild. "Last night I had an idea." His voice was uncertain.

"Perhaps . . . perhaps the name is on the restricted list, Comrade General."

Dimitri frowned. The restricted list was one of several items of ultrasecret information available only to very few top KGB officials. It could be accessed on the office computers by a special code word, changed weekly and distributed to the high officials in sealed envelopes.

"Why the restricted list?" Dimitri muttered. "He was not a head of state or a party official, just a bloody Jewish scribbler!"

"It was just an idea, Comrade General," Sevliev muttered, and awkwardly got up from his chair. An ingratiating smile tentatively touched his quivering mouth. "If you don't need me anymore, I'd like to return to my office. Perhaps my men have found something."

Dimitri dismissed him with a curt nod. After the diminutive colonel left the office, he turned on his own computer, which he used very rarely. He unlocked his safe and took out an envelope stamped with two purple stripes and marked Top Secret. He tore it open. This week's code word was *Nepobedimaya* — unvanquished. He chuckled. The political commissars didn't miss an opportunity for their propaganda. Lately they'd been pounding it into everyone's head that Russia had never been vanquished, which was false, of course.

He typed the preliminary orders on the computer keyboard, entered *Nepobedimaya*, his own code name and secret identity number, consulted the assistance directory, and typed the command for the restricted list.

READY, the computer flashed.

He typed: "Wolf, Victor, 1949."

The screen went dark, then a single phrase flashed across its surface, a long string of green, pulsating letters.

"I'll be damned," he gasped. His mind refused to digest the message. It was amazing, it couldn't be true! But the green phrase was there, announcing the astounding news, waiting for his response.

As the tremendous meaning of his discovery permeated his mind, a wave of savage joy surged inside him. Now I've got you, Alexander Gordon, he muttered. I've got you by your bloody balls. He punched the intercom button. "Get me the Raoul Wallenberg file," he said urgently.

*　*　*

ANGEL SOLTERO entered the small cubicle that served as Alex Gordon's headquarters in Manhattan. "Grimaldi's last report," he said, handing him a typed sheet of paper. "Just arrived by special courier from Langley; the witches had it decoded this morning."

The witches — the decoders — were Soltero's last addition to his glossary. Alex nodded absently. He was standing bent over his desk, examining the first draft of Gorbachev's itinerary for his forthcoming visit to America. He had underlined, with a red marker, Gorbachev's main stops: the United Nations and the Soviet embassy in New York; then, in Washington, the White House, the State Department, the Mint — why the Mint, of all places, for Christ's sake! — Arlington national cemetery, Capitol Hill, the Kennedy Center. A skilled marksman positioned near any one of these sites had a good chance to shoot the Soviet president. An army of policemen, FBI, and Secret Service agents would be deployed along Gorbachev's route, and still there could be no foolproof guarantee against a clever assassin.

Alex raised his eyes. "Let's see what Grimaldi has cooked up for us this time," he said, his glance taking in Soltero's smart suede jacket, gleaming with a dozen or so zippers, shiny buttons, and flaring epaulets. "Where are you going, to a bamba contest?"

"Tonight is salsa night, gringo," Soltero drawled.

Alex took the report from Soltero and perused it quickly. Reaching the last phrase, he winced, then grasped the desk for support. The room swayed around him, and he sat down heavily, staring at the document in amazement.

"Anything wrong, Señor Rambo?"

Alex didn't react, his eyes glued to the report. He swallowed hard and took a deep breath, trying to check the wild thumping of blood at his temples.

Grimaldi's report read:

Next week a Kremlin spokesman will publicly admit the assassination of Swedish diplomat Raoul Wallenberg in 1954, when he was a prisoner at the Vorkuta camp. The execution of Wallenberg was carried out in front of three other prisoners. The witnesses were kept alive, in total seclusion, probably to be used as pawns in the infighting of the Soviet secret services. Wallenberg's execution was carried out by the MVD, which was protected by future prime minister Nikita Khrushchev and Foreign Minister Andrei Gromyko. The KGB, which was the MVD's main rival in the

Soviet intelligence community, succeeded in getting hold of the witnesses, whisking them to a secret location, and protecting them for twenty-six years. Their testimony could be devastating for the MVD and its political allies. It could prove, if published, that the MVD was a bunch of assassins who didn't recoil before murdering a celebrated foreign diplomat.

All the records of Wallenberg's death were destroyed and even the executioners put to death, but two of the witnesses survived. The third witness, Pavel Michurin, died seventeen years ago.

With the release of the report on Wallenberg's death, the two surviving witnesses will be freed from prison and confined to the Siberian city of Pecora, which is located in the restricted zone, beyond the Arctic Circle. The survivors are Genadi Korchagin and Victor Wolf.

He stared at the paper. Victor Wolf. His father. Alive.

It was too good to be true. It was a trap. It had Morozov written all over it. Dimitri wanted to snare him. Dimitri knew of Alex's attachment to his father, of his admiration for Victor Wolf's views and his poetry. Dimitri would assume that the report about Victor Wolf being alive would ignite an overwhelming desire in Alex to see his father again. He would have no other choice but to try to penetrate Russia and reach Victor Wolf.

Alex clamped his jaws in anger. The entire Wallenberg story had obviously been conceived by Dimitri. Just for him. Dimitri had then used Grimaldi to transmit the report.

On the other hand, he thought, Dimitri certainly knew he would thoroughly examine the information. The KGB knew that Alex had other sources in the Soviet Union beside Grimaldi. If it was a lie, or a hoax, he would know it in twenty-four hours. Dimitri wouldn't have thrown him this bait if there was no truth to it.

He sat very still. What if the story wasn't a lie? What if Victor Wolf had indeed survived? And if his father had survived . . . he would be a man of seventy-eight today. Not impossible.

He raised his eyes. Soltero was watching him closely.

"Did you read this?" he asked.

Soltero nodded. "I've heard of Wallenberg, but not the details. . . ."

Alex leaned forward, clasping his hands to conceal their trembling. "Raoul Wallenberg was a Swedish diplomat posted in Budapest during the war. In 1944 and '45, in the last months of the Nazi occupation of Hungary, he saved thousands of Jews by giving them diplomatic protection. He disappeared when the Red Army marched into Budapest."

Soltero puckered his brow. "He was captured by the Russians, wasn't he?"

"He was abducted to the Soviet Union. The Russians apparently wanted him to spy for them after the war. He had excellent contacts in Switzerland, knew the chief executives of the Red Cross, had met the Pope, and was a man with a great future in Sweden." He drained the last drops of coffee from his paper cup and grimaced in disgust. "But Wallenberg refused, and vanished."

"He was never seen again?"

"Well," Alex said, "actually he was. Reports kept reaching the West that Wallenberg was alive. These were mostly eyewitness reports, saying he'd been seen in a prison or a gulag."

"And what did the Russkies say?"

Alex shook his head. His mind was still dazed with the news about his father. He visualized a snowbound field in the endless night beyond the Arctic Circle, a heavily patrolled gulag, dogs barking and searchlights rotating from watchtowers, a prisoner facing a firing squad, and three men dressed in rags watching the grisly scene. One of them was his father.

Soltero's voice repeating his question brought Alex back to reality. "What did the Reds say?"

"The Kremlin denied everything. They never saw Wallenberg, never heard of the man. But in the meantime, Wallenberg became a sort of folk hero, and a cult grew around him. Jewish survivors' organizations, the Swedish government, Wallenberg's family, and a very active Raoul Wallenberg Society kept assailing the Soviet Union with letters, petitions, newspaper campaigns. Wallenberg's life became the subject of several books and movies."

Soltero nodded.

"I personally believed he'd been murdered long ago. The Russians wouldn't keep such an embarrassing prisoner in their secret cells — he could only cause them trouble. But lately they started leaking strange stories to the press. Last year, Russian sources spread the rumor that in 1944 Wallenberg had acted as intermediary between Beria — the KGB director — and the chief of the SS, Heinrich Himmler. This year they broadcast another rumor — that Wallenberg had been a personal friend of Adolf Eichmann and other Nazi officers. He was also portrayed as a playboy and a womanizer."

Soltero spread his arms. "They wanted to discredit him."

Alex nodded. "Exactly. Which means they had something to hide." He paused. "Finally, as international pressure grew, the KGB invited some of his relatives to Moscow, handed them Wallenberg's passport, and informed them he had died of a heart attack in 1947, in the Lubyanka Prison."

"No better place for a heart attack."

"And now there's this report," Alex said softly, "informing us of his murder. One of the two surviving witnesses" — he took a deep breath — "is my father."

Soltero stared at him, speechless, utter stupefaction stamped on his face.

THE CONFIRMATION of Grimaldi's report came early on Friday afternoon, shortly before Alex flew home for the weekend. Following his request, the political officer of the Moscow embassy had called the newly appointed KGB spokesman — another sign of Gorbachev's glasnost — and was informed that the Soviet government, after a thorough investigation, had finally discovered the truth about Wallenberg's death. Yes, indeed, the affable KGB spokesman said, next Monday it would be officially confirmed that Wallenberg was murdered by the KGB. He had no knowledge, though, about any witnesses to the murder. That was probably just speculation, the cheerful spokesman said.

Alex read the cable again in the car that took him to La Guardia through the bustling streets of Manhattan. With Christmas approaching, the department stores glowed with thousands of electric bulbs, the shops displayed evergreens, trinkets, and artificial snow, and Santa Clauses in cotton beards rang their bells at street corners. The excitement was marred, though, by the grim newspaper headlines announcing that war in the gulf was imminent.

That evening, after Tonya had gone to sleep, Alex lit the fire in the living room, poured cognac in two large bell-shaped glasses, and brought them to the couch, where Claudia was curled up, staring into the flames. Since that horrible night in Baltimore, they spent as much time together as they could. Claudia stayed in Washington, because of Tonya, but once a week she flew to New York to spend a night with him, and he came home every Friday for a long weekend.

Since Victor's death, they both felt a strong need to be close to each other. They talked a lot, went out for long walks together, made love with long-forgotten tenderness. It was like a revival of their former passion. But Alex hoped it wasn't only an artificial explosion, caused by the death of their child. He was determined to do all he could to win back Claudia's love.

"I have something to tell you," he said now, sitting beside her. She snuggled against him, warming her cognac in her palms. He told her about Grimaldi's report. When he mentioned Victor Wolf, he felt her stiffen; then she turned back and looked at him with eyes full of anguish. Her face was deathly pale.

"Your father . . ." she managed. "Your father's alive?"

"Do you see what this means, Claudia?" he said softly. "It's a trap, I know it's a trap. This is my brother's ultimate weapon. He found my father and he's going to use him against me."

"I can't believe it," she said. "Your father is alive. Just think — the two of you meeting, hugging each other — " She stopped abruptly, looking at him in horrified understanding.

He nodded. "That's exactly what Dimitri has in mind. He believes that after I learn the news, I'll become obsessed with one thing — finding my father."

She got up, went to the window, and looked down at the dark street. "You think he knew all along that your father was alive?"

Alex didn't answer right away, trying to figure out his brother's strategy. "No," he finally said. "If he knew Victor Wolf was alive, he would have used him against me long ago. He wouldn't have tried to kidnap the children."

She looked at him sharply. "Why not?"

"The kidnapping was a desperate attempt, carried out on foreign soil, involving tremendous operational and political risks. He wouldn't have done that if he had an asset like Victor Wolf. He must have found out about him only recently."

"How could he find out?"

"Perhaps he stumbled on my father's name while reviewing the Wallenberg file. The Wallenberg affair is still a pain in the neck for the KGB; they always have to repel new accusations by world leaders. When he discovered that Victor Wolf is alive, Dimitri probably convinced his superiors to publish the truth about Wallenberg's murder and release the surviving witnesses. I bet he personally chose this city, Pecora, where my father lives now."

"Where is it?"

"In Siberia, close to the Arctic Circle. It's deep in the military zone; civilians from other parts of Russia are not allowed to go near it."

"Why?"

"The area is full of gulags and military bases." He paused. "Dimitri probably chose it to make sure I'd be completely in his power if I tried to rescue my father. He probably laid his trap, transferred the old man to Pecora, then dictated the report to Grimaldi. Dimitri might be in Pecora already, waiting for me."

She returned to the couch and sat beside him again. "He's sure you'll come?"

He nodded. "This report is my death warrant."

"If you play his game. He wants you to go to Russia to save your father." She puckered her brow in thought. "Only a madman would rise to this kind of bait." She left her glass on the carpet, then took his face between her two hands and looked at him. "You're going, aren't you?"

He didn't answer.

"I'm coming with you," she said.

He looked at her beautiful face, her stubborn mouth. "You must be out of your mind, Claudia."

"I'm coming with you," she repeated.

He shook his head. "No way. This is risky business, it could become very nasty."

But seeing the defiant look in her eyes, he realized it wouldn't be easy to dissuade her. He had to reason with her, but how could he when his own reaction was so utterly devoid of reason? Still, what could he do, leave his father to rot in a lost Siberian village? He had no choice, he had to go. But if he rejected Claudia now, he might not find her when he came back. If he came back.

"When Victor died," he said, "I swore to myself that I'd never leave you again. And I'll never again give you a reason to leave me. Do you believe me?"

They spoke for a long while, and only after midnight, when the logs in the fireplace had long turned to ashes, did they reach a shaky compromise: Claudia would accompany him to the point of entry to the Soviet Union and wait for him there.

The next morning he called Angel Soltero. "Hi, Señor Rambo," his incorrigible assistant chirped into the receiver.

"I want you to find out how I can get to Pecora," Alex said.

Chapter 20

THE FERRY WAS FULL of boisterous, jolly Finns on their way to Leningrad for a weekend of cheap drinking and gambling in the hotel lobbies that had been turned into casinos. They had boarded the ferry in their cars and buses, huddled in warm parkas and tasseled hats, and had begun drinking and singing even before the boat had started its short voyage.

Alex was dressed in a bright blue, fur-lined windbreaker, and a knitted ski hat with white, red, and blue stripes. He was carrying a Swedish passport in the name of Arne Blom. He had prepared meticulously for his trip, spreading misleading rumors, setting decoys, using every trick he knew.

His Austrian resident had leaked a report to a KGB stringer in Vienna, saying that Alex Gordon was arriving in Moscow on a Tarom flight from Bucarest; he was carrying a Yugoslav passport. Other reports placed him in a train coming from Prague, a tourist bus that had left Berlin the night before, a car crossing the Polish border, a physicians' delegation bound for a congress in Odessa. Simultaneously, a dozen Company veterans, carrying questionable papers, had arrived in the Soviet Union, using different ports of entry. Each of them could be Gordon; each one was submitted to a long and tedious interrogation by the authorities. They had been dispatched with a single goal — to draw Morozov's attention, and allow Alex to make his way into Russia unperturbed.

While his agents were busy playing hide-and-seek with Morozov's men, Alex planned to enter Russia by sea, on the Helsinki-Leningrad ferry. The northern seashore was the least guarded of Russia's borders; the passport control at Leningrad's pier 14 was a mere formality.

He had left Claudia on the snow-covered pier in Helsinki. He stared for a long while at her tall figure, beaten by the north wind at the edge of the pier as the ferry plowed the black waters of the Gulf of Finland. He couldn't help thinking that he might be seeing her for the last time. For a moment the rosy-cheeked, laughing face of little Victor surfaced in his mind, and his hands clawed in his pockets, as they had so many times in the past. Oh, Dimitri, he thought, if only I can lay my hands on you, I will make you pay for all you've done to me.

As the flat coast of Finland disappeared in the feathery patches of mist behind them, most of the passengers deserted the windswept decks to seek warmth in the cozy cafeteria below. But Alex couldn't stand the company of people. Not now, when he was approaching for the first and probably the last time the land of his birth. It could be the land of his death as well; Dimitri was certainly waiting somewhere behind the curtain of fog and low clouds that had settled on the Russian coast.

He stood alone on the freezing deck, peering into the grayness, and his whole life unfolded in his mind. He thought of the years he had spent at the CIA, devoting his energy, his knowledge, his ideas, to the endless combat against Soviet Russia. Was it worth it? he asked himself, then tried to banish the question from his mind. For the answer was an unequivocal no, it hadn't been worth it; nothing had been worth the cost in deceit and bloodshed. Not this foolish secret war, waged ruthlessly for so many years, nor the sacrificed agents, the bought spies, the double-crossed dead, the false traitors and the phony heroes. And for what? The Russians themselves had destroyed their empire, and we, with all our sophisticated weapons, alliances, missiles, and satellites, had precious little to do with it.

An icy wind blew at him from the south, and the gray fog wavered, breaking into trembling patches then fusing again. The contours of the Russian shore gradually emerged out of the mist, and his father's poem echoed in his mind. "I'll gladly die a thousand deaths . . ." He, too, would gladly die a thousand deaths to see his father just once in his life.

He had a dream, to publish his parents' poems one day, in their English translation. He already had the book's title: "The Pure at Heart." He was going to dedicate it to his living Tonya and his dead Victor. But the other Victor, his father, would Alex actually see him again? Would he hear his voice? How would it feel to call someone "Father"?

A lonely sea gull dived low over the deserted deck, then disappeared in the fog. Alex's heart was pounding a merciless beat, and he bent forward to gaze into the receding gray wall. Where are you, Dimitri? a forlorn voice called in his heart. Where are you, my brother, my enemy? Are you waiting for me at Leningrad's pier, in some dark alcove over the arrivals hall, watching the berth of the Helsinki ferry with a pair of binoculars, ready to whisper the order to shoot in your walkie-talkie? Or will you lie low until nightfall, then sneak into my hotel room and snap my neck as you did to my Tatiana? Will you stalk me on some lost highway in the frozen wastelands of Siberia, or wait in ambush by a roadblock with a team of your assassins, armed to the teeth?

Stop this daydreaming, he said to himself. Think, Alex, think! You know him, you know you're heading into his trap, you know his perverse methods of playing cat and mouse with his victims, luring them into his lair, delaying the kill until the last moment. He will let you get in, he'll make you feel secure, he'll let you surmount all the obstacles, and at the very end of the road he'll be waiting to destroy you.

They sailed into Leningrad harbor, preceded by black waves that shattered against the tall piers in clouds of murky spray. Small harbor tugs passed close by, spooky shadows gliding in the thick fog, hooting their mournful warnings. The sky was low and somber; he strained his eyes, looking for the famous landmarks of Leningrad — the rostral columns and the towering Peter and Paul Fortress — but the thick fog hovered over the noble city like a dark curtain. A huge sign, in Russian capital letters, proclaimed from the top of the Arrival building: ETERNAL GLORY TO THE HEROIC CITY OF LENINGRAD. The scarred waterfront was deserted; the bitter cold had driven away even the dockhands and the customs officials.

As the twin engines of the ferry roared in reverse, a half-dozen men in worn-out parkas and boots ran out of the customs building and spread out along the wharf to busy themselves with the boat's ropes and chains. Alex couldn't spot any KGB officers, in uniform or plainclothes. But the

KGB was relatively invisible these days, he thought. You didn't see them in the streets and the airports, didn't run into them when attending an opposition rally on Moscow's avenues; even the Kremlin guard had been handed over to the city police.

The only KGB officials you heard about were a handful of clowns, busy improving the public image of their murderous organization. They published second-rate, outdated secrets as proof of their goodwill; they starred at press conferences claiming their innocence, conducted organized tours in the Lubyanka, or feted on TV the newly elected "Miss KGB," a pretty, big-breasted, twenty-three-year-old woman named Katya Mayorova, who was supposedly very good on the firing range, in the karate gymnasium, and in the kitchen.

It all made good public relations, while the real KGB, the 400,000 officers, agents, and spies of the organization, made themselves scarce, waiting for their hour to strike. They hadn't been affected by the wave of poverty and hunger that swept Russia. Their privileges were intact, their apartments and cars untouched; their special stores still offered plentiful food and high-quality clothing. In the midst of the chaos that devastated Russia, the KGB kept its iron grip on the army, the Church, the Communist party. It secretly supported Pamyat and other nationalistic organizations. The KGB waited for Russia to collapse, weak, famished, and exhausted; then the secret police would step in, grab the reins and raise the whip again.

The only KGB employees he would see this morning were four overwhelmed officers in the immigration booths, busy stamping the tourists' passports. The morose clerk who inspected his papers waved him through without granting him even a single glance. Alex had no luggage, just a vinyl overnight bag. His maps, weapons, and alternate IDs had been smuggled into the country by other means. His bag was haughtily ignored by the customs officials, a few middle-aged men in gray uniforms, clustered around a samovar that dripped steaming drops on the cement floor. Their transistor radio was broadcasting a news bulletin from Geneva, announcing the failure of the talks between the American and the Iraqi foreign ministers. War was inevitable, a Kremlin spokesman concluded.

Outside the arrivals building, black marketeers were selling tins of caviar and fur hats, and buying American dollars. A tan cab, driven by an unshaven boy with a runny nose and pointed ears, took him to the

Pribalteiskaya Hotel, on the windy western beach.

He waited patiently in line until he reached the check-in counter. The reservation in his name had been made by Finntours, a big agency that handled most of the tours originating in Helsinki. He received a card with his name and room number, 1134, on the eleventh floor. He wasn't given a key, though. According to the Russian system, where surveillance was more important than the tourists' convenience, he was supposed to receive his key from the "floor matron."

Instead of getting on the elevator, he strolled in the modern lobby, studying the displays of the duty-free shops. By the Beriozka showcase, he bumped into another tourist, dressed more or less like him. He was of the same height as Alex, with blue eyes, a blue bag, and a knitted ski cap. They smiled and apologized to each other. Nobody noticed the quick exchange of cards each man held in his palm. As the other tourist turned away, his hand slipped a small package into Alex's unzipped bag.

In a corner of the crowded lobby, Alex studied the card his contact had handed him. It was in the name of Leif Svedelid, another Swede, staying in room 872 at the Moskva Hotel, near Alexander Nevski Church. He checked the package that had been dropped in his bag. It contained a Swedish passport, duly stamped, in the name of Leif Svedelid. Alex went out of the hotel and took a taxi to the Moskva. The first cut-out move had been flawlessly performed. There was no longer any connection between him and Arne Blom, who was probably walking right now into his room at the Pribalteiskaya. Henceforth he was Leif Svedelid, another perfectly legitimate Swede, who had already checked into the Moskva Hotel.

HE COULDN'T SLEEP that night, so he broke the primary rule of behavior in enemy territory and set out to explore Leningrad. The city seemed to him anything but enemy territory. He knew he might die tomorrow, perhaps even tonight, but this was his first night in the land of his birth, his first night in a city that his parents had visited and loved. He walked along the broad Nevski Prospect and stopped for a light meal at the Literaturnoye Café, where Pushkin had been challenged to the duel that would cost him his life; he strolled along the frozen canals, and stood alone in the center of Palace Square, where a handful of soldiers and workers had massed before storming the Winter Palace and launching the Bolshevik revolution.

He got lost among the squares, palaces, theaters, and mansions that gave the city its noble allure. A tram took him across the Neva, to the two columns that guarded the flanks of the towering naval museum. Across the bay loomed the spire of the Peter and Paul Fortress. A poster of the Leningrad Ballet announced a performance of *Swan Lake* at the Maly Theater. A group of teenagers passed by, chatting merrily in soft Russian. Some of the girls had pink and baby-blue ribbons woven pertly into their flaxen hair. He was in Russia, he kept telling himself; after all these years he had returned to Russia. The land of his fathers. And of his vilest enemies.

Shortly before dawn, cold, tired, but deeply moved, he returned to his hotel for a couple of hours of sleep.

His travel alarm clock woke him at seven-thirty. He bought a ticket for the organized tour of the Hermitage Museum, boarded the tourist bus, and left his bag on the rack above his seat. Their guide was a middle-aged blond woman who told them in heavily accented English that she was a member of the Communist party, but thought that Lenin's mausoleum should be burnt to the ground and the city of Leningrad should resume its ancient name of Petrograd. He left the bus together with the other tourists and, for the next two hours, strolled through the magnificent museum, where some of the world's greatest masterpieces were on display. At the end of the tour, he boarded the bus and took the same seat. When they arrived at his hotel, he picked up his bag, added his contribution to the driver's tip, and walked inside.

The bag he held looked exactly like his own, but its contents were different. The switch had taken place while he was exploring the Hermitage galleries. He locked himself in a cubicle in the public rest room and unzipped the bag. Inside he found, neatly packed, the uniform, cap, and boots of a major in the Red Army. In the bottom of the bag lay two leather pouches. One of them contained the identity papers of Major Lavrenti Selukin, his orders, his permit to travel in restricted areas, and an Aeroflot ticket for the afternoon flight to Murmansk. Alex's photographs were stapled to the military booklet and the officer's pass.

In the early afternoon, wearing his major's uniform, Alex took a taxi to Leningrad airport and boarded the Murmansk flight. Forty minutes later the Tupolev landed at Murmansk. Alex briefly glanced at the huge

naval base. His department had paid a heavy price for a set of photographs, taken by a Polish officer who had spent a year at the submarine
basin. At the terminal he waited in line for fifteen minutes before locking
himself in the rest room again and switching identities one more time.
From the second pouch in his bag he took the identity papers, lieutenant
bars, and artillery insignia of Lieutenant Vladimir Zolotov, and a ticket
for the Aeroflot flight to Uchta, which left at six-thirty P.M. and landed
in the snow-covered steppe in the middle of a roaring storm.

In the parking lot outside the rudimentary airfield was a huge Zil army
truck. The keys in Alex's pouch opened the driver's door and started the
ignition. The truck had a full tank of gas, and the oil level was satisfac-
tory. The heavy-duty heater coughed twice, then slipped into a reassuring drone. The headlights carved a bright path into the darkness.

He was on his way.

A BLIZZARD swept the frozen tundra. Across the bleak plain, the howling winds chased opaque clouds of swirling snow that covered the flat
wastes and piled onto the narrow asphalt road. Visibility was almost zero.

Bent over the steering wheel of the military truck, Alex slowly drove
east, the headlight beams breaking against the snowy wall before him.
He had been on the road for six hours already, heading north in a
landscape of white desolation, all alone except for the savage roar of the
Arctic winds. He had come all this way, slipping through Dimitri's net.
He was going to reach Pecora, even if it would be the last thing he did
on earth.

Pecora was deep in the restricted zone, where the towering chains of
the Ural Mountains loomed over the frozen flatlands. Gulags were the
only human outposts in that desert of snow and ice, and the region was
out of bounds for civilian travelers. That was why Alex was using the
army truck. One or two travelers in a civilian car would certainly raise
suspicion, while an army supply truck would be waved through the
roadblocks. His men had stolen the truck a week ago, substituted its
registration plates, and equipped it with food, gas, warm clothes, and
blankets. Two virgin passports for his father were hidden in a secret
compartment under the driver's seat, along with a camera for his passport photographs and two Tokarev handguns.

He had spread the map of Pecora on the dashboard. His men had pinpointed the location of the released prisoners' house, and highlighted it with a green fluorescent marker. They had checked the information and confirmed its authenticity. Victor Wolf was alive. He'd been released a few days ago, as the report said. The disclosure about Raoul Wallenberg's murder had come later in the week. It all fit together.

Nevertheless, Alex was haunted by a dark premonition. Everything had been too easy. His men had obtained the information without any particular effort. He hadn't been bothered, not even once, since his departure from Helsinki. Even when he'd landed in Uchta six hours ago with a planeload of military personnel and government officials, nobody had asked for his papers. The two KGB officers at the gate waved him through, barely glancing at him. That was strange; he knew the Russian mania for papers, permits, and official authorizations. They should have checked him, at least for the record.

Perhaps it was all Dimitri's doing. Perhaps he had managed to penetrate this far inside Russia only because his brother had wanted him to. Alex was almost certain that Dimitri Morozov was waiting for him. And if he was, then Alex knew he was heading for certain death. But he had no choice. What else could he do? He had to try and rescue his father, even at the risk of his life.

On his right a row of dim yellow globes flickered behind the white snow curtain. He leaned forward until his forehead touched the cold windshield, and peered outside. Behind the lights, large rectangular shapes loomed in the dark. Houses.

He was in Pecora.

BARELY A MILE AWAY, in a car parked behind a brown apartment building, Dimitri Morozov was waiting. Tonight he was wearing his general's uniform. The engine was running, to heat the interior. Grimaldi was slumped in the back, huddled in a wolfskin coat.

Dimitri hadn't tried to interfere with his brother's voyage. His people had gotten the warning signs, and the operations room at Yasenevo had been flooded with bogus reports. Excited agents breathlessly reported they had sighted Gordon crossing the Polish, German, or Czech border. Dimitri had ignored them all. What was the use? he thought. His brother was bound to surface at Pecora. All he had to do was wait for him there.

Dimitri had arrived in Pecora the night before and set up his command post at the local militia station. His staff, and the KGB assault units that he needed for the operation, had been stationed at the Inta cavalry barracks, twenty-eight kilometers to the north; they had joined him after nightfall. An hour ago he received a report about an army truck, driven by a lieutenant, which had been cleared through a roadblock east of Uchta. That must be him, Dimitri thought, that was his method. Alex Gordon and his agents always used official vehicles, uniforms, and papers for cover. In Russia people respected authority, and sentries never checked military papers too zealously. Alex's advantage, Dimitri thought, is that he knows us better than anybody else. His flaw is that I know him.

He leaned back, briefly closing his eyes. He could visualize his brother, clutching the steering wheel of his vehicle, fighting the storm on the way to Pecora. It must have cost him a tremendous effort to infiltrate Russia, obtain military papers and uniforms, steal a military truck, and penetrate the restricted zone. And all of that just to enter the trap Dimitri had laid for him.

In an hour, maybe less, their private war would come to its end. Dimitri had planned this moment for years, dreaming of his revenge, tasting in advance the humiliation of the Jew who had stolen his woman. It would be a useless victory, though. When the brothers' vendetta had started, American and Russian agents were fighting a bloody war all over the globe. Today, however, nothing could change the ugly truth — the Soviet Union was falling apart, its empire was collapsing, the cold war had been lost. Uselessly he would be dealing the CIA a devastating blow, the capture and destruction of its most glorious hero.

Dimitri glanced at Victor Wolf's windows. They were still dark. The old man was across the corridor, visiting his friend Korchagin at his apartment. These old prisoners were all the same, they had gotten used to living together and couldn't stand being alone. Besides, Wolf didn't suspect how popular he was with the KGB tonight. He certainly hadn't noticed the military vehicles that had taken positions around the building. The storm and the snow had come just in time. Dimitri had thought of visiting Wolf earlier in the evening, but finally had decided to wait for his brother. It would be more interesting that way.

A shadow materialized by the car window. Dimitri recognized his orderly. He rolled down the window, letting in a gust of glacial air. A few snowflakes landed on his sleeve.

Sereda's broad Ukrainian face was flushed. "He's coming, Comrade General."

ALEX PARKED THE TRUCK in a dark vacant lot, locked it and trudged in the deep snow toward the housing block. The icy wind whipped him mercilessly, and he doubled up, holding his cap to his head. He straightened up only when he reached the small entrance lobby of number 19. It was cold and neglected, bathed in crude yellow light from a bare bulb hanging on the ceiling. The cement floor was cracked and dirty, a small mound of litter was piled in a corner, and the paint was peeling from the walls in large tan flakes.

From the dark well of the staircase a clumsy figure came toward Alex. He immediately recognized the heavy gait.

"Grimaldi," he said. "I didn't expect you here." By coming to meet him in Pecora, Grimaldi was admitting his betrayal. It was a senseless thing to do. In a flash Alex recalled their operations together; he had hoped, like a child, that the sad story of Grimaldi's betrayal would fade away and Napoleone would become his ally again. Still, seeing him now, Alex didn't feel surprise or disappointment, only a dull lassitude.

Grimaldi, standing before him, nodded his head. "Hello, Alex. I guess this is the end of the road."

Alex stared back at him, ignoring the cliché. If Grimaldi was here, Dimitri couldn't be far behind. The place was probably swarming with KGB troops. It was a trap, as he'd suspected all along. There was no way out for him, and even if there were, he wouldn't run away without seeing his father. Dimitri knew all that. The game was over, and Dimitri had won.

"It's not what you think," Grimaldi said incongruously. His hand came out of his pocket, holding a cheroot.

"Isn't it?" Alex said.

"I didn't betray you," Grimaldi said quickly. "I didn't tell them anything. You can check, Alex. Just . . . just this Gorbachev affair. He is a danger, Alex. For all of us."

Alex looked at the staircase. There was nobody there. He knew he would be arrested; he knew he wasn't going to leave Russia alive. He hoped that at least they'd let him see his father.

"You and I, we belong to a dying breed," Grimaldi went on, his lips curling in a wan smile. "We are the last of the samurais, the princes of the cold war."

"Quite poetic tonight, aren't you, Franco?"

"Under Gorbachev, Russia is no longer the enemy," Grimaldi said. "So they won't need the Company anymore, don't you see?"

Alex didn't answer. He watched Grimaldi light the cheroot.

"They won't need us," Grimaldi went on, "not you, or me, or anybody. We'll end our lives in some dusty government office, stamping building permits or tracking drug peddlers. That's the end, Alex. The end of the big game. If Gorbachev isn't removed, we're all washed up. No more thrills, no right to exist. They'll sell Langley Woods to some insurance company and turn the Farm into a vacation resort."

"So you did it for the Company, did you?" Alex pushed him aside and walked toward the staircase.

"Alex, wait, we should talk." Grimaldi took a few steps after him, then stopped. "Wait."

He climbed the staircase to the next landing and turned into a drab, faintly illuminated corridor. There were doors on both sides. On the third door on his right a small rectangle of cardboard was fastened with thumbtacks. VICTOR WOLF, it said.

He took a deep breath. He didn't know what awaited him behind the door. He turned the handle.

The apartment was dark. The silhouette of a man, sitting on a rocking chair, cut against the bare window, and the smell of pungent tobacco hung in the air.

"Welcome, Alex," his brother said, and chuckled. "Nice uniform. Take a seat. Your father will join us shortly."

ALEX LINGERED for a moment on the threshold, then stepped inside. The room was stuffy, and he unbuttoned the collar of his uniform. He was suddenly disgusted with this masquerade; he wished he could discard the Russian uniform. How stupid he'd been to think he could outwit his brother in his own backyard. The game's outcome had been decided from the start.

As his eyes got used to the darkness, he pulled a chair out from the table in the middle of the room and sat down, crossing his arms. Dimitri continued to rock in his chair by the window. They waited in silence, without exchanging a single word. There was nothing to talk about. Alex felt that any exchange of words between them would lead to a murderous fight. What could he ask him? "Why did you kill Tatiana? Why did you kill my little son?"

The best thing is to remain silent, he thought. Silent and resigned. Dimitri had laid a trap and he had knowingly walked into it. Still, there seemed to be a tacit agreement between them that nothing would be done until the meeting with Victor Wolf was over.

A few minutes later the door opened and a stooped figure appeared in the doorway. Alex held his breath. A light switch was flipped and weak yellow light drenched the poorly furnished room. Both Alex and Dimitri rose and moved toward the door. Alex's thighs were stiff and trembling. He couldn't help thinking how ridiculous they must look in their uniforms — uniforms that represented humiliation, cruelty, and death to the old man.

The old man was hollow-chested and completely bald. His gaunt face was wrinkled, and his skin had the grayish tinge caused by heart disease. He had a thin, delicate nose, and his parched lips badly concealed broken uneven teeth, a few of them crowned with some black metal. From his scrawny neck protruded a large Adam's apple. Victor Wolf was wearing thick glasses, fastened to his bare skull with an elastic band. His black suit, made of cheap wool, hung loosely on his skeletal frame. His gray shirt was collarless. My God, Alex thought, is this the romantic poet who bewitched Tonya Gordon? The passionate, handsome man Nina described, with the rebellious shock of hair, the sensuous mouth, the overwhelming charisma? Is this the author of "A Thousand Deaths"? The man who wrote "brothers forever are one"? My father?

The old man didn't seem surprised to find the two officers in his room. Squinting in the raw light, he peered at both of them. "Yes?" he said. He had a rasping, tremulous voice.

Alex's heart was beating wildly, an iron ball swung inside his rib cage. "My name is Gordon," he managed, impulsively unbuttoning the tunic of his uniform. He shouldn't face his father in this hateful uniform. "I am Alex Gordon."

"I am Dimitri Morozov," his brother said.

The old man's hand darted to his chest. He swayed and reached to the wall behind him for support. His breath was shallow, his black eyes darting between the two brothers, his lips trembling. Finally he straightened up again and approached them, dragging his feet on the floor. He was staring closely at Alex. His face was cracked into wrinkles that snaked across the entire surface of his skin. Wolf took a step toward Morozov, then turned back to Alex.

"Tonya Gordon was my mother," Alex said. "I am your son."

Wolf studied his face. His eyes were intensely black. He reached for Alex with his right hand and gently touched his face.

"No," he said, and pointed at Dimitri Morozov. "He is my son."

IN THE STUPEFIED SILENCE that invaded the room, Alex and Dimitri were two pillars of salt, unable to move, unable to utter a sound. Only their eyes followed Victor Wolf, who shuffled painfully across the bare wooden floor, toward Dimitri. "He is my son," he repeated, looking at Alex over his shoulder.

Alex was the first to regain his senses. "What are you talking about?"

"I told you," Dimitri said in a shrill voice. He cleared his throat. "I am Dimitri Morozov. I am Boris Morozov's son."

But the old man shook his head, and Alex could swear he discerned a faint, strangely amused smile on his cracked lips. "I didn't expect us to meet this way," he said. "I didn't expect us to meet ever, actually. But you are my son." He took another couple of steps toward Dimitri. "You're not Dimitri Morozov. You are Alex. Alex Wolf. Or Alex Gordon, if you wish . . ."

"You must be out of your mind," Dimitri muttered, taking a step back, as if he feared the old man.

"No, I'm not." There was a lot of force in that frail body, and the black eyes suddenly became alive. He was speaking to Dimitri. "Why don't you look at yourself in the mirror? You'll see the resemblance." His hand fluttered in the air, outlining the contour of an imaginary face. "Same chin, same frame, same mole over your upper lip." He touched his own face, his voice warming up. "You're my son, all right. You're not Dimitri, you're Alex. Little Alex, Aliosha. You're my son, and I never laid my eyes on you before. God, did I long for you, child."

Alex followed their conversation, utterly astonished.

"Nonsense." Dimitri's voice quivered, and he planted his fists on his waist. "Outward resemblance doesn't mean anything."

"Of course." the old man nodded. "Of course." He swayed on his feet, and leaned on the near chair. He was silent a moment, catching his breath. "You see, Aliosha," he finally said in his rasping voice, "I met Boris Morozov before his death, back in 'fifty-three. We shared the same cell for a couple of weeks."

"I don't believe you," Dimitri snapped. He was white as a sheet. "That's too much of a coincidence. There were one million prisoners in Siberia at that time."

Wolf was nodding repeatedly. "I didn't say it was a coincidence, Alex." It was so strange, Alex thought, to hear the old man address his brother as Alex. "It was no coincidence at all. Morozov still had some connections in the KGB. Old friends, people who owed him favors. He asked to be brought to my cell. He was going to be shot, he wanted to meet me. He had nothing to lose."

He paused, breathing quickly, his hand clutching his throat. Alex quickly crossed the room and entered the minuscule kitchen. There were no glasses, just an earthenware mug drying by the sink. He filled it with water and carried it to the old man. Wolf gulped it down, some of the water trickling down his chin. "Thank you," he said, patting Alex's shoulder, then turned back to Dimitri.

"Morozov told me what had happened to your mother," Wolf went on. "He said to me that when he saw her die — he actually saw her die, you know — he swore to save her boy. His only son. He knew that somebody at the KGB might order the child killed. They often murdered the families of traitors, you know. Or, if they let the boy live, they were going to make his life miserable."

He spread his thin arms. "He couldn't foresee that Russia would change, you understand? And besides, he was so bitter, so deeply disappointed with Russia. He was a communist, a believer, and where did he end up? Waiting for his death in this sordid camp, his wife shot, his family destroyed, his life wasted. He swore to give his boy a chance to grow up free, in America."

Alex Gordon swayed in sudden realization. "He gave his child your son's name," he whispered.

"Exactly," the old man said. "He was sure Nina would take care of the boy as if he were her own child."

Dimitri was shaking his head, his fingers plowing his hair, his eyes focused on the old man. "Rubbish," he spat furiously.

"It was easy, don't you see?" Wolf slumped heavily into a chair. "It's very hard to tell a two-year-old from a three-year-old. He brought you, my boy" — he was looking at Dimitri — "to the orphanage, and registered you under the name of Dimitri Morozov. He didn't care very much what might happen to you there. It was convenient for him that the child at Panfilov would be known as his son, Dimitri Morozov" — he took a deep breath again — "while the real Dimitri was sent to America, under the name of Alex Gordon."

Alex's eyes shifted from Wolf to Dimitri. Everything was reversed. Black was white and white was black. He was the Russian, the Gentile. His brother, the Russian nationalist, the fervent anti-Semite — was the Jew.

Strange thoughts assailed him. If Dimitri had been the one sent to America, wouldn't he be a different man today? And he, what kind of man would he have become if he had grown up at Panfilov? Dimitri might have loved poetry if he had grown up with his parents' poems at his bedside. He might have abhorred violence if he had not been forced to live by it. He might have been gentle and warmhearted if he had been raised by Nina, instead of in the hell of Panfilov. He might have been proud to wear the Star of David on a chain around his neck; he might have loved his Jewish mother if he hadn't considered her the source of his misery.

And he, Alex, if he had been in his brother's place, might have become a killer.

DIMITRI GAZED OUT at the large snowflakes that fluttered by the window. On a night like this his mother had stood before her cell window, watching the snow fall, waiting for her executioner. She had died because she was Jewish. He was Jewish, too; he was one of the people he hated most, those he held responsible for all his suffering.

Nothing had been the way it had seemed. It was his Russian stepfather who had kicked him into Panfilov to save his Russian boy. Could Boris Morozov have been so devious? The man he admired, whose picture he carried in his wallet, could he have been so cynical, so heartless? He shuddered. No, that couldn't be true. Wolf was lying through his teeth, trying to hurt him because he was Morozov's son.

But what if the old man was telling the truth?

He could not accept this sudden reversal of his identity. He recalled a story Alex had told him in Paris, about an Argentinian Catholic, one of the pillars of the Church in Buenos Aires. He had incidentally discovered that he was a Marrano, a descendant of converted Jews. He had shot himself.

Was he indeed a Jew? No, even if his blood was Jewish, he was different; he had grown up far away from them. But if so, it wasn't a question of race or genes, only of religion and way of life. Perhaps religious Jews were different, perhaps they led a different life from his own? Yet how many such Jews had he met? How many vile Jews had he ever known?

Next week he was to chair a meeting of Pamyat in Moscow. What would he say to them? That he was Jewish? That he was resigning? Perhaps he shouldn't return to Moscow, perhaps he should run away. But where? Where on earth could he hide from the Jew who lived in his flesh?

No, it couldn't be true. The old man must be lying.

"You're crazy," he said to Wolf. His voice cracked. "You've lost your mind. That's what the gulags did to you. You shouldn't be here, you belong in a nuthouse. Forty-one years in the gulags drove you mad. Nobody would believe you. I don't believe a word you've said."

"I do," Alex said quietly.

The old man suddenly smiled, a sad, bitter smile. "There is an old question, very ancient, actually, that has always haunted my people," he said. "Who is a Jew?"

He stood up and faced both of them. "Who is my Jewish son? You?" he pointed a trembling finger at Dimitri. "You?" he turned to Alex.

Laboriously breathing, he took a neatly folded handkerchief from his pocket and wiped his brow. "Alex and Dimitri," he said in wonderment. His voice was low; he seemed to be speaking to himself. "You are both my sons. One of you carries me in his blood, and one in his soul. It's more than I could hope for." His legs gave way and he slumped back into his chair, his chest heaving, his breath coming in quick, short rasps.

Dimitri took a step toward the old man, and briefly raised his hand, reaching for him. But he regained control of himself and turned away.

Alex stood behind Victor Wolf and gently placed his hands on his shoulders.

Finally Dimitri spoke. "You still want to take him away?" he asked Alex, without turning around.

Epilogue

ALEX GORDON and the old man crossed the border into Finland forty-eight hours later. Claudia was waiting for them in Helsinki. The same day, the three of them boarded a plane bound for New York. On arrival, Alex Gordon signed his letter of resignation from the CIA and applied for a teaching position at Brown.

Two weeks later Dimitri Morozov disappeared from his Vienna hotel. Rumors said he had defected to the West.

On January 16 war broke out in the Persian Gulf. As a result, President Gorbachev's trip to Washington was postponed until several months later. But Dimitri Morozov, the driving force behind the assassination plan, had vanished; the plot against Gorbachev's life was therefore aborted. The KGB and the Red Army hawks hastily adopted a different strategy, and on August 19 they seized power in Moscow, putting Gorbachev under arrest in his Crimea residence. The coup was short-lived, though; in the absence of Morozov, the most ruthless and dedicated of the plotters, the conspiracy was stillborn.

The remaining conspirators were at a loss when Boris Yeltsin, the president of the Russian Republic, led the people of Moscow into a defiant confrontation with the army and the KGB. The junta hesitated, recoiled before the use of force, and finally disintegrated sixty hours after the coup.

A huge, angry crowd marched on the Lubyanka and brought down the black statue of Felix Dzerzhinsky, founder of the Cheka, forefather of the KGB.

Still, the dramatic events in Moscow justified a decision made by the United States on the eve of the Gulf War. In a widely acclaimed speech before both houses of Congress, in January 1991, President Bush announced he would maintain the Star Wars project. He was following the assessment of some White House experts that *perestroika* might backfire and the cold war break out again.

A few days after the KGB's ill-fated coup, Franco Grimaldi was killed in a hit-and-run accident in Moscow. The reckless driver was never found.

General Oleg Kalinin retired from active duty. His life story, discreetly censored, was described in a best-selling book by Vladimir Dubrovin. The book was made into a movie entitled *Secret Warrior for Peace.*

Claudia Gordon's exhibit opened in a Soho gallery in June. Victor Wolf proudly posed beside his portrait, painted by Claudia. His memoirs, *To Die a Thousand Deaths,* were scheduled to be published the following spring.

The guests at the opening of Claudia's exhibit noticed that the artist's waist had thickened slightly. She was expecting a baby in late fall.

About the Author

MICHAEL BAR-ZOHAR is the award-winning author of eleven novels, including *Enigma* (which was made into a film starring Martin Sheen and Derek Jacobi), *The Unknown Soldier*, and *A Spy in Winter*. He is also the author of many nonfiction books; the most recent was *Facing a Cruel Mirror: Israel's Moment of Truth*. Bar-Zohar is the official biographer of David Ben-Gurion, the founder of the modern state of Israel.

Michael Bar-Zohar lives in Tel Aviv, Israel, with his wife and son. He is currently Visiting Professor of History at Emory University in Atlanta.